T0363716

INTRIGUE

Seek thrills. Solve crimes. Justice served.

Bounty Hunted
Barb Han

Captured At The Cove
Carol Ericson

MILLS & BOON

BOUNTY HUNTED
© 2024 by Barb Han
Philippine Copyright 2024
Australian Copyright 2024
New Zealand Copyright 2024

First Published 2024
First Australian Paperback Edition 2024
ISBN 978 1 867 91768 3

CAPTURED AT THE COVE
© 2024 by Carol Ericson
Philippine Copyright 2024
Australian Copyright 2024
New Zealand Copyright 2024

First Published 2024
First Australian Paperback Edition 2024
ISBN 978 1 867 91768 3

Published by
Harlequin Mills & Boon
An imprint of Harlequin Enterprises (Australia) Pty Limited
(ABN 47 001 180 918), a subsidiary of HarperCollins
Publishers Australia Pty Limited
(ABN 36 009 913 517)
Level 19, 201 Elizabeth Street
SYDNEY NSW 2000 AUSTRALIA

Cover art used by arrangement with Harlequin Books S.A.. All rights reserved.

Printed and bound in Australia by McPherson's Printing Group

MIX
Paper | Supporting
responsible forestry
FSC® C001695
www.fsc.org

Bounty Hunted

Barb Han

MILLS & BOON

USA TODAY bestselling author **Barb Han** lives in north Texas with her very own hero-worthy husband, three beautiful children, a spunky golden retriever/ standard poodle mix and too many books in her to-read pile. In her downtime, she plays video games and spends much of her time on or around a basketball court. She loves interacting with readers and is grateful for their support. You can reach her at barbhan.com.

Visit the Author Profile page
at millsandboon.com.au.

DEDICATION

All my love to Brandon, Jacob and Tori, my three greatest loves.
How did I get so lucky?

To Babe, my hero, for being my best friend, greatest love and
my place to call home. I love you with everything that I am.

CAST OF CHARACTERS

Crystal Remington—Can this US marshal keep her witness in the program, or will he ditch her and try to do everything on his own?

Wade Brewer—Can this wounded veteran stay alive long enough to testify?

Trent Thomas—This buddy is a lifesaver, but can he be counted on?

Victor Crane—This head of a criminal organization will stop at nothing to keep Wade from testifying.

Damon O'Meara (aka Damon the Devil)—Who is he and, better yet, who does he work for?

Chapter One

Crystal Remington repositioned her black Stetson, lowering the rim, after she opened the door of the Dime a Dozen Café off I-45. She scanned the small restaurant for Wade Brewer. At six feet, four inches of solid muscle, the thirty-three-year-old former Army sergeant shouldn't be too difficult to locate against the backdrop of truckers and road-tripping families.

In the back left corner, Mr. Brewer sat with his back against the wall. His position gave him an open view of the room. As a US marshal and someone who was used to memorizing exits, Crystal appreciated the move. At his vantage point, no one would have an opportunity to sneak up on him from the side or behind.

He glanced up and then locked onto her, not bothering to motion for her to come sit down. In fact, he looked down-right put out by her presence. What the hell?

Tight chestnut-brown-colored hair clipped close to a near-perfect head and a serious face with hard angles and planes, she didn't need to look at a picture to verify her witness's identity. This was the man she was scheduled to meet. After deciding she wasn't a threat, he leaned forward over the table and nursed a cup of coffee as she walked over to join him.

He picked up a sugar packet and twisted it around his

fingers. "Marshal Remington, I'm guessing." Most would consider him physically intimidating, but she'd grown up around a brother and a pair of cousins similar in size, so it didn't faze her.

"That would make you Wade Brewer." Crystal sat down, then signaled for the waitress before refocusing on Brewer. Even with facial scars from an explosion during his time in the service, the man was still beautiful. "Ready for the check so we can get out of this fishbowl and I can get you to a safe place?"

"Do I look like I need your help?" he shot back with daggers coming from his eyes. She wasn't touching that question. "Remind me why I agreed to this when I'm fully capable of taking care of myself?"

Crystal waved off the smiling waitress who was unaware of the tension at the table. And then she turned all her attention to her witness. "First of all, two of the people I love most in this world are lying in hospital beds fighting for their lives while I'm sitting here with you, so have a little respect."

Brewer didn't flinch. Instead, the most intense pair of steel-gray eyes studied her. The unexplained fear that he might pull something like this had been eating at her since she'd learned about his background. Tough guys like him generally didn't go around asking others for help. They handled life on their own terms and, generally speaking, did a bang-up job of it. She'd dismissed her worry as paranoia. Then there was the fact of her grandparents' serious car accident that had been weighing heavily on her mind. Didn't bad events usually occur in threes? If that was the case and her witness decided to bolt, she had one more to go. Lucky her. "Now that we have that fact out of the way, you are the key to locking away a major criminal who—"

"Is currently in jail," he interrupted without looking away from the rim of his cup.

From here on out, Wade was Brewer to Crystal just like everyone else she referred to. Using last names was a way to keep a distance from people. First names were too personal.

"And has a very long reach on the outside with two lieutenants and more foot soldiers ready to kill on command than you can count on both hands." She needed to get him out of this café and on the road to Dallas if they were going to get there in time to pick up the key to the town house tonight. "Why are we talking about this? I thought this issue had already been decided. It was my understanding that you agreed to enter into my protective custody. Has something changed that I haven't been informed of since six a.m.?"

"I've had time to sit here and think." Brewer took a sip of black coffee, unfazed by the emotions building inside her and emanating from her in palpable waves. "Maybe it's time to change my mind."

"Why is that, Mr. Brewer? What possible thought could you have had that would cause you to do an about-face right now?" If he said the reason had to do with her being a woman, she might scream. She'd come across perps who'd believed they could outrun or outshoot her due to her having two X chromosomes. They'd been wrong. If that was the case with Brewer, she could assure him that she was just as capable as any man to do the job or she wouldn't be here in the first place. Brewer didn't give her an indication this was the issue, but she'd come up against this particular prejudice a few too many times in the past and it always set her off.

To his credit, Brewer didn't look her up and down. Instead, he stared into his cup. "It's simple. I'll be able to stay on the move a lot easier if I'm alone. Being on the move doesn't make me a sitting duck."

"I can offer a stable safe house, Mr. Brewer."

The look he gave said he wasn't buying it. "You have no guarantees." Didn't he really mean to say she wasn't strong enough to cover him if push came to shove?

"Not one witness to date has died while following the guidelines under the protection of a US marshal," she pointed out. "I can't say the same for folks who decided they could do it themselves." She folded her arms across her chest and sat back in her chair. "Our track record speaks for itself."

Brewer didn't seem one bit impressed. The terms *dark* and *brooding* came to mind when describing him.

She needed to take another tack, offer a softer approach. "First of all, I want to thank you for your service to this country." She meant every word. "And I realize your training provides a unique skill set that most who come under my protection don't possess." Pausing for effect would give him a few seconds to process the compliment and, maybe, soften him up a little. "I have no doubt you were very good at your job, Sergeant. But make no mistake about it—my training is suited to this task. And I'm damn good at my job. If you have any doubts, feel free to contact my supervisor or any of the other marshals I've worked with over the years. This isn't my first rodeo."

He dismissed her with a wave of his hand, which infuriated her.

Taking a calming breath, she started again. "If the fact

I'm a woman bothers you, say so upfront and let's get it out of the way."

His face twisted in disgust. "I've served alongside a few of the most talented soldiers in the Army, who happened to wear bras. The fact you do has no bearing on my decision whether or not to strike out on my own."

Embarrassed, heat crawled up her neck, pooling at her cheeks. She cleared her throat, determined not to let this assignment go south. "You have no reason to trust me other than the badge I wear. You don't know me from Adam. I get that. Not to mention your military record is impeccable. If we were at war, you'd be the first person I turned to. This situation is stateside, and you have no authority here."

"I have a right to defend myself," he countered.

"Same as every citizen," she pointed out. No doubt he packed his own weapons, not that he needed a license to carry any longer. Scooting her chair closer to the table, she leaned in and lowered her voice. "Did you take care of your aunt?"

"Yes, ma'am. She has been relocated to a secure location," he said. Taking care of his elderly aunt had been his first priority after Victor Crane had been taken into custody and was the reason they were meeting north of Houston, his home city. "Without your help, by the way."

"Fair enough." Crystal could see she was losing him. Was it time to cut bait? Leave him on his own? The way she saw it, there wasn't much choice. His mind seemed made up. Then again, there was no harm in trying. She'd throw out a Hail Mary anyway and see if it worked. "At least make the drive to Dallas with me. Consider changing your mind about protective custody. What's the worst that can happen?"

He flashed eyes at her.

She put a hand up to stop him from commenting. "How about we get inside my vehicle and you can consider your options on the highway heading north?" she said. "You change your mind, I'll personally drop you off anywhere you request. No questions asked."

Brewer gave her a dressing down with his steel gaze. If he was testing her, she had no intention of backing down.

With the casual effort of a Sunday-morning stroll, he shifted gears, picked up his mug and drained the contents. After reaching into his front pocket and peeling off a twenty, he slapped it onto the table, shouldered his military-issue backpack, then stood. "Let's go."

A celebration was premature. Crystal stood up, turned around, and walked out of the diner, keeping an eye out to make sure no one seemed interested in what they were doing. She didn't like meeting this close to Galveston, Brewer's childhood home, or Houston, where he currently resided. Victor Crane would no doubt have someone on his or her way down to make certain Brewer couldn't testify. With a pair of loyal lieutenants, Crane wouldn't even have to make the call himself if Brewer's name got out as a witness. He'd been Crane's driver, so the odds of that happening were high now that Brewer had disappeared.

He followed her to her government-issue white sedan parked closest to the door without taking up an accessible parking spot. She half expected him to keep walking right on past and was pleasantly surprised when he stopped at the passenger door.

It was too early to be excited. She'd given him the out to change his mind anytime during the ride to Dallas in order to convince him to get into the car.

"I should probably hit the men's room before we continue north," he said, breaking into her small moment of victory like rain on parade day.

"All right." On a sharp sigh, Crystal took the driver's seat, figuring it was a toss-up at this point as to whether or not he would return. She tapped her thumb on the steering wheel after turning on the engine as Brewer headed inside the restaurant. What was he going to do? Sneak out the bathroom window to throw her off the trail for a few minutes? Were negotiations over? His mind made up?

She'd give him five minutes before she gave up and called it in.

BREWER CONTEMPLATED DITCHING the marshal for two seconds in the bathroom. Getting far away from Galveston and Houston was a good idea. Dallas? Was it his best move? He'd only been out of the military for six months now and hadn't come home to a warm welcome in his former hometown other than his aunt despite his service to his country.

In all honesty, he'd brought the town's reaction on himself. He'd barely graduated high school due to the number of fistfights he'd been in. He'd worked two jobs to help provide for his elderly aunt, who was technically his great-aunt, which had tanked his grades. He could have been more focused in school, except that he'd hated every minute of sitting in class. Before he'd shot up in height, he'd been bullied. And then, he'd gotten angry. The football coach, in an attempt to court him, had given Brewer permission to use the weight room before school, which he'd done religiously to bulk up and then use his newfound muscles to punish. By junior year, he'd taken issue with anyone who'd looked sideways at him and had the power to back it up.

And he'd done just that a few too many times for the principal's liking and pretty much everyone else in town whose kid he'd beaten up.

The military had given him a purpose and an outlet for all his anger, not to mention a target to focus on. He'd gone from hating the world and blaming everyone for his hard-luck upbringing to being able to set it all aside and compartmentalize his emotions. His childhood had had all the usual trappings that came with a drunk for a father who apparently couldn't stand the sight of his own child. As for his mother, she'd been a saint to him until she'd up and disappeared. The Houdini act had made Daniel Brewer hate his son even more. The man could rot in hell for all Brewer cared after what he'd ultimately done. As far as his mother went…what kind of person left a five-year-old behind to live with a drunk? Her sainthood had been short-lived as far as he was concerned. It had died along with all his love for her.

Brewer fished his burner cell out of his pocket. He fired off a text to his buddy to say this was him on a new number and to pick up. Then, Brewer put the phone to his left ear and made a call. The burner phone was new since he'd turned his old one over to the US Marshals Service for safekeeping. It was too late to regret the move now.

His buddy picked up on the second ring. "Trent, hey, it's me."

"Dude, I tried to call you." Trent Thomas breathed heavy like he was in the middle of a run. "What happened to your phone?"

"I borrowed this one." He hoped Trent wouldn't ask any more questions. They'd been military buddies early on in Brewer's career, Trent having been the closest thing to a friend in basic training when they'd both had their backsides handed to them.

A disgruntled grunt came through the line. "I had no idea what that bastard was really up to, Brew."

"Figured you didn't," Brewer reassured his buddy. The two had gone to the same middle school, high school, and boot camp. They hadn't really gotten to know each other until the latter. They forked in different directions after basic.

Then Trent had been a godsend when Brewer had medically boarded out of the Army. He'd been the first to make calls to find work for Brewer, work that had given him a reason to keep going after his life-changing injury. And now the job put his life in jeopardy. There was no way Trent could have known Crane wasn't the head of a legitimate company as they'd been told. Brewer's buddy would never do that to him.

"I feel like a real jerk for putting you in that position, dude. Especially after what you've been through and all."

"Don't sweat it," Brewer reassured. "Besides, this'll all be over in two shakes, and I'll be on the hunt for a new job."

"What can I do to help?"

He knew Trent would come through. "I need a place to hide out for a few days until I can figure out my next move. Somewhere off the grid, if you know what I mean."

The line went quiet for a few seconds that felt like minutes as Brewer turned on the spigot to wash his hands.

"I can help with that, Brew. No problem." He rattled off coordinates that Brewer entered into his cell after telling his friend to hold so he could dry his hands.

"I'll owe you big-time for this, Trent."

"Consider it payback for the position I put you in," Trent

said with a voice heavy with remorse. He wasn't normally an emotional guy, so the intensity registered as odd.

After what he'd been through in the past twenty-four hours that had led him to standing in front of a bathroom mirror in a roadside café made him more than ready to get off the grid, where he could catch his meals and cook his own food. Civilization wasn't as civilized as he'd wanted it to be.

"I'll be in touch when I can." He ended the call on the off chance someone was listening. Freedom was near. All he had to do was ditch the marshal sitting in the parking lot and get on the road.

After entering the coordinates into his map feature, he smiled. This place was so remote, all that showed on the screen was a patch of trees. Near the Texas-Louisiana border close to Tyler, he could easily see himself getting lost and finally finding some peace until time to go to trial.

So why was his first thought that he didn't want to disappoint the blue-eyed, ponytail-wearing marshal sitting out front?

Chapter Two

Five minutes blew by too fast. She had a few more to give. Eight minutes ticked by with no Brewer. She'd lost her witness. The man had probably opened a bathroom window and escaped out the back like in the movies. *Great.* She checked the clock again and tapped her finger on the steering wheel. Nine minutes. Time to call it in. Crystal reached for her cell as the door to the café opened. Out came Brewer. He strolled to the passenger side, casual as anyone pleased before opening the door and claiming the seat.

"Let's do this," he said causally, like she hadn't been sitting here sweating bullets the entire time he'd been gone.

"Good." As she put the gearshift in Reverse, her cell buzzed. "Do you mind if I get that?" She checked the screen and then flashed eyes at him. "Family emergency."

"Be my guest." He glanced around and then unbuckled. "Should I drive?"

Crystal shook her head and refrained from calling him out for being irritating. After pulling over to the side of the parking lot, she answered her sister's call. "Everything okay, Abi?"

The line was quiet, which sent Crystal's stress levels soaring.

"Abi?"

"Hi, yes, everything's fine now, considering the circumstances." Abi cleared her throat like she did when she was hiding the fact she'd been crying.

Abilene Remington was not a crier. Despite being five years younger, she could hold her own in a fight too. The fact that she'd been crying triggered alarms inside Crystal's head. "Did something else happen this morning?"

"Gram coded," Abi supplied before quickly adding, "but her heart is beating again."

Crystal frowned as a moment of panic seized her. Holding back the swell of emotions gathering in her chest like a storm, she muttered a stream of curse words. "Oh, Abi. That's not good. Are you there right now?"

"No," Abi admitted. "I had to leave. Which makes everything so much worse, right?"

Yes, it did. The imagination ran wild when a loved one was sick or in the hospital and you couldn't be there to see how the person looked, breathed, rested with your own eyes, or to ask the doctor questions when you caught her or him in the hall. Gauging someone's reactions on a screen only went so far. It was better than nothing, but there was no replacement for being physically present.

Crystal and Abi were in the same boat as far as not being at the hospital. Her siblings and cousins were also US marshals. They couldn't all leave the job at the same time with their caseloads, so they'd worked out a system. Her brother, Duke, had been able to arrange to come back to the ranch first, then Crystal hoped it would be her turn. A selfish part of her wished Brewer had disappeared out that bathroom window a few minutes ago so she could head to Mesa Point. "This setback will complicate her recovery, won't it?"

"I thought we were going to lose her, Crys." Abi rarely called Crystal that name. "And Duke was back at the ranch with Nash." Shiloh Nash was the ranch foreman.

Pinching the bridge of her nose with her free hand, she exhaled. "I'm sorry you had to be alone at the hospital when that happened." Crystal had been assigned to pick up Brewer, which also wasn't going as planned. "That's my fault, and I—"

"Work happens," Abi interrupted. "We all agreed to this. You couldn't have known what would happen. Besides, everything was stable four hours ago. Being here is essentially like watching paint dry until it isn't."

"I'm still sorry that I wasn't there, Abs." Another rarely used pet name they'd developed joking around with each other after Krav Maga class. Hitting Abi in the abs had been like slamming a fist into steel.

She glanced over at Brewer, who was pretending to check his cell phone instead of listening. Why did that worry her? "This assignment might wrap up sooner than I originally believed, so I might be back before you know it."

"Camden can take a few days off." Their cousin was the oldest of the six. Crystal was second oldest. "Said he'll be here after he files papers on his last assignment." Abi paused. "It's just hard sometimes, you know?"

"I do," Crystal reassured. "Our grandparents are lucky to have you there to make sure they have everything they need."

"Just wish they would wake up. Then again, while I'm wishing, I may as well wish this was all a bad dream."

"Words can't express how much we all want that to happen."

Their condition after a near-fatal car crash had been stable over the past few days, but Dr. Abel had warned anything could happen. Their advanced ages weren't helping matters, and the doctor had no guesses as to how long the two might be in a coma. The only comforting thought was that the two of them were going through it together. They functioned like hydrogen and oxygen, and one wouldn't be able to breathe without the other. The fact that Duke had arranged to have them moved into the same room provided a small measure of comfort in a dire situation.

"Let me know when Camden gets there. Okay?" she said.

"I will." Abi's word was as good as gold. "You have to go, don't you?"

"I'm sorry," Crystal said for the third time. She'd say it a thousand more if it meant their grandparents would wake up.

"It's fine," her sister reassured, even though it wasn't. It might never be fine again if they lost Lorenzo and Lacy Remington, and they both knew it. "Call me later if you want to talk."

Crystal promised she would before saying goodbye and ending the call. Without another word, she put the gearshift in Drive and navigated onto I-45. Normally, she wouldn't allow her personal life to interfere while on an assignment, but this was life-or-death and she couldn't perform her job to the best of her ability without staying plugged into what was happening in Mesa Point.

For the next couple of hours, Brewer tilted the seat back and closed his eyes for the ride while Crystal ruminated about the accident that had left her grandparents fighting for their lives. She should have been the one on the back road leading to their property instead of them. She should have been the one to find them after the accident instead of Audrey Newcastle, soon to be Remington, but that was hardly the point. And she should have been the one sitting in the blue chair on top of nondescript blue carpet in a blue waiting room when her beloved grandmother had coded instead of out here negotiating with someone who figured they could save their own life better than she could protect it.

Halfway to Dallas, Brewer stirred. He sat up and hit the button to make the seat back rise. His intense gaze fixed out the front windshield. She hadn't intended for him to know anything about her personal life while on the job. It was the reason most US marshals she knew didn't wear a wedding ring or have screen savers of their husbands, wives, or children. Not that she had any of those things. Still. That wasn't the point. The less others knew, the better. This situation couldn't be helped. He needed to know that she might have to check in or take calls from home but she had no intention of abandoning him.

"There's something going on with my family that won't affect my job," she said.

He didn't respond.

"I just thought you should know I'm dedicated to your safety until I see this through no matter how long it takes." Work came first. It had always come first. Nature of the job. "And I will need to take a personal call from time to time." She prayed not one with bad news. "But if you're uncomfortable with this arrangement, I can call my supervisor, get myself replaced." It would take time. It would take some shuffling. But she might be able to pull it off.

Nothing.

BREWER DIDN'T HAVE the heart to be a jerk to Crystal after overhearing her side of the phone call. "I don't have an issue, ma'am." He figured once they got to Dallas and settled in, he'd find a way to ditch her and get to Trent's location off the grid anyway. Brewer had no idea what he'd find once he got there, and that suited him just fine. Could be nothing more than a campsite. But he needed to figure out transportation since he'd left his vehicle with his aunt in case she needed it.

Either way, he'd make do.

"Okay," she said. "You can call me Crystal. Every time I hear *ma'am* or *Ms. Remington*, I check over the shoulder for my grandmother." Her voice hitched on the last word.

Was it his place to say anything?

Why the hell not. "I'm sorry to hear about your family situation, ma'am… Crystal." Calling her by her first name would take some getting used to.

"Thank you." Those two words were spoken with genuine appreciation. Brewer had become good at reading people after being in charge of interrogations for a stint. He'd learned to listen for subtle clues. For instance, liars usually spoke slower, paused for longer periods, and spoke with a higher pitch. Crystal's voice filled with warmth rather than her usual straight-to-the-point tone. "My grandparents have always been the rock of our family, so it's unnatural for them to be so…helpless."

"What about your folks, if you don't mind my asking."

"Gone." The word came out so easily that whatever had happened must have been a long time ago. "I have two siblings and three cousins, but we're all like siblings because we grew up together. My father abandoned us after Abi was born."

"I'm sorry."

"Thank you," she said, keeping her eyes forward on the stretch of road in front of them.

"Your mother?" he asked.

"Died during childbirth with Abi." Some of the tension eased as she relaxed into her seat. "I'm the oldest, and my brother, Duke, is in the middle."

"It must have been hard growing up without a mother." He should know.

"We had our grandparents. That made a huge difference in our lives. In fact, I'm not sure where any of us would have ended up without them." She tapped the steering wheel with her right thumb. A nervous habit? "They raised us and our three cousins who, by the way, now all work as US marshals, same as our grandfather did once."

He made a face. "That's odd, isn't it?"

"We're not that much different than military families," she stated. "Our grandfather started off his career as a US marshal but left as soon as he saved enough money to start his paint-horse ranch. He couldn't stand being away from our grandmother for even a few days."

"Makes sense." Brewer understood military often ran in families but couldn't relate to being in the kind of relationship with someone that would make him want to overhaul his life so they could spend more time together. It boggled the mind.

"What happened to your aunt and uncle?" he asked.

His aunt had been his lifeline and probably the one person in Galveston who didn't have a bone to pick with him from something he'd done during his time there. Getting her out of harm's way had been his first priority when he'd learned Crane's arrest had gone down. Aunt Rosemary had taken him in when no one else would. She'd never once turned her back, no matter how much he'd deserved it. He owed her.

"My aunt took off a few months after my cousin Dalton was born, we still don't know why," she informed. "My uncle died when we were all young. And then there's my own father who split after my mother died."

"Sounds like a real jerk."

"Agreed," she said with authority. "He's remarried with a new family and no time for the old one. Although, my brother said our dad called recently, probably sniffing around to see if there was an inheritance in the near future."

Exactly the reason Brewer had no plans to tie the knot with anyone. Marriage was antiquated. The idea had had its day. Long-term commitment had proven to be impossible and overrated. His own parents were all the proof he needed.

Brewer glanced down to where his left shin used to be. Underneath his cargo pants, it was impossible to see the prosthetic leg. He knew part of himself was missing now and would never be replaced no matter how many advances were made in medicine. No one would want to spend the rest of their life with a partial man.

"I've been going on and on about my family. I'm not usually this talkative. I apologize." Crystal blushed, and it only served to make her more attractive.

"Don't," he said. "It's making the time pass faster, and I'm interested in hearing more. Takes my mind off my current problems."

"It's just not what I do when I'm working. Better to keep a hard line between personal and professional. I hope you can understand."

He leaned his head back. "Do I ever. The only way to survive in the military is to push all thoughts other than survival out of your mind. Right before a mission, I used to take a few minutes to think about what I'd be doing once it was over. Plant the seed that I was confident that no matter what I faced that day, I'd be back in a few hours, days, or weeks, playing a pickup game with one of the guys in my unit after chow time."

"Sounds like a good strategy."

"It kept me alive this long," he mused. Even though he hadn't exactly come home whole. "Other than Aunt Rosemary, I didn't have anyone else to come home to like some of the men. They'd stare at a picture of their girlfriend or wife. Some had kids. They would memorize those smiling faces and take that into a combat zone with them. It was enough to assure they came out alive."

"It's good to have something or someone to look forward to."

She had to have read in his file there was no one in his life. "What about you? Anyone special you're going home to?"

He half expected her to remind him that her personal life was none of his business. Instead, she shocked him by saying, "Not in a long time."

A beautiful, intelligent woman like her shouldn't have to be alone. "Too busy?"

She opened her mouth to speak before clamping it shut again. He'd crossed a line he shouldn't have.

"Sorry," he said. "You don't have to answer that. I get it. Your personal life is on a need-to-know basis, and I don't need to know."

"Something like that."

"I'm just killing time." He checked the burner cell. Two people had the number, Aunt Rosemary and now Trent. "Didn't mean to step out of bounds with my questions." He was more curious about Crystal Remington's life than he had a right to be. He wanted to know what brimmed under the surface of that serious facade. Did she have a sense of humor to go with her determination and intelligence?

"If we're going to spend twenty-four seven together over the next couple of days until the hearing, it might not hurt to get to know each other better," she said. "Relationship status is the only topic out of bounds, as you said."

He didn't feel good lying about his plans to ditch her and head toward Tyler. But what could he do?

"A name came up in the investigation into your case. Who is Damon O'Meara?"

"Damon the Devil?" he asked.

"Sure," she said. "I guess that's the same one."

"He's been showing up with the Lithuanian lately," Brewer said.

"Who is the Lithuanian?" she asked.

Brewer shrugged. "You got me. That's the only name I ever heard him called by. I think he's close to Victor Crane. A confidant or right hand. He didn't interact with me. I only ever managed to see him from behind."

"Interesting," she noted.

That was all he had about the Lithuanian, so he steered the conversation back to personal life. "You were telling me about your family. Was there some kind of accident that caused your grandparents to be in the hospital?"

"Car crash," she answered. "Did you know that in Texas there's at least one traffic fatality every day?"

"I didn't, but after growing up driving on country roads I'm not exactly shocked."

Crystal nodded. "My grandfather is getting older." She gripped the wheel tighter. He noticed she did this every time she spoke about her grandparents or the accident. "He's too stubborn to give up his driver's license no matter how many times we try to ease into the subject."

"A person like him would fiercely guard his independence, I'm guessing."

"Yes, and I get it on some level."

"Aunt Rosemary refuses to drive over thirty-five miles an hour no matter what the speed limit is." Brewer's biggest fear was that she would cause an accident. "She knows better than to go out at night, though. Her eyes aren't what they used to be."

"Does she still drive?"

"Only if it's an emergency," he said. "For the most part, I finally got her to give up her keys."

"How on earth did you do that?"

He shook his head and cracked a smile. "It won't work with your grandfather."

"How do you know?"

"Trust me."

"That's a two-way street," she quipped, full of sass and vinegar. "That trust thing. Why not trust me enough to tell me in case it could help me figure out how to keep my grandfather from ever driving again once this is over?"

"Because I seriously doubt the man wants hot firemen, as my aunt puts it, driving him to run errands or to take his wife to a doctor's appointment."

"You hired off-duty firemen to drive your aunt?" she asked with what sounded like a whole new respect for him and more than a little admiration.

"Damn right I did."

The fact she cracked a smile shouldn't cause his heart to squeeze. But it did.

Chapter Three

Crystal cracked a smile. "Sexy firemen definitely won't work with my grandfather. Brilliant idea, though." She had to give that one to him.

"What can I say? Aunt Rosemary got a kick out of it, and it got her off the road." From the sound of his voice, he was smiling too. Why did that strike her as a rare occurrence? More importantly, why did it warm her heart so much?

Based on Brewer's current situation, he hadn't had a whole lot to be happy about lately either. She'd read in his file that he'd lost part of his leg before being offered medical retirement from the military. She knew he'd refused psych help, saying he would take care of it on his own. And now he'd learned he was working for a crime-ring leader.

To say he'd been through a lot lately was like saying Texas summers were brutal. Yes, they were. End of story.

As strange as it probably sounded, even to her, she liked opening up to Brewer and talking about her family. The reason was probably more related to all the pressure she'd been under and not that there was chemistry between them. Reading too much into it would be a mistake. He was a captive audience, and she needed to get a few things off her chest. Normally, she would talk to her grandmother if something was eating at her. Since that wasn't an option, Brewer was the closest person in proximity and didn't seem to mind.

When he spoke, he had the kind of honest, direct voice that put her at ease. Too much so?

It also wrapped her in warmth and created all kinds of sensations in her body best ignored and forgotten. She'd never experienced sensations like those simply from the sound of someone's voice.

Crystal reminded herself not to get too attached. This assignment would be over in a matter of days, a week tops since the district attorney was trying to push through a speedy trial date. The case against Crane was cut-and-dried, and a witness was at risk. Judges tended to be more accommodating under those circumstances. Court dates magically opened up while other cases languished.

It was good this would be over soon. She needed to get to the hospital in Mesa Point.

GPS let them know the turnoff was one mile ahead. I-45 turned into North Central Expressway. They had a town house waiting for them in University Park, a ritzy area just north of Dallas. It had been finagled by Crystal's supervisor, who'd told her not to get used to living in the lap of luxury. She didn't see how that was possible considering the family horse ranch in Mesa Point was enough to keep anyone's feet on the ground. Not to mention a marshal's salary wasn't exactly putting her in the top one percent. The paint-horse ranch barely made ends meet, but the home and land were paid for and it had provided for six kids while keeping her grandparents fed and happy. They'd always intended to divide the ranch equally among all six of the grandkids. Crystal couldn't begin to think about a day when her grandparents didn't live there and work the business they'd built together after Grandpa Lor's stint as a marshal.

"It'll be good to get in and get settled before it gets too late." She was still surprised Brewer had come out of the restaurant when she'd been about to call it in. He'd taken his sweet time in exiting, though, which said he'd probably been in the bathroom thinking seriously about his options. "We'll have to stay indoors once we arrive, but I think you'll find the place easy on the eyes. We don't normally get such a swanky safe house."

"Don't I feel special?" He'd shifted gears and was now staring out the passenger window in quiet contemplation. Why did she get the sinking feeling he was considering ditching her?

She blew it off as a combination of stress and nerves.

"Your file gave me information about the situation you're currently in," she started, changing the subject, and turning the tables. "What made you go into the military?"

"My high school guidance counselor said I had a lot of anger." He surprised her in talking about his past. "Tried to get me to join the football team."

"I'm guessing you said no."

"Organized sports were never going to be my thing." He rubbed the strap of his backpack in between this thumb and forefinger. "Plus, I wouldn't have known when to stop if someone came at me hotheaded. It would have gotten ugly fast."

"What did you do instead?" she asked. "To get out your anger."

"Got suspended mostly." He chuckled. "I'm not exactly proud of some of the things I did when I had too much testosterone and not enough common sense. I read somewhere once that the decision-making filter in the front of the teen brain takes a break for a couple of years. I got out of hand a few too many times, but never unprovoked. I'm not saying that makes it right, but I didn't start fights. Not even then. Although, looking back, I can admit to overreacting too much of the time."

"What made you so angry?"

"The usual predictable stuff," he continued. "Had a drunk for a dad who used to beat the hell out of me for no reason except sometimes I breathed too loudly. A mom who couldn't take living with an abusive husband, so she bolted without looking back, saving herself and leaving me with a monster."

"You didn't tell anyone about the abuse?"

He shook his head without missing a beat. "Ever hear the saying about the devil you know being better than the one you don't? It's the reason most kids don't turn their parents in. They have no idea what will happen to them if they do."

"Did your aunt step in at some point?" Crystal asked. "Is that why you take such good care of her?"

"Yes, ma—" He stopped himself. "Yes, she did. She's an angel in my book. She started off asking my father if I could come to her house after school. Then, she would come up with an excuse to keep me later, like I wasn't done with my homework. Once eight o'clock hit, he'd been too drunk to care where the hell his son was. If she could keep me until then, we were home free. I spent most nights there and then weekends with him until she had me living with her full-time by sophomore year. No matter how bad I was, she saw a piece of good in me." He shrugged. "I'll never understand it because I sure as hell didn't deserve or appreciate her enough at the time."

"The world needs more Aunt Rosemarys." She would add her grandparents Lorenzo and Lacy to the list too. It amazed her that they'd taken on six kids who were within seven years of each other. The teenage years had seen a whole lot of doors slamming and arguments that had needed interventions. The Remingtons had been good kids, but no one would call them angels. Those angsty temperamental teenage years had left no prisoners. "And grandparents like mine."

"I'll second that," he concurred. "Your grandparents must have had their hands full with all… How many did you say there were of you in total?"

"Six," she answered. "I was just calculating our ages in my head. We're all within a seven-year span. Working from the youngest to oldest, Dalton and Abi are the same age. They're both twenty-eight years old. They were close growing up since they were in the same grade. Then there's my brother, Duke, who's thirty now. He just got engaged. Jules is thirty-two. Her real name is Julie. I'm thirty-three." She shot major side-eye at him. "Don't you dare say anything about me getting old."

He put his hands up, palms out, in the surrender position. "Wasn't planning on doing anything of the kind."

"Good. That leaves my cousin Camden, who's thirty-five."

"Which also makes you the second oldest, if my calculations are correct." He put his hands down and returned to working the strap of his backpack between his thumb and forefinger.

"That's right," she agreed, pulling into the parking lot of the town house. After finding a parking spot away from the street, she texted her contact to let him know they'd arrived. The response came a few seconds later. "He's on his way. Should take about fifteen to twenty minutes."

Brewer leaned his seat back again. "Guess we have time to get comfortable, then."

She wasn't touching that statement with a ten-foot pole. There was never a moment in this job where she felt like she could ever relax. After work? Sure. Never during work hours. She cut off the engine. "You were telling me about your family."

The look he shot almost made her laugh. Turned out the intense former military sergeant had a sense of humor.

"Nice try, Crystal." The way her name rolled off his tongue shouldn't have sent goose bumps across sensitized skin. He had one of those voices that she was certain had seduced every woman he'd set his sights on.

It wouldn't work on this one, all sense of professionalism and code of conduct aside. A man like Brewer was dangerous. She had no doubt he had a *take no prisoners* approach to love.

Love? Since when did she begin thinking about the love life of those in her charge?

This wasn't the time to start.

BREWER NEVER HAD a problem cutting bait and moving on in any situation he'd been in, until now. He tucked his cell inside the pocket of his rucksack, secure in the knowledge he had the coordinates safely in his phone for when he needed them. There was a wad of cash inside a zippered pocket. It was enough to get him through a couple of weeks if he needed that long, which he didn't expect to. Still, survival took planning.

Leaving Crystal wasn't something he wanted to do so

Bounty Hunted

much as needed to at this point. Depending on others hadn't proven to be the best plan. Staying meant being responsible for her life in addition to his own. Although she wouldn't see it that way.

Brewer knew the kind of man he was up against. He knew who the lieutenants she'd mentioned were. Hell, he'd driven his boss—someone he'd believed to be a successful businessman when he'd taken the gig while fresh out of the military—to meetings with those men. Brewer could name all of them. He wished his word could put them all behind bars, but the DA had said he could only prove an association if Brewer had witnessed a crime. Overhearing information about a crime was circumstantial evidence and wouldn't hold up in court.

With his background, he was probably lucky the DA hadn't locked him up in the same cell as Crane. But then, Brewer had gone to the district attorney's office with proof of a crime. He'd witnessed Crane order a hit. Better yet, he'd recorded the meeting once he'd realized what was happening.

As a driver, Brewer had built trust with Crane based on his background and military experience. Trent had vouched for Brewer, so there'd been no reason for distrust. He certainly wasn't a plant from the government. In fact, he was still angry about the bad intelligence his superior officer had acted on that had cost two of his friends' lives, part of his leg, and hearing out of his right ear.

The explosion, the losses, still haunted his dreams.

He'd known the job he'd been signing up for in the military. In many ways, going into the service had saved his life. It had certainly changed his perspective and the man he'd become. Given him honor and a reason to hold his head up high.

Didn't mean he would do a few critical things over if he could go back in time. It should have been him driving the Humvee that day, not Randal. It should have been him who'd had to be pieced back together to ship his body home after the IED had blown up. And it should have been him who'd come home in a box.

Randal had volunteered to drive that sweltering day. He'd argued it was his turn even though everyone had known it was Brewer's. Thanks to a raging headache, Brewer had gladly turned over the keys. Beer pong out of boredom the night before had cost a man's life. Brewer had gone to the back of the Humvee to lie down and cover his eyes from the unforgiving sunlight while they'd driven on their mission. Only two of the four had returned to camp alive.

Brewer didn't care about Crane's men coming after him. He only had to live long enough to ensure the bastard spent the rest of his life behind bars. The men were ruthless and would show no mercy in the event they found Brewer first. He had news for them—they weren't the first ones who'd tried to kill him. Knowing his luck, they wouldn't be the last.

"You got quiet on me." Crystal's voice pulled him from his deep thoughts.

He shook his head like he could somehow shake off his frustration at coming home to Texas a broken man who was now a witness, tricked into working for a bad man. "What do you want to talk about while we wait? Or should we get out of this car and stretch our legs?"

"It's probably not a good idea to be seen, unless you have a cramp you need to work out." She glanced over and then immediately returned her gaze to the patch of windshield directly in front of her. Was she curious about what the prosthetic looked like?

Brewer wasn't in the mood to talk about it or what had happened to cause the injury.

The woman was intelligent and beautiful. He'd rather learn more about her. "I get that your job runs in the family, but why did you decide a career as a marshal was the right job for you?" he asked.

"Why do you question it? Because I'm a woman?" She'd mentioned that before, and he honestly didn't care one way or the other.

"No," he said, deciding not to go down the road of explaining his viewpoint a second time when the first apparently hadn't taken. "Of all the jobs in the world, why this one? You grew up on a horse ranch. I see why your grandfather started in law enforcement and then moved to the country for peace. The other way around doesn't make as much sense to me. This doesn't seem like the logical next step."

"I guess not," she conceded, rubbing her temples. She'd been through hell with the accident. It was easy to see how much she loved her grandparents.

The only way he could relate was because of Aunt Rosemary. She'd been the first person to stick up for him and tell him that he was better than his actions. It might have taken a bit for him to believe it too, but he'd finally gotten there.

"The respect I have for my grandfather set the stage for me and the others to follow in his footsteps," she said. "But you're right. Every law enforcement officer I know has a story as to why they decided on this job."

"Do you?" It was probably not the best question. "I'm guessing so."

"Stick around and I might tell you mine."

"What's that supposed to mean?" he asked. She couldn't possibly have read his mind.

A navy blue Tahoe pulled into the parking lot and parked two spaces away.

"Save it for later?" she asked with a wink. The move was most definitely not flirtatious. It was more like *I've got your number.*

Had she figured out that he planned to disappear after she went to sleep? How? It wasn't like she had a crystal ball or mind-reading capabilities. Was she that good at reading people? At reading him?

A man in his late forties who looked dressed for the golf course stepped out of the Tahoe.

Crystal exited the driver's side of her sedan. Before closing the door, she said, "I'll be right back."

The exchange took less than three minutes, according to Brewer's watch—a watch he never went anywhere without.

After the driver returned to his seat and the Tahoe pulled out of his spot, Crystal motioned for Brewer to join her. She walked to the back of her vehicle and popped open the trunk before retrieving an overnight bag. She'd done this before. Many times if he had to guess.

When he left tonight, he'd tape a note to explain himself on the fridge. He owed her that much after she'd talked to him on a personal level. It was the right thing to do.

A quick tour of the two-story town house convinced Brewer this was probably the fanciest place he would ever stay in. It was tempting to stick around for the primary suite alone, which had a bathtub the size of a two-person hot tub. The mental image of Crystal joining him in there naked needed to go.

After setting his rucksack down in·that room, once Crystal had made it clear she wouldn't have it any other way, he joined her in the living room.

"Are you hungry?" she asked, picking up the TV's remote.

"I could eat." Brewer could go without food longer than most. But there was nothing to do except kill time, so he might as well go along with the idea.

A moment later, Crystal's expression twisted to fierce determination as she dived toward him, knocking him off his feet. The move surprised him because she knew exactly where to aim to knock him off balance—not an easy thing to do.

The hearing loss in his right ear made him miss the sound of the shot until the bullet had pierced the front window, which was a few seconds too late.

Chapter Four

"Stay down," Crystal said to Brewer, cursing the fact their safe house had been compromised.

It was unlikely they'd been followed but not impossible.

Dealing with a high-level long-standing criminal operation raised the stakes. She was good at her job, but so were they. And they didn't get to be one of the top crime organizations in Texas by being sloppy or allowing witnesses to make it to trial to testify.

Despite keeping vigilant watch, she couldn't be one hundred percent positive she hadn't picked up a tail. *Dammit.*

Was she too distracted by her family crisis to do a good job?

Diving on top of Brewer had been instinct. In that split second, reason hadn't kicked in to tell her that he used to be military and could handle himself. Brewer rolled out from underneath her in one swift move. It happened so fast she landed on the hardwood flooring with a thud.

"They'll expect us to come out the back door," she said, belly crawling away from the kitchen. The town house had a typical shotgun layout with a bathroom to the right.

"Bathroom?" he asked. He must have already memorized the layout. She should have known he would get the lay of the land in a matter of minutes. She did the same.

Memorizing exits was the curse, or blessing, depending on how you looked at it, of working in a job that could get you killed on a daily basis.

"Yes," she said. She'd already pulled her Glock from her shoulder harness and was army crawling while holding her weapon out in front of her.

Brewer managed to gather and then slip his rucksack onto his back without missing a beat. His clear thinking and presence of mind wasn't something she was used to in a witness. Protecting a former Army sergeant was virgin territory. The guy could hold his own, but she had better resources at her disposal—resources that he was going to need to stay alive and make it to trial.

At this point, Crystal was following Brewer's lead. He navigated them to the bathroom. The window next to the toilet was shaped like a cruise ship's. Could Brewer fit through the octagon shape?

"Here, let me," she said.

He spun around until he was back-to-back with her as she stood up and took a peek out. She lifted her head barely enough to survey the area. A man wearing all dark clothing moved around the side of the town house. He was carrying, and she suspected his target practice was decent if he'd been selected for this job.

A long-range shot would make for quick and easy witness removal. No one would even get their hands dirty handling "the problem" in that manner.

Crystal got a good look at the shooter's profile. A bounty hunter? Protecting Brewer just got a whole lot trickier.

"There's a bounty on your head," she whispered to him, just in case he decided to get cute and ditch her in the chaos that was bound to follow.

Brewer muttered the same curse she was thinking.

"You're a high-value target," she said to him as the bounty hunter rounded the back of the town house. "And I have a feeling this guy is about to come in through the back door in a matter of a few seconds, so we'd better get the hell out of here if we both want to stay alive."

Brewer moved to open the window. "You want out first?"

The sound of the back door being kicked in echoed through the home.

Without saying a word, Crystal climbed out the window and then landed hard on prickly shrubbery that wrapped its arms around her. She bucked before rolling onto the hard soil. A few scratches never killed anyone.

Once again, she was left holding her breath to see if Brewer would follow. Had she made a mistake in going first? She couldn't exactly call out to him.

The thought that he might be in trouble stopped her cold as she stared at the small window.

"Dammit," he said with a grunt. His voice traveled out the window into the still night air.

Crystal couldn't climb back in the way she'd gotten out, so she bolted around to the back door and then into the kitchen. The bounty hunter had kicked the door in, just like she'd suspected. At this point, she assumed he worked alone, like most in his profession. Profit sharing wasn't exactly a common business practice.

Bounty hunters were the lone rangers of the twenty-first century. They weren't bound by laws like marshals and others who worked in law enforcement. They weren't above them either. In general, they were end of the line, the last resort in trying to locate someone. Did Cane's men want Brewer alive? Did they want to mete out their own form of justice?

A thud shook the walls of the town house. Crystal turned off lights as she carefully, methodically moved through the town house.

A series of grunts and curses twisted her stomach in knots. From this vantage point, she had no idea if Brewer was winning the fight.

At least no weapons had been fired, which was part of the reason she believed this might be a "bring 'em back alive" order. Proof of death would be easy enough if the bounty hunter shot Brewer and then took a photo.

Photos could be doctored, but even the most dishonest person would realize sending in a fake would cost their own life when dealing with someone like Crane.

A bounty made a difficult protection detail a dozen times harder. If they weren't so short-staffed at the marshal's office already, she would request help. Several marshals had turned in their badges, saying the public didn't appreciate their service any longer so they didn't see the need to put their lives on the line.

If being a US marshal wasn't in her blood, she might feel the same way.

Another crash sounded, tightening the knot. She took another step toward the bathroom. At least she had on her Kevlar vest underneath her suit jacket.

The light flipped off in the bathroom, casting the place in darkness. There was a little light from the street streaming in between the mini-blind slats. It was enough.

As she approached the bathroom, a body came flying out.

"Put your hands where I can see 'em," she demanded the second she realized it was the bounty hunter and not Brewer.

He appeared next, taking up the door frame before launching himself toward the bounty hunter. You'd think both had just run a marathon for their heavy breathing.

In the next second, Brewer had the bounty hunter pinned to the floor with his knee jammed into the guy's back. "Who sent you?"

The bounty hunter turned his face to the side and grinned.

The question had to be asked, even though she would have been more surprised if he'd answered.

"It's your death sentence," Crystal said, keeping a watchful eye on the doors. "Are you by yourself, or should I break out the charcuterie board for company?"

The bounty hunter chuckled at her sarcasm, then winced when Brewer ground his knee harder into the man's back.

"What's your name?" she asked, moving toward him to relieve him of his wallet so she could retrieve his ID. Folks in this line of work didn't always carry identification in the event that, well, something just like this happened and they got caught on the wrong side of the law. Checking pockets was still mandatory.

Still no word from the bounty hunter.

"Cat got your tongue?" she goaded. On occasion, one of the folks' ego swelled when she poked the bear so to speak. Most weren't exactly reading Shakespeare in their time off. Muscle people like this one rarely read much more than texts with names of their targets and the price on their head. Speaking of texts, she searched him for his phone.

This guy was shrewd based on the fact he'd left any identifiers either in his vehicle or at home. He didn't have a cell on him, which was rare, but she'd come across his type in her line of work.

Only an experienced bounty hunter would take a job like

this one. If a hunter left any ties leading back to the organization, they would be erased. Crane ran a tight ship—one that had escaped the scrutiny of law enforcement for the past seven years. Well, guess what? Time was up.

BREWER FINALLY CAUGHT his breath as Crystal heaved a sigh. Being dramatic must've been part of playing a role.

In battle, there were rules that had to be followed. Brewer figured home was no different. As much as those rules got in the way of forcing someone to speak, they were as much the reason he took pride in his military service as backyard barbecues and families huddled around shiny trees on Christmas morning. For better or worse, rules protected people. He'd had a bird's-eye view of countries without order. Chaos. It gave him a new appreciation for home. That and the fact bullets weren't flying over his head every five minutes.

"Talk, sonofabitch," Brewer managed to grind out the words.

"It's all good," Crystal said to him. "Dallas PD will have a good time arresting this one." With that, she pulled out her cell phone and called 911. She walked away before she identified herself to Dispatch.

The bounty hunter Brewer had pinned to the floor was trying to kill him and not her. Although this jerk didn't look like he would mind a little collateral damage.

The man was half a foot shorter than Brewer, so five feet, ten inches of a tank of a man. The guy bleached the top of his short, spiky hair, leaving the sides black. Brewer had stared into the eyes of folks with no souls. Folks who would use women or children without a thought as a means to an end, strapping a bomb to them and sending them into enemy camp. Evil always showed through the eyes.

This sonofabitch had no conscience and was greedy. He hadn't shot Brewer when he'd had the chance, so the bounty must've been to bring him in. Brewer didn't have to be one of them to realize what that meant. Torture. Make an example out of him in case anyone else in the organization grew a conscience and decided to testify against the boss. Or if the feds had put pressure on some of the "employees" of the organization, had anyone close to turning state's witness.

People needed a leader. Some might view Brewer's actions as leadership. They might be tempted to follow suit.

Crane would want to squash that instinct like a cockroach.

The bounty hunter tried to buck Brewer off to no avail. He might have gotten in a few good punches, but Brewer was strong as an ox and about as heavy as one too. Going to the gym, pushing himself to the limit with endless burpees that he hated doing and pull-ups along with weights and about a dozen other exercises made all the body parts he had left strong.

Within a matter of minutes after the call, the town house was flooded with law enforcement officers. After exchanging what looked like a coin with the lead officer on the scene, Crystal turned to him. "We need to talk."

With the bounty hunter under arrest, Brewer could finally catch his breath, think about his next step. "Okay."

She walked into the kitchen area where a handyman had just arrived to fix the back door.

"I understand if you don't trust my ability to keep you safe, but—"

"Whoa," Brewer said, interrupting her. "What gives you that impression?"

Crystal-blue eyes studied him as she folded her arms

across her chest. "The safe house was compromised minutes after we arrived." She shrugged. "I figured after almost getting ditched back at the diner that you'd definitely want to be rid of me now."

"I'm alive because of your quick thinking," he corrected. He knew a good teammate when he encountered one. He brought his hand up to his right ear. "I'm sure you've read my file. I can't hear out of this side. It's the reason I never heard the bullet. If you hadn't jumped me, I would likely be dead right now. If anything, this has shown me that I do need someone else to have my back."

Crystal was good at her job. She'd proven her abilities. They made a good team. And a growing part of him didn't want to let her down in return. Could he take her off the grid with him? Would she agree?

Chapter Five

"First of all," Crystal shot back, appreciating the first break in tension and show of trust in her abilities since meeting Brewer this morning, "I didn't 'jump' you." She flashed eyes at him. "You'd know it if I did."

Her sarcasm brought out a smirk. It wasn't exactly another smile, but she could work with it. The fact that the mood could lighten so quickly after what had just happened told her that he'd been one damn fine sergeant. He was used to bullets and battle. After seeing him in action, she was a little less offended that he'd tried to cut her out of the equation. The man was capable of taking care of himself.

Still, she had resources available that he didn't. It gave her an edge, and he'd finally conceded as much. She could exhale now despite the fact her heart pounded at the thought of spending time alone with Wade Brewer.

She shoved the unprofessional reaction out of her thoughts.

"This bastard is facing a third-degree-felony charge," she said to Brewer to get the conversation going again.

"Think there's a snowball's chance in hell that he'll talk?" he asked, leaning a slender hip against the counter. The sleeve of his shirt was ripped, displaying a peek of a tattoo on his bicep. The man's arms were thick, tan, and muscled. She had a thing for men with well-placed tattoos despite her squeaky-clean image and the fact she had none of her own. The right one could be sexy as all get-out. Too many and it came across as a doodling on someone's body. Most of the time, it looked like a hot mess.

Brewer's fit into the *sexy* category from what she could see.

Good for him. He probably had no trouble dating, whereas Crystal had been in a drought of her own doing. Ever since her breakup with Lucas Mahone, she'd been content to spend Saturday nights at home with a good book and a glass of wine when she wasn't on the job. Lucas had been "the one" on paper. He was good looking. Was a solid marshal who worked a different district than hers, despite putting in a bid to transfer. Never been married. No kids. Not that she minded either, but he wasn't hung up on the past or tied to someone he didn't want to be with any longer.

And yet dating him felt a lot like drinking milk. Plain. Probably even good for you. Last Christmas, though, he'd given her a new seat for her bicycle. Had she needed one? Yes. Did it make riding her bicycle more comfortable? Yes. Was it practical? Yes.

Therein lies the problem. He was a practical choice. He was comfortable. He was measured.

Did he make her palms sweaty? No.

Did he make her stomach flip-flop? No.

Did he make her skin sizzle with his touch? Absolutely not.

So, she'd done the only kind thing she could think of. Rather than draw out the relationship another few months or, worse yet, years, she'd cut him loose so he could find someone who would be a better match.

Lucas had another trait. This one had become annoying. He was stubborn, said he'd win her back. Six months later, he was doubling down despite her best efforts to handle the breakup in a professional manner.

Crystal had learned a valuable lesson through this experience—never date anyone even remotely connected to her job.

To make matters worse, Lucas's transfer had been approved since they were so short-staffed in her district. He'd made the move last week.

"Hey," Brewer said, snapping his fingers in front of her eyes. "Anybody home?"

"Yes, sorry," she said, giving herself a mental headshake. "Did you say something?"

He studied her a little more intensely now. "I have a place where we can go off the grid."

"I have to be in contact with my supervisor at all times," she said, shaking her head. Brewer might've been fully capable of taking care of himself, but she couldn't let him take over. "In fact, she's coming up with a new plan for us right now."

"Excuse me for saying but this one didn't exactly work out," he said, twisting his face in disdain. "To be clear, you're good at what you do, but my trust in the process ends there."

She couldn't argue his point even though she wanted to.

"I have a certain protocol to follow, Brewer." She shrugged. "If you want me, you'll have to go along with it." Her cheeks flamed. "I didn't mean *want* me." Words came out all wrong when she got flustered.

The freakin' smirk returned for a split second before his face morphed to all business. "Give me one good reason to trust your organization again."

"Simple," she said. "Me."

Brewer exhaled sharply. "You do come in handy when a bullet shoots past my right side."

"Give me another shot, and if I fail, I'll figure out a way to go to your safe place," she offered. "Are we good?"

"Good." The one word spoken with finality said there'd be no going back if her second attempt didn't pan out.

To be fair, his life was on the line. Would she handle the situation differently if the shoe were on the other foot? Would she blindly trust someone else with her life? Probably not.

So, she could cut him some slack for digging his heels in and leaning into his stubborn side.

"Give me a few more minutes and I'll have a plan for us," she said. "Deal?"

His nod was almost imperceptible. He was agreeing against his better judgment, according to the questioning look in his eyes. What could she say? The man had beautiful eyes. Eyes she could stare into for days.

And probably a whole lot of women said the same thing. Did the same thing.

Anyway, moving on. She didn't have time for stargazing.

Within seven minutes, she had a new plan. It required a new vehicle, which would also show up in seven minutes. One more seven and she might believe her luck was starting to change.

Her cell buzzed. She checked the screen. Her supervisor was calling, so she answered.

"Marshal Remington here," Crystal said. It was her standard answer, confirming with her superior officer, Elise Fissile, that she was still in charge of her phone. It was their code.

"Everyone all right?" Elise asked.

"Perp is in cuffs, and the witness and I are fine," she

confirmed. "My witness lost a shirt in the process. He'll need more clothing aside from the few things he has in his bag." He couldn't exactly blend in with a ripped shirt. It was bad enough that his hot bod and chiseled jawline drew attention if they had to be in a public place. He didn't exactly make it easy to travel incognito.

"Done," Elise said. "I have a dark blue Chevy Tahoe heading your way. In the dashboard will be a folder with cash and new identities inside."

"Okay," Crystal said. "I'll confirm as soon as I have the vehicle in my possession."

"I'm putting you in a motel off Harry Hines Boulevard for the night," Elise informed.

She groaned. Talk about a fall from grace. They were going from a spacious town house with hardwood flooring and granite countertops to a roach motel. *Great.* Looked like Crystal would be sleeping with one eye open tonight. She hated cockroaches.

"We can do that," she finally said, searching her thoughts for other options. Checking into the motel didn't mean she had to sleep there. Once she was alone with Brewer, she would ask if he had another idea.

"The bounty on your witness's head is half a million dollars, by the way." Elise was probably picking up the roll of Tums sitting on top of her desk. Every time she delivered bad news, she popped one.

"That's a lot of money for a starting bid." The price would go up.

"The FBI is involved, so watch out for one of their agents," her boss continued without missing a beat.

"Do I get a name?" Crystal asked.

"I'm working on it," Elise supplied. "But they aren't in full cooperation mode after Mahone outed one of their agents by accident last month. The director and I are barely on speaking terms right now."

"Which is understandable under the circumstances."

"Mahone tried to get himself reassigned to assist you in case this gets bigger than one marshal," Elise said, then paused. Her supervisor was no doubt waiting for a reaction. There were rules against two marshals in the same division having a personal relationship. Rules that were in place for good reason.

"Do we have enough personnel to put two marshals on this case?" Crystal asked, keeping her voice as level as possible. Unaffected. She had to come across like she didn't care one way or the other.

"No." Elise's suspicions had been raised since Lucas wasn't exactly being discreet about his attachment to her. The last thing Crystal needed in her file was a reprimand for dating a coworker. Not to mention the fact they weren't a couple any longer and hadn't been since before his transfer.

And she had bigger priorities in her personal life right now. Her grandparents needed her, and she felt guilty as hell for being here and not there. She needed to go home to Mesa Point and park it until they were better. The doctor had no idea how long that might take or if it would even happen in all honesty, but Crystal refused to give up hope when hope was all she had.

"So, you're okay on your own with the witness?" Elise continued.

Crystal wasn't sure *okay* was the right word to use, but she'd figure it out. "No problem."

THE FIGHT WITH the bounty hunter marked the first time Brewer had been physically challenged since losing part of his leg. He'd come out all right. A spot the size of a base-ball on his left rib cage where he'd taken a knee already hurt like hell. The bruise would make twisting and bend-ing painful. At least his rib wasn't cracked. Or at least not that he could tell.

He'd become good at assessing his injuries over the years. Adrenaline had gotten him far this evening, but the boost was already wearing thin. Exhaustion settled in as a replacement. Brewer was bone tired.

Crystal joined him in the kitchen where he'd propped himself up, back against the wall. His eyes were closed, causing every other sense to come alive to make up for the momentary sight loss. Bodies, when he really thought about it, could be amazing. Too bad they couldn't regrow broken or missing parts.

"What's the plan, boss?" he asked when she stopped a couple feet in front of him.

Slowly he opened his eyes, doing his level best not to no-tice full, kissable lips. Or the way her tongue slicked across them before she spoke, leaving a silky trail.

Crystal made eyes at him. "I have a new place, but I'm not sleeping there." She shivered.

"That bad?" He barely held back a chuckle at her physi-cal response. Must've been bad if she was having this kind of reaction to it.

"Roach motel," she said, then winced. "I can't."

"Do you have a better idea?" he asked on a laugh. Move-ment hurt. The bruise forming was going to be a doozy.

"Figured I'd ask you first," she admitted. He appreci-ated the trust she'd given in that statement.

"I have the place I mentioned before, but it might be too far away," he stated. "It's completely off the grid."

Crystal shifted her weight from her left foot to her right. He'd never noticed feet as much as he did now. It was a strange fact. Once he'd lost his foot, he couldn't stop checking out everyone else's. Brains did interesting things sometimes. He figured he could study his for the rest of his life and still know a fraction of its capabilities.

At least she was considering the option.

"*Off the grid* sounds really tempting right now," she said after a thoughtful pause. "But I should probably stay in range so I can provide updates to my boss. Otherwise, we could end up stranded with no support or backup."

"You've proven to be all the backup I need," he muttered.

"Thanks for the compliment." Her cheeks turned three shades of red, which shouldn't have been as sexy as hell.

"How about taking a drive and seeing where we end up?"

He didn't hate the idea.

"Okay," he said.

"My superior is having a Chevy Tahoe delivered in the next—" she checked her watch "—two minutes."

"We're ditching the old ride?"

"Just in case we were followed," she said. "I didn't see anyone." The look of failure that crossed her features was a little too familiar.

He was about to be a hypocrite but decided to say it anyway. "If we were followed, it wasn't your fault."

"Doesn't matter," she quipped. "It was my responsibility."

For once, Brewer didn't have a comeback. In fact, he understood her logic completely. Hell, it was the same logic he used to beat himself up over what happened overseas. The guilt was real. The sense of failure was real. The losing sleep at night over past mistakes was real.

The only thing he could say in all honesty was "You're

good at your job. No one is perfect. Not even you. This could have happened to anybody. This could have happened to me if I'd been out here alone. And then where would I be?"

"You?" The look of surprise on her face caught him off guard. "No. You would be just fine."

Without expanding, she turned toward the back door. "No reason to stick around here any longer. Our Tahoe is pulling into the alley now."

As much as Brewer appreciated the vote of confidence, *fine* wasn't the word he would use to describe not hearing a bullet whiz past his ear. He'd never needed anyone in his life, so this new reality had him off his game.

Did he need Crystal Remington? Or could he still strike out on his own and keep himself safe?

Chapter Six

Crystal met the driver in the alley, thanked him, and then climbed into the driver's seat. Walking away from Brewer when he was busy complimenting her had been necessary. The fact that he felt the need to bolster her confidence shouldn't have irritated her. But it did.

Being on edge had more to do with her grandparents than this high-profile case. Their conditions weighed heavily on her thoughts. Guilt sat like a wet blanket around her shoulders for working while they were in the hospital. Grandpa Lor wouldn't have had it any other way, though. He would give her a hard time for taking work off—even if she could—so she could sit around a hospital room and watch him breathe. The knowledge made being on the job a little easier.

Brewer appeared at the back door, once again taking up the entire frame. The man was like looking across a lake, placid on the surface with a whole lot brewing underneath. It was the stuff underneath that concerned her.

At least they'd built a tentative bridge of trust today. She couldn't say for certain that meant he would stick around, but she had more confidence that he was giving witness protection a chance. Giving *her* a chance.

Without a whole lot of ceremony, he slipped into the

passenger seat, placed his rucksack at his feet, and then buckled in.

"Hungry?" she asked, thinking a burger and fries sounded almost too good right now. They could swing by a drive-through if she had him hide his face.

"Yes," he conceded. Quiet Brewer was back. Brooding?

"Whataburger sound good?"

"Sure," he said, distracted.

Crystal was an overthinking specialist, so she recognized the trait in others. But right now, she sat at the mouth of the alley unsure of which way to turn. "Left or right?"

"You're asking me?"

"Never mind," she said, turning left as she remembered it was the long way out of the neighborhood. She tapped the steering wheel with her thumb. Going out a different way in a different vehicle was good. There would be more bounty hunters stepping up to the challenge as word spread, especially with a price as high as the one on his head. Keeping him alive to collect worked in her favor.

She mentally shook off the thought.

There was no way Crystal was losing Brewer. "Tell me more about the guy who hooked you up with the job."

"Trent Thomas?"

She nodded.

"We grew up in the same town. Although I wouldn't call us friends. I wasn't exactly Mr. Popular back then."

The file on Brewer said he'd confused himself for a boxer in his youth. "You ever consider going pro?" she quipped.

"Pro?"

"Boxing. I read that you liked to punch first, ask questions later," she said. It wasn't a judgment, just fact.

"Growing up a punching bag for my old man gave me

enough practice." His voice held no emotion. He could have been reading the contents of a cereal box for how little feeling came across.

"You ever reconcile with your father?" she asked.

"Why would I? He wasn't there for me when I was growing up," he said with brutal honesty.

Crystal could relate.

"You got quiet all of a sudden," Brewer pointed out.

She nodded. "Let's just say that I can relate to having a deadbeat for a dad." But didn't a little piece of everyone wish their parent could be there for them? "I never thought about the man until the accident."

"You said he called but did he show up at the hospital?"

"Not to my knowledge. He's too good to darken the door of Mesa Point," she said, then realized she'd just said her hometown out loud. Normally she kept personal information to herself with a witness. "That's where my grandparents live, and it's where I'm from."

"Forgive me for saying but the bastard doesn't deserve to know you or your family if you ask me."

She couldn't argue his point. Even though a growing part of her wanted to let go of the very real pain in her chest at the mention of her father. He might not have deserved her forgiveness, but she wanted peace. Would forgiving the man bring her peace of mind?

Since this was going nowhere, she circled the conversation back around to Trent. "Tell me more about your buddy."

"What's to tell?" He fidgeted with the strap on his rucksack. "Like I said, we weren't buddies back in Galveston—but then I didn't have friends then. I was classified as a loner by my guidance counselor."

"Were you?"

"A loner?" The question was rhetorical. "Hell yes. I went from this skinny kid who got picked on to someone who could snap a neck like that." He snapped his fingers for emphasis. "Kids left me alone after that."

"But you still fought," she said.

"Anyone and everyone who had a bone to pick with me." Brewer talked like that was as normal as day and not a cry for help. Her heart went out to him. With two siblings and three cousins all close in age, she'd been insulated from bullying except for the snide comments about her dad and being an orphan. Kids could be cruel. No one got out of childhood without having their feelings hurt by their peers at one point or another. Outright bullying, relentless bullying was a different story. She tensed thinking about the cruelty and the damage it left behind. She'd seen the effects. Depression. Teen suicide.

"I'm sorry that happened to you," she said and meant it.

"It's fine," he said with forced conviction.

"No, it's not. It's never fine. It's awful, and no one should have to deal with it, least of all teenagers who already have enough pressure."

"I survived," he said. His voice a study in measured calm. Forced calm?

BREWER CHECKED THE side-view mirror as he bit back a yawn.

"Whataburger is a couple of blocks from here," Crystal said. "Then we can figure out a place to grab some sleep."

"Sounds like a plan to me," he said. The other subject was closed. He'd had a bad childhood; one he wouldn't wish on his worst enemy. It happened. He wasn't the only one. Sitting around being angry didn't change it. Which was why he'd moved on.

No other words were spoken as Crystal drove the few blocks and then pulled into the drive-through. Even at this hour, there was a long line.

"How do you know Dallas so well if you're from Mesa… wherever?"

"Point," she supplied. "It's Mesa Point. And I come here all the time for work."

"Hiding witnesses?"

"That and other things," she said.

"I thought that's all marshals did," he said. "Witness protection, right?"

A smile broke across her face. "We do a whole lot more than that, but that's what everyone thinks." She glanced over, and those simple few seconds stirred something deep inside his chest. He dismissed the feeling as being overly tired.

"What else do you do?"

"Protect federal judges," she continued with the kind of pride he'd felt at serving his country once he'd gotten over his anger. "We track down felons and arrest them, bring them to justice. Then there's prisoner transport to add to the list." She pulled up to the order box as she turned to him. "What'll it be? Dinner is on me tonight."

He couldn't help but chuckle before giving his order of a jalapeño burger with the works and fries. What could he say? The marshal was intelligent and funny, not to mention one of the most beautiful women he'd laid eyes on. If he complimented her on her looks, she would probably deny them.

Crystal ordered the avocado-and-bacon burger along with an order of fries.

"You said the blood on your shirt is from the bounty

hunter," she said once out of earshot from the order box. "Have you checked your right shoulder?"

"I did while you were on the call," he admitted.

"And?"

"It's not much more than a scratch," he said, dismissing the fact it could be a real injury. He'd been nicked by the bullet his right ear had failed to warn him about. He glanced over at the blood stain slowly flowering on his shoulder. Okay, maybe more than a scratch. All he needed was a needle and fishing line to sew it up. "You have a first-aid kit somewhere in the supplies you requested, right?"

"Yes," she said, drawing out the word.

"That's all I need to take care of it," he responded. "It's nothing a good Band-Aid can't fix." Softening the injury wasn't an outright lie so much as meant to put Crystal's mind at ease. Right now, all her focus needed to go toward keeping them both alive. If Crane got his way, Brewer would be dead by morning. Or worse, alive and tortured to the point that death would be a relief.

Men like Crane showed no mercy. Something was missing inside that made them ruthless. Heart? Conscience?

Those came to mind first, but it was even deeper than that. A soul?

"Your file says you were on the job for six months," Crystal said, shifting the topic.

"Give or take," he admitted.

"Why didn't you just quit?" she asked. "You could have saved yourself all this stress and drama if you'd walked away. You could have relocated and started a new life. Gone off the grid like you mentioned before."

"Good questions," he said. "Quitting was never an option for me."

"Why not?" she pressed. "A whole lot of people, probably most, wouldn't dare go up against someone like Crane. And for good reason. He's one of the worst. He has long reach. The only person in the area who could hold his own against the man is Michael Mylett's organization."

"True," he agreed. "Everything you said is fact."

"Have you ever had interactions with Mylett?" she asked.

He shook his head. "I know of him, but I didn't have a reason to speak to him."

"How does Trent know Crane?" she pushed.

The vehicle in front of them moved up a car length and she advised him to keep his face hidden as they neared the window.

"Through a second cousin," Brewer said. "I reached out to Trent to see if he knew anyone who was hiring. He got back to me a couple days later after putting out a few feelers with his relatives."

"Trent wasn't aware of his criminal enterprise?" she asked, not buying that he wasn't. Crane must have trusted Trent's cousin or he wouldn't have taken him up on his suggestion to hire Brewer.

"Said he wasn't and I believe him," Brewer said, sounding defensive. "You asked me why I didn't just walk away from Crane. Believe it or not, I didn't have a lot of honor in my actions growing up," he admitted. "There my aunt was, though. Standing beside me. Telling me that I would do better next time." The memories brought tears to the backs of his eyes. Brewer didn't cry. "How would I ever be able to go home again, look her in the eye if I ran away when I could save lives?"

"That's an honorable thing to say," she said. "Even more honorable to stand by your words."

"It's the right thing to do," he said dismissively. He never thought of himself as anything but a normal human doing his best to stay on the right track, make his aunt proud.

"Which doesn't exactly make it easy," Crystal pointed out.

"It's simple when you break it down to what's right or wrong," he countered. "Walking away, letting this man continue to get away with murder, would have kept me awake nights. Being killed would be better than never sleeping again."

"Still, there's a lot of honor in what you're doing," she said.

The respect in Crystal's voice did little to tamp down his growing attraction to the marshal. A part of him was starting to wish there could be something between them no matter how impossible that might be.

Or was it?

Chapter Seven

Crystal was thoroughly impressed by her witness. She protected everyone with the same integrity. However, it wasn't uncommon for her to be charged with keeping a criminal alive to testify against an even bigger criminal. Low-level criminals sometimes turned against their bosses. There was always a story behind the reason that often times ended up being about self-preservation. The low-level criminal had messed up, and then his or her head ended up on the chopping block. Or their family was threatened. WITSEC was self-preservation for those types.

Then there were innocent folks who'd been in the wrong place at the wrong time, causing them to witness a crime in process. Protecting someone who hadn't asked for any of this always hit Crystal square in the chest.

The vehicle in front moved up, so Crystal did the same. She rolled down her window. The food smell filled the cab of the Tahoe and made her stomach growl.

And then there was Brewer. He had experience with war. He'd unwittingly gone to work for a criminal, figured it out, and then turned state's witness to lock the bastard behind bars for the rest of his life.

Brewer had to be fully aware that he could be hunted long after the trial. Crane had long arms, in a manner of speaking, and a man like him would lose all street credibility if he allowed Brewer to get away with testifying and then staying alive.

All Brewer had in the world was his aunt, who was safely tucked away. He could go into the program when the trial was all said and done. He could be given a new identity, a new job, a new lease on life.

Or—and this was the most likely scenario—he could disappear all by himself. He could disappear off the grid. She had no doubt he would survive. There were still remote places in America where a person could go to get lost. Then there was Canada. He could set up camp in the vast wilderness there. Facing wildlife had to be more appealing than always looking over his shoulder for someone in the scumbag organization he'd worked for to find him and kill him.

Would he be able to walk away from his aunt? Leave her without knowing if she would be all right? He wouldn't be able to afford twenty-four-hour security. Not even if he handed over his entire paycheck while he slept on the soil and ate from the land. With her age and general health, he wouldn't be able to take her with him.

"Hey," he said to her, breaking through the noise in her head.

She looked over at him. He nodded toward the front of the Tahoe. Oh. Right. She'd been so lost in thought she didn't realize it was her turn to move up.

After paying for the food and drinks, she pulled up and then found a parking spot.

"Mind if we eat right now?" she asked, not waiting to dig into one of the bags.

"I was thinking the same thing," he said with a smile

that most likely had women forming lines for the chance to spend time with him.

For the next few minutes, nothing mattered but devouring burgers and fries.

Since she hated the smell of food lingering in a vehicle, she grabbed the bags and then headed to the trash can positioned next to the door of the fast-food joint. From the cab, she heard Brewer protest, saying he could do it. She waved him off, needing to stretch her legs a bit. Plus, she was stalling for time.

No magical ideas came to her on the walk back and forth, but it was still nice to get fresh air.

"What had you so quiet in the line earlier?" Brewer asked after she reclaimed her seat.

Crystal might as well come clean. "I was just thinking about how a lot of the witnesses I protect come to me in order to save themselves. I'm the lesser of two evils, if that makes sense."

He nodded that it did.

"And here you are truly placing yourself in harm's way in order to do the right thing," she said.

Risking a glance, she could have sworn his cheeks flooded with embarrassment. It was fleeting, and he regained composure within seconds.

"It's the right thing to do," he said. "It's not hard."

"Oh, but it is," she countered. "And you deserve credit for being an honorable person."

He sat there quiet for a long moment. "I had a lot to make up for from my youth."

With his father treating Brewer like a punching bag instead of a person, she was surprised all the goodness hadn't been beaten out of him. She'd come across plenty of folks in her line of work who used a bad childhood as the reason they'd turned to crime.

Everyone had a choice. Everyone experienced trauma in one way or the other. Everyone had the ability to determine right from wrong.

So, she never let someone off the hook easily.

"Since we're talking about the past," he hedged. "Do you ever wonder what your life would have turned out like if your mom was still alive?"

"No," she said, surprised at how quickly he'd turned the tables on her. "Why would I? It would only be a waste of time."

He nodded, but it was more like concession.

"My dad was another story," she continued. "I made up all kinds of stories in my head about why he had to leave, like he was some kind of saint who was out making the world a better place and had to keep us in a secure location. I used to wake up on my birthdays certain the man would walk through the door with an armload of presents. I gave him all kinds of jobs. Adventurer. There were times when I decided he couldn't contact me because he was in some kind of remote jungle, saving someone's life. He was always the hero who would ride in on the white horse someday to rescue us."

Brewer reached over the console and took her by the hand. Hers was small by comparison. The moment of silence between them after her skin's reaction to his touch felt like the most intimate moment of her life.

How could that be?

Since this man possessed superpowers that scared the hell out of her, she pulled her hand back and thanked him.

This time, when he nodded, she saw hurt in his eyes.

"We should get back on the road," she said. "It's a mistake to sit in one place too long."

"Okay," he said, his voice sounded gruff now. His deep timbre sent warmth all through her body. Even now. Even when his voice was clipped and there was a trace of hurt in his tone.

Had another wall come up between them?

BREWER HAD NO idea why Crystal had withdrawn her hand but after making physical contact decided the move was probably for the best. Electrical aftershocks still rocked his hand and arm even after a minute passed.

"Do you consider yourself an outside person?" Crystal asked.

"I can camp with the best of 'em. Why?" Was she about to ditch the Tahoe and head for the woods? They were in Dallas, so there were no mountains. Everything here was flat, which worked to their advantage. No twisty roads to make them worry about something or someone lurking around the next bend. No fog to blind them until they were right up on someone. And not many trees to hide behind.

There were, however, wide-open skies. Even at night, he felt the openness. And there were vehicles everywhere, day and night. It didn't matter. Someone was on the roads, making it easier to blend in.

The Tahoe had blacked-out windows despite the otherwise soccer-mom look. Glancing at the fast-food line, there'd been exactly three Tahoes with soccer emblems on the back window along with the names of the players scrolled underneath.

If Brewer ever had kids, their names would not be stamped on the back of the family vehicle. It seemed like the easiest way to get his kid stolen. The kidnapper already had the kid's name and some information about him or her. The more information a perp had, the easier it would be to convince the kid that they already knew each other. Or that the perp knew the kid's parents.

Brewer caught himself right there and stopped the train of thought. Him with a kid? He'd never once considered it. Karma was hell, and he'd racked up too much bad karma during his youth. His own kid would most likely have personality traits that would be payback.

Plus, he'd never once envisioned himself as a father. His bad genes needed to die with him. And now that he wasn't a whole man any longer, he couldn't imagine anyone would want to spend their life with him.

"I was thinking we could find a spot, park, and lean the seats back," she said. "The problem is going to be finding a place out of the way enough not to draw attention."

"Or we could do it the other way," he stated. "We could find a small neighborhood that has cars lined up on the streets and slip in between a couple of big trucks."

"That would be Garland or Richardson," she said with a spark in her voice that shouldn't have caused the knot in his chest to tighten as much as it did.

Adding to Crystal's positive traits was her voice. She had the kind of laugh that was like waking up to a spring morning after a rain shower, the air clean and crisp.

Before he tripped down that rabbit hole, he cleared his throat and grounded himself in the reality that she was there as his protection from a ruthless criminal.

Brewer glanced at the rearview mirror and could have sworn he recognized someone a couple of cars back. "We might have picked up a tail."

Crystal muttered a curse. "I made a mistake keeping us in the area too long." She smacked the wheel with her right palm. "I shouldn't have done that."

Was she always so hard on herself?

"We're a team," he corrected. "Your mistakes are my mistakes. Got it?"

"We can talk about that later," she said, cutting a hard right at the next light as it turned red. "Let's see if this sonofabitch follows."

The vehicle made the turn, squealing the tires as it rounded the corner.

"At least we know what we're dealing with now," she said. "I need to call this in and get some help."

"Or we could handle this on our own."

"You're not used to following protocol," she said. "I get that. But my job is on the line, and it's all I have right now. I won't risk it."

Crystal cut a hard left, entering a quiet neighborhood. A cul-de-sac?

Brewer grunted. "Ever hear of soldiers following orders?"

"Of course," she admitted.

"They're not called suggestions for a reason," he quipped, more offended than he probably should've been. Hell, everything put his guard up since the blast. A little voice in the back of his mind asked if he was starting to get tired of always being tense. The answer would be yes.

Being chased brought back a flood of memories. Brewer reached for the grab handle and then wrapped his fingers around it until his knuckles turned white.

"Everything all right over there?" Crystal asked after glancing over at him.

Pride kept him from admitting just how not okay he was right now. "Fine."

"What's happening, Brewer?"

"Nothing."

"We can't work well together as a team if you lie to me or keep me in the dark," she countered.

Damn. She was right. He knew it. But opening up right now would lead to a whole can of worms being dumped out when she needed to focus.

"I can handle it," he reassured. "But yeah, a lot's going through my head right now." It was the best way to describe what was happening. Flashes, memories, panic. Those three words instantly came to mind as a fresh wave of guilt assaulted him. *Stay in the present, Brewer.*

This was his cross to bear since he was the one to survive when the others hadn't. He reached down for the strap of his rucksack. Rubbed it in between his thumb and forefinger on his left hand. And then had to repeat the move with his right hand. Next, he touched the dashboard with one hand and then the other before reaching for the grab handle again.

The urge to continue what he'd just done in a repetitive cycle was almost overwhelming.

"Whatever is going on is okay with me," Crystal said in a calm, reassuring voice. "You don't have to talk about it. I just want you to know that I'm here if you change your mind or if talking helps."

Man, was he embarrassed to admit the level of psychosis battling it out inside him. More than anything, he wanted to repeat the touch cycle. The fact that he'd stopped himself from touching everything in sequence revved up his stress.

He glanced at the side-view mirror as a pair of headlights came charging toward them. "You have bigger problems to worry about right now instead of what's going on inside my head."

Crystal checked her rearview and muttered the exact same curse he was thinking. "Hold on, okay?"

It was dark on the street she'd turned down save for one streetlight at the curve of the cul-de-sac.

How the hell was she going to get them out of this mess with his brain being absolutely no help?

Take a deep breath, Brewer.

Chapter Eight

Crystal saw no other out as she reached the cul-de-sac. The yards here looked to be decent size—quarter of an acre to half acre. Fences weren't the normal eight-foot privacy fences like much of Dallas and surrounding cities had.

This might've been a trap, but she was short on options. So, she cut the wheel right onto the paved driveway that led to the back of a random person's house. Destroying civilian property could get her in more trouble than she wanted to consider, so she didn't. She blocked that out of her mind and went into sheer survival mode.

Keeping her witness alive trumped everything else.

Making a hard right, she drove beside the house with no lights on. The sleepy neighborhood looked to be one of those that rolled-up the streets after eight thirty every evening, a place where parents still allowed their children to play out front in the yard.

Roaring through their backyards at half past midnight would scare the neighbors, not to mention wake them. The law would be called. She was putting a spotlight on her activities, which could end up putting her in the hot seat with her boss.

Losing a witness was far worse than any punishment Elise could devise.

As she cut around the back of the house, she gunned the engine. Navigating around trees and bright yellow-and-blue toy cars before almost landing in the pool, she gripped the steering wheel tighter.

It dawned on her based on how quiet Brewer became that a battle was going on inside his thoughts. This must've taken him back to the incident that had ended his military career. She almost blurted out another curse as she swerved around the house and risked a glance back.

The chorus of dogs barking set against the backdrop of lights flipping on inside the homes tightened the knot in her chest. The knot warned that not everything was going to turn out all right.

It had been lodged there since hearing about her grandparents' vehicle accident and was determined to take root inside her chest.

Risking a glance behind as she made the turn, she saw the moment the car that had been following her nailed a tree. She pumped a fist in the air before quickly returning both hands to the steering wheel.

An adrenaline boost collided with dopamine release, giving her a euphoria that only sex with Brewer could beat. Cancel that thought—she wasn't now or ever having sex with her witness. Not only would that be unprofessional but having the best sex of her life with someone who would disappear wasn't her best idea.

Crystal shoved those unproductive thoughts aside and focused on the stretch of road ahead as she navigated back onto the street.

Before the car could untangle itself from the tree and catch up to her, she flew out of the neighborhood. This future write-up caused a wave of dread to wash over her.

The behind-chewing that was coming would be worth it, though.

They were safe from threat.

"Good driving back there," Brewer said as she navigated back to a main road. Laced with respect, she appreciated those words coming from someone like him. The man was no stranger to battle and had, no doubt, been in worse situations.

"Thank you," she said. "We're not out of the woods yet."

"No, but sticking together was a good decision on my part," he admitted.

She didn't want those words to reach into her and warm the cold places in her chest—places that had caused her to leave every past relationship.

"That means a lot, Brewer."

"Bounty hunters are going to come out of the woodwork," he surmised.

"True."

He was right. No doubt about it. The amount of money on the line would draw out a whole lot of scumbags looking to make a buck and not afraid to break a few laws or heads in the process.

"Don't tell me that you're giving up," she said.

"Never," came the fast response. He studied the sideview mirror. "It just means we have to be more careful. And, as much as I hate to say it, lose the Tahoe and any other vehicle related to the Marshals Service."

"Why is that?" Every marshal on the job had a plan, one they incorporated when everything had gone to hell in a hand basket and they needed to disappear. Inside the trunk of her service vehicle, Crystal kept her real passport, a fake-identity passport that would get her through any major international airport without being stopped, a wad of cash, burner phone, and keys. The keys were for a safe vehicle to drive to and from the airport. Since going through proper channels wasn't paying off, should she circle back and use hers so her witness could make it to his court date?

Something niggled at the back of her mind. She couldn't quite put her finger on it.

"How did the guy back in the car know we'd changed vehicles?" he asked.

"Are you suggesting someone on the inside could be handing out information about us because—"

"I'm not disagreeing that could be the case," he interrupted. "Or someone has figured out how to get through the encryption in your cell phone to follow us."

"That's it," she said out loud.

"What?"

"Give me your cell phone," she stated, holding out a hand.

"Why?"

"Because you might be the one being tracked," she said. "Have you made any calls with it since we've been together?"

"No," he denied. "Not to anyone who would compromise our position."

"Does that mean yes?"

"Yes," he retracted. "I called my buddy Trent back at the diner so he could set me up with a place off the grid."

"The one who got you the job in the first place?" she asked, shocked.

"Yes," he said. "But I don't see how that—"

Brewer cursed.

"They might have tapped his cell phone," he said out loud after muttering a few choice words.

"They would absolutely tap into his line to see if you

reached out to him," she said. "But if he has a connection to them, they would probably tap his line anyway."

"There's one way to test the theory."

Crystal glanced over at Brewer to see if he was serious. The answer came quickly—yes, he was.

"What are you proposing?" she asked as the knot tightened.

TRENT'S LINE WOULD be encrypted. Hacking into his phone would require skill. Then again, a multimillion-dollar operation would have the funds to hire the best. And Trent had been a foot soldier, not predictable in the military. His skill set would be no match for an experienced tech person's, and he couldn't match what the organization could afford to pay for an individual, which was the reason the person with the most money usually won.

But this wasn't the time to debate economics.

"We need to find a spot where we can leave the burner phone and then watch to see who shows up," he said.

"I knew you would say something like that," she stated. "Isn't it just easier to ditch your phone?"

"Not if I need to get into contact with Trent again," he pointed out. His friend felt bad enough for getting Brewer into this mess. Not knowing whether Brewer was alive or dead would cause more unnecessary stress. Plus, he intended to have Trent check on his aunt at some point to make sure she was fine and didn't need anything. Trent was all he had.

"Doesn't seem like a good idea, Brewer."

"Why not?" he asked.

Crystal didn't respond to his question. Instead, she kept

her gaze on the stretch of road in front of them. "You need sleep."

"So do you," he said. "Neither of us will get it until we find out if my phone is causing a problem for us."

"How about this," she said after a thoughtful pause. "We put the phone somewhere safe, and then we find another location to get sleep. How does that sound?"

"We could figure out a way to find out if anyone showed up," he said.

"It's too late for a bank vault, but we could set up a camera to see who shows," she said. "I haven't had a chance to circle back to find out the first bounty hunter's name yet. Or get the debrief."

"You expect a man like him to talk?" he asked.

"I guess not," she said. "Depends on his situation, though. If he has a kid who needs medical attention, you'd be surprised at what we can get from a person."

"What are the odds?"

She sighed sharply. "I guess not so good, but I always circle back. Once in a blue moon, you hit a jackpot."

"While you play the slots over there, I'll use my phone as bait," he said. "We'll see who gets something on the other end of the line first."

"Is that a challenge?" she asked as a smile fought to replace the frown that he was beginning to believe might be permanent.

"You always this sarcastic?" she quipped.

"Why? Does it bother you?"

"No," she said. "I prefer to talk to someone with a sense of humor." She paused a beat. "Looks like I'll be waiting a long time now that I'm stuck with you."

Brewer laughed, and it broke up some of the tension

block—tension that felt like hardened concrete—in his chest that had made it so hard to breathe a few minutes ago. "How about we compromise?"

"What do you propose?" she asked.

"Like you said, hide the phone, set up cameras, and let's get some sleep." He might not've needed it, but she certainly did. The news about her grandparents affected her despite her arguments to the contrary. It didn't make her bad at her job, but the worry lines etched into her forehead weren't about him and his situation. The only person who would put those there for him was his aunt, so he couldn't imagine if she was in a coma and her future uncertain. He owed it to Crystal for all the sacrifices she was making for him.

It was odd when he really thought about it. His military career had been about doing the same for others. Volunteering to put his life on the line to preserve a way of life for others came down to putting a face to the why. His aunt was the reason he'd gone into the military in order to get his act together. Her face came to him before he entered into a situation that put his life on the line.

She had no one to look out for her if he didn't come home. And now he was the reason she was in danger. Talk about a hard pill to swallow.

"Do you have a location in mind?" she asked.

"Why not make this easy on ourselves? Why not secure my phone where there will already be cameras? I'm sure you could finagle getting a hotel manager to show us video if you flashed your badge."

"I can get more than that for flashing my smile," she said, causing a wave of jealousy to stab him in the heart. What was that about?

"No doubt," he said, trying to tamp down his reaction to

the suggestion. There was no sexual innuendo about it, but he was certain her smile could open a lot of doors. Doors he didn't like sitting back and watching as they opened.

He had no designs on Crystal Remington. *Marshal Remington*, the tiny voice in the back of his mind corrected.

This seemed like a good time to remind himself she wasn't here as a volunteer or a date. Protecting him was her job—a job that she seemed to be very good at and took very seriously. Because of that job, the two of them would part ways once he was safely delivered to trial on a date yet to be determined. Reading anything else into the situation wouldn't just be foolish, it would be dangerous. Getting his hopes up was a risk he didn't intend to take. One more disappointment and he'd be wrecked. He'd already lost too much in the men who'd been like brothers. In his own body with his leg and his hearing.

Brewer sensed that losing Crystal, if he opened his heart to her, would be the last straw. The one thing to break him.

No way. No matter how strong the pull toward Crystal might be. No matter how difficult fighting the attraction might be. No matter how much he wanted to lean into it and claim those pink lips of hers as his.

He wouldn't.

Couldn't.

Refused.

Chapter Nine

Crystal needed to get them out of the Tahoe. They'd been circling around downtown Dallas for twenty minutes now. One-way street after one-way street. The DART Rail came to mind. The Pearl/Arts District Station was the closest to their current location. If memory served, that one was located on Bryan Street.

Stopped at a red light, she grabbed her cell phone and pulled up the map feature. From the corner of her eye, she noticed Brewer staring at her with a curious look on his face. "I have an idea."

She pulled over after making the next right turn.

"We need to ditch this vehicle," she pointed out.

"Agreed," he said. "What's the idea?"

"How do you feel about riding a train?"

"Cool with me," he said. His tone told her he was smiling.

She parked the Tahoe. "Grab all your stuff. We're not coming back to this vehicle again." The fact that someone was on their tail so quickly after the town house unnerved her. Standard measures weren't enough to stay ahead of this organization. Everything about her plan needed to rise to the next level in order to survive.

Crystal led them to the train station, then hopped onto

the next train. The ticket machine had been too exposed for
her to risk standing there to buy tickets. Her badge would
be enough to get them by if anyone checked.

The train was empty save for a couple of guys who
looked like they'd spent the evening out drinking. Better to
have them on the train keeping to themselves than driving.

Both got off on the next stop. For the rest of the ride to
the end of the line, it was only Crystal and Brewer in the
car they'd chosen. A lucky break.

Those had been too few and far in between for her liking, but she was developing a new plan now.

"Once we check to see if anyone is tracking that phone,
we need to find a place to sleep," she surmised.

"Agreed," was all he said, using the word for a second
time. He was down to one- or two-word responses at this
point. Was he tired? Or losing confidence in her ability to
keep him safe? Tired she could live with because exhaustion wore on her too. Loss of confidence might mean he was
evaluating his options again. That frustrated her to no end.

Time would tell. In the meantime, she intended to keep
a close eye on him.

They exited at the Parker Road Station and then located
a parked vehicle in the well-lit parking lot. A Ford truck
would do.

"Hand me your cell," Crystal said, standing at the tailgate of the silver Ford F-350.

Brewer fished it from his pocket. "Let me wipe out the
contacts, just in case." He tapped the phone screen a few
times before handing it over.

Crystal tucked it into the bed of the truck close to the
taillight as Brewer studied the area. They needed a good
place to hide and a possible quick getaway. The chain-link

fence surrounding the parking lot was a good place to get on the opposite side of.

"If someone is watching my phone, we'll know soon," Brewer said, finally using more than a phrase to speak to her. Had he been in deep concentration before, calculating the best plan of attack? Was that the reason he'd become quiet, and not because he wanted to ditch? His aunt must've been on his mind as well. Crystal knew firsthand how difficult it was to be separated from loved ones. Speaking of which, she needed to check in with Duke. The fact that there hadn't been any updates on the group chat worried her.

Brewer's gaze locked onto a point at the northeast corner of the parking lot.

"Let's give it an hour tops before we take off," she said, not liking the exposure. If this convinced Brewer to lose his phone and confirmed her suspicion, it would be worth the risk. She needed to get a little breathing room in between them and the bastards who always seemed a step behind. At this rate, they would catch up. No one could keep outsmarting an enemy with the kind of reach this one had forever. "Okay?"

"Deal," he said. His word was as good as gold, so she wouldn't question the lack of commitment in his tone.

As they walked away from the truck and phone, a couple of figures jumped the fence and headed across the parking lot. Males. Lanky. Teenagers?

The lot was lit up like it was daylight. The last thing Crystal wanted was to have witnesses see her and Brewer, so without debating her next actions she turned to face him. "Go with it, okay?"

Before he could open his mouth to respond, she pushed

up onto her tiptoes and pressed her lips to his. Looping her arms around his neck was probably a mistake since it caused her breasts to press firmly against his solid wall of a chest. The electrical impulses zipping through her body promised the best sex of her life if things moved forward between them.

They wouldn't. But the sudden ache in her body didn't care one way or the other. The spark of need that threatened to engulf her in flames wasn't doused in the least.

Crystal liked the feel of Brewer's lips moving against hers as the young people gave them a wide berth. The move prevented the teens from seeing her and Brewer's faces, and it awakened parts of her that she hadn't realized existed.

Even with the scars, he was gorgeous. Getting to know him had only served to make him even more attractive if that was possible. For once, Crystal knew exactly what she wanted and wanted to go for it, career be damned.

She wouldn't.

Gathering all her willpower, she pulled back enough to break apart. Her heavy breathing matched his.

"Get a room," one of the teens shouted before they both laughed and then took off running.

She couldn't help but laugh. If only it was that simple.

"They're gone," she said to Brewer, who leaned forward and rested his forehead against hers as they both caught their breath.

"I know," he said, his voice a low rumble that sent more of those sensual shock waves rocketing through her.

What could she say? The man's touch, his voice were the equivalent of Fourth of July fireworks to her body. Her soul?

She stopped herself before she could go all-in with the thought.

"We need to get out of here," she whispered, despite the fact her feet refused to move from this spot.

"I know," he repeated.

Neither one budged.

Crystal had to pull on all the strength she could muster to move. To calm the rising panic in her chest, she dropped her hand to reach for his and then linked their fingers. She could say the move was to sell the fact they were a couple to anyone who might be watching. The truth, however, was that no one was around.

Didn't mean they wouldn't be.

BREWER DIDN'T WANT to think too much about the kiss that had just happened—that had *needed* to happen. He'd immediately understood why Crystal had made the move. Blocking their faces from any passersby was a smart move. No witnesses.

A US marshal would be keen on not leaving witnesses who could be pressed for information or, in some extreme cases, tortured. At this point, the young men could honestly say the only folks they saw in the parking lot had been lovers who'd needed to get a room.

The ache in Brewer's body would subside. He tried to convince himself the tsunami of need had a simple explanation. It was because he'd stopped having sex altogether since losing part of his leg, part of himself. He'd come back from overseas less than whole and didn't want to freak someone out by thinking he was something he was not. Seeing his metal shin and foot for the first time had shocked the hell out of him, and it was his body.

Anyone else would likely flip out too. He couldn't talk about it either. How would that come across? *Hey, we've been getting along. Think we should move to the next level? And, uh, by the way, want to see my fake leg?*

He wouldn't be able to stomach the look of rejection in someone else's eyes he'd seen in his own.

No, thanks.

Shaking off the reverie, he kept a firm grip on Crystal's hand so she could hop the chain-link fence. She used it as leverage and easily cleared the obstacle. She muttered a curse after landing on the prickly hedges on the opposite side of the fence.

With a one-arm hop, Brewer followed suit. The hedges scraped his good leg, reminding him that he was still alive. That was pain's job, he reasoned. It told folks when to stop. Without it, where would he be?

Pain was the reason he pulled his hand from a hot stove before it burned to the point that it was useless. Pain was the reason he knew when he'd had enough during a wrestling match with one of his brothers in arms. And pain was the reason he was still alive when others were dead.

Trying to shake off the heavy thoughts, he crouched down low as Crystal tugged at his jacket. She had on a navy blazer and jeans. The light blue button-down shouldn't stand out. She had on dark shoes too.

Was it enough to keep her warm on this chilly night?

"You okay?" he asked, checking her for a reaction. Her body had been warm against his, but that could've been for another reason. When they'd been standing with their bodies flush, warmth had flooded him too.

No doubt in his mind it would be amazing to bury himself inside her and forget the world for a few hours. Days?

As much as he wanted...*craved*...her touch, he couldn't allow it. People who got too close to him died. The fact had him stressed about his aunt. So far, so good there. But Brewer was always waiting for the other shoe to drop. How long before it would? How long before more bad news struck?

"I'm good," Crystal responded.

He glanced over and realized she was studying him.

"Everything okay, Brewer?"

"Yeah," he said.

"I'm sorry about the kiss," she continued. It must've been the reason she thought he was upset.

"I'm not," he whispered loud enough for her to get the message. "That's the best thing that's happened to me in too long."

The admission embarrassed him. But there it was.

"Me too," came the response. He probably didn't need to hear that because it spurred him on.

Reaching over and taking her hand in his, he brought her palm up to his mouth and planted a kiss there. "I know nothing could ever happen between us."

"Parallel universe maybe," she offered.

"Doesn't mean I don't want it to," he admitted. This time, he wasn't embarrassed.

She squeezed his hand.

"Same here," she whispered. "We both know an attraction might cause a dangerous distraction."

"And yet the body wants what it wants," he countered, and he could almost feel her smiling. Blushing?

"I have no doubt the sex would be amazing," she said in the voice that had a way of breaching the walls erected around his heart.

"That it would," he said quietly. "Except for the fact…"

He started to open up, talk about the fact he wasn't

whole, then decided against it. What good would it do? How did he even start?

"For what?"

A vehicle pulled into the parking lot, moving slowly. It cut its lights off and then circled the interior once as they buried themselves deeper into the hedge. A branch was cutting into the scratch on Brewer's shoulder, a scratch that he'd only recently stemmed the bleeding from.

The vehicle was a white Camry.

The Camry pulled up behind the truck, keeping the lights off. A red flag if ever there was one. Brewer reached for his weapon inside the pocket of his rucksack. Crystal's hand went to the Glock inside her shoulder holster.

Just in case.

He palmed the handle of the SIG Sauer inside his rucksack, noticing how his hand started shaking. That wasn't like him. Stress only made it worse. He'd been a good shooter before. Was everything being slowly taken away from him?

Brewer bit back a curse and tried to will his hand to stop shaking. He'd refused to see the military psychiatrist because they would have told him what he already knew… he had to learn to deal with this new reality, this new person he'd become.

Someone who couldn't depend on his reflexes. Someone who wasn't whole. Someone who didn't deserve to be alive when two in his unit were dead.

Frustration welled up, filling his chest. At that point, something magical happened. His hand stopped shaking.

Thank the stars for small miracles. This new superpower wouldn't bring the rest of his leg back, but it would keep his hand from moving while he fired off a shot. It might keep him alive.

Crystal shifted position, ending up on his right side.

A female exited the driver's side of the Camry, wearing all black. She crouched down low as she moved around the truck. Did she believe they were inside, asleep?

The way she moved stealth-like and with precision said she did this for a living. A female bounty hunter? From this distance, Brewer couldn't get a good look at her facial features. But no one showed up in all black and moved like her unless they meant business.

Was she assessing threat? Trying to confirm her suspicion that they were asleep? Was she about to try the door and shoot?

She had to think there were two of them inside even though she didn't peek into the windows. Not yet anyway.

They should probably disappear before they drew attention, but Brewer was too interested in seeing what this mystery woman planned to do next.

Chapter Ten

The bounty hunter—and that was the only reasonable explanation for the woman's skill set—circled the truck twice before reaching her hand underneath the truck's bed. GPS would pinpoint the phone's location without being exact. She wouldn't know the difference between the bed or the cab based on a tracking app.

What was she up to? Feeling around for the phone?

A second later, she withdrew her hand and then climbed into her vehicle before backing away from the truck. Then, she sat. Waited.

For what?

Crystal's mind conjured up several possibilities. Before she could go down that road too far, a small explosion sounded.

The truck. The woman. An explosive device.

It took all Crystal's self-control not to stand up and go after the woman. There was no movement in the vehicle she drove.

The bounty hunter was trying to flesh them out of the truck. The explosion wasn't big enough to set the truck on fire or cause much of a scene. It was, however, loud and jarring enough to wake anyone who might've been asleep in the truck.

"We shouldn't stick around here," Crystal whispered. How long would it be before the female checked the immediate area in search of them?

Their question has been answered as far as Crystal was concerned—Trent's phone was being monitored.

Again, she questioned how much Brewer could trust his friend. How close were they?

Brewer nodded as he stared at the truck, his gaze intense. Was he wondering the same thing?

"He's in trouble," he whispered before turning to follow her.

They could discuss Trent later. The chill in the air turned to a biting wind. They needed shelter. Looking at her phone wasn't an option. She couldn't afford for the light from the screen to alert the female bounty hunter.

Still in the parking lot, she inched her Camry toward the truck. She must have been expecting them to come out by now. What would she do next?

The entrance to the parking lot was on the opposite side of Crystal and Brewer's current location, which would buy time because they needed to get the hell away from there. Their dark clothing would help them blend into the night as they continued east.

Crystal shivered in the cold as they made their escape, wishing she'd worn more than her standard navy jacket.

Brewer looped an arm around her waist, and she leaned into his warmth as they moved farther away from the parking lot.

"Thank you," she said, praying they wouldn't draw attention as they crossed Avenue K.

"It's two-fold," he commented. "One, you'll stay warmer. And two, the bounty hunter isn't looking for a couple. She's looking for a marshal and me."

Her chest deflated a little at the practical reasoning. He was right on both counts. She was instantly warmer being nestled in the crook of his arm, and this position would be considered unprofessional under different circumstances, so it would throw off Ninja Woman back there if she happened to drive this way.

Crystal prayed the woman headed in any other direction, but especially west, since it was the opposite way they were headed. "Shelter would be nice. Any ideas there?" She knew he would have a few. They could check into a motel along US 75, which would require them circling back the opposite direction. Crossing the station again wasn't an appealing idea. They needed a place close by.

"Can I see the map feature on your phone?" Brewer asked now that his was gone. For his sake, she hoped Trent came out clean despite her suspicions. She decided to hold her tongue until they received more information about Brewer's friend. According to the file, Trent appeared to run an honest landscaping business. She made a note to get a copy of his client list to see if Crane's name was on it. Without a warrant, she would have to ask for it.

Crystal located her cell and then handed it over. Skin-to-skin contact sent more of that electrical current racing through her hand and up her arm.

He studied the phone for a minute, no longer, and then handed it back. "This way."

Walking side by side, she tensed as several vehicles passed by. Brewer reacted by pulling her closer to him in a protective manner. Crystal couldn't remember the last time someone had done that. Needing someone to protect her versus allowing someone to take the lead were two different things. It was nice to feel like someone could handle whatever came their way. Mahone, her ex, was a marshal; he should have made her feel safe in the way Brewer was. They'd spent time together, been in a relationship. And yet she'd always been on alert with Mahone.

What was it about Brewer that had a calming effect on her?

He led them across a busy intersection toward a residential neighborhood and then onto a quiet street. Cars lined both sides. She was just about to ask what the plan was when he turned to the third house they passed. She saw the wisdom. A covered motorboat. They could slip underneath the tarp, which would get them out of the wind, and grab a few hours of sleep before the sun came up.

And then they would have to talk about Trent.

Crystal slipped onto the motorboat. It had a curved bench seat in the back near the motor. The vinyl covering was cold and caused her to shiver as Brewer positioned himself on the floorboard. He grabbed a life vest to use for a pillow and pulled a sweatshirt out of his rucksack. He spread it out beside him.

"You can slide in here next to me if you want," he said, turning onto his side. "Body heat will help keep us from getting too cold. Might even be able to grab some shut-eye."

"Being warm is too good to pass up right now," she admitted as she was hit full force with the memory of how incredible his lips had felt against hers. Crystal cleared her throat to ease the sudden dryness. She'd never acted in an unprofessional manner when it came to her career and had no plans to begin right now. Not even for someone as tempting as Wade Brewer.

The attraction was strange when she really thought about it. Tattooed and looking more like a rebel than anyone she'd

ever get close enough to call a friend, Brewer was not her
typical type. Not on the surface. Okay, the man was hotness on a stick, so he was pretty much everyone's type.
Who wouldn't fall for a bad boy who looked straight off an
underwear-model billboard? Or at the very least drool over
the man?

Crystal normally dated clean-cut men who opened doors
and probably called their mothers every weekend. Family
was important to her and had to be a priority for anyone
she dated as well. She might not have spent as much time
with hers as she wanted to or probably should've, but that
was going to change once this case was over and she delivered Brewer safely to trial.

Facing losing her grandparents had made her realize
how precious time was and how fragile life could be. She'd
thought they had all the time in the world, that there would
be a slow decline and ample time to spend together before
it was too late.

A tear spilled from her eye as she positioned herself
in the crook of Brewer's arm again. This time, their bodies were flush with each other, providing much-needed
warmth. With the canopy pulled taut, they were safe from
the winds. No one knew their location.

For the time being, at least, they were safe. With that
thought, Crystal closed her eyes and gave in to the exhaustion tugging at the back of her mind.

BREWER IGNORED JUST how right the marshal felt in his arms.
Once again, he chalked up their chemistry to going too long
without companionship. The kiss they'd shared had barely
scratched the surface and yet had turned the moment in the
parking lot into something much more.

So much for playing it cool with Crystal Remington. *Marshal Remington*, he felt the need to keep reminding himself.

Her steady, even breathing told him she'd fallen asleep within minutes of settling in next to him. The fact that she was comfortable, out of the elements, and asleep shouldn't have made his chest puff up with pride as much as it did. There was something deep inside, primal, that brought a smile to his face for being able to protect Crystal. Sleeping in someone's presence was the ultimate act of trust.

Maybe he wasn't completely broken, useless to others.

Once this ordeal was over, he needed a new job. The fact that he'd been paid by a corporation had him believing that, early on, Cane's organization had been legit. To be honest, Brewer's head hadn't been on straight when he'd first boarded out of the military. Six months had made a difference. He'd joined a gym and started working out almost immediately. He'd been so focused on what he'd lost and trying to find a way to live as less than his former self that warning signs had slipped past him.

The meetings with all manner of folks should have tipped him off that Victor Crane wasn't on the up and up. What CEO met with guys wearing warmups?

Brewer had driven Crane to cafés. Those made more sense. There'd been breakfast meetings, lunch meetings, and dinner meetings. None of those were red flags in and of themselves.

In the first few weeks, Brewer had been too inside his own head to notice the man he drove around was meeting with thugs as well as others wearing suits. The job had been *ask no questions, get no answers* kind of work. His military training had taught him not to question. The need-to-know policy had trained him to mind his own business and focus on his task or mission.

He wasn't naive. Looking back, he'd been in too much of a brain fog to question Crane. As he'd started to become more aware of his surroundings again, the red flags had popped up. He'd been too invested at that point to walk away without a plan, a plan to ensure his aunt would be safe long after he was gone.

Right now, though, he was more worried about Trent than anything else. Would there be a backlash against him since he'd been the one to recommend Brewer to the job in the first place? Was Crane keeping Trent alive in order to use him to find Brewer?

He needed to have a conversation with his pal about relocating once this was over. Or, at the very least, lying low. Trent now knew that Crane was the head of an organized crime business.

Brewer needed to figure out a way to keep Trent safe. So far, he'd been concerned with his aunt.

His thoughts bounced to Crystal and her grandparents. She wasn't with them because she was with him. The fact was a bitter pill to swallow.

Could they swing by Mesa Point? Visit the hospital without being detected?

Brewer's injury marked him. Made him easier to pick out of a crowd if he wore shorts instead of jeans.

The Lithuanian must have seen Brewer or had his physical description. He might've been too high up in the organization now that Crane was behind bars to risk going after Brewer himself.

Crystal shifted in her sleep, causing her body to press harder against his. She mumbled something he couldn't quite pick up.

Was it about an ex? Someone she was interested in?

Why did either of those scenarios cause his chest to deflate as fast as it had puffed up? Crystal was a beautiful woman who was intelligent and sharp-minded. There had to be someone in the background despite her saying she wasn't interested in anyone.

Was he being sexist in his thinking that just because she was beautiful there had to be guys around? Maybe.

Still, he couldn't imagine there wouldn't be half a dozen guys circling the stunning marshal, waiting for a green light from her in order to make a move. A woman like her didn't come around but once in a lifetime. On that point, he was certain.

Any single man who knew her but wasn't interested had to be a fool. If Brewer had had a remote chance under different circumstances, he wouldn't have hesitated. She deserved someone in her life who was decisive about being together, who wanted to be with her more than he wanted to breathe air.

Brewer was amused at the rabbit hole he'd just gone down with the marshal.

"Hey," she whispered in a sleepy voice that brought more of him to life than he cared to admit.

"Morning," he said. Hours had passed while he'd been in deep thought, dozing on and off.

The squeak of a screen door opening caused them both to tense.

"I said I'd take out the trash, and that's what I'm doing," a male voice barked.

Were they about to be caught?

Chapter Eleven

Crystal bit back a curse. She held her breath as she listened. The sound of plastic tires on the brown city-issued trash cans against concrete rolled too close to the boat for comfort. Had they closed the tarp properly?

Folks were known to keep shotguns and other weapons on hand despite living in a suburban area. The whole *shoot first, ask questions later* mantra hit a little too close to home. Would she be able to identify herself in time? More importantly, would the man believe her?

It was dark enough to realize clouds had rolled in overnight. The temps had dropped.

Trash Man started whistling. At least it was easier to follow his movements after he situated the trash bin at the end of his front-entry driveway. He made his way back up the short drive, stopping next to the boat.

"I'll be damned," he muttered, the whistling stopped. "What in tarnation is this?"

Crystal felt around for her Glock, palmed the handle. Brewer moved too, stealth-like, no doubt locating his weapon same as her. Glock out, finger hovering over the trigger mechanism, Crystal was ready if it went down.

Of course, she would identify herself first as a US marshal. It went without saying.

Her cell vibrated. Frustration at the timing seethed. It was followed by fear this might be bad news about her grandparents.

On the other hand, the message could be good news about a trial date. The sooner, the better—except for the fact her case would close and she would walk away from Brewer forever. Crystal pushed the thought out of her mind and craned her neck to hear.

She prepared herself for the tarp to go flying off or a shotgun barrel to be stuck inside.

Trash Man picked up whistling again. Whatever had caught his attention must have passed. She slowly exhaled, not budging.

A dog barked rapid-fire. The pet came barreling up to the boat and jumped as it barked.

"What's wrong with Butch?" a female voice shouted.

Crystal imagined Butch was some kind of bully dog, like a pit bull. Something that latched on when it bit and its jaw couldn't be pried open with machinery once it locked.

"Probably another squirrel," Trash Man said, dismissing the dog's attempt to warn them that people were inside their boat.

"Get in here, Butch," the female demanded. "If you want your breakfast."

Butch cared more about the contents of the boat than his meal. Until his owner yelled one word: "Treat."

The panting and scratching halted almost immediately as Butch turned tail toward the house and rocketed back inside.

Was Trash Man still outside?

Crystal didn't dare move. Her question was answered a few seconds later when she heard a truck door open and then close. Almost immediately after, the engine roared to life. She exhaled and, for the first time, noticed how cold her fingers had become.

"I need warmth," she whispered to Brewer. "Like real warmth. A fireplace or, hell, I'd settle for a campfire at this point. My fingers are going numb."

She flexed and released her fists a couple of times. Was she being dramatic? Probably a little. Being hungry, tired, and cold had a way of giving her a flair for drama.

"I'll check it out," Brewer said with a smirk. "See if it's safe to slide out of here so we can go somewhere and eat."

"While you do that, I'll check my phone for a nearby diner or breakfast place," she supplied. Scrambled eggs and hash browns sounded amazing to her right now. Add a cup of coffee and she would believe she'd died and gone to heaven.

There were no messages from her siblings, even Duke, which she took as a good sign that things were stable at the hospital. The text from Elise requesting a phone call tightened the knot in her chest. A phone call generally meant bad news.

According to the map feature on her phone, a diner was a fifteen-minute walk from their current location.

"It's safe to exit," Brewer decided.

Crystal wasn't looking forward to getting out into the biting wind again. Winter had arrived at the same time as fall, lacing the wind with ice. They'd made it through the night unscathed and in one piece, which had been no small feat. This case was shaping up to be the most difficult of her career.

Challenge accepted.

Crystal could call her boss from the restroom of City

Diner on Avenue K. She wasn't looking forward to the walk, but she could do anything for fifteen minutes, including brave the cold.

Brewer slipped out of the tarp first and then stood guard while she followed. Both crouched down low. Beside the wheel of the late-model Jeep parked next to the boat sat a basket. A picnic-type basket. What the…?

He held her back with a protective hand. While she appreciated the gesture, she was here to protect him, so she stepped forward and scanned the street. Out of the corner of her eye, she caught a dark image in the window across the street.

Crystal turned her head to get a better look. The person immediately shifted out of view.

Before Butch caught on to the fact strangers were in his driveway, Crystal nudged the basket with the toe of her boot. She cringed, half expecting the thing to explode.

When it didn't, she crouched down and grabbed a stick. Using the end of the stick and keeping as much distance as possible, she flipped the basket open.

Food. There were breakfast bars, individually wrapped muffin packs, and two coffee-in-a-can drinks.

Brewer grabbed the basket handle as they stayed crouched behind the Jeep. It was only a matter of time before Butch came perusing the front windows or was let outside to do his business. The dog had a set of pipes that would wake the neighbors.

"We need to move," she whispered to Brewer before hitching a thumb toward Butch's house.

"I know," he said. "Should we return the basket to the old lady who's been watching us from behind the curtain across the street?"

"She's a senior citizen?"

"Afraid so," he informed.

"Then we weren't exactly stealth in our hiding place, were we?" She'd seen someone in the window but hadn't been able to make out the outline to determine male or female, let alone age.

Turned out Brewer had a superpower—exceptional eyesight.

He shook his head. "Although to be fair, the reason we didn't pick that side of the street was because the light was on inside the home."

"True," she agreed. "I need to return my boss's call, and I'm freezing out here. Let's return the basket sooner rather than later, okay?"

"We can do it right now," he said, crawling on all fours to the end of the driveway.

Crystal followed, then popped to her feet in a swift motion once she reached the sidewalk. She linked her arm in his and leaned into his warmth as they crossed the street.

The front door across the street cracked open.

"Eerie," Crystal said out loud.

Rapid-fire barks sounded as Butch charged the chain-link fence behind them. They'd narrowly escaped that one.

"Do you want to stay back?" Brewer asked Crystal.

"No," she immediately responded. "I have no plans to sit on the back burner while you take all the risks."

BREWER COULD RESPECT Crystal's decision. He respected her even more for it. To be fair, she was law enforcement and, therefore, used to taking risks. "I'm used to working with a familiar team," he said. "We know each other's moves almost better than our own."

"I won't do anything other than identify myself as a US

marshal to begin with," she stated. She had the badge and gun to back up the statement. That should help make this conversation go easier. The bigger question had to do with the older woman. "What do you think she wants from us?"

"People randomly bake food for me all the time," Crystal stated like it was common knowledge. "If you're not getting the same treatment, that's on you." She shot a soft elbow into his ribs.

He laughed, which made him cough. Sharp pain shot through his chest. He'd taken damage but would live. His shoulder where the bullet fragment had grazed could use some TLC to keep it from getting infected. He'd experienced that before while on a mission—almost lost his pinky finger because of it. So, no thanks on an infection festering. Best to nip it in the bud before it became an issue.

The open door sent a bad feeling rushing through him. It could've been muscle memory, though. The last time he'd walked through an opened door, he and his unit had been immediately bum-rushed by the enemy. Brewer had ended up with the pinky cut and Philly—because John Padulla was from Philadelphia—had left the scene with a gash in his shin so deep they could see bone. Not a pretty sight.

It had been a sure way to make Hanson Baker, comms guy, lose his lunch when Philly had pulled up his pant leg to reveal tissue and bone.

The other thought still lurking in the back of his mind was curiosity about what Crystal's boss had to say. After last night, maybe her SO was checking in to see if they were still alive. The bounty on his head complicated matters.

He stepped onto the wooden stairstep leading to a porch. The screen door was propped open, and the interior door was still cracked. What the hell were they about to walk into?

"It's open," a fragile-sounding voice said. "But you can leave the basket on the porch if it suits you better."

Brewer turned and locked gazes with Crystal, who had the same *no clue what's going on* look on her face. She reached inside her jacket, no doubt going for her service weapon just in case.

"Ma'am, my name is Marshal Remington," Crystal started.

"Oh?" came the confused voice.

"Who am I speaking with?" Crystal asked.

"Name's Dorothy," she replied. "The military man can bring anyone he pleases with him inside. I don't care too much for the law, but I can make an exception."

Crystal stepped into the door frame and then pushed open the door using her toe. "So, you don't mind if I enter your home?"

"Already said I don't," Dorothy pointed out. Brewer liked her candor, and there was something else he trusted about the older woman. There was something in her voice that said she could be trusted. His instincts had served him well…and they'd been on alert the day he'd lost his buddies and part of his leg.

Inside Dorothy's house was dark, and the place looked as expected. Vintage wood pieces in various states of wear and tear were covered in doilies and porcelain figurines that had, no doubt, been collected over a lifetime.

"Ma'am, thank you for allowing us inside your home," Brewer immediately stated as he stepped a foot in the door. Heavy flowery curtains covered the windows, keeping most of the light out. There were stacks of magazines and books everywhere—on the floor, on top of bureaus. This wasn't exactly at the level of *hoarder*, but it measured pretty close in Brewer's book.

"Well, close the door, or you'll let all the heat out," Dorothy quipped. The older woman had a full head of white hair cut short and brushed spiky. Although the style looked matted to one side of her head, so he wasn't certain the spiky part was on purpose. She sat, hands folded in her lap, wearing an almost ear-to-ear grin. She had on what could only be described as an old-school dressing gown complete with pockets that looked sewn on after the fact, socks, and fuzzy slippers.

Dorothy beamed up at Brewer.

"Thank you for your service," she said to him.

"You're welcome," he replied. Hearing those words never got old.

"My Joseph served," she continued before glancing around. "Where are my manners? Would you like something to drink? Coffee? Tea?" The older woman pressed a button that caused her recliner to push her to standing, easily.

"Something warm," Crystal said. "Coffee would be amazing."

"You can eat what's in the basket," Dorothy said with a smile. The fact she had several teeth missing didn't dim her smile. She reminded him of his aunt. Not in the physical sense, but attitude. You couldn't get much sassier than his aunt. He might have just found her match.

"There's no poison in there if that's what you're worried about. And I hate to burst your bubble, but there's no 'coke' in Coke anymore either—not like when I was young." Dorothy winked, and it caused Brewer to crack a smile. He couldn't help himself. She was feisty.

"I'd like coffee too, if it's not too much trouble," Brewer said, amused.

"Is there a place I can make a private call?" Crystal asked.

"Bathroom's over there," Dorothy said, pointing to the hallway.

All business, Crystal thanked her before crossing the living room. Her demeanor stressed him out if he was being honest.

He followed Dorothy into the kitchen, where she instructed him to sit at the eat-in table before getting to work on her Mr. Coffee machine. The old model vibrated and hissed as it filled the room with the aroma of fresh brew.

Dorothy inhaled. "Doc says I can't drink more than one cup a day. What does that bastard know?"

Brewer laughed. "You should probably listen to him. The world needs more Dorothys." He wanted to add *and less people trying to kill me*, but it would require explanations he didn't care to give. Being inside in the warm house was too good to pass up, and Dorothy's hospitality might end abruptly if he explained his situation.

"Take a muffin," she urged as she set a mug filled with coffee on the table in front of him. She motioned toward the basket.

"If you insist," he said, taking a blueberry one.

Brewer took his first sip of coffee as Crystal joined them. One look at her expression tied a knot in his chest. "What is it? What's wrong?"

Chapter Twelve

Crystal glanced at Dorothy and then back to Brewer. For a second, she wondered if it was a good idea to discuss what her boss had just told her in front of their host. On balance, she decided Brewer deserved to know. "Your friend is MIA." Keeping names out of the equation was for the best for all involved.

"What does that mean exactly?" Brewer asked, his gaze intensifying upon hearing the news.

"You know what it means," she stated. "He didn't show for work today and is no longer answering his cell."

A muscle in Brewer's jaw ticked. "We're going after him. We have to find him. He's in this mess because of me."

Crystal wasn't so sure, but Brewer's loyalty to his friend was admirable. "Absolutely not." Plus, she was pretty certain he had it backward.

She didn't want to discuss this further in front of Dorothy. She turned toward the elderly firecracker of a woman. "Thank you for your hospitality."

"Oh, where are my manners—please sit down," Dorothy said, motioning toward the chair opposite Brewer.

"We should probably get—"

"Don't be silly." Dorothy waved her off. "If you had somewhere to go you wouldn't have been sleeping out in the cold in Cranker's boat. If he'd have caught you, I'd be plugging up bullet holes too."

"How did you know where we were, by the way?"

"Got one of those Rings," Dorothy said with a smirk.

"I didn't see one on the door." Crystal had looked too.

"It goes anywhere. It's on a battery." The older woman's smirk widened. "I stick one on my camper out there, and it picks up what's happening on the road." She waved her hand like she was presenting her kitchen as a showpiece. "Don't have much here to steal unless someone wants to pawn old coffee mugs." She had quite the collection displayed in a box-type frame with enough cubbies for twenty or so cups hanging on the wall. "Got one from every state after my husband retired. Put my favorites up on the wall. We took to the road every summer." She put a hand over her heart as she spoke. "Those were good times."

"I'm sorry for your loss," Crystal said.

"Thank you." Dorothy fixed a cup of coffee for her. "Sugar? Milk?"

"A little milk if you have it," Crystal responded.

"Sit down and I'll get it."

She took a seat. "If it's not too much trouble."

"Nah, I don't get the pleasure of much company these days." Dorothy went to work, looking happy as a lark. "Don't get out much either."

Brewer had been quietly stewing. Plotting?

"Grab something to eat while I pour the milk." Dorothy started humming.

Crystal's toes finally thawed out. She wiggled them to make sure they still worked. Thankfully, they did. She took one of the muffin packets marked *Blueberry*, along with a banana. While she wrangled with the packaging—she would never understand why manufacturers made it so hard to open bottles and packages—Dorothy set a cup of coffee on the table.

The senior citizen glanced at the clock hanging on the wall. It was a black cat with big eyes. For every second that ticked by, the cat's eyes moved. "I better watch my show. If you'll excuse me. I like to watch it first thing and I'm days behind. Go ahead and eat while I'm in the next room."

The move was clearly meant to give them privacy.

Dorothy padded out of the kitchen and returned to her recliner. She clicked on the TV and turned up the volume to *80s boom-box blast* level. Again, was she giving them the opportunity to speak? If so, Dorothy was an angel.

Brewer took the package out of Crystal's hands and then ripped it open, using his teeth. He handed it back and leaned forward. "What happened to Trent?"

"That's what my boss is trying to find out," Crystal answered.

"I have to find him," he said.

"Not a good idea." She leaned in too. "Or do I have to remind you how dangerous it's been out there for us?"

"Doesn't matter." He shook his head. "He wouldn't leave me to rot either."

"Have you considered the possibility he's done that already?" Crystal regretted saying those words out loud the minute Brewer's face dropped. She was walking a tightrope here with her witness. Push too far and he would disappear and go rogue. "Look, I'm not saying that's what happened."

"Sounded like you were to me."

"I'm sorry if I offended you," she continued. "It's my job to consider every possible outcome."

"He's loyal."

"Possibly," she stated. "Either way, it's still my role to think outside the box."

"You don't know him."

"No." But she could say that she knew of him. She also knew he was being investigated due to his involvement with Crane in the first place. That wasn't what Brewer wanted to hear after finding out his friend had gone missing, though. He was under the impression that Trent was innocent in all this. Trent might've been. He might have been duped by someone he believed to be in legitimate business. He might have been helping a former associate down on his luck. "There is another possibility when it comes to Trent."

"Which is?"

"He went into hiding." It was plausible. "Your friend might have realized the hornet's nest that has been stirred up and decided to disappear until it blew over."

"I know where he would go," Brewer said after a thoughtful pause. "Hell, I'm pretty certain he told me exactly where to meet him."

"The place off the grid?" she asked after taking a bite of muffin. Questions were mounting, like whether or not the location would be compromised because Trent had been the one to give it to Brewer, but her growling stomach won out.

"Yes," he said.

"Where is that exactly?" She realized they'd gotten rid of his cell phone, which was where the information was stored.

"East Texas," he supplied.

"That's vague," she said.

"There was no map so I memorized the coordinates," he stated like that was a common thing to do. His military training served him well. It was also serving them both right now because Crystal was certain Dorothy's kindness had to do with his cargo pants and military-issue rucksack.

"Why doesn't that surprise me as much as it should?"

The depths of Brewer shouldn't shock her. Her physical reaction to him threw her off balance.

"Let me see your phone," he said before extending his hand.

Would he give her the wrong coordinates? Ditch her?

Time would tell. She had a feeling time was about to be up.

No doubt Trent was in over his head because of Brewer. He pulled up coordinates on Crystal's phone after she handed it to him, nabbed a screenshot before handing it back. Those coordinates were an hour south of Trent's location. She would be safe there.

In the meantime, could he lose Crystal?

After getting to know her, the thought of placing her in danger sat like a hot branding iron against the center of his chest. No one else would die because of him.

He handed back the phone. "That way you'll have the location in case we get separated."

Crystal eyed him. Based on her expression, she'd read between the lines. "Are you counting on that happening?"

"No," he defended. Too fast?

His answer was written all over her face. "I don't intend to let you out of my sight. So, I won't need these coordinates." She deleted the screenshot.

He had to give it to her, she'd caught him red-handed. "I'd feel more comfortable if you'd let me give you the coordinates."

The look she gave him could have shot daggers at him.

"We both know that will lead me off the trail." She paused long enough to take a sip of coffee. "My coffee hasn't had time to kick in yet, so I'm real cranky right now. For the sake of argument, let's pretend you didn't just try to pull the wool over my eyes. Okay?"

"Got it." More than ever, he was impressed with Crystal. No one had read his intentions so easily. The fact should've freaked him out more than it did. Crystal was unique, a one-off. She wasn't the norm, or he wouldn't have survived this long. He chalked up their connection to thinking along the same frequency and promised himself it wouldn't happen again.

The TV shut off, and the hum of the chair's motor in the adjacent room replaced it.

"I'll be darned if the one person who shouldn't win always seems to," Dorothy exclaimed from the next room. She padded into the kitchen and sized up the breakfast table. "Neither of you have eaten squat. Unless you're telling me you're not hungry or there's something wrong with my food, eat up."

"The muffins are amazing," Crystal said, turning her attention away from Brewer and toward their host.

"I have to admit, I assumed you were homeless," Dorothy said. "The way our military is treated after their service is inexcusable."

It made sense why she'd left the food basket now. Her husband had served. She'd had a ringside seat to the sacrifices that entailed. Hell, military wives deserved medals as much as their spouses. They brought up children as single parents until their husbands came home on leave and messed with the schedules. They acted as head of the household before stepping aside, in most cases, to give their husbands room to make decisions. And it worked the other way around too. Military husbands were just as deserving while their wives were away. The burden of running the house fell onto the parent at home. Being away, missing family was another issue. Brewer had seen that side and heard his buddies talking about it while on missions together or in the mess hall.

Military service wasn't always an easy life.

Being single had its benefits. Brewer didn't have anyone back home to answer to or miss for that matter. He didn't have to worry about whether or not his kids were listening to their mother since he didn't have those either.

His life was uncomplicated.

Was it lonely?

Brewer could admit to himself that the past year had felt like he was missing the boat. The feeling went against everything he'd convinced himself he prized. And he didn't buy into the whole *I need a relationship to complete me.*

Brewer was a complete, fully formed human. He glanced down at the metal shin underneath his pant leg. At least, he had been fully formed once. Now he felt more like patchwork, but that was a whole different mental slippery slope he didn't need to go down right now.

"Who wants a breakfast sandwich?" Dorothy's voice interrupted his thoughts.

"I don't want to eat you out of house and home," he countered, even though a sandwich sounded better than good to him. He'd trained himself to get by on very little food, to conserve when the situation called for it. He could survive on a couple of muffin packets. Being back on US soil, he'd gotten spoiled by having coffee every morning. Without it, he became a cranky pain in the neck. One of many signs he was getting weaker, not stronger. And another reason he didn't need to think about entering into any serious relationship. He'd come back broken. Who needed that in their life?

"It's no trouble." Dorothy eyed him up and down. "You'll need two."

Brewer cracked a smile. "Then, yes, ma'am."

He made a mental note to have groceries delivered to replenish her supplies. Her generosity was much appreciated. It was the very least he could do.

"How about you?" Dorothy asked Crystal. "Will you be having one or two?"

"One is good," Crystal said after thanking her. "Can I help?"

"No." Dorothy waved her off. "It'll give me something to do besides sit in front of the box." She referred to the TV. "Doc says I should exercise more."

"I'm not sure this counts," Crystal said with a laugh. "But we'll take it."

Seeing a light in Crystal's eyes was a powerful draw. She was even more beautiful when she smiled if that was possible.

Dorothy turned around and winked before getting to work on the sandwiches.

"We're being spoiled," Crystal said. "Would it be all right if I poured another cup of coffee?"

"Help yourself," Dorothy said, looking pleased with herself.

It dawned on Brewer why the woman might peek out her window or spy on others, help strangers. Everyone needed a purpose. Without purpose, it was easy to get lost like a boat in the sea during a hurricane.

Being in the military had given Brewer purpose until

the incident. He refused to call it an accident or blame it on bad intel. The incident had been his fault. He'd made widows out of two young women. Dorothy seemed to have had a long life with her husband before he passed. Hadn't the others deserved the same?

Because of him, several children would grow up without their fathers.

And now Trent was missing. He had a family. Had his wife and kid disappeared too?

Chapter Thirteen

Crystal polished off her sandwich in no time. She wasn't in a hurry to leave the relative safety of Dorothy's home. The US Marshals Service couldn't match this woman. Then there was her generosity. Crystal would make certain groceries showed up in the next day or two. Dorothy could be the millionaire next door for all Crystal knew, but she didn't live like she had anything more than a fixed income to get by on.

A spitfire in every sense of the word, Dorothy was the opposite of Gram Lacy. Lacy was the softest, kindest person Crystal had ever met. Grandpa Lor had a firm but kind way about him.

To be fair, he would have been happier if she'd stayed back and worked the paint-horse ranch, but Crystal had wanted to make her own way. Now none of her siblings or cousins truly knew how to run the business, and they might be faced with making decisions none were qualified to make. At least they had Shiloh Nash, the foreman, to lean on. He'd worked the ranch for decades. Based on age, he probably should have retired five to ten years ago. But the man was still strong as an ox and determined to "be useful to others," as he'd put it. Long ago, Grandpa Lor had given Nash the property he lived on along with the home he'd built. Most times, Nash stayed in the bunkhouse to be close to the horses. He had a reputation for being able to hear the horses' thoughts just by touching them.

Nash was like a favorite uncle to Crystal. She couldn't imagine Remington Paint Ranch without him working there.

Crystal shook off the mental fog as Dorothy set plates down in front of her and Brewer.

"Everything okay?" Brewer asked.

She looked up to realize he'd been studying her. "Yeah." The word came out despite the frog in her throat. "Sure. I was just thinking about my family's ranch, got lost for a few minutes."

"Have there been any updates?" He picked up the sandwich and took a bite before chewing.

"No," she admitted with a headshake. "I'm taking the no-news as a good sign."

Dorothy joined them at the table with a muffin and cup of yogurt. Her forehead wrinkled in concern.

"It's my grandparents," Crystal explained, figuring it couldn't hurt. "They were in a serious car crash and are in the hospital."

"I'm sorry," Dorothy said with a look that said she understood and sympathized. The pair of cobalt blues staring at her had seen loss. It was the kind of look Crystal imagined would be on either of her grandparent's faces if one lost the other.

"Thank you."

A rogue tear welled in Crystal's eye. She tucked her chin to her chest, turned her face, and coughed. Trying not to be conspicuous, she brought her hand up to wipe away the tear as more emotion welled up inside her.

What the hell was happening? Her tear ducts threatened to turn her into a faucet, which was the last thing she needed. Brewer was already questioning whether or not he wanted to stick with her for protection. Considering the dangerous near misses they'd had in less than twenty-four hours together, could she blame him?

"We should probably head out soon," Crystal finally said, rejoining the conversation. Brewer's plate was clean. She polished off the last few bites of her sandwich, chasing the food down with coffee that was warm on her throat and almost too good to be true.

"I hope everything works out all right for your family," Dorothy said with the kind of sincerity that brought another wave of emotion coursing through Crystal.

"I appreciate the good thoughts," she responded. Prayers, good thoughts, healing crystals…she didn't care what folks used for comfort. She was grateful for the sentiment all the same.

Dorothy nodded.

Crystal needed to get them out of there and to the white four-door sedan parked down the street, waiting for them by now. Her SO had supplied another vehicle after Crystal explained why she'd detoured from the roach motel plan.

With Brewer's cell phone gone, she figured they were going to be a whole lot luckier about not being followed or attacked every few hours. A new safe house had been set up in McKinney, which wasn't far. Elise was banking on the fact Crane's crew and the bounty hunters would bet Crystal would head south with Brewer. That or north to Oklahoma where there were plenty of fishing cabins dotting Lake Texoma. Staying near the area where they were last tracked should throw everyone off track. If they knew about the coordinates from Trent, it might be assumed they were fake to throw people off course.

At least, that was the logic. Fingers crossed. Crystal's plans hadn't exactly worked out so far.

They'd spent the night in the boat without being detected unless you count a harmless nosy neighbor. Dorothy wasn't actively trying to kill them, so that was a plus.

When the last drop of coffee was gone from Brewer's mug, he turned his attention toward Dorothy. "I can't thank you enough for your hospitality."

"You're more than welcome," Dorothy said, her voice surprisingly soft. She practically beamed at Brewer, her eyes filled with appreciation. In the sprinkling of photos around the cozy living room, her husband was young and in uniform. Dorothy's eyes filled with moisture. She blinked a couple of times. "You take care of each other, now."

"We're only together for a short time," Crystal immediately said, not wanting to give Dorothy the wrong impression of the relationship between herself and Brewer. Without being able to explain the reason life had paired them up, Crystal had nothing else to add. She bit down on her bottom lip to stop herself from overexplaining and inviting more questions.

"We promise," Brewer interjected. His answer was the one that seemed to satisfy Dorothy.

"Good," she said.

"What's the best way to leave here without being seen?" The last thing Crystal wanted to do was draw attention to Dorothy. If there were others in the neighborhood who liked to peek out their curtains and take notes on their neighbors' activities, she didn't want to give them a reason to get out their camera phones. Being stealthy and staying stealthy was becoming more and more difficult given new technologies. Crystal felt the need to add, "Or heard."

"Butch across the street is pretty active this time of day," Dorothy pointed out after a thoughtful pause. "He'll bark at his backside when he passes gas."

Crystal couldn't help but laugh at the image.

"These houses are front entry and the backyards, I'm guessing, are chain-link fence," Brewer added.

"That's right," Dorothy confirmed. "But you knew that from last night when you climbed into the boat."

"Folks look out for each other here?"

"That, or need something to gossip about," Dorothy stated with a cackle, clearly amusing herself. "If you climb out the window by the trailer, you should be able to wind around the other side of it and get on the sidewalk without anyone realizing this is where you came from." She caught Crystal's gaze. "That is what you're worried about, isn't it?"

Crystal nodded. No use trying to snow this lady.

"And they say you can't believe cop shows." Dorothy shook her head. "It's how I figured you for law enforcement."

"Guilty," Crystal said, not pointing out that she'd identified herself as a US marshal when they'd entered Dorothy's home a couple hours ago. "But I need you to forget we were here, okay?"

"Done," the woman said without fanfare. "Besides, who am I going to tell? My son moved to Colorado with his granola-eating girlfriend. Barely see them once a year at the holidays."

"It's important that you forget what we look like too," Crystal pointed out. "And maybe erase us from your Ring if you can."

Dorothy nodded.

"Thank you again for everything," Crystal said. She wasn't normally a hugger but gave Dorothy a hug anyway. They would've been a whole lot colder, hungrier, and crankier at this point if it hadn't been for Dorothy. Plus, who knew what else. Dead? "If anyone stops by asking if you've seen us, you haven't."

"I'm clear on what I need to do, and believe me, I can handle myself," Dorothy reassured.

Good. Because Crystal would never forgive herself if harm came to this sweet, albeit feisty, woman because of her actions.

"My advice is to cozy up to one another," Dorothy said. "Folks will look away." The move would have the added benefit of making their faces harder to be seen or recorded on more of those Ring devices.

Brewer stood up. He'd been too quiet for Crystal's liking.

"Will do, Dorothy," he said, taking a couple of steps toward the older woman. He bent down and planted a kiss on top of her head. "You're an angel."

Dorothy blushed. She shooed him away. "Go on now so I can forget I ever saw you."

Crystal knew how impossible it would be for her to forget Brewer. It was going to be hell once this witness was successfully delivered to trial. Because it would signal the end. And she wouldn't be able to wipe him from her mind like she'd done so many others before him.

A BATTLE RAGED inside Brewer's head. On the one hand, sticking with Crystal would give him more resources to work with. On the other, being with her put another good person at risk. And she was a good person. There was a long list of other things she was too, but this wasn't the time to go into how thoughtful or intelligent she was.

Crystal stood at the bedroom window. She stepped aside. "You first this time."

He limped over, thinking how much it would stink if his good ankle/leg stopped working properly. Then again, the other was made of metal, so he probably shouldn't worry too much. He opened the window, shaking off thoughts of what happened the last time they'd stood in a similar position. His shoulder still needed medical attention, but the longer they stuck around Dorothy's place, the more danger they brought to her doorstep. Bounty hunters wouldn't care a bit about murdering an elderly person to get what they really wanted…him.

Brewer climbed out the window, straddled it for a second to scope out the area, and then finished exiting. At this point, he could probably bolt and outrun Crystal. Or could he? His so-called good leg was giving him fits. It might be a sore joint, or he could have tweaked it. Then again, the cold front that had moved through went straight through his bones. It was probably just his imagination taking over, but he would swear the cold went right through his metal leg.

Being part metal, part man was going to take some getting used to.

"Hey," Crystal said as she climbed out the window. "Where did you go just now?"

"It's nothing," he said, embarrassed he'd lost focus even for a few seconds when he should've been vigilant about watching the area. His mistakes were piling up, costing lives, and risking safety. "I'm good."

Brewer refocused as Crystal moved to his side. He opened his jacket, figuring it would cover more of her that way. She'd lost track of her Stetson yesterday during the fight with the first bounty hunter, so neither had head coverings, which would have both provided a screen and warmth.

"It's even colder outside now," Crystal said, looping her arm inside his coat. Contact sent more of that electricity rocketing through him. "But if we wait ten minutes, the weather will change."

He didn't react to her attempt at humor. He couldn't let himself off the hook so easily. This time, he wouldn't allow any distractions. "Where are we headed, by the way?"

"Down the block," she said, palming her cell phone. The map feature was open, and there was a red blinking pin on the street behind them and down the block.

"Another vehicle?" he asked.

"White four-door sedan," she supplied.

"And another safe house?"

"That's right," she confirmed. "McKinney. In an area called Adriatica. It's a house this time, with a garage and small courtyard. It should be private."

"Sounds good," he said.

"I can't wait for a shower and change of clothes," she admitted as they turned the corner toward the vehicle.

Could he disappear while she was in the shower? He wouldn't leave her without a vehicle, so he'd have to figure something out there. With no cell phone, he couldn't exactly make a call. Not that he knew anyone around these parts who would drop everything and lend him a vehicle anyway.

He could hot-wire a motorcycle if he could find one. That might be an option. And while he was wishing, maybe there'd be a helmet and leather jacket too.

A thought almost stopped him cold. Crystal would try to find him. She would do her level best to hunt him down.

Would that bring more danger to her than if he brought her along with him?

It was a valid question. Would Elise reassign her if she lost her witness? Would she be able to take leave and go to the hospital to be with her family? Or would her file be marked from now on, considered a risk.

Once they got to the house, he could case the situation. Plan. Think. Figure out the right time to make a move. Because it was only a matter of time before he brought death to the marshal's doorstep, and her grandparents needed her.

Taking off would be for the best for everyone involved. No matter how much he tried to convince himself of that fact, the annoying voice in the back of his mind tried to argue.

Brewer could get himself to a trial date without help. More than that, he needed to prove to himself that he still could. When the time was right, he'd break off and find Trent.

Chapter Fourteen

The key was exactly where Elise had said it would be, sitting on top of the back tire on the driver's side. Crystal held the key fob on the flat of her palm. "Catch."

Brewer's reaction time was ridiculous. He caught the key with ease, like he'd expected the toss all along. His reflexes were finely tuned. The man didn't even blink.

"You drive," she said to him. The lack of communication from Duke about their grandparents was probably a good sign. Still, Crystal wanted to check in, and after a rough night in the boat, she selfishly wanted to shower and sleep the minute she and Brewer were in a secure location. The cold had a way of zapping her energy.

"You sure about that?" he asked.

"Yes," she confirmed. "Why?"

Brewer shrugged before unlocking the doors. As he put his rucksack in the back seat, he said, "Figured this was a government vehicle and that you'd have to drive for insurance purposes, or something like that."

Those were good points. "We're making up our own rules now."

It took two minutes to program the address into the car's navigation system. The drive to McKinney was a straight shot up US 75.

Once on the highway, Crystal informed Brewer that she needed to make a call. He knew enough about her situation for her not to feel like she needed to do so in private.

Duke answered on the second ring. "Crystal, hey."

"How's it going in Mesa Point?" she immediately asked.

"It's been calm since we last spoke," he responded, and she exhaled the breath she'd been holding.

"That's good, right?"

"Neither one has coded, which is a good sign," Duke explained with a hesitation in his voice she didn't like.

"What has you worried, Duke?"

"All of it, if I'm being honest." Her brother made a good point. "The fact that their recovery might take weeks or months if they recover at all. The fact that this in-between state could drag on, leaving them both in limbo. And then there's the unthinkable that could happen." He stopped right there. He didn't say that one of them could wake up only to realize their best friend and lifelong partner had died, leaving them all alone. Crystal and the others would ensure the survivor was well cared for and had plenty of company, but she couldn't imagine losing someone she'd loved her entire life.

She mentally shook off the possibility.

"I get it," she said. "I feel the exact same way."

Duke exhaled. "Didn't mean to unload on you like that, sis."

"You didn't say anything we aren't all thinking," she pointed out.

"How's your case going?"

"It's interesting." She couldn't say much else, and her brother of all people would understand why without needing an explanation. "Congratulations again to you and Audrey, by the way. The fact that you found each other almost makes me believe in love."

"We have you to thank," he said. "If you hadn't given me a heads-up that she might be in danger, I never would have stopped by her cabin that day to check on her."

"I'm just happy you caught the bastard in time," Crystal said. Audrey had been the target of a serial killer who'd cut the ponytails off female deputies after murdering them. The man was one twisted sonofabitch who was going to spend the rest of his life behind bars, where justice would be served for the families of the innocent victims he'd brutally killed.

"At least something good has come out of me being here," he said. "I feel like I'm failing our grandparents by not being able to do anything to help them recover."

"Being there is enough, Duke. You're helping Nash keep their livelihood going and making sure they have a business to wake up to. That paint-horse ranch is their life. They started it together and built it to what it is today. They poured their hearts and souls into that ranch. If you ask me, you're doing the most important work right now."

There was a long pause on the line.

"Thank you, sis. I needed to hear that today."

"I should be there with you," she said.

"If I don't get to feel guilty, you don't either," Duke countered. "We made an agreement to take turns, which we're all doing. Besides, physically being here isn't going to make them wake up or get better any faster."

He was right. She knew he was right. And yet guilt still sat heavy on her chest just the same. It wasn't just guilt for not being there today. It was a long history of guilt for not making it home for birthdays because of work. Then there was that one Christmas where no one had made it home. She remembered hearing the disappointment in Grandma Lacy's voice, disappointment her grandmother had tried to mask.

That had been last year. Possibly their last Christmas together.

Moisture gathered in Crystal's eyes.

"Sis?"

"I'm here," she said, hearing the frog in her own throat.

"It would be just like you to comfort me as you're headed down a slippery slope of guilt," Duke said with compassion. "Try not to, okay?"

He really knew her.

"I won't," she promised. "Everyone else good?"

"We're all rowing the same boat," he said. She understood what he meant.

Brewer turned onto Mediterranean Drive, where they were transported to the small Croatian village this area had been built to resemble. The house at the end of Seaside Lane would give them several possible exits should their location be compromised once again.

"Duke, I have to go."

"Take care of yourself, and we'll see you soon," her brother said. She'd read middle children were the peacemakers, negotiators. As tough and stubborn as Duke could be, he was also usually the one who brought reason into a heated situation.

"See you soon," she echoed before ending the call.

"Your brother?" Brewer asked. It was more statement than question.

"Yes," she said as he tapped a button and the garage door opened.

"Sounds like you guys have each other's backs." Brewer surprised her with the observation.

Then it dawned on her. He didn't have siblings. Who had his back?

"I WASN'T EAVESDROPPING on purpose," Brewer felt the need to point out.

"It's okay," Crystal said. "I wouldn't have made the call in this small space if I was concerned."

He nodded before pushing the button one more time to close the garage door behind them.

"I should probably go in first to check the place out, just in case," Crystal said.

"We're a team. Remember?"

There was no way he was letting her go in alone after everything they'd been through together. Plus, it wasn't like he could ditch her right now. She would make a phone call that would put a tail on him in two seconds flat. It might have been the reason she'd entered their destination into GPS, so her SO could keep tabs on them if something happened to Crystal's phone.

Brewer was taking no chances. He'd bide his time until it was safe to make his quiet exit. Trent was either in trouble or in hiding. The thought occurred to Brewer that if his friend was in trouble, he might have already given away the coordinates he'd shared with Brewer. There was no amount of torture that could persuade Brewer to turn on a friend, but everyone was different. Trent had a family, whereas Brewer had no idea what that might be like.

"Let's do this, then," Crystal said with a half smile that caused his chest to tighten.

She drew her weapon and headed toward the door into

the home. He located his and followed, sticking so close he might was well have been her shadow.

The three-bedroom home was impressive to say the least. The feel of the neighborhood transported him back to Europe during a couple of his furloughs. The cobblestone streets and Mediterranean flare made this area look like it had been here for centuries. In reality, it was all probably new builds from within the last five to ten years. He had to hand it to the developer, though. This area didn't feel like he was in Texas anymore.

The home was easily worth a million dollars. The place was done up to the nines with coffered ceilings. In the kitchen were white marble countertops with a gas range that had six burners plus a grill plate. The building itself was stone, along with a Mediterranean-style roof. The living room had a stone fireplace with a flat-screen mounted above the mantle. There were hand-scraped hardwood floors throughout with large windows. The courtyard, filled with flowers and plants, sat behind an iron gate.

"When can we move in?" he teased once they'd cleared the place.

"Right?" she answered, just as amazed as he was by the details. "I'm a country girl at heart, but I could make this place work." She smoothed the flat of her hand across the marble in the kitchen. "Too bad I'm not much of a cook. This would be wasted on me."

"What do you eat?" he asked, surprised there were people out there who didn't know their way around a kitchen. It wasn't a sexist thing either. It was a survival thing.

"I heat," she responded like he should've been doing the same. "The grocery store has a lot of precooked meals, and I don't have a lot of downtime. I eat on the road a fair amount. I've always wanted to learn but never made it beyond baking cookies during the holidays."

"That counts for something," he offered.

"They're the kind you break off from a roll," she said with a laugh that could brighten the darkest room. Or soul, he thought.

But that was a conversation for a different time.

"I know the heat works fine in here, but do you mind if I light the fireplace?" Crystal asked as he checked the fridge for food. He wasn't hungry but needed to assess the situation to see if they should go out at some point or have food delivered.

At least a week's worth of meals were in various restaurant to-go containers inside along with makings for sandwiches and breakfast. There was bread in the pantry. All right, then. This place was a go.

Crystal struck one of the oversize matches in a box next to the hearth and then turned the gas on. The fire lit immediately. Sure saved a whole lot of trouble cutting firewood, drying it out, and then using up half a newspaper as kindle. "Is it wrong that I want to take a shower and brush my teeth more than anything else right now?"

"No," he responded. While she showered, he might do the same, but not before checking all the window latches. "Does this place have an alarm?" He'd seen a box by the door to the garage.

"Yes," she said. "Matter of fact, it does." She rattled off the code to arm and disarm it. "I didn't want to set it until we got everything from the car."

He nodded.

Sneaking out while Crystal showered wouldn't give him enough time to figure out new transportation, so he would stick around until she fell asleep. Disarming the alarm might wake her if she was a light sleeper. But then, the main bedroom was upstairs, far away from the door to the garage.

"Take the main bath," he said to her.

"Are you sure?" she asked. "The shower in there could fit two people." She cleared her throat as she realized how that might sound. "I didn't mean us two or anything."

Brewer shouldn't be as amused as he was. "Didn't think you did."

He disappeared for a minute to grab his rucksack and an overnight bag that had been placed inside the trunk, locking the vehicle for good measure. Once back inside the house, he set the alarm, paying close attention to how loud the beeps were after arming it. Normally, the beeps lasted thirty seconds, enough time for the person who set the alarm to get out the door without triggering it. He counted. Yep. Thirty seconds. This was a standard system. It would be monitored, of course. The person who lived in a million-dollar home would take precautions.

"Here you go," he said, handing over Crystal's overnight bag.

She took it, not immediately budging from her spot on the hearth. "These fake logs might look pretty, but they sure don't give off a lot of heat. You have to sit right on top of them if you want to get warm." She studied him, asking a question with her eyes. Did she have to sit on him? Or was she sitting in a false sense of security?

Brewer wasn't a liar. He threw his hands out. "I'm here, aren't I?"

She smiled. Let her guard down a little? "Yes, you are."

Not providing the whole answer could be considered deception. Nothing had been black-and-white since leaving the military. In all honesty, there'd been gray area there too. Life in the civilian world was the gray area. But he wasn't an outright liar and it mattered to him she knew that about him before he took off.

Chapter Fifteen

A shower, a toothbrush, and clean clothes were better than Christmas morning as a seven-year-old.

Crystal finished dressing before checking the closet to find it full. Dresser drawers were the same. She located a fleece sweater and then put it on. After last night, she couldn't get warm enough. Unless the kiss she'd shared with Brewer stamped her thoughts. Then, all of a sudden, she was on fire.

She had to push that unprofessional thought aside and force her gaze to stay off those thick lips of his, lips that had covered her mouth and moved in a way that caused her stomach to freefall just thinking about it. How was that for keeping her cool?

At this point, it was dinnertime. The sun was descending, so she walked around and closed the blinds in all the upstairs rooms before heading back down.

Brewer was studying some fancy espresso-slash-coffee machine that was all chrome and stainless steel.

"Need a hand?" she asked.

"I probably don't need any more coffee," he said with a shrug. He'd showered and changed into low-slung jeans with no shirt. Her fingers itched to trace the muscles on his broad shoulders and back.

The shirtless image of him wasn't helping her tamp down the attraction.

"I can give it a try if you want," she offered.

He stepped aside and turned, leaning his hip on the marble countertop. Lucky marble. "One of us should figure out how to use this thing. You don't want to know me without my caffeine fix in the mornings."

The man was lethally gorgeous.

She cleared her throat and walked in front of him, bending down to study the machine. She'd seen something like this before when she'd protected a chef once. He'd been reluctant to leave home without his machine. People and their fancy coffee-slash-lattes. The brown liquid was a means to an end for her. Turned out, her tastes when it came to coffee weren't all that sophisticated. She could make instant work when she had to. It wasn't great, but it got the job done. "Let me see." She ran her finger along the back of the machine, found the On switch. Tapped it.

The machine came to life.

"How'd you do that?" Brewer asked, clearly impressed.

"Protected a chef once," she said. "He showed me the ropes on his machine. I figured these were probably all similar once you get over a certain price point."

Brewer didn't respond. He folded his arms over his chest and watched. Jealous?

No. There was no way Wade Brewer would be jealous of her protecting another man. Not to mention the fact Chef Gerard wouldn't measure up in any way, shape, or form to the former Army sergeant.

She located the well to put beans in. "I'm not sure if this is for espresso beans or regular coffee."

"Why don't we test it out, see what it makes?"

"Sounds like good teamwork to me," she stated, pleased with herself for getting them this far.

Her stomach picked that moment to remind her it was dinnertime. Loudly. It shouted at her.

"Or we can wait until after dinner," Brewer said.

She turned to face him, which ended up being a big mistake this close. Her fingers wanted to run their tips along the tattoo on his left shoulder and down his arm. Was it some kind of tribal tattoo?

"What sounds good?" he asked, stepping away to open the fridge door.

"If there was some form of pasta inside there, I wouldn't hate it," she stated. "And if it had seafood mixed in, even better." They were nowhere near the coast, but her stomach didn't know that.

"I have the answer to your prayers right here." Brewer held out a box from Sea Breeze Fish Market & Grill.

At this point, Crystal's mouth was practically watering. "I've heard of that place." She took a couple of steps to close the gap between them and took the offering. "There's enough inside here for two people if you're game."

"Tee up," he said by way of response. "What do you want to drink?"

"Water," she said. "We should probably both drink more of it. Best to stay hydrated."

She heated and plated their meals while he set the table rather than eat at the marble counter with bar chairs. "It's nice to have a sit-down meal tonight."

"Agreed," he said, "but I should put on a shirt."

"Don't bother," she said. She cleared her throat. "It's just us. You should be comfortable."

Considering he had on jeans and no shirt, it struck her as

odd that he had on socks. She remembered his injury and figured he must've been hiding his prosthetic. Was he embarrassed by it?

"I was giving my shoulder a chance to breathe," he said, glancing at the cut there.

Now she was embarrassed. She'd been so distracted by his hot bod that she'd complete forgotten about what had happened in the bathroom last night.

Had it really only been last night?

Time always seemed to slow in a case like this, and this one took the cake as far as danger was concerned. "There will be supplies here to take care of the injury on your shoulder. I'm decent at cleaning wounds if you'd like my help."

"I'll let it breathe for now," he said. "As long as you don't mind that I'm not wearing a shirt to dinner."

"No," she said quickly. Too quickly. She could feel her cheeks heat.

The food smelled amazing, so she picked up her fork and took a bite before she could stick her foot in her mouth again.

Plates were clear in a matter of minutes. Actually, they were more like bowl-plates and had been perfect for seafood pasta.

"I've got dishes," she said.

"You heated the food," he argued.

"Really, it was no trouble. I pushed a couple of buttons on the microwave." It was dark outside, and sleep tugged at the corners of her mind. "Plus, I need to figure out this fancy dishwashing machine before I head to bed." She almost added the word *alone* but stopped herself in time, saving herself at least that much embarrassment. Tonight had been one for the books when it came to speaking before thinking. "What does your tattoo mean?"

"It's the mark of my unit, which essentially is my tribe," he said, examining his injury. "Only two of us are still alive. One if Crane's men have their way."

"That's my job," she said. "I'm here to deliver you safely to the courtroom."

"And then what?" he asked, surprising her with the question. He had to have thought of the consequences of testifying before now.

"Witness protection program, if you're interested," she supplied, wondering how the suggestion would go over.

"I'm not worried about myself," he said quietly. "But my aunt doesn't deserve to be targeted, and she will be. Even after the trial."

"Normally, these bastards have short memories," she said. "Once we put a leader in jail, the fight for who takes his place is enough of a distraction. But in this case…"

"They want me dead," he supplied in a blunt manner.

"Badly," she said, hating the thought he would disappear after the trial. WITSEC or no, Brewer would disappear. He knew better than to show his face unless he had a death wish. "You'll want guarantees for your aunt."

"Can she go into the program without me?" he asked.

"It doesn't really work that way," she said.

"I figured as much." His deep timbre took on a reflective quality. He was considering his options. She couldn't blame him. "How successful is your program in keeping folks alive after they've testified?"

"Of the ones who stay in? One hundred percent alive. There are those who leave the program because they miss loved ones or the old neighborhood. Those instances don't usually end well. Once they leave the program, they leave our protection. There's nothing we can do because there isn't a budget to have marshals watching over individual homes twenty-four seven."

"Makes sense." He winced as he ran his finger along the cut that would leave a scar.

After loading the dishwasher, Crystal located a first-aid kit and rejoined Brewer in the kitchen. She opened the latch to find fairly extensive supplies. There was enough in there to stitch someone up, if needed.

"Mind if I take a look at your injury?" she asked, catching his gaze. The second their eyes locked, she knew she was in trouble. The pull toward Brewer was strong. Too strong.

Forcing herself to look away was her only hope at breaking the magnetic force.

"Go for it," he said after clearing his throat. The move gave her the impression that he struggled as much as she did when they stood too close to one another. The fact shouldn't have made her smile. It did anyway.

Crystal rummaged around in the tackle box–style kit. On the top level were antiseptic wipes. She would need those, so she pulled several packets out. And then there was a tube of antibiotic ointment. She would definitely need that.

She examined the cut, noticing the other scars on his chest, arms, and neck. "What happened here?" She ran her finger along a two-inch scar near the base of his neck running down his back.

"Gun fight," he said before clarifying. "A piece of shrapnel caught me above my body armor. The darn thing bled like you wouldn't believe. One of the folks in my unit turned white. Didn't think I would make it home." He laughed, which only caused his stomach muscles to flex. "Turned out to be a scratch."

"Looks like more than a scratch to me," Crystal said, thinking they could use up the rest of the evening talking about all the marks and scars on his body. Did he have half this many on his heart?

Forget the question. She didn't need to wonder about Wade Brewer's romantic life.

"It's nothing."

"Either way, I'm sorry this happened to you," she said, refocusing on the wound. When he didn't respond, she continued. "I'm going to clean the wound with an antiseptic wipe first. Okay?"

He mumbled an okay.

"I won't do anything without giving you a heads-up first."

"Good," he said. "I don't like surprises."

She figured that statement covered more than just this moment. Good to file away the piece of information. It made sense that someone in his former line of work who followed orders to a T and willingly went into hostile situations wouldn't like to be caught off guard. He had enough evidence on his body to prove he'd experienced more than his fair share of them.

Crystal ran her finger along a line on his tattoo.

"We designed our own," he said. "During one of our fireside late-night chats with too much time on our hands, we realized we all had Celtic blood running through us. So we decided right then and there the basis for the tattoo should represent Celtic tribes."

"That must be the knot here in the center," she said as she went about the work of cleaning his injury. Getting him to talk about the artwork on his arm was two-fold. First, it distracted him from the sting of cleaning the wound that was pink and angry. Second, she could learn a little bit more about him. Tattoos usually had a meaning behind them. It made sense when she really thought about it. If she was going to put permanent ink on her body, she would want it to mean something beyond the surface.

He craned his neck to look, and the scent of peppermint toothpaste filled her. Toothpaste had never been sexy in her book until now. Then again, anything would be sexy on this man.

This seemed like a good time to remind herself that he was dangerous too. And he wasn't exactly opening up to her. Even if they were in ideal circumstances and this was a romantic getaway instead of a safe house, he was a closed book.

"These kinds of tattoos have deep ties to nature and the elements of fire, water, earth, air, and space," he continued, sharing the most about himself that he had since they'd met. "Four of us were in a unit together, so we determined which element fit our personalities. The knot symbolizes life, death, and the afterlife too." He paused as though it was difficult to talk about this.

"We don't have to—"

"No," he said, cutting her off. "I want to. I never talk about the men in my unit, which is shame."

"Why not?" she asked as she applied antibiotic ointment to the deep gash.

"There hasn't been anyone I wanted to talk about them with," he said. Those words, his deep timbre, caused warmth to burn through her. "Philly disappeared once we came back stateside. My best guess is he's living off the grid somewhere, refusing to talk about what happened or the unfairness of the two of us still being alive."

"Thanks for trusting me," was all she said. All she could say.

"Talking to you is easy," he admitted, surprising her once again.

"Believe it or not, I never talk about my family life with someone I'm protecting," she said, figuring he deserved to know the feeling was mutual. "Opening up isn't my strong suit, so I'm told that I don't talk to most people. At least, that's what my last couple of boyfriends said when we were breaking up."

"They were fools to walk away from a woman like you," he said before catching himself.

"If it makes you feel any better, they didn't." Why was she sharing any of her personal life with Brewer? The lid was open—she might as well spill the drink. "I broke up with them. They, of course, pointed out that I'd kept my running shoes on from our first date."

"Then you've been dating the wrong type," he said. "Because I'd make sure they came off with everything else you were wearing if you were mine."

The possessiveness in his tone gave her the same sensations as the first drop on a big roller coaster. She had to stop herself from pointing out that that could never happen considering he was a witness in her care. He wasn't offering. Still, the comment caused her knees to go weak for a few seconds.

Crystal needed to change the subject while she still had control.

Chapter Sixteen

Brewer cleared his throat to ease some of the dryness.

"Do you want a bandage to protect the antibiotic ointment?" Crystal's voice broke through the mental image stamping his thoughts of her naked and the two of them tangled in the sheets. Her touch was tender as she worked on his injury. He could imagine those same hands gripping his body, fingers digging in so she could brace herself for the ultimate…

Glancing down at his prosthetic shin and foot, he couldn't imagine anyone would want him now. He clenched his teeth. "Sure."

Eyes forward, he forced himself to stop noticing the way her hands felt on his body. What good would it do to go down that road—a road that would only lead to heartache and pain? Pain of missing out. Pain of having no prospects. Pain of having a lonely future.

Pain of regret?

With the right mindset, Brewer could grind through anything. He'd made it this long. He could grind out the rest of life too with sacrifice and discipline.

"You got quiet on me again," Crystal said. She'd let her hair down and had taken on a more casual tone with him. Most likely, she was too tired to keep up the stiffer professional front. They'd been through a lot in the past day and a half. This was the point where folks started mentally breaking down.

This was the point where Brewer's training kicked in. He doubled down on shutting out emotion and hyper focused on the goal. This was the point where discipline kicked in.

"It's a training technique so I won't focus on the pain," he said, motioning toward his shoulder. A truer statement had never been made. It might not have been the same pain she thought he was talking about, but it was pain.

Crystal bit back a yawn. With a full stomach and a warm home, she wouldn't be able to fight exhaustion much longer. Once asleep—and he'd paid attention to her habits last night—he would be able to slip out.

She slept hardest when she first fell. Last night, she'd tossed and turned after about an hour, so he had a decent window to play with after she went down tonight. An hour, maybe. That would give him plenty of time to get his act together. His rucksack was already packed and ready to go. Nothing was stopping him from a quick exit when the time was right.

"Or we could talk," she said as she gingerly placed a patch on the wound. She then used medical tape to secure it.

"That's good work right there," he said, thinking he needed to grab some of the supplies and slip them into his rucksack before heading out. He was decently trained at field dressings and would need to stay on top of the injury.

"Thank you," she said with a self-satisfied smile. It tugged at his heartstrings, but he was determined not to allow it to change his mind about leaving. In fact, he was even more determined to keep her out of harm's way.

The niggling feeling he might end up hurting her career

with the move had him wanting to rethink his strategy. But he couldn't allow the thought to take hold. In the long run, she would be better off without him dragging her down. A small note in her file would be better than dying.

Everyone he cared about—and the list was small—was in danger or dead. He'd come home less than and was a cancer to everyone around him.

"I'm so tired my bones ache," Crystal admitted, taking a step back to admire her work. "But this looks good. I think you'll be able to save this arm." She shot a look of apology and then diverted her gaze.

It was common now and the reason he wore socks. He always kept his feet covered and wore long pants. Pants easily hid the area from beneath his knee to his ankle. He'd mistakenly put on running shorts to go for a jog out of habit when he'd first been cleared for exercise.

There were two types of folks in the world to him now— the ones who stared and the ones who couldn't look at him. Most fell into the second category, like Crystal right now.

Disappointment weighed heavy on his chest.

"You should go to bed," he stated.

Crystal hesitated before lifting her gaze to catch his. "I'm taking my work hat off with this next request." Her cheeks flushed and made her even more beautiful if that was possible.

He steadied himself for whatever might come next. "Go ahead. What do you want to ask?"

"For you to stay with me until I fall asleep," she admitted before quickly adding, "I'd totally understand if that's crossing a line for you and would respect your decision." She exhaled a long, slow breath. "With everything going on at home and the events of the last day and a half, I don't think I'd be able to relax enough to fall asleep without someone in the room with me." She paused. "Is that a strange request?"

He shook his head. "Not really." On some level, he understood needing comfort, reassurance after a near-death experience. Or in this case, a couple of them strung together.

"This place feels like a fortress in some ways, but…"

"In others it feels penetrable. Vulnerable." He finished her sentence for her.

"Yes," she said as her eyes brightened. Those beautiful eyes. He would say yes to pretty much any request if he stared into those long enough.

Being her comfort made him feel…useful again. For the first time in a long time, he felt needed. There was something primal about still feeling like he could protect someone. And about her asking him to be the one to do it. The fact that she felt safe with him caused a little bit of pride— and hope?—to sneak in.

"We can curl up on the couch if you'd like," she offered. "Might feel less personal that way."

He thought about how that might mess with his plans. "You'll sleep better in a real bed after last night."

"That's probably true," she admitted. "You know, this is bigger than last night and yesterday morning. My whole world tilted on its axis after my grandparents' accident. It's like the ground is shifting underneath my feet and I can't do anything to stop it."

He glanced down at his leg. "Believe me when I say that I know exactly what you mean."

"Right. Sorry. Of course you do. You've been through hell and back—and then got a job. I'd imagine you were putting your life back together after what must have been the absolute worst possible thing that could have happened to you and your unit. Only to find out you're working for a criminal." She paused. "I know I've said it before, but most people wouldn't do the right thing. They would cash in their losses with Crane and do their best to forget they ever worked for him."

"What would that solve?" he asked. "Crane would still be out there, shifting the ground underneath even more people's feet. I would still end up in hiding for the rest of my life. And nothing would be gained for the sacrifice."

"It's still honorable, Wade."

Was this the first time she'd used his first name? Somehow, it made those words strike a little harder, a little deeper in his chest.

"Well, I had and still have a lot to make up for," he finally said. Before she could say anything else that might make him want to stick around, he stood up. "We should get ready for bed."

CRYSTAL MIGHT'VE BEEN misreading Brewer, but she figured the minute she fell asleep he'd be gone. It was the reason for the request. Or maybe that was the lie she told herself—because she'd never crossed a professional boundary before.

Either way, keeping him close would alert her if he tried to slip out of bed. Generally, she was a light sleeper. Her plan should work, especially if she stayed awake until he fell asleep. Could she? She made no promises. She would fight sleep as long as she could before giving in and hope for the best.

Brewer not agreeing to curl up on the couch had her concerned. She would've been able to hear the alarm if disarmed from there. The move to give her the main bedroom—the farthest one from the garage door—wasn't lost on her. This wasn't her first rodeo.

After brushing her teeth, she met Brewer in the bedroom. Sleeping in her current outfit would be fine sans the sweatshirt. Shrugging out of it, her T-shirt rode up. Quickly, she dropped a hand to hold it in place and not give a peep show. Without a bra, she would be bearing all.

There might not have been much of a show, but her dignity was still intact as she dropped the sweatshirt onto the chair in the corner and then slid underneath the covers. The bed was bigger than any king she'd ever slept on. Must've been a custom job. Of course, it would be. Everything about this safe house screamed *custom* and *expensive*. Her SO had set them up well. Crystal reminded herself not to get too used to these kinds of digs. These places were rare and normally a favor being called in.

They were 0–2 when it came to safe houses, hoping to improve the numbers with this one.

Brewer changed into sweatpants, no shirt. The thought of being skin to bare-naked skin with that chest sent sensual shivers racing over her body. Warmth spread over her and through her as she met him in the middle of the oversize bed.

"I need to ask where this bed came from," Brewer said with a smile that tugged at her heartstrings. Too bad he was most likely plotting his exit. "It's the most comfortable thing I've slept on in ages. Then again, that's not difficult considering what I have to compare it with."

"Tents and hard dirt are most definitely the opposite of sleeping on a cloud," she said on a laugh, trying to break up the sudden tension in her chest. Her gaze dropped to his lips again. She couldn't regret the move, but it definitely wasn't helping stem the almost overwhelming pull of attraction.

"True," he said, his voice low and sexier than any man's should be.

"Is it okay if I get closer like last night?" she asked, not wanting to overstep her bounds. Last night, the boat had forced them to be crushed together and the cold had made being as close as possible an even better idea. Tonight was a different story. They had heat. They had room.

She'd had to make being close about something else. Since she made a terrible liar and had never acquired the taste for it, unlike her father, she'd gone with the closest thing to the truth. Everything she'd said had been from the heart. Her world was upside down, spinning out of control fast.

Brewer was a tether to reality. So, yes, she needed him and had been honest in every way that counted aside from the plea being a strategic move.

"Go ahead," he said, turning onto his back.

She moved into the crook of his arm and then he looped his arm around her, pulling her closer. His spicy male scent filled her senses, bringing awareness to every intake of air. His body was silk over steel. There was an intensity about Brewer that put ideas in her mind about how incredible he would be if they gave in to attraction and had sex. A voice in the back of her head reminded her it would be a bad idea. Not just for professional reasons, although that was a big one. But because he would raise the bar for sex. For what she should expect in the bedroom and, she suspected, out of it too, based on the way he'd treated her so far.

Crystal realized there was more to her attraction than circumstances. Brewer was intelligent, intense, honorable.

He had a smokin' hot bod that made her hands ache to roam all over it.

"Thank you for doing this, by the way," she said to him, attempting to guide her thoughts back onto a professional track and the real reason she'd asked for this. Being able to track his movement should he decide to bolt made suffering through a physical ache to be with this man in the biblical sense worth it.

"No problem," he said, but his gruff voice gave him away. A trill of awareness shot through Crystal along with a small sense of triumph at the fact he seemed just as affected.

A one-way attraction this intense would feel awful. Not that she would act on a mutual one.

"I forgot to mention earlier with the kind of day it's been," she started, realizing she'd neglected to share one of the most important pieces of information to him after receiving a text from her SO while showering. "The trial date has been set for Monday."

"Today's Friday," he immediately said.

"That's right," she agreed. "We only have to stay alive through the weekend, and I have to get you safely to the courthouse. Come Tuesday or Wednesday of next week, you and your aunt will be able to put all this behind you."

Based on how quiet he'd gotten, she had no idea if this information was good or bad. For the case, it was positive because it gave Crane's men less time to find and kill Brewer. She would be able to get to the hospital sooner rather than later, which was also a plus.

After spending time alone with Brewer, she needed to go home and hit the reset button. Not once in her professional career had she been tempted to cross the line with a witness. Zero. Granted, she had no intention of this being the first, no matter how much her heart protested.

"Good," Brewer said. "You'll finally be rid of me, and I can't make any more mistakes that could get us both killed."

"You? Mistakes?" she asked, shocked. "What's my excuse? You turned your original phone in but I should have taken your phone the minute I realized you had a second one."

"It's blown to smithereens now," he said as a quiet settled over Brewer. Intensity practically radiated from him. Nothing was going to get through.

They were both tired. They needed sleep. They would have a better perspective in the morning.

Crystal repositioned, moving her leg next to his. He immediately moved his out of reach. Had she struck a nerve?

Silence hovered like a thick cloud. Crystal fought the urge to give in to sleep. Something told her the news she'd just delivered made Brewer even more resolved to leave. Was she overreacting?

Ten minutes in, fighting to keep her eyes open, it finally happened. Brewer's breathing slowed to a steady, even pace. She could hear his strong heartbeat as she let go and drifted off to sleep.

Chapter Seventeen

The sun peeked through the slats on the blinds as Brewer blinked his eyes open. He immediately noticed the bed was cold where Crystal had been.

Had he nodded off? Slept the entire night? Dammit.

So much for slipping out while Crystal slept. He also realized it was the first time he'd trusted someone enough to sleep in their presence in a long time.

Tossing aside the covers, he threw on a shirt and headed toward the bathroom. Not five minutes later, he followed the smell of coffee to the kitchen. The clock on the wall said it was seven forty-five.

"Good morning," Crystal said with a smile in her voice. She had on a long T-shirt that fell to midthigh and not much else.

The fireplace was going, and the heat was on in more than one sense of the word.

"Hey," he responded, still trying to process the fact he'd fallen asleep. "I can't believe I slept the whole way through." He hadn't had a true night's sleep since the incident if he was being honest. After, there'd been nightmares. Then, waking up with phantom pain in part of a leg that was no longer there. That had been fun.

Crystal crossed the kitchen and went for a robe she'd

hung on the back of one of the bar chairs. She shrugged it on and tied the cinch to the point he wasn't certain she'd be able to breathe. "I didn't hear you coming downstairs."

Good to know he could still pull off being stealthy when necessary. "Didn't mean to catch you off guard."

"Not a problem," she said before crossing the kitchen. "I figured out the machine. What'll you have? I can do coffee, but that's boring. I can do a latte and I can do a cappuccino. Or the machine can, rather. I know what buttons to push, though, so that makes me the boss."

There was a spring in her step he hadn't noticed until now. Then again, their situation hadn't exactly called for lightness up to this point. And yes, it was great they'd had a real bed to sleep in last night in a million-dollar home. Who wouldn't be happy?

Happiness was fleeting. Brewer had learned the lesson firsthand. Would he ever be truly happy?

It was probably surviving a life-and-death situation together and being in close proximity that had him believing he and Crystal could make a life together.

Whoa there! Slow down, Brewer.

"Coffee with a shot of espresso works, if you can manage." His imagination was getting the best of him. Because they weren't a real couple and this situation was temporary. The fact that he was going to testify on Monday put his aunt and Trent in even more danger.

As it was, Brewer had no idea what was going on outside the bubble of this million-dollar home.

"I just had the same myself," she said with a satisfied smile.

He walked over to the fridge and started rummaging,

opting for a bowl of cereal. "Have you heard anything else from your SO today?"

"Nothing," she said as the machine hissed and groaned while it spit out brown liquid. "You like yours black, right?"

"Yes, ma'am," he said, realizing how military he just sounded. Force of habit.

"It's too early to be so formal," she teased before producing a mug that almost smelled better than she had last night. He could still remember the lavender scent that had filled him up and reached deep inside him, reminding him of fields of fresh flowers and the reason he thought this country had been worth putting his life on the line to protect.

"Sorry," he said, taking the offering. He inhaled a breath and ended up with more of Crystal's lavender soap in his body.

"Don't be," she said before grabbing her own mug. She lifted it up in a toast. "To us both waking up here today."

The way her voice slightly caught on the word *here* had him wondering if she'd figured out his plan last night. And then the reason she'd wanted to sleep together dawned on him. She was onto his plan. Or at the very least, she feared he would pull a stunt like the one he planned. Since they were way past being coy, he asked, "How did you know?"

"I didn't," she admitted. "I suspected."

He studied her for a long moment before shaking his head and grabbing his cereal bowl.

"I can make something better than that if you'd like," she offered.

"Thought you couldn't cook," he reminded her. Had she been playing him then too?

"Does breakfast count?" she asked. "I can do a mean

avocado toast, which technically involves a toaster, not an oven or stovetop."

"Do you cook an egg?"

"You got me on that one," she admitted, joining him at the table.

"Then you lied to me before," he said with more heat than intended.

"I didn't," she said. "I wouldn't." Catching his gaze, she added, "I couldn't do that to you. Plus, I'm a terrible liar."

It was probably his ego that wanted the statement to be true.

"Are you saying you've never had to lie in the course of doing your job?" he pressed, knowing he should probably quit while he was ahead.

"Is that what we're really talking about here?" she countered.

Brewer laughed and put a hand up in defeat. "Touché."

"Guess it's my turn to apologize."

"Never apologize to me for being honest," he said. The world had become too comfortable with lies as far as he was concerned. He'd heard plenty while rehabbing after surgery. Some folks might've called it optimism. The doctors and nurses had been full of it, telling him that he could still live a full life despite his permanent damage. They'd said it was up to him and that he could get the rest of his mobility back. As for the loss of hearing in the right ear, there wasn't anything that could be done there, but he was supposed to be thankful for hearing on the left side.

His frustration wasn't due to throwing a pity party for himself. The hand he'd been dealt was punishment he deserved.

"Okay, then," she started. Suddenly, the rim of her coffee

mug became very interesting. "Since we're being honest. Why did you pull away from me last night?"

"I didn't," he defended. At least, he didn't remember it.

"My leg touched yours," she continued without missing a beat. "It was innocent on my part, but you couldn't move away fast enough."

"You were on my left side," he explained, surprised when her eyebrow shot up in confusion. "My bad leg."

Crystal sat there for a long moment. Her expression revealed the moment she made the connection. "Your 'bad' leg. You don't like anyone to touch it?"

He nodded.

"Or see it," she continued.

It was time to change the subject, but he filled his mouth with a bite of cereal instead.

"Is that why you always wear socks?" She dropped her gaze again, not making eye contact.

"Trust me, you don't want to see my feet." Or should he say foot?

"It wouldn't bother me one way or the other."

"That's what you say now because I haven't taken my sock off," he pressed. Which person would she be? Someone who stared? Or someone who refused to look?

"WHY DON'T YOU take it off right now?" Crystal probably shouldn't continue down this line with Brewer. As it was, he'd shifted in his seat three times.

"Because I'm eating."

"Then let me do it." Crystal caught his gaze. "What's the harm?"

She wanted to see his leg and his foot—not out of some morbid curiosity, but it occurred to her that he was hiding them. He was ashamed or embarrassed, which burned her to no end. The man had fought for his country. He'd been in battle. In her book, that made him a hero. And heroes shouldn't have to be ashamed of their body parts for being missing or broken.

Brewer's gaze intensified, almost daring her.

"Not without your permission," she clarified.

"You won't look at me the same."

"How about allowing me the opportunity to prove you wrong." It broke her heart that he thought he had to hide parts of himself from her, from the world.

"If I wanted this to become awkward, I would have taken my sock off already," he snapped.

Her body reacted to those words similar to a physical slap. "I wouldn't... I couldn't." And then it dawned on her that others might have. "It's okay, Brewer. Never mind." Crystal didn't easily accept defeat, except that she knew when she'd lost a battle, and there was no use beating her head against a wall.

Brewer set his spoon inside the bowl. He bent down and rolled up the jeans he'd changed into, stopping just above the knee. Next, he peeled off the sock.

"How does it work?" she asked. "When you have shoes and pants on, I can't tell a thing."

"That's the idea," he said. "A Texas-based company donated the materials. This works off muscles the same way the real thing would."

"It's kind of cool looking," she said. "Like the stuff superheroes are made from."

"You've seen too many Marvel movies," he said as a smile played with the corners of his mouth.

"You're still the sexiest man I've ever seen wearing jeans

and not much else," she said, then immediately realized she'd said the words out loud instead of inside her head as usual.

The look on her face after the slip must have amused him because his full lips broke into a wide smile over straight white teeth.

"Okay, I didn't mean it like in the unprofessional way," she quickly countered, rolling her eyes. "And don't let your head swell so big you can't make it out the door when we get the signal to leave."

"I'm a hot-air balloon at this point for how much my head is swelling," he teased. This time, there was a sparkle in his normally too-serious eyes that she hadn't seen before. It was nice, and she wondered if this was what he'd been like before the incident that had taken part of his leg. "We lift off after breakfast."

Crystal laughed.

Despite everything, it was funny. And it was good to laugh. There'd been too little laughter in her life up to this point.

"Eat your cereal, and then we'll talk." Based on his reactions so far, she was dead-on about him trying to sneak out last night. It was only Saturday. How on earth would she keep an eye on him twenty-four seven until Monday morning?

Glancing at the clock, she had roughly forty-eight hours to cover between now and then. Could she stay awake? Not go to the bathroom?

Okay, the bathroom part was pretty extreme. Could she get him to stay put might've been a better question. This home might've just been their ticket to staying alive until he needed to testify. Favors had been called in to get on the docket Monday.

He reached down to unroll his jeans.

"You don't have to do that for me, by the way," she said.

His eyebrow shot up.

"Cover up," she clarified. "I don't care one way or the other."

He looked at her like she couldn't possibly mean that. It dawned on her that he wasn't used to being treated like he used to be. He should've been. But she'd protected a witness who had a little girl in a wheelchair from cerebral palsy. The witness had said the worst part was how no one ever looked his beautiful little girl in the eyes or said hello. No one spoke to her in the grocery line or when he took her out in the park. It was the bit that broke his heart because his little girl deserved to be seen. She deserved to have people say good-morning to her when he dropped her off at school instead of the blank straight-ahead stares she got.

"You're the same person to me, Brewer."

He was almost fully hovered over his cereal bowl at this point, face down. When he looked up, he had a smirk on his face a mile long. "Still as hot?"

Again, Crystal laughed.

"Yep," she quipped. "Same level of hotness."

"Good," was all he said, but she heard so much relief in that one word it caused her heart to break a little more for him.

He polished off two bowls of cereal after rolling his jeans leg down. He kept the sock off, which she appreciated. She'd seen all the physical scars on his body from his time in the service, feared she'd only seen the tip of the iceberg when it came to the ones on the inside.

Brewer needed to know he was still gorgeous, hot beyond her wildest imagination, and…whole.

Was there any way to convey that to him in a way that could help him see it was true?

Crystal gave herself a mental headshake. She had to keep him alive until he could testify on Monday. Beyond that, professionally speaking, it wasn't her job to care what happened to Wade Brewer.

So, why wasn't she able to let it go?

Chapter Eighteen

Brewer glanced down at the metal foot as light bounced off what should have been the top of his arch. Superhero?

No. Bulletproof?

No. Special?

No.

He shouldn't get a medal for surviving when it should have been him behind the wheel that day. Today, though, he couldn't afford to jump on that hamster wheel of shame and guilt. Because he had a chance to save another friend's life. In order to accomplish the task, he needed to focus and put all distractions behind him. Which included Crystal.

Right now, he wanted to stay with her more than anything. Not because of the words she'd said a few minutes ago. He genuinely liked being with her. At the table, he'd laughed for the first time in a year. Probably longer than that if he was being truly honest. He'd joked. That wasn't something he was used to doing anymore either.

For a few seconds, Brewer had felt like himself again. As much as he wanted to hold on to that feeling a little while longer, Trent could end up dead. Not having contact with the outside world to know what was going on was driving him to the brink.

Leaving her was going to be one of the hardest things

he'd ever done. She would resent him for ditching her. She was also onto him. She was watching. He had to bide his time and find the right moment to make his exit. All he could do at this point was wait.

Crystal's cell buzzed. She retrieved it and answered the call.

"Hey, boss, what's going on?" She sounded surprised to get the phone call, which got Brewer's attention. "I see." She hesitated before finally swinging her gaze around to meet his. "Okay." She paused a beat. "No. Don't do that. There's no need." Another pause. "Seriously. I'm good. We're good." A final pause. "I'll let you know if anything changes. Thanks for the information." She ended the call.

"What's going on?" he asked.

"Damon has been sighted in the Dallas area," Crystal informed.

"Which means he's on the hunt for me." Brewer wasn't sure if he should take that as a good sign for Trent or not. It would be useful to know if his friend had gone into hiding or had been abducted. "Did your SO say anything about Trent?"

Crystal shook her head. "My SO would have said something if she had new information. She did, however, mention sending a replacement for me."

"No," he argued. "Absolutely not. I don't trust anyone else to get the job done. It's you or no one."

"I talked her out of it for now," she said. "But she wants to send him anyway."

"Why?"

"Said something about this assignment being bigger than one person and that it might be easier if we were able to take shifts so one of us could sleep," she continued.

"You told her not to do that," he confirmed.

"That's right." Crystal issued a sharp sigh. "This is a high-profile case. It's not uncommon to assign two marshals when we have the resources."

"But you don't," he interjected. "Do you?"

"Not really," she admitted. "I have history with the marshal she wants to send. History that is no one's business but ours."

"Why do I get the sense he's trying to get himself assigned to this case to get back on your good side?" Brewer didn't like that one bit. He didn't have a right to feel one way or the other when it came to her personal life. The kiss they'd shared, as electric as it had been, wasn't personal. Okay, he could admit it had felt personal in the moment, but there had been a tactical reason for it too.

"You would be correct."

"Has he been trying to contact you since we've been here?" he asked.

"Yes," she admitted. "But I haven't been responding. I do my best not to introduce my personal life into my work. The exception, of course, being with my grandparents. Mahone is crossing a line here."

Brewer studied her for a long moment. "Your SO doesn't know about your history with Mahone, does she?"

"No," Crystal said. "I think she suspects something, but when we first got together, we worked different districts, and he got himself transferred to mine after the breakup."

"Sounds persistent." Brewer's whole body shouldn't have tensed at hearing this even though it did. In the back of his mind, he was trying to work out the threat level now that they knew Damon was near.

While holed up in the million-dollar home, Brewer as-

sumed the threat was low, but it was dangerous to underesti-
mate Damon. The rival to Crane's organization was Michael
Mylett. Based on the intel Brewer had gathered while working for Crane, Mylett wanted to take over. Could Brewer
go to Mylett and spill more "company" secrets? Help him
take command of Crane's men in exchange for protection
for Trent and his family, Aunt Rosemary, and himself? He
would only bargain to keep himself alive so he could take
care of his aunt in her later years. Abandoning her to live
out the last years alone was wrong. He couldn't do that
after she'd welcomed him into her home and protected him.

Mylett hung out in Austin at the Roasted Bean. He considered himself a true businessman. Apparently he woke
at five forty-five every morning to go to the gym. After
a workout, he stopped off at the Roasted Bean, where he
sometimes met with his associates over breakfast. His office, much like Crane's, was the back of a blacked-out SUV.

His home would be a fortress. Not to mention the fact
Mylett might have Brewer shot for betraying his former
boss.

Brewer reserved this option as a last resort. At this point,
he needed information. He needed to know where Trent
was and if he was hiding or captured. He thought about
his aunt. Should he have her moved? Was it safe for her to
stay in the same place for very long?

Now that he'd tucked her away, he didn't want to disturb her any more than necessary. She'd trusted him when
he'd asked her not to question why she'd needed to move
temporarily. She'd been able to take her cat, Tiny, with her.
Tiny, the twenty-pound cat who'd outgrown his name, had
sealed the deal.

"Talk to me, Brewer."

"There's not much to say." He tried to sell the line but couldn't. He couldn't sell what he didn't believe himself. He put a hand up. "Okay, there's a lot to say, but I don't know where to start."

"Then throw anything at me, and I'll do my best to answer."

"What about Aunt Rosemary? Is she safe where she is? Being targeted? Left alone? Should she be moved to another location for preemptive purposes?"

"I can take care of that." Crystal made a note on her phone. "What else?"

"What did you just do?"

"Put in a request to have her moved as I'm capturing your concerns," she said. "That might be something as simple as asking for a wellness check or extra local manpower to patrol your aunt's new location. Or alerting my superior so she can track down resources just in case." She looked up at him and blinked. "I'm on your side, Brewer. Or haven't you noticed that already?"

"You're doing your job," he pointed out. "This is my life we're talking about. I don't punch out and go home when this is over. Or have you forgotten?"

Those words landed with the equivalence of a physical punch. Crystal drew back and sucked in a breath.

Brewer felt like a real jerk.

"MAYBE YOU'RE RIGHT about me," Crystal started, wondering where she should begin in defense of what he'd just said. "Maybe I do get to 'clock out,' as you put it, at the end of the day and go home. Last I checked, I was here with you trying to keep us both alive. Oh, and that's not all. I just got off the phone with my SO, who wants me to 'clock out,' but

I refused because protecting a witness is personal for me and I don't walk away just because a case is high profile or classified as the most dangerous of my career. I'm not here for my own health or to get some kind of gold star in my file. I'm here to protect you." She was starting to get heated. Emotion was overtaking logic. But since she was already strapped to this runaway train moving at full blast, she continued. "And do you know why I'm still here against my SO's better judgment?"

Brewer folded his arms across his chest and gave a slight headshake.

"Because I don't walk away from a witness who needs me."

"I need you?" he asked. His gaze narrowed and his lips thinned.

"That's right, Brewer. Believe it or not, you need me," she stated with more of that heat in her tone.

"Why is that?"

"Because no one is going to care about you and Aunt Rosemary as much as I do," she continued. "This is personal for me because I've gotten to know a little bit about you in the past forty-eight plus hours, and guess what? I like you. Despite the fact you look ready to walk out that door the minute I turn my back, I actually think what you're doing is noble. I think you're an honorable human being, and not just because you came home from a war you didn't start with battle scars."

"Then why?" His face was stone, giving away none of his emotions.

"Because you've been to hell and back, which could have turned you into a bitter jerk," she continued, spilling the truth like water from a fountain. "You're intense—don't get me wrong. You're not easy to get along with all the time. But you're strong, and I don't just mean in the physical sense. You're the kind of person kids need in their lives to have someone to look up to."

"More of that superhero nonsense."

"Maybe," she said. "But there aren't nearly enough people left in this world who are worth of looking up to, and you're one of them." She threw her hands in the air. If he couldn't see it at this point, she would never be able to convince him with words.

As she stood there, fuming, Brewer broke into a wide smile.

"What about being hot? You forgot to add my hotness to your list of good qualities," he said.

She wanted to wipe the smirk from his face. "You're also infuriating!"

"So, where do we stand on the hotness scale?" he continued, unfazed by the fact she was a teapot about to boil over. "Am I a nine or ten?"

"Jerk. How about that scale? Because right now I'd definitely say you're a ten." She cut across the room and tapped his good shoulder. He captured her wrist. "Quick. I'd give you a nine on the quickness scale."

Against her better judgment, she locked gazes with him. The moment their eyes connected, lightning struck. Was her heart in trouble? Hard yes. Was there anything she planned to do about it? Harder no.

The air in the room crackled with electricity. The heat between them could be a furnace for all of downtown Dallas. The only thing she could do under the circumstances was take a step back and drop her hand in order to break his grip.

She had no doubt he could have tightened his hold, but

he seemed to know this was a bad idea as much as she did. "I need air."

Without looking back, she disarmed the alarm and then walked into the garage, welcoming the cold on her heated skin.

She could think clearly in here, away from Brewer.

It was only a matter of time before he made his move. Should she have allowed Elise to send Mahone to double up on keeping watch over—and on!—Brewer?

His main concerns seemed to be around the safety of his aunt and his friend. There wasn't much she could do about Trent, considering she had no idea where he was and hadn't gotten back definitive intel as to which side he was on.

Having Brewer's aunt moved should ease some of his concerns. If Crystal was in control of his aunt's situation, that would also give Brewer extra incentive to stick around.

They had…she checked the time on her cell…forty-four hours to get through before she needed to safely deliver him to the courtroom. Had Brewer figured out this assignment only got trickier from here? That the danger increased dramatically the closer they physically got to the courthouse?

Should she prepare him?

Crystal reminded herself to get a grip. This was Wade Brewer she was thinking about. The man was former military. He would have thought through all the possibilities, assessed the risks by this point.

Was that the reason he wanted to ditch her? She could see in his eyes that he did. It was in the words he wasn't choosing to say.

The man had a unique ability to get under her skin. He could throw her off balance by existing in the same room with her. She might not have experienced anything like this before with a witness, or anyone else for that matter, but that didn't mean she wouldn't find a workaround.

Brewer wasn't the only one good with strategy and tactics.

A noise inside the house made her heart leap into her throat. He wouldn't be climbing out a window right now... would he?

Chapter Nineteen

Brewer bent down to pick up the dish he'd dropped while emptying the dishwasher. The plate had broken into four big chunks and more tiny pieces than he cared to count.

Crystal came rushing into the room from the garage. "Everything all right in here?"

"Peachy," he said, not bothering to hide his frustration. "It slipped right out of my fingers." He issued a sharp sigh. Was this another sign his body was no longer listening to him?

"It happens," Crystal said, checking the pantry before joining him with a broom and dustpan. She held them out. "I'll leave you to your work."

"You're not helping?" he asked, surprised.

"You can't clean up by yourself?" she asked, turning over the items.

"I didn't say that," he said a little defensively.

"Good," she quipped. "I figured you weren't helpless."

He didn't know whether to hate her or revere her for the fact she refused to help. On the one hand, it meant she believed he was fully capable of cleaning up his own mess. The operative words being *fully capable*. Even Aunt Rosemary had wanted to baby him after the incident. She hadn't offended him on purpose, but he'd been prickly as hell. The more she'd wanted to do for him, the less of a human he'd felt. So, he'd left after a few days, checked into a nearby motel—if it could be called that—and figured out how to fix his own meals. The dollar menu at the fast-food place within walking distance had been a lifesaver during his recovery.

Aunt Rosemary had insisted she go with him to his rehab appointments, so he'd been stuck in the back seat of a hot off-duty fireman's vehicle next to his aunt. He'd had to hear his aunt flirt with said hot off-duty fireman. It had been the only time that plan had backfired on him.

Brewer decided he respected Crystal for not helping. She was telling him that he didn't need it.

He would take Crystal's actions as a compliment.

Leaving her was getting more difficult by the minute. Say, for argument's sake, he did find a way to slip out. Where would he go? What would he do?

He had cash stashed in his rucksack, so he could pay for items without leaving a trail. That fact didn't help much when it came to ordering a car service. Those needed an app. Without a phone, his options were limited.

He picked up the broken pieces of the plate and set the four large pieces on the countertop. With the right glue, he could probably piece this thing back together again. Using broom and dustpan, he collected the smaller pieces. "Have you seen any glue around?"

"Glue?" Crystal echoed in a surprised voice like he'd just asked her to marry him. She didn't need to worry about that one even though she was exactly the kind of person he could see himself settling down with for the long haul.

"Turn up your hearing aid," he quipped. Teasing her was a lot more entertaining than it should be.

She joined him in the kitchen. "Why would I know where glue is? Does it look like I live here?"

"You should," he said. "Live here. This place suits you."

Crystal couldn't shake her head fast enough. "I'm a country girl through and through. Did you see how close the neighbors are?" She made a dramatic show of shivering. "Way too close for comfort."

"What are you trying to hide?" he continued, enjoying the momentary break in tension.

"What's gotten into you, Brewer?" She eyed him with amusement.

"Cabin fever?"

"We haven't been here a full twenty-four hours yet," she said with an eye roll.

"What can I say?" He threw his hands out wide. At least he had both of those and they still worked properly. Most of the time anyway. "I'm an outdoor person."

Crystal's laugh was the cliché. It was angels singing to Brewer's good ear.

He finished cleaning up the mess as she checked drawers.

"Everyone has to have a junk drawer in the kitchen, right?" she asked when she was coming up empty.

"Apparently people who live in million-dollar homes keep their drawers organized." Pretty much all of his kitchen drawers fell under the category of junk drawers. No wonder he hadn't made his first million yet—he didn't know the drawer trick.

Everything in this house had a place. Glue would be no different. "What about the garage?" he asked. "Did you see a toolbox in there?"

"I'll go check," she said.

He hadn't been paying attention when they'd first arrived yesterday and had yet to go out there today. In fact, when she came back inside, they should probably arm the alarm. He wasn't kidding about staying inside. On their initial tour, he'd seen a workout room. Could he get a good sweat going in there? Work off some of the tension building inside him?

The gym had been a lifesaver during his recovery. Even more so now. Weights didn't care who lifted them. The gym was equal opportunity. A private gym would stop others from sneaking looks through the mirror when they thought he couldn't see what they were doing.

But first, could he piece this plate back together?

Crystal returned, beaming. A small tube sat on the palm of her hand. "Beast Glue."

"Only the best," he said with a smile.

"Can you imagine yourself living in a place like this?" she asked. "Seriously?"

"No." He didn't have to think about his answer. "I wouldn't be happy. There's way too much concrete for my liking outside the door. Speaking of which, we should arm the alarm."

"Oh, right," she said, moving to the pad and then punching in the magic numbers that started the beeps. They momentarily took him back to hearing a similar sound in the hospital when he'd woken after the incident. The shock of glancing down to find he only had one foot. Then the slow process of being able to sit up again on his own. Patience wasn't exactly his middle name.

He pushed to be able to do more, against medical advice. What did doctors know about him? They knew generalities. They were schooled in what the average person could expect. They had no idea what would go down for each individual. Despite all the years in school and the experience in the field, it turned out that medicine wasn't an exact science.

Then came the tests, the fittings, the recovery. The learning to live with a new reality. The rest, as they say, was history.

He took the glue and fitted the pieces back together as best he could. "It's not perfect, but it's better than nothing."

Crystal studied the patchwork. "It's better than before."

"How so?"

"It used to be a plate just like all the others in the cabinet," she surmised. "Now it's an art piece."

Brewer glanced down at his body, wishing the same could be true.

CRYSTAL WALKED TO the living room and then plopped down onto the couch. She picked up the remote control and pressed a large green button. A cabinet opened above the fireplace, revealing a massive flat-screen. "Whoa."

It was Saturday, which meant college football.

"Do you want to watch a game?" she asked, figuring him for the football-watching type. She hoped the distraction would buy some time.

"I'm going to hit the gym," he said. "The door will be open if you want to work out together."

The invitation caught her off guard. She stretched out her arms and then legs. "I'll be there in a few minutes."

Fifteen minutes later, she pushed off the couch, having flipped through the channels and found nothing worth settling on despite having more options than she knew what to do with. The term *choice paralysis* applied here. More

than not, trying to find a movie to watch at home took longer than actually watching a movie. By the time she found
one, it was time for bed.

In the gym, beads of sweat rolled down Brewer's neck
to pecs that bulged against his cotton T-shirt.

Crystal shook her head as she moved to a treadmill. This
home gym was something. The room had a circular shape
with a flat wall of mirrors. There was a treadmill, rowing
machine, elliptical, and weight bench. There were various
weights to choose from along with a few resistance bands.
A couple of rolled-up yoga mats were tucked inside a basket, making it look almost like a floral arrangement. And,
of course, there was another flat-screen TV mounted on
the mirrored wall. She was half-surprised the room didn't
have one of those exercise bikes that had been all the rage
a couple of years ago.

Crystal located the remote and flipped to a music station that was the perfect for a workout. She glanced over
at Brewer to see if her choice was okay, got a thumbs-up.
Hard rock wasn't something she normally listened to, but
it worked when she needed to get her blood moving either
for a run or a workout.

Being a marshal meant passing annual fitness tests as
well as shooting tests. She always had to be ready to fire
her weapon when chasing dangerous felons or protecting a
witness. This job wasn't like a suburban beat cop who might
fire a weapon once or twice during their entire career. As
a marshal, she had to fire frequently on assignment when
she chased felons who had nothing to lose. Once caught
and convicted, they weren't likely to step outside a prison
gate for the rest of their life.

Those kinds of perps were notorious for shooting first,

asking questions later. And running. They liked running. Not in the going-for-a-friendly-jog sense. They were more in the vein of running-for-your-life runners. The boost of adrenaline that came with being so close to arrest gave them a superpower.

So, yes, Crystal trained. She hit the gym. She worked out.

Because she always had to be ready to catch someone on an adrenaline- or drug-fueled high.

An hour ticked by before they took a break. Of course, a million-dollar home would have a water cooler with cups like at the gym. She grabbed one for herself, then one for Brewer and filled both before handing his over.

"This was a good idea, Brewer."

"Always helps to get a good sweat going," he said through heaves. He looked around. "Who keeps fresh towels in their home gym?"

"Not anyone I know," she said. "But then we're all backyard-barbecue-and-beer type folks. This is a champagne-and-caviar lifestyle and definitely not a typical safe house. Someone important must live here."

He smiled as he wiped sweat from his face and neck. "Sounds awful, but then I don't eat raw fish either."

"You don't eat sushi?" she asked.

"Nope," he informed. "I like my food cooked all the way through." He made a face. "Too much bacteria otherwise."

"I'll take my dry chicken any day over single-celled organisms."

"Someone paid attention during biology class," he teased.

"A-plus student right here," she bragged.

"So, what's next?" he said to her when his breathing calmed down to a normal pace.

"We go to court," she said. "I thought you were in on the plan."

"I can't risk Trent's life," he stated.

"My SO is doing a little more digging into his background," she said, then held up a hand to stop him from going off. "Before you say anything or tell me what a great guy Trent is—and that might be true, by the way—at least listen."

Brewer shifted his gaze up and to the corner of the door frame before giving a slight nod for her to continue.

"We wouldn't be doing our job if we didn't investigate the man who put you in this position," she explained.

"You said something similar before," he pointed out.

"I meant it then too." Crystal took a sip of water. "Trust me?" She practically held her breath waiting to see how he would answer.

Chapter Twenty

"Fine," Brewer said to Crystal. "For the record, I believe in Trent. He wouldn't put me in this position on purpose."

"How can you be so certain?" she asked.

"Because we're part of a brotherhood that none of us would betray." The answer was just that simple. "We made a commitment to each other and our country. Those commitments create an unbreakable bond."

"Ever hear the name David Berkowitz?" she asked.

"Yes."

"How about Jeffrey Dahmer?" she continued.

"Of course," he replied. Where was she going with this?

"Dennis Rader?"

"He was BTK," Brewer responded. "What do these men have to do with Trent?"

"They all served in the military," she said. "And then became predators in the very country they swore to protect."

"That's not Trent," he argued.

"The list goes on," she said. "Serving in the military doesn't make him innocent."

Brewer shook his head. "Doesn't make him guilty either."

"Some people leave the military with scars you can see, like you," she gingerly pointed out. "For others, those scars aren't so visible." She paused. "You don't know which kind

Trent picked up or what might have been going on in the back of his mind before."

Arguing would do no good and she'd made one helluva point, so Brewer bit his tongue. Was he being naive when it came to Trent? Did he know the man as well as he believed he did? "Do what you need to do."

"Thank you for understanding." She wiped more sweat from her neck. "Even if I know you don't agree."

"I need to grab a shower," he said as she walked out of the room. With Crystal, he feared he might agree to pretty much anything she said. Brewer was convinced Trent wouldn't walk away if the situation was reversed. She hadn't heard Trent's voice on the phone like he had. She hadn't heard the regret or his apologies or the way he'd blamed himself and taken full responsibility. She didn't know how much Trent wanted to help Brewer get out of the situation he was in *because* of him.

A cold shower helped clear Brewer's mind.

The time was nearing when he needed to make his escape. Leaving tonight gave him time to get to east Texas and the spot Trent had practically said he'd be hiding. Brewer stood at the window in the upstairs spare bedroom where he'd placed his rucksack, staring out. This area of Adriatica Village housed villas. There were apartment buildings too—plenty of them. Which meant he should be able to find a motorcycle to hot-wire.

A plan was taking shape. If he was lucky, there'd be a helmet with the motorcycle. There was no hiding his rucksack. It was the one thing that could give him away. Then again, a motorcycle would get him to the destination off the grid much quicker than most cars, especially with the speed limits in Texas. *Limits* was a loose interpretation.

Drivers took the term *limit* more as a suggestion or a starting point than a limit per se.

If he disappeared, though, what would that do to Crystal's career? Would losing a witness put a mark on her file?

Could he do that to her after everything she'd done for him? After he'd told her more about his past than anyone else?

Brewer rejoined Crystal in the kitchen in time for a late lunch. They heated a Tex-Mex favorite—fish tacos. Sitting across the table from her, he wondered if finding Trent would go a lot smoother if he let her in on his plan rather than go behind her back?

After getting to know her, walking away was less appealing. Plus, he didn't want to be the reason she got a mark on her file.

"I think I know where we can find Trent," he admitted. "If he's hiding, that is."

She cocked her head to one side. "The coordinates you gave me were fake, weren't they?"

Not much got past the marshal.

He shook his head. "They were close but far enough away that I doubted you'd hit the target." He still held on to the idea that he could go to Mylett if everything fell apart.

"Why put me in the area at all?" she asked.

"Because it was more believable that way," he admitted. "Then there's the fact I can't lie to you."

"I hope, for your sake, Trent is clean," she said. "I need to get approval from my SO before heading out."

"Does that mean we're going?"

"Only if I get the green light," she informed. "Otherwise, I'd be putting my career on the line to find someone who might be guilty as sin."

"If Trent is hiding, this is where he'll be," Brewer said. "I owe it to him."

"What if he set you up?" she asked. "Do you still owe him?"

"We'll cross that bridge when we come to it." Until proven otherwise, Brewer had to give Trent the benefit of the doubt.

Crystal issued a sharp sigh as she picked up her phone. "Here goes nothing."

LEAVING THE PROTECTION of the current safe house would be considered unprofessional if there was no threat. In truth, Damon was in Dallas and she'd received a text saying he was last seen on the train heading north. He was tracking them, and it was only a matter of time before he found them.

Which brought Crystal to her next point. They should've been heading south to Austin, where the trial was set to take place. Except that might be exactly what Damon would be thinking. She might be able to sell her SO on the fact they needed to do something unexpected if she was going to deliver her witness in one piece.

Going off the grid would be a hard sell, but Crystal would promise to check in frequently. Would her promise be enough?

Elise picked up on the first ring. "Give me good news."

Crystal argued her case before rattling off the coordinates. To Elise's credit, she listened quietly before making any judgments.

"It's a risk," she finally said.

"What isn't?" Crystal pointed out. "We stay here, Damon might find us in a matter of hours. We leave, we could get caught. My witness has a location that is unexpected. I think the risk is worth taking."

The rattle sound was most like Elise picking up the bottle of Tums on her desk and shaking it. The habit meant she was thinking hard.

"Do what you need to in order to keep your witness safe, Remington. I'd send backup if we weren't so short staffed." Elise was quiet for a beat. "Get him to court alive. I don't need to remind you how important this case is for our district."

"You can count on me," she promised, not liking the fact she was being asked to re-avow.

The phone was silent for a long moment.

"I have information coming in," Elise warned. "Hold tight."

Crystal didn't like the sound of this. She waved a hand to get Brewer's attention while he was putting away dishes and reloading the dishwasher. One look at her expression and he abandoned the job he'd been doing, immediately switching gears to erasing their presence. She didn't normally work with a witness who could hold their own. It was a nice change of pace.

Before Elise was back, he made a beeline for the stairs.

"My bag is in the bedroom, and I have a few toiletries in the bathroom," she said, covering the receiver with her free hand.

"Got it," he said before disappearing a moment later.

"You there?" Elise asked, coming back to the conversation.

"I'm here," Crystal confirmed.

"I've just received word Damon is in Adriatic Village," Elise informed. "You have to move. Now!"

Crystal immediately ended the call and jumped into action. By the time she reached the bottom of the stairs, Brewer was already coming down them. He'd shouldered his rucksack and had her bag in hand. "Damon's here."

"Go," he said, not wanting to waste a second.

She turned, grabbed her purse, and fished out the keys as she bolted toward the alarm pad. She punched in the numbers. A burst of adrenaline caused her hands to shake, but she kept it to a minimum as she grabbed the door handle.

In the next few seconds, she was behind the wheel, all thought of Brewer driving flew out the window as he hit the button that opened the garage door.

Crystal feared Damon might be standing on the other side of the door as it lifted, AR15 or some other rapid-fire weapon in hand, finger on the trigger.

It was too soon to revel in relief when the coast appeared to be clear. Damon was on the property, hunting them like a skilled hunter stalking prey. Lack of a phone to trace had bought them time, just not enough for her liking.

"You know what he looks like," she said to Brewer.

"Yes, ma'am," he responded, kicking into full-on military mode. He dropped his hand inside his rucksack and pulled out a Glock, keeping it low as he bent forward as if doing something as simple as tying a shoelace. The man wasn't breaking a sweat.

Staying calm under pressure saved lives. Considering the skill level of the folks they were up against, she needed Brewer's assistance if they were going to survive.

Rather than gun it and draw unwanted attention, Crystal navigated around the empty pathway out of the villas and into the restaurant and apartment area of the village after entering the small roundabout with a waterfall in the center.

Brewer casually surveyed the area, but there was nothing relaxed about the intensity of his gaze. Crystal worked the rearview and side mirrors, keeping vigilant watch to ensure no one seemed too interested in them. At this point in the afternoon, people stood outside a popular restaurant and more vehicles were on the internal streets.

Her best hope was to blend in.

Slowly, she made her way to the exit of the village, hooked a right-hand turn toward the highway. So far, so good. She'd learned a long time ago not to get comfortable too fast.

On Virginia Parkway, traffic thickened. It was another good sign.

Crystal navigated onto the highway without a tail. "It's too early to celebrate, but I need you to program in the ultimate destination or, at the very least, start talking. I don't have more than a vague idea of where we're headed."

"Maybe it's for the best if we take it one step at a time," he said. Didn't those words send an icy chill racing up her spine.

Did he trust her?

The reason dawned on her a few seconds later. If Damon caught up and captured her, she wouldn't be able to give him more than a general direction. Brewer was operating on military philosophy—need-to-know basis.

It was smart but also left the door open for him to lose her if they made a stop for gas or took a bathroom break.

Disappointment sat heavy on her chest at the thought that he didn't trust her after everything they'd been through together. After how much of their personal lives they'd shared. Hell, after working out together. She'd mistakenly believed they'd formed a bond.

Way to stay neutral on her witness.

Brewer was a special case. There were depths to him that were rare in an individual. From the minute they'd first met, she'd wanted to know more about him.

This seemed like a good time to remind herself that he'd been planning his escape all this time. He might've had depths that interested her, but that didn't mean he would let her inside. He was used to relying on himself and seemed to prefer it that way.

Still, it was difficult not to be impressed by the man. Their attraction burned. And a growing piece of her wanted to know how that would play out if it was allowed to run its course. After boyfriends like Mahone, she had a feeling Brewer would blow her mind, reach parts of her that she never knew existed.

And then what?

Walk away? Leave her heart shattered into a thousand flecks of dust?

On second thought, keeping a safe emotional distance made far more sense.

Step by step, Brewer provided directions moments before an exit needed to be taken. After just shy of two hours on the road, he told her to find a good place to hide the vehicle and park.

"There aren't exactly parking lots around here," she said.

"You're going to have to take this vehicle off road," he pointed out.

And get stuck? Break the only vehicle they had for a quick getaway? No thanks.

"Is there a plan B?" she asked.

"On second thought, we need to circle back and grab a few supplies from the gas station," he said. "Water, for one."

Had this been his plan all along? Get her out here in the boonies and then ditch her at the gas station?

Crystal was about to find out.

Chapter Twenty-One

"This might be the last real restroom you see for hours, possibly all night. Might be a good time to take care of business." Brewer fully intended to use the facilities.

Crystal shot him a wary look. He immediately caught the meaning. Telling her that he had no intention of ditching her wouldn't do any good. She needed to see it. So, he skipped the part where he would try to convince her. It would be a waste of breath anyway.

Brewer headed to the bathroom while she stood in the aisle. Waiting?

It dawned on him they'd come full circle with bathrooms. This time, he didn't have a phone or the intention of sneaking away. A small wave of disappointment that she didn't trust his word tried to take hold in his chest.

What reason had he given her to believe him?

Brewer washed his hands and pushed those thoughts out of his mind. They had a hike through maple, oaks, and river birch ahead of them, not to mention a person to find. After exiting the restroom, Brewer was surprised that he didn't see Crystal anywhere. A moment of panic struck like lightning on a clear day.

He grabbed half a dozen bottles of water and cleared out the power bars before heading to the cashier. On the way, he glanced out the window to realize Crystal waited in the car. Maybe she trusted him after all? Or maybe she had no choice.

After paying, he placed the supplies inside his rucksack and then headed toward her. As he neared, he realized she was on the phone. More bad news about them being followed? He picked up the pace.

She glanced up and nodded. A good sign?

Brewer opened the passenger door after placing his rucksack in the back. He eased onto the seat as she finished up the call. "Everything okay?"

"I called to let my brother know I might be out of range for a couple of days," she supplied.

"Once we find Trent, we can head to your hometown," he offered, not liking the wrinkle in her forehead. The crease was deep, meaning she was concerned more than she wanted to admit.

"Can't," she said. "Wouldn't be professional of me to bring a witness to the hospital on a personal errand."

Why did those words hit the center of his chest like bullet fragments?

"I understand," he said, needing to kick the relationship back to a professional level. Logic said they'd only known each other a matter of days. His heart argued it was already too late. He'd met enough of the wrong people to realize who the right ones were by this point in his life. Right people, wrong time? They wouldn't get a chance to know each other before he had to disappear for a couple of years, maybe more. A woman like her wouldn't wait. She would move on. The thought shouldn't strike like a physical blow. It did. "We should head out and find a good spot to stash the car."

"Right," she said, her tone all business as she gripped the steering wheel. She dropped one hand long enough to fish out her cell and hand it over. "Lead the way."

Brewer opened the map feature and studied it. "Head out this way." He pointed as he continued to focus on the map.

"All right, then," she said with no enthusiasm in her tone. "Time to get this party started."

Was she regretting putting her life on the line for someone like him? A broken-down soldier?

Either way, they were off to the races.

After finding a suitable place to hide the car, Brewer exited the vehicle and shouldered his rucksack. He noticed a couple of bags in the floorboard filled with water and packaged food.

"I have water and power bars," he supplied.

"Then we'll leave these here so we have something to come back to," Crystal said. "I got a text while we were back at the station. Michael Mylett's eighteen-year-old son was picked up on felony charges."

"What the hell for?" Brewer asked. He'd been betting on being able to go to Mylett as a backup plan should this one blow up in his face. How else would he keep Aunt Rosemary safe? The government?

"Aggravated assault," she supplied. "Looks like the kid will do time if the charge sticks."

Mylett would be in no mood to dole out favors if his kid was looking at prison. Time to pivot once again. Brewer was running out of options. He didn't have a whole lot of faith in one entity. He'd planned on stacking the deck.

After the trial, he could grab Aunt Rosemary and disappear. He knew how to stay off the grid. But his aunt? Now that he thought about it, she needed medication. She had her doctors in Galveston. Sure, leaving for a couple of days or a week was fine.

But months? A year? Two?

How would he make certain she could see her doctors in confidence, have access to her diabetes medication? There was no amount of hot firemen that could solve every issue. If Brewer went into hiding without her, they would use her to draw him out eventually.

Attachments left him vulnerable and hurt anyone who cared about him. At least Crystal would be safe once this was over. No one would come after her once Brewer was out of her protection. The only reason she was in danger now was because she could end up caught in the crossfire. No one would target her specifically. In fact, he'd noticed folks were going out of their way to isolate him in their attacks.

Crystal checked her cell phone. "I'm officially out of range."

Being off the grid had its uses. Although pointing that out to her right now when she had grandparents lying in the hospital fighting for their lives didn't seem like the right play.

"I apologize," he said to her, stopping long enough to look her in the eyes. It would be dark soon and they would have to move slower toward the spot, but this was important and he wanted her to know how he felt. "I'll get us out of here and back into cell coverage as soon as humanly possible. I know how important your phone is to you right now, and I hate being the cause of you needing to be out of touch in case your family needs you."

"None of this is your fault, Brewer." She folded her arms across her chest and studied him. "Is that why you think

I'm tense? Because I blame you for what's happening?" Before he could answer she added, "I don't, by the way. I'm a grown woman. I have a job that causes me to take risks."

Then, he was confused.

"I'm on edge because I half expect you to ditch me at any moment and it frustrates me to no end because I won't be able to find you," she explained on an exhale. "I will have disconnected from family to end up lost in these woods with no witness to show for it."

"If I gave you my word, would you believe me?" he asked, caught off guard at her reasoning.

"Yes," she said. That one word caused his chest to squeeze. It was important to him that she trusted him.

"I'll get us both out of these woods alive," he said. "That's a promise."

"Together?"

"Yes," he confirmed. "Together. I'm not leaving you, Crystal." He realized his mistake the minute her first name rolled off his tongue. He shouldn't use a familiar name with the marshal. He'd already crossed too many lines as it was. He needed to find a way to maintain a safe distance. Being personal wasn't the way to do it.

"Okay, Wade." Hearing his name roll of her tongue lit a dozen campfires inside him.

He vowed to do whatever it took to ensure he kept his promise.

SEALING THE DEAL with a kiss would be unprofessional, so Crystal wouldn't request it no matter how much her heart protested. She'd been concerned Brewer would ditch her and disappear, leaving her out here to fend for herself. Granted, she was a country woman at heart and she had a weapon, along with a backup. She'd strapped on her ankle holster while waiting in the car at the gas station.

"We better get to it before all the sunlight is gone," she said with a little more confidence this time. Having his word meant something to her. It touched her in a deep place. Now they just needed to stay alive so she could deliver him in one piece come Monday morning.

In a surprise move, Brewer reached for her hand and then gave a reassuring squeeze. The small touch provided so much relief. They were still a team—a team that worked well together. Good.

He let go, turned, and led her deeper into the trees. She couldn't say how long they'd been hiking when he stopped for a water break, but it was long since dark. She had no idea if they were on public or private land—one could get them shot. Of course, his friend would provide a location that wasn't easy to get to. If it wouldn't have been too noisy, she would have asked for a chopper ride.

As it was, her legs burned. The workout from earlier in the day might not have been the best idea considering she'd pushed herself. Then again, she'd been under the impression they were going to stay locked inside a cushy private home until it was time for the trial. Or driving to their next stop.

Lesson learned.

She should have known something like this would end up happening. At least it was cold enough to keep the mosquitoes away. Making this trek during the spring or summer months would have gotten her eaten alive.

Brewer leaned toward her, whispered, "Listen carefully to anything that sounds out of the ordinary. We're close."

"Okay." She could see his face clearly now that her eyes had adjusted to the darkness.

He turned and moved, slowly, methodically, deeper into the trees.

Crystal did her best not to make unnecessary noise. She'd turned down the lighting on her screen and put her phone on silent not long after they started the trek.

Brewer froze. He knelt down, indicating she should do the same without taking his eyes off whatever he'd seen up ahead. Did they find it? Was Trent here?

Crystal followed suit, reaching for and then palming her backup weapon. The SIG Sauer fit in her hand easily and provided a decently accurate shot. All bullets killed the same when they struck in the right place. In this case, size made no difference.

Brewer held a hand behind him, indicating she should stay put. So, she did as he disappeared into the thicket to their left. No doubt he would circle the perimeter. Minutes later, there was no sign of Brewer. No sound either.

For a split second, she feared this was it. This was the time he would ditch her in the woods and leave her to her own devices in the name of keeping her safe. The man could circle back to the vehicle and disappear for all she knew. Could he hot-wire a car? She had no idea but didn't doubt his skills for one minute. Doubting a man like Brewer would be a mistake. Underestimating the soldier in him wouldn't be smart.

And then she heard voices. Not much more than a whisper at first.

The sounds of movement alerted her to the fact Brewer at the very least was heading her way. Should she hide? What if it wasn't Brewer? What if he'd been stabbed and this was Trent? What if Trent was in league with other men and they accounted for the voices, not Brewer?

Crystal ran through all the possibilities, decided for better or worse she needed to move. She could gauge the reaction of whoever was coming once they arrived. So, she climbed the tree before they could get too close. From her vantage point, she would be able to get a visual on who was with Brewer before they knew where she was.

The thought that he could be in trouble, walking toward her with a gun to his back, struck. She dismissed the notion. Brewer wouldn't lead someone directly to her. He would lead the person the other way and then strike the second he believed he had an advantage. Brewer had the kind of patience that won wars. If he was walking her way with someone, he'd deemed the encounter to be safe.

Still, she would wait to see with her own eyes before making a decision to reveal herself.

The scent of pine tickled her nostrils. It dawned on her that she was allergic and it was only a matter of time before she sneezed. She'd been fine on the ground since it was cold outside. Grandma Lacy had moved to fake trees after Crystal's allergies had gotten so bad she couldn't be in the same room with the Christmas tree. To this day, Crystal lit a pine-scented candle to make it feel like Christmas in the small apartment where she resided.

This seemed an odd time for her to realize she hadn't felt the Christmas spirit in years. She lit the candle and put a wreath on her door, but that was the extent of her decorations. Growing up at the paint-horse ranch, the holidays had been magical.

More of that regret for abandoning her grandparents these last few years strangled her, causing her throat to close up.

Or maybe it was the smell of pine doing the trick. Either

way, the jig was about to be up. Crystal took in a long, slow breath and then held it, praying she wouldn't sneeze. Would it give her enough time to assess the threat?

Chapter Twenty-Two

A sudden sneeze drew Brewer's attention to the trees. He clamped his mouth shut and put a hand on Trent's chest to stop his friend from overreacting.

"Crystal?" he whispered as fear gripped him. He's been certain that she would still be in this spot.

"Here," came the familiar voice—a voice that dropped his pulse back to near-normal levels. She must have panicked when he hadn't immediately returned.

She climbed down and then sneezed again.

"This is Trent," he said once she'd settled down.

"I'm Marshal Remington," she said, taking the hand being offered.

"It's good to meet you," Trent said. "Looks like the cavalry has finally arrived."

"Where's your family?" Brewer asked.

"Safe," he responded. "For now."

Those were two words no person wanted in the same sentence when it came to protecting their family members.

"Your aunt must be—"

"Somewhere she won't easily be found," Brewer said, cutting Trent off. "Shall we head back to the car?"

"Sure," Crystal said. "What's the plan now?"

"Once we get back into cell range, I was thinking your superior could provide a safe house out here," Brewer said.

"How about we find a fishing cabin to spend the night in?" Crystal said. "According to the map, there are several lakes around."

Trent was shaking his head. "Bad idea. We should definitely get back to civilization."

"Why is that?" she asked.

"We can't stay in one place for too long," Trent quickly said. A little too quickly?

"Maybe we can join your family," Brewer stated. It was probably all the talk from Crystal about not knowing whether or not they could trust Trent that had Brewer questioning his friend's motives. His buddy hadn't done anything so far to cause alarm. Brewer would keep an eye on the situation, though. If Trent made a wrong move, they would leave him on the side of the road to fend for himself.

"Another bad idea," Trent said.

"I need your phone," Crystal said to him.

"My what?"

"You heard me," she said, calm as anyone pleased. "It's protocol. We can't risk anyone tracing us."

Trent's gaze bounced from Crystal to Brewer. Was he looking for some kind of intervention on Brewer's part? Because after what had happened, Trent would be waiting a long time. "Is that really necessary?"

"After reaching out to you with a new cell, our location was compromised," Crystal said matter-of-factly. "Now that might have been a coincidence, and for your sake, I'm hoping it was. But I'm not taking another chance like that."

If Trent's phone had been compromised, Crane's people should have been able to find them all this time.

"Okay, okay," Trent said a little more defensively than Brewer would have liked.

"What's the big deal?" he asked. "Hand over the phone."

"When will I get it back?" Trent asked. "I have a family to think about. If my wife can't get a hold of me, she'll panic."

His reasoning was solid. Keeping in touch with his family would explain why Trent hesitated to give his phone over. A twinge of guilt stabbed Brewer for not trusting his buddy's intentions. Trent stood to lose people close to him too.

"Once this is all over, you'll be welcome to retrieve it from the gas station bathroom where I intend to hide it," Crystal said.

Brewer leaned in so only she could hear. "Is that necessary? The man has a family to consider."

Crystal took a step back and caught his gaze. "Then let's do everything in our power to get him home safely so he can be reunited with his loved ones."

He couldn't argue her point, so he turned to his friend. "This is the best way for now."

Trent studied Brewer. His face morphed. "I shouldn't complain, man. I know. I still can't believe I got you into this mess in the first place. I guess my family will be safer if they can't get a hold of me until this is all behind us."

"That's the right attitude," Brewer said. "We'll get through this together. In the meantime, Crys... Marshal Remington has done a damn fine job keeping me alive." He put a hand out like he was presenting himself to the world. "I'm still here despite a few close calls and against the odds."

"Teamwork, Mr. Brewer," Crystal said, switching back to being formal.

Brewer's chest deflated a little even though he understood the need for them both to be as professional as possible now that Trent was in the picture.

Trent handed over his cell so the three of them could get on the move. Crystal tucked it inside her left pocket after turning the power off. Brewer doubted that would help in terms of security, but it might keep Trent from panicking if a call came through once they hit a patch with service.

"That's not all, sir." Crystal shot a look of apology to Brewer before shifting her gaze back to Trent. "I'm going to need to pat you down."

"You better believe I'm carrying," Trent stated, lifting his hands in the air. "And we're on the same team here."

"Even so, sir. It's protocol," she informed, her voice steady, even, and authoritative. "Nothing personal."

Trent shot a look at Crystal that could freeze water in hell before slowly turning his back, spreading his legs, and anchoring his hands against the nearby tree trunk. "You'll find a Glock tucked into a holster in the waistline of my jeans. That's all I have on me."

Brewer noted how formal Crystal was with Trent as she patted him down. Her guard was way up when it came to his military buddy. Did she have good reason?

Deciding an extra layer of precaution never hurt, Brewer filed the information under the *interesting* category and moved on. He would keep an eye on Trent too. The man was a bundle of jitters and nerves. Under the circumstances, it was understandable. Crystal might've been making a mountain out of a molehill. Either way, they were covered.

Crystal thanked Trent. "Do you need to pack up any supplies at your campsite before we head back to my vehicle?"

"Nah," he said. "I'll just leave everything here. No reason to waste time, and there's nothing that can't be replaced or retrieved at a later time."

"All right, then," she said, nodding to Brewer before turning the direction they'd come and hoofing it back.

It was past midnight by the time they located the car.

"Think we should grab a few hours of sleep before heading out?" Brewer asked, thinking of Crystal. They'd slept last night. In fact, he tried to forget just how right she'd felt in his arms and how fast and hard he'd fallen asleep. He couldn't remember the last time he'd slept so well.

"I'm good," Crystal said quickly. "I'll drive. You can do whatever you want in the back seat."

"I'm riding shotgun," Brewer argued.

"Not this time, champ," she said. Was it easier for her to keep an eye on Trent in front?

Crystal's moves were always tactical, so he didn't put up an argument. It would be easier for him to subdue Trent from the back seat, though.

"We'll both ride in back," he said, making a production out of opening the door for his friend.

Trent nodded, did as told. There was no humor in his eyes. Was he concerned about what would happen to his family if they were found?

Crystal claimed the driver's seat, then placed Trent's cell inside the console.

"Man, I'm just so glad you found me," Trent said to Brewer.

"How long were you waiting?" Brewer asked.

"Not long," he supplied. "Since last night after I stashed my family away. What about your aunt?"

"Same."

"She's good, though?" Trent continued.

"In good hands," Brewer stated.

"I sent someone to check on her, and they reported back that she wasn't home," Trent stated. He leaned back in the seat and swiped a hand over his face. "I've been worried sick ever since I tried to call you back and got nothing." He motioned toward Crystal and lowered his voice. "I'm guessing she's to blame for your phone going missing."

Brewer wasn't sure how he wanted to play this. On the one hand, he could pretend to be the victim here in a *good cop, bad cop* way. Trent already didn't like Crystal. It was obvious from his expression every time he looked at her and his reaction to her demand to turn over his cell.

But did they have more to worry about than Trent not being able to get in touch with his family? Or was there someone else waiting on a call?

THE PIT STOP at the gas station hadn't taken long. Crystal had hidden Trent's phone and was now the only person who knew the exact location of the cell. It was neater that way, especially when it came time to retrieve the piece of tech.

At this point, she was the only one with a cell. Hers had bars again, so she was finally in range for service. She had several texts from family members that she'd scrolled through while Brewer filled the gas tank. No news wasn't exactly good news when it came to a loved one being in a coma for an extended period of time.

The text exchange had been her siblings and cousins checking in. Since all six worked in different districts for the US Marshals Service, their jobs weren't nine-to-fives. They had to be ready to travel at a moment's notice when a felon was located or believed to be located because you never really knew until you arrived on scene.

One look at Brewer said he was relieved they'd found Trent. She didn't have history with the man, so there was no attachment for her, making it easier to be objective. Brewer was intelligent. He had street smarts. Under normal circumstances, she would trust his judgment on a person. He seemed to have the ability to read others well. Bias might get in the way, though.

Back on the road, she wondered if they could make a detour through Mesa Point on their way to the next safe house. Being a caring granddaughter was beginning to win over following exact protocol despite her need for perfectionism in her work. Crystal's SO needed time to find a good location. Elise wanted them closer to Austin, so she'd thrown out Round Rock as a possibility. The sprawling suburb north of Austin could be a good place to blend in.

Another front entry garage–type house would work until Elise figured out what she wanted to do with Trent, now that she was aware he was along for the ride. The best news so far was that Aunt Rosemary was in an upscale nursing home having the time of her life. Not even the promise of hot firemen would be able to pry her out, according to sources. It was a good place to tuck her away until this whole ordeal was over.

Then what?

Crystal hadn't given Brewer the sales pitch for WITSEC just yet. The subject had been brought up. The thought of Brewer disappearing, gaining a new identity and new life, sat hard on her chest.

The other message she hadn't seen fit to return was from Mahone.

I miss us.

Those three words twisted up her insides. She'd been clear. He wasn't *the one*. He needed to move on for his own sake. He deserved to find someone who could love him back. During their relationship, Crystal had believed she was broken somehow, that she was incapable of loving anyone. Was it the curse of her father's DNA? How much could he have loved her mother if the man couldn't stick around to bring up their children after she'd died giving birth?

Until meeting Brewer—and it was ridiculous when she really thought about it because the kiss had been so short—she'd thought what she'd had with Mahone was as far as she could go.

Her ex deserved better than mediocre feelings toward him. Crystal cared about him, but that wasn't the same thing as being the cliché head-over-heels in love with someone. The kind of love that made her stomach free-fall when he was near. The kind of love that made her so in tune with his presence, she knew the second he walked into a room. The kind of love that caused an electrical storm in the space between them and fire to burn low in her belly and warm the insides of her thighs.

Now that she'd experienced those things, there was no going back. Which was also ironic because there was no going forward with the only man who'd ever made her feel that way either.

"I might as well grab some sleep while I'm in good company," Trent said, shifting down in his seat farther, reminding her of a sullen teen. He tucked his chin to his chest and folded his arms across his chest.

"Go ahead, man," Brewer stated. "We'll keep watch for anything out of the ordinary."

Trent's phone was back at the gas station, so he couldn't

be trying to make a secret call for help or to give away their location by slinking down in his seat. She'd patted him down but hadn't found a wire either.

Then again, devices could be small enough to miss. Could they trust Trent?

Chapter Twenty-Three

A text came through on Crystal's phone from her boss. Brewer read it out loud.

New plan. Go to Waco.

"That's it? That's all she says?" Crystal asked.

"Hold on," he said as three dots appeared on the screen. Then, a link to an address. "She sent a link to a hotel."

He tapped on the link and rattled off directions.

"Guess my SO wants us to go antique shopping," she quipped before glancing at Trent through the rearview and buttoning up the look on her face. He must have shot a look of confusion because she added, "Magnolia Market." She studied him for a couple of seconds in the rearview. "C'mon. Don't tell me you haven't heard of Chip and Jo-anna Gaines."

He shrugged.

"Seriously?" she asked. Then came, "Oh, right. You've been out of the country and then probably not in the mood to care about a home-renovation show even if it swept the country for a while."

"Can't say that I have," he admitted. "Or that I care."

She feigned disgust, and it made him chuckle. Brewer

missed the easy way they had with each other, but he needed to ensure Trent's safety. Until when? Would Damon punish Trent for being with Brewer? Hurt the man's family to prove a point?

Damon might get backlash from others for going that deep. Trent might've been fair game because he'd been the one who recommended Brewer to the job. Not on Brewer's watch. He would ensure his friend was safe. Maybe even cut a deal with Crystal to be one hundred percent certain of the fact.

From Palestine, the drive was a little less than two hours long. By the time they reached Waco, the sun was coming up. Brewer was wide awake. Trent, on the other hand, was snoring.

Crystal pulled behind a newer-looking hotel. She parked next to the service entrance. After sending a text, she cut off the car engine. As if on cue, a worker opened the back door and then waved them in. "Do you want to wake Sleeping Beauty over there?"

Brewer stifled a laugh. "On it."

He shook Trent, who immediately made a move to wrestle him. In a heartbeat, Crystal had her weapon drawn and pointed at the center of Trent's chest.

"Calm down, Trent. It's me. Brewer."

Trent mumbled a curse as his eyes blinked opened and he seemed to realize where he was. The look he shot Crystal for having a gun pointed at him would have scared most. She didn't budge.

"Everything okay back there?" she asked.

"Yeah, fine," he mumbled. "Now get the barrel away from me."

"As long as we're all good, I don't have a problem with

that." She eased the weapon down before holstering it. "Ready?"

"Where are we?" Trent asked through a yawn, looking disoriented.

"I'll tell you all about it inside," Brewer said, wishing he could check on his aunt. He'd feel a whole lot better if he could hear her voice, know that she was doing well.

The trio exited the vehicle and headed upstairs. They were led through the employee hallways to a room near the exit. No doubt this had all been planned out by Crystal's superior. The fact calmed Brewer's nerves slightly.

"I'll bring breakfast," the employee said. He didn't introduce himself, but he seemed to know Crystal when he touched her arm and asked to speak to her privately.

Brewer didn't like it.

"PLEASE TELL ME you didn't volunteer for this assignment," Crystal said to Mahone.

"Is it wrong that I want to know you're safe?" he asked.

"No," she answered. "But interfering with my case crosses a line."

"We're not together anymore," he countered. "Unless..."

"Same answer as before." Crystal needed to shut this down before Mahone got any more ideas. Letting him go down that path, giving him hope, would only hurt him more in the long run. Besides, she needed all her focus to make it through until Monday morning. "The last thing I want to do is hurt you. Believe me when I say I'd only hurt you more if we tried to keep this thing alive. I can't do that to you and understand if you don't want to be friends."

Mahone's face was turning redder by the second. Crystal hated being the one to do this to him.

"I need to get back into the room," she said. "Tomorrow's the big day, and neither one of us slept last night. I have to stay sharp."

"Fine," he said, but his attitude said he was angry.

She'd been honest. She hadn't led him on once she'd realized the relationship meant more to him than it did to her. She'd let him down as easily as humanly possible. Beyond that, there wasn't much else she could do.

"But this is not over," he mumbled as he turned to walk away.

Crystal exhaled a long, slow breath before heading back to the room. A distraction right now was the last thing she needed. She glanced at the time, performed a quick calculation in her head. Twenty-five hours and ten minutes to go.

The blackout curtain was pulled closed, the coffee machine percolating and brewing. The TV was on.

Shoes on, Trent took up the bed closest to the door. Should Crystal see it as an omen? His legs were crossed as he flipped through channels.

Brewer stood, leaning against the wall next to the coffee maker. "The first cup is ready." He motioned toward a full cup sitting next to the machine. "It's yours if you want it."

There was so much she wanted to say but couldn't. Hell, she didn't even know if it would be welcomed by Brewer. She would start with the fact she hadn't asked for Mahone to be assigned to this case. Nor did she want him here. Being defensive in front of Trent was a bad call. She took the coffee and settled on "Thanks."

Then there was the issue of Trent. She didn't trust the man. Nothing personal. She was doing her job—a job that had trained her to be suspicious of people first and trust them later. The trust part was a work in progress.

"Do you want to grab a few hours of sleep after breakfast arrives?" she asked Brewer.

"Not hungry," he supplied. "I had a power bar while you were in the hallway. It'll get me through until we can order a pizza or figure something out."

"Room service is going to provide meals," she said. "We're less than two hours from Austin, though traffic is unpredictable, so…" She glanced at the clock and performed another mental calculation. "We'll be safe if we leave by five o'clock in the morning."

"That leaves us a lot of time to play with," Brewer said.

"Maybe we should go over how this is going to go down." Plans had a way of changing in the heat of the moment, but it was good to have one at least.

She heard the toilet running in the next room, figured Trent—who looked a little too comfortable on the bed—had taken care of business while Brewer had made coffee.

"Go ahead." Brewer's voice was as stiff as his body language. Once this was over and he'd safely been delivered to court, could she talk to him about the possibility of seeing each other again off the job?

Or had she been reading too much into their bond? At least the bond she'd picked up on before meeting up with Trent. Now Brewer was cold as ice.

A knock at the door startled them. She immediately reached for her weapon, as did Brewer. Reflex?

It was most likely Mahone at the door with food.

"I've got this," she said, moving to the door before checking the peephole. Sure enough, he stood behind a room service cart on the other side.

Crystal opened the door. "I can bring this inside on my own."

Mahone nodded. "I'll be around in case you need me."

Having backup was probably a good idea. She would rest easier tonight. Rest? Crystal rolled her eyes. The final hours were the hardest in tough cases. Time seemed to slow to a drip. And she couldn't sleep until she'd delivered her package safely.

After thanking Mahone and requesting their next meals arrive around one o'clock, she took the cart and brought it inside. Everything smelled amazing, but she picked at her plate. Her stomach was queasy, but that didn't stop her from finishing her coffee. Without it, she highly doubted she would survive.

Trent passed out again. The man was awfully comfortable. But then, he trusted Brewer. The feeling was mutual despite evidence.

They watched back-to-back movies and one of those comedy specials on pay-per-view. Neither did much laughing, but the comedian's voice was better than silence. It was a decent enough distraction.

Brewer had been sitting there, quietly stewing. His mind was somewhere else altogether. And then he sat up ramrod straight. "Something has been bothering me, but I couldn't figure out what it was."

"Go on," she urged. She'd been having a similar feeling, but that wasn't uncommon in a case like this one.

"It just dawned on me what the problem is," he said, glancing over at a still-sleeping Trent. "He wasn't worried about calling his family on his cell."

The pieces all fit together for her now. The fact that Brewer had been found after making a call to Trent meant the man's line had been traced. "He should be very worried about Damon finding his family. But he was downright angry that I took his cell."

Brewer raked a finger through his hair.

"What did you do when I was out in the hallway with my coworker?" She lowered her voice on the last part and caught Brewer's gaze.

"Made coffee," he said. His pupils dilated as it dawned on him that Mahone was a marshal.

"Anything else?" she asked.

His eyes lit up. "Used the restroom."

"Leaving Trent alone with a landline," she supplied. "We have to get out of here."

"What about him?"

Trent sat up. "What about me?"

A knock at the door caused them both to jump. It occurred to Crystal that Trent was the only one who wasn't startled by the sudden noises. She drew her weapon and headed to the door with Brewer behind her for reinforcement.

Checking the peephole, she saw Mahone with more food. Crystal checked the time. It was close to one o'clock.

"Right. Food," Brewer said.

She opened the door. A random foot wedged inside. In the next second, a man came into view. With one hand, he wrapped his fingers around Crystal's neck as cold metal pressed to her forehead.

"Don't shoot." Brewer raised his hands in the surrender position.

"Set your weapon down," Damon ordered.

Crystal glanced over at Mahone, who shot a look of apology. Trent, the bastard, walked up behind Brewer and took his weapon.

"Sorry, man," Trent said. "It was you or me, and I have a family to think about."

"You're a sonofabitch," Brewer ground out. "I trusted you because of the bond I shared with the others in my unit. You didn't deserve it. You don't deserve the loyalty I've given you. And you sure as hell don't deserve to be treated like one of us. You're a damn traitor to the promises we all made to each other overseas. I hope you rot in hell."

Crystal wanted to scream. She glanced over at Mahone, who gave a slight nod at the food-service table that he was still gripping with both hands. She instantly knew what he was going to do.

In the next second, he rammed it into the back of Damon before the man could take Crystal's weapon. Her Krav Maga training kicked in.

In one swift movement, she brought her hand up as the cart rammed into Damon. The move caught him off guard. She took advantage of the moment to snatch his weapon from his hand and turn it on him instead.

Brewer fired off a headbutt. The crack against Trent's forehead echoed. He groaned and then dropped to his knees as blood from his now-broken nose splattered everywhere. A second later, Brewer had already spun around and managed to get his weapon back.

He used the butt of the gun to deliver a knockout hit.

Trent fell to the floor and slumped on his side.

Mahone pinned Damon to the wall. "Get out of here. Now!"

"Will you be—"

"Okay?" he asked. "Damn right I will be. Now, go!"

Brewer had her bag and his rucksack, urging her into the hallway before she could argue.

"I owe you one," she said.

Mahone smiled before handcuffing Damon, finally getting the message they could only ever be coworkers and friends.

She and Brewer bolted down the stairs and out the employee entrance. She claimed the driver's seat as Brewer scrambled into the passenger side.

As he pulled his seat belt over his chest and then locked it into place, she pulled out of the parking lot and onto 35. "Get my SO on speaker. We have to get him some help."

The call was quick. Mahone already had hotel security by his side. More help was on the way. All was under control.

"The only thing left to do is get your witness to the courtroom on time," Elise informed.

"Yes, ma'am," Crystal promised. "I'm headed there now to be close to the courthouse. Any chance we can have early access to the building?"

"I'll see what I can do," Elise promised.

Waco to Austin was a three-hour drive with late afternoon traffic despite the distance on maps. Crystal found paid parking on the street three blocks from the courthouse.

They stayed there until half an hour before time to report when the text came from her SO indicating they would have assistance. Four squad cars encased them as they made the short drive to the courthouse.

"So this is what it feels like to be president," Brewer stated, smiling for the first time in what felt like days. "I think I'll pass."

They pulled up to the front of the courthouse, where they were met with a squad of officers.

"This is where we part ways," she said to him. "Go in there and put the bastard away with your testimony. Okay?"

"I'll do my best," he said before reaching over and running his finger along the back of her hand. It shouldn't have been as sexy as it was. "Will you be out here when I'm done?"

"Maybe," she said. "I have something to take care of."

Brewer nodded, saluted, and then disappeared into the small army of officers escorting him inside.

Epilogue

Two days later

"Do I have your word?" Crystal had no plans to hang up this call without confirmation. There was too much at risk.

"You do."

"Thank you," she said into the receiver. "I only wish I could have been the one to set it up. Hear the words, the commitment with my own ears."

"You know you can trust me. Right?"

"Of course," Crystal stated. "With my life."

"Good. Do me a favor."

"Anything," she promised.

"Go see your family and forget about this place for a while."

"That's a deal," Crystal said before adding, "What happened to the bounty hunters?"

"Larson Figgs is going down for attempted murder," Elise informed. "The woman is known as The Widow for her proclivity to wear all black, and was last seen heading over the border to Mexico. I imagine she'll stay there until the situation cools off. We'll catch her when she attempts to cross over again."

"Good," Crystal said. "Both need to be locked up."

"Agreed," Elise said. "I had Mahone pick up Trent's cell from the gas station and admit it into evidence. There's nothing left for you to do except go take that time off."

"Will do," Crystal said. "I'll take care of informing Wade Brewer of the update."

She ended the call with her SO after perfunctory good-byes and then walked into the private room in the court-house where she knew Wade would be. "It's over," she said to him. "Really over. You did your part, and the jury will send this bastard away for a very long time."

He sighed relief as he studied her. Then came, "They'll come for me when I'm not looking. I'll never be safe as long as I'm on the grid. And since I can't leave Aunt Rosemary alone, I'm a dead man walking." He shrugged, looked re-signed.

"There's another solution," Crystal said. "But before I tell you, I'd like to inform you that you're no longer my witness. You can walk out that door anytime."

Wade crossed the room. She took a step back and an-chored herself against the wall. And then she grabbed a fistful of his shirt and tugged him toward her until their lips were barely an inch apart. "Does that mean what I think it does?"

"I hope so," she said, smiling. "You did it, Wade. You testified. From what I hear Crane is going to be locked up for a very long time. Damon will be sent to a different prison, as will Trent."

Wade's gaze locked onto hers, causing a literal fire-works show to explode inside her chest. "I wasn't sure I'd ever see you again."

She swallowed to ease some of the sudden dryness in her throat to no avail.

"You have quite the effect on me, Wade," she said, staring into eyes filled with the same ache she felt.

"You called me Wade," he pointed out, surprised.

"I guess I did," she admitted.

"That's a big deal for you," he said.

She smiled and said, "Yes, it is."

"I'd like permission to kiss you," he said.

"Granted," was all she said before his lips came crashing down on hers. He kissed her with the kind of intensity that lit a wildfire inside her. She parted her lips for him after his tongue tested the barrier.

He tasted like a mix of dark-roast coffee and peppermint toothpaste…better than Christmas morning.

Wade closed the gap between them, his body flush with hers, her back against the wall. She brought her hands up to his shoulders to anchor herself as she got lost in the kiss.

She dropped her hand to the center of his chest and could feel his rapid heartbeat against her palm.

A noise in the hallway brought them back to reality too fast.

Wade pressed his palm against the wall as he rested his forehead against hers. They both tried to calm their rapid breathing. "I have to go soon."

"You don't," Crystal said. "Not if you don't want to."

He drew his head back and caught her gaze. "I think we both know the hand I've been dealt."

"Yes," she began, "but what if I was able to reshuffle the deck?"

"I'd have to hear you out, wouldn't I?"

"I already mentioned that Michael Mylett's son was arrested for aggravated assault," she stated.

"Ri-i-i-ght."

"My SO was able to negotiate on your behalf," Crystal

continued, unfazed. She could scarcely wait to tell him the news. "In exchange for lessening the charges against his son to essentially a slap on the wrist, we were able to get a commitment from Mylett that no one would harm you or your aunt. You'll be under his protection for life."

Wade stood there for a long moment, his expression unreadable stone.

"I thought you'd be happy," Crystal said, confused by his reaction.

"What if I don't want to be under his protection?" he asked.

Crystal wasn't sure what about the arrangement didn't make sense to him. "No, this is a good thing. Mylett is the top dog now that Crane's been arrested. No one will go against him. You'll be safe to walk down the street and do as you please."

Wade's lips compressed. Was he frowning?

She brought her hands up to cup his face, deciding to put her heart on the line. "We could see each other, if you'd like."

Wade shook his head. Her heart fell, landing with a *thud*.

"I thought you—"

He shushed her by covering her mouth with his and kissing her so thoroughly that she almost forgot where she was.

Was it a kiss goodbye?

"The reason I'm not okay with the arrangement is because if I'm under anyone's protection, I want it to be yours." Wade broke into a wide smile. "I've spent a long time on this earth without even realizing someone like you existed. I never believed in love at first sight until I met you. Because you proved to me that I can trust my eyes. I may not be able to hear out of both ears, and I don't have…" He motioned toward his prosthetic leg. "All of me. But what's left belongs to you. Heart and soul. I mean it, Crystal. I've dated enough people to know when I've found the real deal. It's you. I fell in love with you. And there's no one else I'd rather be with than you. For life."

"You might not see yourself as a whole person anymore, Wade. But I do," Crystal said, tears gathering in her eyes. "Because what really makes a person whole is their heart. Their brains. Their mind. The mold was broken when you were made. But you weren't broken when the mold was damaged." Crystal stared up into the eyes of the man she loved. "We're all damaged in some way or another, Wade. I'm not perfect. You'll figure that out soon enough. What counts, what makes a whole person is what's in here." She placed the flat of her palm against his heart. "You're whole. You're perfect. I'm madly in love with you. Only you. It's only ever been you."

Wade picked her up off her feet and kissed her.

"Promise me one thing," she said when they broke apart.

"Anything," he said. "Name it."

"You'll give me your heart forever," she said.

"It's yours," he said. "Before we even met, my heart belonged to you. I just didn't know it until I met you."

"Good." She beamed. "Because I'm asking for forever."

"On one condition," he countered.

"Okay," she said.

"Forever starts today."

A rogue tear streaked down her cheek. Wade dipped his head and kissed it. He feathered kisses on her eyelids, the tip of her nose, her chin, until finding her lips.

Wade pulled back first. "Should we head to Mesa Point after picking up Aunt Rosemary?"

Crystal laughed. She felt lighter than she could remember. It would change when she got to Mesa Point. She realized the heaviness in her chest would return. And that was okay. Finding happy moments was even more important to her as she realized how truly fragile life could be. But that wasn't why she'd laughed. "I got an update on your aunt."

"Oh?"

"Turns out she started a wet T-shirt contest for the male orderlies," she said, covering her laugh with her hand.

Wade's laugh was a low rumble in his chest. Sexy as hell. And now hers.

"Sounds about right," he finally said. "Guess we should give her another night or two in paradise."

"I think she'd appreciate that," Crystal said as she reached for his hand. He was reaching for hers at the same time. Their fingers met in the middle.

It was time to go. To get out of the courthouse. To start living.

And it was time to go home to Mesa Point, where the rest of her heart resided. With Wade by her side, she could weather any storm. This man was her lifeline, and she couldn't wait to spend the rest of their lives together, side by side, as partners and equals.

"By the way, when you said you were playing for forever, I hope you meant it because I fully intend to ask you to marry me," Wade said, causing her heart to sing.

"I don't need a piece of paper to prove this is the kind of love that will last a lifetime," she said. "But a wedding is a good place to start."

* * * * *

Captured At The Cove

Carol Ericson

MILLS & BOON

Carol Ericson is a bestselling, award-winning author of more than forty books. She has an eerie fascination for true-crime stories, a love of film noir and a weakness for reality TV, all of which fuel her imagination to create her own tales of murder, mayhem and mystery. To find out more about Carol and her current projects, please visit her website at www.carolericson.com, "where romance flirts with danger."

CAST OF CHARACTERS

West Chandler—Dead Falls Island's new sheriff comes with a strong desire to eradicate the drug trade on the island...and a past; when the son of a pretty local Realtor emerges as a possible witness to a murder, West must overcome his past fears and his attraction to the boy's mother to save him.

Astrid Mitchell—As a single mom with a corrupt ex, a former police officer in WITSEC, she has her hands full; when her son becomes entangled in a murder case, she has to turn to another cop for protection, but the new sheriff in town is nothing like her ex.

Olly Crockett—Astrid's son steals the drone his mother borrowed to use for work, but his theft has consequences far worse than a time-out.

Chase Thompson—The murder of this local drug dealer sets off a chain reaction of terrifying events for Astrid and her son.

Naomi Wakefield—Chase's girlfriend may have some ideas about who killed her boyfriend, but will she live long enough to reveal them?

Monique—This mystery woman is connected to Chase in more ways than one, and West needs to find her before she meets the same fate as Naomi and Chase.

Michelle Carter—Astrid's new client shows an avid interest in one of Astrid's listings, a notorious property where a family massacre occurred, and Astrid needs to determine if she's really interested in the property... or its reputation.

Chapter One

Astrid's breath came in short spurts as her gaze darted among the Dead Falls Spring Fling crowd, searching for Olly's bright blond hair. He'd promised to be back before the fair ended. She'd been giving him too much freedom since his father had entered the Federal Witness Protection Program. Just because she couldn't find Russ didn't mean he couldn't find her…and Olly.

"I'm a sucker for sprinkles."

Astrid's head whipped around to confront her customer, a tall, dark and handsome…cop. Her lips stretched into a smile across her gritted teeth. Pointing at the cupcakes arrayed on the trays, she asked, "Vanilla or chocolate frosting?"

He wedged a finger against his impossibly square jaw and cocked his head. "That depends on what's underneath."

"Excuse me?" She raised her eyebrows. Typical cop—always with the flirty double entendre. Did they teach that at the academy? She hadn't seen this deputy around the island. Must be new.

He had the grace to duck his head as a blush touched his cheeks. "I meant the cake part. If the cake is chocolate, I like a vanilla frosting and vice versa."

"You're in luck." She poked a plastic fork in the direction of a chocolate cupcake with white buttercream frosting and sprinkles. "This one is chocolate. I also have carrot cake with a cream cheese frosting."

"Sprinkles?" He ran a hand through his short, dark hair, as if this were the most important decision of his day.

It might very well be, given he belonged to the crack Dead Falls sheriff's department. The residents of the island had been hopeful the new sheriff would turn things around after the disaster of Sheriff Hopkins, but Astrid wasn't holding her breath. Cops—if they weren't inept, they were probably corrupt. At least in her experience.

She sighed. "I can add sprinkles to a carrot cupcake, if you like."

"That would be great…if it's not too much trouble." He took a step back from the table as a middle-aged couple swarmed him.

The woman beamed. "Just wanted to say welcome to Dead Falls Island, Sheriff Chandler. I'm Lydia Feldman, and this is my husband, David."

As Astrid dipped at the knees to grab the plastic bottle of sprinkles, she kept one eye on the exchange between the new sheriff and the Feldmans. So that's why he was at the Spring Fling—meet and mingle with his constituents.

She screwed off the lid of the multicolored sprinkles and shook the bottle over the cream cheese frosting on one of the carrot cupcakes while she watched the new sheriff's easy banter with the couple. He had them wrapped around his little finger.

"Ah, I think that's good." He nodded at the cupcake in the tray, smothered with sprinkles.

"You're the new sheriff." She narrowed her eyes and thrust the cupcake toward him. "That's one dollar."

He carefully took the cupcake from her, the fingers of his left hand pinching the silver sleeve. He extended his right hand. "That's right. West Chandler."

Placing her hand in his, she said, "Astrid Mitchell. Welcome to Dead Falls."

She'd had sprinkles stuck to her fingers and had transferred them to his hand during the shake. They both eyed the sprinkles for an awkward second, their hands still clasped.

"Nice to meet you, Astrid." He slid his hand from hers, sprinkles and all. "Did you make these?"

"Yeah, I did." She wiped her hand on a napkin as if he had cooties. "The Spring Fling is a fundraiser for Samish Elementary, and my son is a student there."

"I knew that—I mean, that this was a fundraiser for the school. It's great to see parents involved in their kids' education. Do you and your husband do a lot of volunteering for the school?" He retrieved a dollar bill from his pocket and handed it to her. Then he peeled back the paper and took a big bite of the cupcake.

She didn't want to talk about her husband, her ex-husband, and a flash of blond hair in the crowd saved her. She waved her hand in the air. "Olly!"

Her son galloped toward her in the booth, his long, skinny legs almost tangling. "Hey, Mom."

"You were gone so long. Where did you end up going?"

He flung his arm out to the side. "You know, just regular places."

He lunged for a cupcake with chocolate frosting, and she smacked his hand. "You have to pay for those. It's a fundraiser."

"I'll get that for him." Sheriff Chandler handed her a crumpled bill.

"Hey, thanks." Olly sank his teeth into the cupcake and asked with his mouth full, "Are you the new sheriff?"

Even her son had figured it out before she had. "This is Sheriff Chandler. Sheriff, this is my son, Olly."

"Good to meet you, Olly." He raised the half-eaten cupcake in the air as he turned away. "Thank you."

Astrid stared after him, the khaki material of his uniform stretched across his broad back as he reached out to shake another hand. He'd only wanted to hit on her and had decided to hightail it out of here as soon as her son showed up. Jerk.

As Olly stuffed the rest of the treat in his mouth, leaving a smear of chocolate on his chin, Astrid noticed his high color and bright eyes. He still hadn't told her what he'd been up to all afternoon while she'd been slaving away at the cupcake booth. "So, where did you and Logan go?"

"Umm, we took our bikes out and rode around, near the cove and stuff." He jabbed a dirty finger at another cupcake. "Can I have that one if I pay you when we get home?"

"Hold on." She turned to Peyton, skipping up to the booth, followed by her mom, Sam. "Hi, you two. Cupcakes?"

"They look delish." Sam patted her curvy hip. "I know I shouldn't, but hey, it's for the school, right?"

"Exactly." Astrid nudged Olly. "Did you say hi to Peyton?"

Olly dropped his chin to his chest, looking up at Peyton through his lashes. "Yeah, hi."

Astrid and Sam exchanged grins as Sam plucked two cupcakes from the tray. Some of the kids were just getting beyond their shyness with the opposite sex, but Peyton and Olly were not among them. Astrid was fine with that. She didn't need to deal with girl problems just yet, not as a single mother.

Peyton swiped her tongue along some vanilla frosting. "I saw you and Logan on your bikes on the cliff over the cove."

"Did not." Olly kicked the leg of the table with the toe of his sneaker, and the remaining cupcakes trembled. Astrid gave him a sharp look from the corner of her eye.

She'd told Olly plenty of times not to ride his bike on the cliff. The lack of guardrails on the edge would result in a sheer drop to the cove.

As Sam peeled back the paper on her cupcake, she asked, "Did you meet the new sheriff? He's here somewhere."

"I did meet him. He bought a cupcake."

"He *is* a cupcake. Or is that beefcake?" Sam wiggled her eyebrows up and down. "And I heard he's single."

"Yeah, he's all right." Astrid stuffed the bills in the cash tin and closed it with a bang. "Let's hope he's better than the last guy."

"Mom." Peyton tugged on Sam's sleeve. "Can we play the game to get a betta fish before they close the booth?"

"Sure. I'll win one for you." Sam gave Astrid a wink before walking away with her daughter.

Still eyeing one of the last of the cupcakes, Olly said, "Fair's almost over, Mom. Can I have that one for free now?"

"You can have it now and pay me later. I baked these to make money for your school, not so you could gobble them all up."

He snatched it up as if he were afraid she'd change her mind.

As she consolidated the remaining cupcakes on one

tray and stacked the other trays, she asked, "Were you and Logan on the cliff above the cove on your bikes today?"

"Peyton doesn't know anything. We weren't up there. Logan's not allowed to ride on the cliff, either." He pulled his cupcake apart at the middle and stuck the bottom half on top of the frosting to make a little cake with icing in the middle. His uncle had taught him that trick.

She decided not to press him but didn't know whether or not to believe him. Ever since she'd told him his father would be away for a long time for his own safety, Olly had been secretive. Her friend Hannah Maddox, who was a child psychologist, told her it was natural for Olly to close down a bit after that news.

Astrid had been trying to give him a little space to process, but she'd been having a hard time of it since her brother, Tate, had left on a special assignment to DC. He'd followed a woman there, and she had no intention of dragging him back here with her whining about Olly. He was her son, and she'd have to raise him as a single mother.

"These are awesome, Mom." Olly rubbed his belly and nodded. "Good job."

She ruffled his shaggy blond hair. "Thanks. Clean your hands off with this sanitizer. Then take this tray with the last of the cupcakes, walk around and try to sell them while I pack up."

She held her breath, expecting pushback, but he squirted a dollop of the clear gel in his palm and vigorously rubbed his hands together. As he grabbed the tray and spun around, she called after him. "And don't try anything sneaky. I know there are seven cupcakes, and I expect seven bucks if you return with an empty tray."

He waved one hand in the air as he delved into the crowd.

Astrid wiped down the table and crouched to grab the box beneath it. She stacked the empty trays inside the box and put the hand sanitizer on top of them, along with a few items she'd brought from home. Lastly, she dropped the plastic bottle of sprinkles in the box.

The new sheriff sure did like his sprinkles but didn't seem to like kids much, or he didn't like women with kids. Sam had mentioned he was single, so that explained a lot. Not that Astrid was looking to date anyone, but if she did, she always thought going out with a divorced dad with kids might be easier than trying to hit a bachelor over the head with family life right out of the box.

She slipped her phone from the pocket of her denim jacket. It might be spring in Dead Falls, but the winter chill hadn't quite dissipated. She tapped Kelsey Monroe in her contacts. Kelsey was the PTA treasurer and all-around volunteer queen.

"Hi, Kelsey. It's Astrid Mitchell. I'm about ready to close down the cupcake booth. Do you want to pick up the money now, or should I drop it off later?"

Out of breath, as usual, Kelsey said, "I'm just picking up the money from the hot dog booth. I'll be right over."

By the time Astrid finished counting the money, Kelsey scurried up, a large duffel bag over her shoulder, weighing her petite frame down on one side. Kelsey flashed a set of dimples. "Your cupcakes were a smashing success. Everyone was raving about them—even the new sheriff."

Astrid cleared her throat. "Good to hear. I sent Olly out to sell the remaining ones. If he comes back with any more money, I can drop it off in your mailbox."

"Perfect." Kelsey shook out a zippered money pouch and

produced a sticky note and a felt pen. "Just write down the amount here and stuff the money in the bag."

As Astrid began to scribble the total for the cupcakes, Olly ran up to them, panting and waving a ten-dollar bill in the air. "Mom, Mom. Sheriff Chandler bought all the cupcakes left on the tray, gave me ten bucks for them and handed them out to some kids leaving the fair."

"Isn't that nice?" Kelsey's cheeks turned pink. "I like him better than Sheriff Hopkins already."

Astrid crossed out the previous amount she'd written and added ten to it. So, Chandler did like kids—just not hers. "He overpaid. There were only seven left."

"Well, I like him even more then." Kelsey zipped up the money bag and dropped it in the duffel with the others. "I think this was a great success, and even the weather held."

Astrid and Olly finished clearing the booth, and she made him carry the box of supplies to the car. Tate had left his Jeep behind when he went to DC, but she preferred her truck although she knew she'd have to trade up if she wanted to be a successful Realtor on the island. Nobody wanted to see a Realtor pull up in a beat-up old pickup.

Olly loaded the box in the truck bed and joined her in the cab. The sugar from the two cupcakes—maybe three— had made him hyper and he yakked in the seat beside her about the games he'd played and the friends he'd seen at the Spring Fling. She let him chatter on during the ride, enjoying his vivacity after a few months of morose silence.

She pulled the truck in front of Tate's cabin, as he'd insisted on calling it, despite its size, comfort and amenities. Olly had the door open before she even killed the engine.

As she stepped out of the truck, she called him back. "Hey, get the box out of the back."

He scampered past her and dived into the back head-first. He then followed her up the porch to the front door, hopping from one foot to the other. He either had to pee or she was facing a long night ahead getting him down from his sugar rush.

She slid the key into the door lock, and then shoved it into the deadbolt lock. It didn't click over, and she tsked her tongue. Had she forgotten to lock the dead bolt?

Bumping the door with her hip, she reached for the security keypad. Her fingers rested against the display with the red light. Had she forgotten to set the security, too? She must've been in a rush this morning.

She tapped the side of the box in Olly's arms. "Take this to the kitchen, and we'll put away the stuff."

She followed him to the kitchen, where he dropped the box on the floor, the metal trays clanging.

"Hey, be careful with that."

"L-look, Mom."

She raised her head to follow his pointing finger and gasped at the broken glass from the side door. She grabbed Olly, digging her fingers into his bony shoulder. "We need to get out now."

Chapter Two

West took a sip of coffee as he stared at the falls, the flavor bitter on his tongue after those sweet cupcakes. His intermittent wipers kept up with the mist that collected on his windshield—barely. He could do this. New job. New town. New start.

After the previous sheriff of Dead Falls Island, the city council had welcomed his urban experience. The small town had recently suffered through a couple of murders and kidnappings, and its location near the Canadian border had put it on the map for the drug trade.

That's how the council members had tried to sell him on the job, by pumping up the excitement and danger. Although a few dead bodies and missing kids couldn't compare to the volume of crime he dealt with in Chicago, he'd taken the job to escape that level of violence and mayhem—to escape the violence in himself before it overwhelmed him.

The Spring Fling had been the perfect opportunity for him to meet and greet the community and enjoy some awesome food. He licked his lips, still tasting the buttery frosting from that cupcake. He didn't know what Astrid did for a living but if she made those cupcakes, she had a future as a baker. She fit right in with the island—tall, athletically slim, fresh-faced with eyes that matched the color of Discovery Bay. When he'd looked into those eyes, he'd felt something he hadn't felt in almost two years. Too bad she had a kid, especially that kid.

The radio in his unmarked SUV crackled to life, and the dispatcher's voice called out a break-in. In Chicago, that call wouldn't even warrant radio chatter. He checked the address on his GPS and discovered he was close to the location. Might as well jump in with both feet. The town had complained about the previous sheriff's laziness, his unwillingness to get involved in the crimes on the island. West had never suffered from indolence, so he got on the radio and indicated he'd respond to the call.

He stashed his coffee cup in the holder and peeled away from the Dead Falls overlook. He didn't exactly have to go code four. Apparently, the burglars hadn't made an appearance yet, but he owed it to the frightened homeowner to get there as soon as he could. The beauty of small-town service and all that.

He followed his GPS back across the bridge and farther into the woods, taking a small road that led to a large cabin—house.

A woman stood at the edge of the drive, clutching a shovel in both hands, her blond hair over one shoulder, a boy standing to the side, kicking a log. West swallowed hard. Had he conjured up Astrid and her son from his thoughts?

He parked his car several feet behind them, down the drive from the glass-and-wood cabin with its wraparound porch and alpine roof. The views from the house must be spectacular.

He stepped out of the car, his boot crunching gravel and dirt. Lifting his hand, he said, "Are you both okay?"

"We're fine." Astrid clamped a hand on Olly's shoulder. "Stop kicking that."

"Any sign of the intruders?" He approached them, his hands relaxed at his sides, away from his holster.

"We didn't see anyone. As soon as I noticed the broken window in the kitchen, we left." She pounded the shovel into the ground. "We made it this far, and I haven't seen anyone leave the house. Of course, they could've slipped out the back and disappeared into the forest."

West's gaze tracked around the perimeter of the house, taking in the greenery on all sides. A barbecue and firepit nestled on one side of the house in a clearing.

He flung his arm at the house. "I can go inside on my own first, if you like, to make sure it's all clear. Then you can join me and let me know if anything is missing. I can have a forensics person out here to dust for prints near the broken window."

She bit her bottom lip and then shrugged. "Sure. That's fine. We'll follow you. I left the front door open when we ran outside."

West strode to the front of the house, his hand hovering over his weapon, Astrid and Olly a safe distance behind. He nudged the door open with his shoulder. He didn't want to add his own prints to the mix.

A quick check of the house confirmed the burglars had vacated the premises. He stepped onto the porch and waved at Astrid and Olly, stationed next to a white truck. "Nobody here."

Astrid hoisted the shovel into the truck bed and marched to the porch. "I can't believe someone got in here. I must've forgotten to set the alarm when I left for the Spring Fling—too preoccupied."

"Cameras?" West jabbed a finger at a camera tucked under the eaves.

"Yes, but not by the side door, which is where they entered. If the security system had been set, the alarm would've sounded when the intruders broke into that window on the side door."

West shook his head. "I'm sorry. Security systems are only useful when they're properly set."

Astrid wedged a hand on her hip. "No kidding. I'll check to see if anything's missing. My brother keeps guns and other items in his safe. I'd better have a look there first."

"Your brother?" His eyes flickered to a black Jeep parked in front of the truck. "You live with your brother?"

"Temporarily, and he's off the island for several months." She held up one finger. "Wait here, and I'll run upstairs to check the safe."

Olly perched on the arm of the sofa when his mom left the room. The boy studied the gun in his holster, and a bead of sweat trickled down West's back.

"My dad's a cop."

West licked his lips. "Really? Do you know what department he works for?"

"I dunno." Olly hunched his skinny shoulders. "He's hiding right now."

West widened his eyes but before he could respond, Astrid jogged down the stairs.

"Safe is untouched, same for my jewelry box." She crooked a finger. "Did you see how they got in?"

He followed her into the kitchen, where she stopped short of the broken glass on the hardwood floor. Whoever broke in had closed the door behind them, but they had busted out the top window and reached in to unlock and open the door.

Pivoting from the mess on the floor, he asked, "Do you want to have a look around down here? Any cash lying around? Expensive gadgets? Looks like maybe a quick smash-and-grab."

"Uh-oh." Astrid covered her mouth with one hand and pushed past him into the step-down living room with the massive stone fireplace and a wall of windows that framed the forest and the bay beyond. She stopped at the coffee table and picked up the single book resting on the shiny wood.

Her head cranked from side to side, and she lunged at the large sectional sofa, grabbing pillows and tossing them aside. "I can't believe this."

"There *is* something missing?" And by Astrid's frantic movements and flushed cheeks, he'd have to guess the intruders took something important or expensive…or both.

"The drone. My company's drone is missing." She threw her hands up in the air. "Olly, did you see it before we left? Didn't I put it on the coffee table?"

Astrid's emotions had gotten to her son. His face paled so that his freckles stood out on his nose as he twisted his fingers in front of him. "I-I think so, Mom. It was right there on the table."

"Your company?" West took a turn around the room, scanning the well-ordered surfaces for the high-tech gadget.

"I'm a Realtor. I just recently got my license and started working for Discovery Bay Realty on the island. I'm putting together a package for a listing and borrowed the drone to get some aerial shots. This is bad." She continued upending cushions and peering under the furniture that couldn't possibly hide a drone.

"I'm sorry. Your company probably has insurance. Maybe it won't be a huge loss for them. You can file a police report, and Discovery Bay Realty can send that along to the insurance company." He wanted to put his hands on her shoulders to steady her, to calm her agitated movements.

"A police report?" Olly's eyes rounded into saucers, taking up most of his thin face. "Is that against the law?"

"Of course it is, Olly." Astrid threw her arms out to her sides. "It's burglary. It's theft."

West cleared his throat. "Is there anything else missing? If they grabbed the drone, they may have made off with similar easy to carry items. Cameras? Phones? Watches? Artwork?"

Astrid crossed the room to some shelving and ran her finger along the edge of each shelf, filled with objets d'art. "Some of these pieces are kind of expensive, but I don't notice anything gone. A lot of my possessions are in storage, and I'm not sure about Tate's stuff. I don't think he has a camera."

"Keep looking. If you spot anything else out of the ordinary, we can add it to the police report. I'll try to get a fingerprint tech out here from forensics to check that door and window, maybe the coffee table if you really think that's where you left the drone." Out of the corner of his eye, West saw Olly scampering toward the kitchen. "Whoa, there, buddy. Where are you going? You'll want to stay away from that door and broken window for now."

Olly tripped to a stop and spun around, his movements jerky. Poor kid was taking this hard.

"What about my bike, Mom? Maybe they took my bike. I was gonna go out to the side of the house where I left it."

Astrid pointed to the wall of windows and a door tucked into the corner. "Go out the back way for now."

When Olly rushed outside, Astrid rubbed her arms. "He seems upset. Maybe I should've sent him out of the house. He's had some…upsets lately."

Like his missing father?

West pulled his phone from his pocket. "I'll give the station a call to find out when the tech can get here. You can drop by any time to fill out the report. The sooner the better. Hey, if anyone starts playing with a drone around here, maybe we can recover it. It might even have a GPS tracker on it, if we're lucky."

"I was thinking about that." She turned toward him, extending her hand. "Thanks so much…"

Like a magnet, he went to her, a loud yell from outside stopping his progress.

"Mom! Mom, I found it!"

Astrid's eyes popped open as she glanced at West. "Thank goodness."

She made her way to the back door, and West followed her. This had to be the strangest burglary ever. They almost collided with Olly rounding the corner of the house at warp speed, his arms wrapped around a large box.

He pulled up short in front of them, panting and patting the box. "Look. I found it."

"Let me take that. It's heavy." Astrid scooped the box from Olly's arms. "Where in the world did you find it?"

"Umm—" Olly jerked a thumb over his shoulder "—it was in the garbage can. I left my bike next to the cans, so when I went to look for my bike, I saw the lid off the can and the box stuck in there."

West cocked his head. "That's strange. Could've been

kids who got spooked and dumped it in the trash before they took off."

"Probably, unless something else was taken." Astrid asked Olly, "Did you see anything else in the trash can or on the side of the house with your bike?"

"No." Olly put his arms behind him and rocked back on his heels.

Astrid screwed up one side of her mouth. "Did you notice anything out there when you rode your bike home? Before Mrs. Davidson gave you a ride to the Spring Fling?"

"No." Olly pressed his lips together, for some reason determined to give his mother as little information as possible.

"Let me take this inside." She hoisted the box in her arms. "It's getting heavy."

"I'll take it." West placed his hands beneath the box, as his eyes met Astrid's over the top. She released it quickly before he had a handle on it, and he stepped back to gain a little purchase so he wouldn't end up dropping the drone and getting her in trouble with her employer all over again.

He stamped his feet before walking back into the house and its gleaming hardwood floors. "On the table?"

"Yes, please."

Olly trailed behind them. As her son closed the door, Astrid came up behind him and wrapped her arms around him. "Thank you. Olly. If you'd never gone to look at your bike, I probably wouldn't have found the drone until trash day."

The boy's face brightened. "Does that mean I can play Xbox before dinner?"

"Go ahead." She tousled his blond mane. "But you're done when I say you're done. You're not going to waste your spring break in front of the tube."

"Okay, Mom." He turned at the bottom of the staircase and raised a hand. "Bye, Sheriff Chandler."

"See ya, Olly. Good detective work."

Olly grinned and hopped up the stairs, two at a time.

West stared after him, scratching his chin. "That was... lucky."

"Maybe not. I'd better call my brother and send him some pictures to see if anything else is missing, but if the thieves crammed the drone in the trash can, I'm thinking it was some teens who got cold feet."

"Whether or not anything is missing, you still need to report it. You can probably make a claim on your home-owners' insurance to get reimbursed for the door."

"Good idea." She waved a finger at him. "See, you're better than Sheriff Hopkins already."

"From what I understand, not such big shoes to fill, but I'll take the compliment." The phone in his pocket rang, and he checked the display. "Excuse me. It's the station. I need to take this."

"I'll sweep up this glass, if that's okay."

He nodded as he fished the phone from his pocket. "Chandler."

"Sheriff, this is George Vickers. We just got a call, and I think you're gonna want to be there for this."

West glanced at Astrid sweeping up the glass on the kitchen floor and rolled his eyes. Was this one going to be a kitten up a tree?

"Yeah, what is it, Vickers?"

"Dog walkers just discovered a dead body at the cove— Crystal Cove."

"On my way." West tapped the phone against his chin before sliding it into his pocket. "So, not a cat up a tree."

Chapter Three

Wiping her hands on a dish towel, Astrid strolled back into the living room, catching the sheriff talking to himself. "Everything okay? If you have to leave, I think we're done here. I'll check with my brother to find out if any items are missing, and I'll go to the station tomorrow to file the police report."

He pocketed his phone and made a move for the door, all of a sudden in a big hurry to take off—kind of like this afternoon. "Yeah, I do have to get going. Not sure I'll be able to get the fingerprint tech out here to dust the side door or the drone box."

"Oh, well—" she bunched the towel in her hands "—that's okay. Olly and I can avoid using that door, but I'll have to get the window replaced tonight."

"Do what you have to do to be safe." He bolted for the front door, not even waiting for her to show him out. He called over his shoulder. "Glad Olly found the drone."

"Yeah, me, too." She strode after him and grabbed the door when he flung it open. "Thanks for all your help, Sheriff Chandler."

"West." Without turning around, he waved a hand in the air on his way to his black SUV.

She closed the door behind him, locked it and set the security system, that broken window in the kitchen relegating the act to a useless gesture. Sheriff Chandler... West had practically run from the house. Just another unstable cop, even though his sincere good guy act had her going there for a while.

Sighing, she used the dish towel to open the back door and carried the dustpan full of glass to the trash cans on the side of the house. She maneuvered around Olly's bike leaning up against the wall and tipped the lid off the first can. She dumped the glass on top of a few plastic garbage bags in the bottom of the can.

She tilted her head. Had Olly found the drone in this one? There wasn't enough trash in here to make the drone box sit on top with a skewed lid. Isn't that what he'd said? No, maybe he'd said the whole lid was off.

She peeked into the can, which was half full. The intruders must've had a change of heart.

As she walked back into the house, her phone on the counter started buzzing. She checked the display as she picked it up. "Hey, Sam. Did you forget something at the Spring Fling?"

"Oh my God, Astrid, did you hear about the dead body?"

Astrid sucked in a short breath. "Dead body? On the island? Oh God, it's not another one of Dr. Summers' victims from his killing spree years ago, is it? I thought we'd found and accounted for all those missing kids. I'll have to tell Tate."

Sam lowered her voice to a whisper. "No, this is a current murder, an adult male. Someone walking a dog at the cove discovered him just this afternoon."

"Why are you whispering?" Astrid pressed her fingers against her chin. "Wait, at the cove? Crystal Cove?"

"Yeah, down by the water." Sam cleared her throat. "I was whispering because Peyton decided to come into the kitchen for a snack."

Astrid flickered her gaze to the ceiling, hoping Olly was too immersed in his game to come downstairs. "What time was the body found? Olly and Logan were out at the cove today before Logan's mom dropped him off at the Fling."

"Not sure." Sam lowered her voice again. "I think it's a drug thing. You know how shady the cove is."

"How do you know all this already? How do you know it's not just a drowning instead of a murder?"

"Well, I *do* live near the cove. Kinda hard to miss the sirens and emergency vehicles flying up the road, and the rumor's out there that the victim was shot—so no drowning." Sam smacked her lips. "I even saw the hot new sheriff."

"Stop calling him that." Astrid's cheeks flamed, and she was glad Sam was on audio only and not video chat. "He was actually at my house when he got the call, but he kept mum about it."

Chandler had hightailed it out of here on his way to the murder scene without telling her a thing. He obviously didn't understand how small towns worked if he thought she wouldn't find out within hours—actually minutes—of the discovery of a dead body.

"Wait, what? The hot sheriff was at your house already? Girl, I thought you'd had it with cops."

"Stop." Astrid perched on the edge of a stool at the kitchen island. "Someone broke into my house today."

"Really?" Sam clicked her tongue. "I swear, this island is suffering an absolute crime wave. What the hell? Did the little punks steal anything?"

"You're already blaming the teens."

"Yeah, those Goth, Wiccan punks who skulk around in their black clothes."

Astrid snorted out a laugh. "I doubt they spend their time breaking into homes. Too busy with incantations in the forest. Anyway, I didn't notice anything gone, but I'll have to check with Tate."

"I'm going to head out there with the rest of the lookie-loos. You wanna join me? We could have a cocktail or two in town after. We worked hard on that damned Spring Fling, and the kids are out on break. We deserve it."

Astrid rolled her shoulders, feeling the tension of the day. "I'd take you up on it, but I'm not dragging Olly out to a crime scene."

"I've got that covered. My mom is coming in a few to boil eggs with Peyton for the Easter egg hunt. She's ordering pizza and everything. Olly can join them." Sam had added a singsong, cajoling tone to her last sentence.

"Okay, we're in. I have to warn you that Olly still thinks Peyton is kind of icky, but he'll be down for boiling eggs and pizza for sure."

"Great. Pro tip. Break off the main road and come up the back way to our house, so Olly doesn't see all the hoopla. I told Peyton some lie about the sirens."

"Gotcha. You're such a good mom." Astrid glanced at the side door. "I do need some time to board up my window. It's broken."

"I'll send Anton over to do that. He needs the work anyway, and he's out your way right now. I'll text him, and he can work on it while you're over here."

"If you're sure."

"Bruce is trying to worm his way back into my life, so his son knows he has to jump when I whistle."

"Must be nice. Tell your stepson I'll give him a bonus for coming out after hours and if this will help you and Bruce fix your marriage, I'm all for it."

"Whose side are you on?"

"Yours. I'll be there in about thirty minutes."

Thirty-five minutes later, she took the back road to Sam's house in a newish tract of homes near the coast, walking distance to Crystal Cove. Olly had whined about leaving his game and whined some more about going to a *girl's* house, but the promise of pizza mollified him.

She'd avoided the emergency vehicles Sam had warned her about on the phone. Would they still be there? West had left her house about an hour ago. If this were a murder, even an accident, the cops would be on the scene for a long time.

She pulled into Sam's driveway, behind her car, and put her hand on Olly's shoulder as he reached for the door. "Remember, be nice to Peyton. This is her house, and we're guests."

"All right, but she'd better not tell anyone I was over here doing Easter eggs with her." Olly jutted his chin out and tumbled from the car.

Rolling her eyes, Astrid followed. She had to remember that this stage was probably preferable to make-out sessions behind Dead Falls. By the time she reached the door, Olly had already rung the bell, and Sam swung it open.

"Hello, you two. You're just in time. Luigi's delivered the pizzas a few minutes ago, and the hard-boiled eggs are cooling and ready to color."

Astrid raised a hand at Sam's mother, Lucy, and Peyton sitting in the living room playing a game of go fish. "Hi, Lucy. How are you?"

"Losing." She slapped a card onto the coffee table in front of Peyton. "Olly, do you want to join us?"

Olly glanced at the three pizza boxes on the counter, caught his mom's eye and said, "Okay."

Sam said, "Don't worry, Olly. We'll bring the pizza to you."

"I'll get the plates." Astrid turned toward the cupboard, but Sam whipped a stack of paper plates from a plastic bag.

"No dishes tonight. I'm on spring break."

Peyton shoved her glasses up the bridge of her nose with her thumb. "You promised soda tonight, Mom."

"I did." Sam mouthed the word *sorry* to Astrid and said aloud, "Is that okay with you, Astrid?"

"Please, Mom." Olly bounced up and down on the couch. A soda was going to send this kid into overdrive.

"I suppose. You've already had about twenty cupcakes, what's a cup or so more of sugar." Astrid stuck out her tongue at Sam.

The kids clapped like a couple of trained seals, and Astrid murmured to Sam. "Are you sure your mom's up for this?"

She winked. "Dad was a prison guard. I'm sure she learned a few tricks from him."

"I heard that, Sam." Lucy snapped her fingers. "And when you bring those sodas out here, bring me a glass of red while you're at it."

"That's how she gets through." Sam nudged Astrid with her elbow.

Astrid took the pizza orders—cheese for Peyton, pepperoni for Olly and the deluxe for Lucy. She surveyed the three open boxes. "You have enough pizza here to feed an army."

Tapping her head, her springy curls bouncing, Sam said, "Ready-made breakfast. I'm always thinking."

When they delivered the food and drinks to Lucy and the kids in the living room, Sam and Astrid settled at the kitchen table with their own slices and sodas.

Lucy raised her glass. "You two not imbibing?"

"We're going to have a drink in town." Sam cracked open her soda. "If that's okay with you, Mom."

"That's fine. Just avoid the cove." Lucy took a sip of her wine, and Sam sliced a finger across her throat.

Olly choked on his soda and wiped the back of his hand beneath his nose. "What's wrong with the cove?"

"I think there was some debris on the beach from a slide." Astrid raised her eyebrows at Sam, who nodded. They'd better get their stories straight. Kids always had a sense when you were lying.

"Olly was at the cove today. On the cliff." Peyton nipped off the point of her cheese pizza with her teeth and then daintily dabbed a napkin to her lips.

"We rode by. We weren't on the cliff." Olly scowled at Peyton and shoved some pizza into his mouth, chewing loudly in her direction.

Astrid snapped at him. "Olly. Manners, please. I'm just going to tell you again. You're not allowed on that cliff above the cove."

"I know. Me and Logan just rode past."

By the time the kids finished their pizza, they'd made a truce and when Lucy told them the eggs had cooled off enough to color, they were practically best friends.

Sam must've figured this was the perfect time to make their escape, as she jerked her thumb at the door. They left Lucy and the kids huddled around the kitchen table dropping colored tabs into bowls under fumes of vinegar.

When they walked outside, they skirted Astrid's truck in the driveway and crossed the street to make their way to Crystal Cove. Astrid pulled her jacket closed as she followed Sam on a narrow trail through a small patch of woods that led down to the rocky beach. People didn't sunbathe at Crystal Cove, even when it got warm enough to do so. They explored the tide pools, took their chances in the caves at low tide and launched boats from the deep-water inlet—usually for nefarious purposes.

A few dead bodies had wound up on the beach from misadventures on the cliff above. That's why she'd given Olly strict instructions to say away from the cliff. He could ride his bike right over the edge and sail onto the beach.

As they clumped down the end of the trail, voices carried back to them, muffled by the trees. Watching the ground for gnarled roots, Astrid almost bumped into Sam when she stopped short.

"I guess we're not getting any closer." Sam waved her hand toward a line of yellow tape stretched between two trees, keeping people off the beach.

Astrid peered around her at the clutch of people where the trail met the sand, craning their necks. She nudged Sam in the back. "Let's find out what they know. I see Charlene Lundstrom. She probably got here to stick her nose in before half of the sheriff's department arrived."

Sam twisted her head over her shoulder. "If Charlene is sticking her nose in, what are *we* doing?"

"Taking a leisurely stroll." She gave Sam a little push between the shoulder blades. "Move it."

They joined the other lookie-loos, the toes of their shoes

touching the sand of the beach. Astrid shoved her hands in the pockets of her jacket and nodded at Charlene. "Do we know who he is?"

Charlene clutched at her sweater. "It's a local."

"A local?" Astrid's pulse ticked up a few notches. "Who is it?"

Charlene's husband spoke without turning around. "It's that Chase Thompson, so probably drug-related."

Astrid bit her lip. Chase was a local, small-time drug dealer. He must've upped his game to warrant a murder at Crystal Cove.

Standing on her tiptoes, Sam said, "I heard he was shot. Is that right?"

A few other people gathered around murmured their assent.

Peering upward at the cliff's edge, Astrid said to no one in particular, "So, he didn't fall from the cliff."

Kevin Badgley, a local fisherman, crossed his arms and leaned against the trunk of a tree. "My guess is Chase was either expecting to shove off in a boat, or he just landed with some drugs and was intercepted. Either way, the new sheriff had better make some inroads into drug trafficking in Discovery Bay. The back-and-forth with the Canadian border is only getting worse."

"Is he here—Sheriff Chandler?" Astrid stood on her tiptoes and scanned the emergency personnel gathered on the beach.

"I think he's still with the body, which we can't see from here." Charlene almost sounded disappointed.

"There he is." Sam jabbed Astrid with a sharp elbow, and Astrid rubbed her arm.

West had walked up from the water and was talking

and gesturing to one of the uniforms on the sand. As he glanced at the crowd of people at the edge of the beach, Astrid ducked behind the solid form of Kevin.

She hissed at Sam. "Let's go."

"Oh, you don't want him to see you snooping around a crime scene?" Sam fanned her face. "Whatever will he think of you."

"I'm leaving." Astrid spun around and clumped back up the trail. She huffed out a breath. "You'd better follow me if you want a ride to the bar."

Sam scrambled after her and hooked a finger in her belt loop. "Lead the way."

When they reached Sam's house, Sam peeked into the window to make sure her mother and the kids were still coloring eggs. Then Astrid drove into town and parked on the main street halfway between the only two bars still open.

"Let's see." Sam wedged a finger against her chin. "Dive bar extraordinaire the Salty Crab, or *upscale* prosecco at the bar at the Grill?"

Astrid snorted. "I refuse to go into the Salty Crab with you. Last time we were there, you almost got into a fight."

"I had an excuse. I'd just found out Bruce was sexting with that...woman."

"That was not sexting, but I'm still not showing my face in there." Astrid shoved open the door of the truck. "The Grill, it is."

Sam joined her on the sidewalk. "We'd probably get more info about Chase in the Salty Crab."

"Don't care." Astrid hooked her arm through Sam's. "This way, missy."

The Grill was about to close the kitchen for dinner, but

the bar would remain open for another few hours. Astrid steered her friend into a cozy booth by the window.

When their waitress got to their table, she said, "The kitchen is about to close, but I can get you some food."

Sam waved her hand in the air. "We just had a bunch of pizza, but you can bring me a glass of the house red."

"Same." Astrid raised her hand.

After they settled in with their drinks and speculated about Chase Thompson's death, Astrid nursed her wine while watching Sam down three of the same as she complained about her husband.

Astrid didn't dare tell Sam some of the stuff her husband Russ pulled. Unlike Astrid's own husband, Sam's was a good guy despite his misstep.

Sam took a breath and tapped her phone. "Should I call Mom and find out how the kids are doing?"

"Sure, let her know we'll be back soon. I'm ready to wrap it up." Astrid put a finger in the air to catch the waitress's attention.

Scooting out of the booth and tossing a card on the table, Sam said, "I'm going to hit the ladies' room. My treat 'cuz I outdrank you three to one."

Sam disappeared down the dark hallway to the restrooms, and Astrid held up her friend's credit card for the waitress.

When Sam returned, she tipped the dregs of her third glass of wine down her throat. "Mom said the kids crashed out on the couch watching TV. She took Peyton up to bed and tucked a blanket around Olly. He can sleep over, if you like. Then you don't have to disturb him and try to get him to sleep again when you get home."

"That's okay. I'm driving you home, anyway. Might as well scoop him up while I'm there."

Sam fluffed up her curls. "You're tall, but Olly is almost up to your shoulder already. I doubt you can scoop up that boy anymore."

When the waitress returned with the card, Sam's eyes widened as she gazed past her shoulder. "What are you doing here, Anton? You're not twenty-one yet."

"Mama Lucy told me where you were and I was eating a burger at Gus's anyway, so I just wanted to let Ms. Mitchell know that I boarded up the glass in her door."

"Thanks, Anton. I'll pay you online when I get home."

"No hurry." He pulled his hat over his short Afro. "Did you hear about Chase Thompson down at the cove?"

"We did." Sam gave an exaggerated shiver. "That's why your dad and I are always nagging you to stay away from drugs. Bad news."

"My friends and I aren't into drugs, Sam. I told you guys that."

"We still worry." Sam snapped her fingers. "Hey, are you going home now? Can you give me a ride? That way Astrid doesn't have to, and Olly can sleep over."

Anton answered, "Yeah, I'm on my way home."

"Only if you're sure it's okay, Sam. I don't want Olly to spoil your plans tomorrow."

"I don't have any plans tomorrow." Sam grabbed her jacket. "It's settled. You can pick him up in the morning."

"Okay, thanks." Astrid patted Anton's arm. "And thank you for fixing my window."

"No problem, Ms. Mitchell."

Astrid grabbed her own jacket. "You two go ahead. I'm going to use the restroom."

They said their goodbyes, and Astrid made her way to the back of the bar, which had cleared during their chat session. When she finished in the ladies' room, she walked through the bar toward the front door, waving to the bartender and the waitress.

Once outside, she plunged her hand into her purse for her keys and strode toward her truck, which sat alone at the curb. This end of downtown Dead Falls rolled up the sidewalks early, even on weekends. The Salty Crab on the other end of the street kept its doors open until two, and several cars were still bunched up in front of the squat building with a pink neon crab on the front. Classy place.

As she approached her truck, the low heels of her boots clicking on the pavement, a dark figure emerged from the truck bed.

She squinted and called out. "That's my truck. What are you doing?"

Gripping her keys between her fingers, her adrenaline pumping her legs, she ran toward the truck. Before she could reach the bumper, the person jumped from the truck bed, swinging something in his hand.

She managed a strangled cry before a sharp pain pierced her brain and everything went dark.

Chapter Four

West rubbed his eyes and sucked down the rest of his Coke. First week on the job and a dead body on the beach. He slapped a five on the bar for the drink and nodded his thanks at the bartender. He hadn't wanted Chicago-level crime, but he didn't want to fall asleep on the job, either.

The Salty Crab, Chase Thompson's favorite hangout, hadn't yielded much in the way of information. Chase's friends had kept mum about the dead man's activities prior to his death, but West planned to dig so deep into their own personal affairs, those friends would come around eventually.

He twisted around on his barstool, eyeing his company, some loudly arguing in the corner, a few playing pool and one guy trying his luck with a couple of women at the jukebox. If this motley crew stayed until closing time, he hoped they had alternate transportation home.

Brayden Phelps, one of the guys West had questioned earlier, stumbled back into the bar through the front door. "Hey, there's a dead chick on the sidewalk."

West shoved back from the bar, his heart hammering. No way did Dead Falls produce two dead bodies his first week of work.

He strode toward Brayden, who was pitching and weaving. The guy was so drunk, he probably didn't know what he saw.

Grabbing Brayden's sleeve, West said, "Show me."

Brayden staggered outside. Obviously, the shock of seeing a dead body hadn't sobered him up. Half the bar cleared out behind them as Brayden pointed down the street at a lone truck parked in the shadows.

Brayden's finger wavered. "Right there. She's behind the truck."

West's mouth went dry. He'd seen that truck before— at Astrid's cabin. He shoved Brayden out of the way and jogged down the sidewalk toward the truck.

He saw a pair of feet in some low-heeled boots propped up on the curb before he saw the rest of the body in the street behind the truck. Astrid's blond hair fanned out behind her on the asphalt.

He crouched beside her, his fingers reaching for the pulse in her throat. When he saw her chest rise and fall, her eyelashes flutter, he finally breathed.

As the bar patrons crowded behind him, he said over his shoulder, "Stay back. Don't touch anything."

"She ain't dead." Brayden hiccupped at his audience. "Prolly hammered."

The pulse beneath his fingertips beat strong and sure, and he scanned her body for an injury. "Astrid? Can you hear me? It's Sheriff Chandler."

A moan escaped from her parted lips, and she raised a hand to her head.

"Are you injured? Can you sit up?" West fumbled for the phone in his pocket and called 911. If she needed medical treatment, he wanted the EMTs here as soon as possible.

She mumbled something and slid her fingers along the

back of her scalp. His flashlight picked up dark wet streaks on her palm.

He shouted. "Someone run back to the bar and get a clean cloth from the bartender—a couple."

Astrid struggled to sit up, and West curled an arm under her back to support her. She leaned into him, and even the blood and the oil and grime from the road couldn't diminish the fresh citrus scent from her bright locks. He also smelled the deeper fruity scent of wine on her breath.

"An ambulance is on the way. Did you fall and hit your head?" He turned to the side and flicked his flashlight at the bumper of the truck. Had she hit her head on the truck on her way down?

She sucked a breath in through her teeth. "Didn't fall. Someone attacked me. Hit me on the back of the head with something…hard."

As the bartender from the Salty Crab shoved two white towels at him, he said, "Hey, Sheriff. There's glass all over the road on the driver side of the truck. Looks like a broken window."

"Yeah, don't touch it." West bunched up one of the towels and pressed it gently against the back of her head. "Here?"

Astrid hissed. "Toward my right."

As sirens whooped down the street, West clenched his jaw. Someone breaks into Astrid's house and now her truck? He didn't believe in coincidences like this. Was there something Astrid had neglected to tell him earlier? Did she have enemies? Did her husband have enemies?

"Did you get a look at the person or persons who attacked you?"

She shifted her head. "One guy. He had a mask over his

face. At first, I just thought it was too dark to see, but he definitely had a mask on."

An ambulance pulled up behind the truck, followed by a patrol unit. This time, he planned to do a little more investigating. He waved his hand in the air at the EMTs as they jumped from their emergency vehicle.

The taller EMT got a hitch in his step when he approached the scene. "Sheriff Chandler."

"Have a look at Astrid. Someone hit her over the head. Knocked her out."

"I never lost consciousness." Astrid dug a hand into his shoulder to haul herself to her feet and promptly swayed.

West popped up beside her and put a light hand on her hip. Tapping the back of his head, he said, "There's a wound here."

"Can you walk, Astrid?" The second EMT took her arm. "Come to the back of the ambulance. We'll treat you there."

"Of course I can walk." She took a few careful steps toward the ambulance.

When West saw her seated on the back, the two EMTs attending to her, he approached one of the patrol officers. "Deputy Robard, you're trained in printing, correct?"

Robard flicked her ponytail over her shoulder. "Yes, sir. We have a kit in the back."

"Just for the heck of it, can you dust the truck? The guy broke in through the driver's-side window before attacking Astrid. She's not sure what he used to hit her, but it might be in the bed. That's where he was when she approached her truck."

She jerked her chin toward Astrid. "Is she okay? It's just that she's been through a lot lately, and her brother's out of town right now."

West cocked his head. "You know about the break-in at her place?"

"What? No." Robard widened her dark eyes. "I should probably call her brother, who's a friend of mine, but she'd kill me if I did."

"Let's just see if we can figure out who's targeting her." He jerked his thumb at the truck, and the female deputy strode back to the patrol car.

Less than an hour later, Astrid's truck had been dusted for prints and her wound dressed. The crowd from the Salty Crab had dispersed, and the EMTs were wrapping up.

Astrid stood next to her truck, kicking at the glass in the street with the toe of her boot.

"We got prints this time, just in case."

"I noticed." She wrinkled her nose, eyeing the smudges on her truck.

"That'll come off easily." He cleared his throat. "Are you okay to drive home? Where's your son?"

"He's at an impromptu sleepover, and I'm fine."

"You did lose consciousness, you know. That guy who came running into the bar thought you were dead."

"He was probably drunk if he was out at this hour." She rolled her eyes and winced. Touching the edge of her bandage, she said, "You're right. I did black out, but just for a few minutes. I guess my attacker just wanted what was in my truck."

"But you said he didn't take anything from your truck. Do you need to have another look? Or maybe save it for tomorrow when you're feeling better?"

Her gaze darted to the bed of her truck. "He did break into the tool caddy. He might've taken something out of there. I'll go through it tomorrow."

"Someone breaks into your house, takes the drone, thinks better of it and leaves it in the trash can. Then that same person, or someone else, breaks into your truck and doesn't steal anything." West scratched his jaw. "Is that about right?"

"What are you implying?" Astrid's blue eyes got icier. "Do you think I'm making things up? Lying?"

"No." He held up his hands. "Why would I think that? I saw everything with my own eyes."

"That's right. You did. I have no idea why this is happening." She dropped her chin to her chest and brushed off her jeans.

He studied the cascade of blond hair hiding her face and knew she was lying—not about the events. He did witness them. But he didn't believe for one minute she didn't have a clue about the motive for these…searches. Because that's exactly what it smelled like to him.

Somebody had searched Astrid's home and now her truck. Either the thief had found what he was looking for this time and Astrid had no intention of telling him what had been taken, or her assailant would look again.

Chase Thompson's dead body on the beach today had reminded West about the drug trade on this island. Was there more to Astrid Mitchell's fresh, outdoorsy mom persona?

Straightening up, she smoothed back her hair. "If there's nothing else, I'm going to head home."

"I'll follow you. You were able to get the broken window replaced?"

"My friend's stepson boarded it for me. I'm sure it will be fine. I'll make sure to arm the security system this time." She stepped over the glass and opened the door of her vehicle. "I don't really need an escort home."

"No problem. I'd rather follow you home than face the unpacked boxes at my place."

"I hear ya." She hopped into the truck and cranked on the engine. "Thanks for your help."

"Just doing my job." When he realized she didn't plan to wait for him to get into his car, he stepped back from the rumbling truck and strode to his vehicle.

Astrid followed all the rules of the road as he tailed her back to her luxury digs masquerading as a cabin. Once he verified she'd made it into the house safely, he backed down her drive and hit the main road.

On his way back to his boxes, West made a detour to the station. Astrid Mitchell exuded an air of mystery, and he wanted to get to the bottom of it to find out why her house and truck had been hit—at least that's what he told himself.

He'd start with her missing husband. He knew he could just ask around. Most likely every deputy working for him could give him the lowdown on Astrid Mitchell and her AWOL husband—but she'd find out about his curiosity, and he didn't want to give her a heads-up.

Seated behind his desk, he logged in to a couple of different databases, searching for a cop named Mitchell initially. His eyes glazed over as he scrolled through the findings. He knew it was a long shot when he started. He cleared that search and tapped his finger on the mouse.

Searching her name would be a better bet, as Astrid wasn't that common. Her real estate listings popped up first, and he perused a few of the houses. He was in a rental now, but if he stuck around, he'd buy something—and he'd use her as his agent. She could use the break.

As he skimmed down the screen, an article seemingly unrelated to Astrid caught his eye. His pulse jumped when he caught the drift of the story—a ring of dirty Seattle cops busted for drug dealing.

He clicked on the link and hunched forward to read the words on the screen. Several Seattle cops had been working in concert with a local drug dealer, Pierre Dumas, giving him a heads-up on busts and stealing drugs and money from raids. None of the cops had the name Mitchell. Why did a search on Astrid bring up this article?

He continued to read, and Astrid's name jumped out at him. Her ex-husband, Russ Crockett, was one of the dirty cops, and Astrid had testified against him. But before Crockett could be sentenced, he made a deal with the prosecution—names, dates, details—invaluable information for bringing down Dumas and his drug ring.

A quick phone call to a friend in high places gave West some insider information on Crockett. In exchange for his testimony, the Feds gave Crockett a new life in WITSEC. So Olly was right. His dad was hiding.

West leaned back in his chair and steepled his fingers. How much did Astrid know about her ex-husband's life? How much had she profited from his ill-gotten gains? Were the recent break-ins of Astrid's home and truck and the dead body on the beach all linked? Had Russ Crockett turned over all the drugs and money when the Feds arrested him? Or had he left some for safekeeping with his wife?

Olly's dad might be hiding, but was Olly's mom hiding something, too? If she was, West had every intention of finding out what that was—one way or another.

Chapter Five

Astrid studied her son spooning cereal into his mouth in front of Sam's TV, Peyton nowhere in sight. "Was he horrified when he discovered he'd had a sleepover with a girl?"

"He took it in stride, once I set that bowl of sugary breakfast food in front of him." Sam eyed her over the rim of her coffee cup. "Looks like his mom took getting conked on the head in stride, too. I'd be a nervous wreck if that happened to me, especially after the break-in."

Folding her arms across her chest, Astrid said, "I am a nervous wreck, but I don't want to telegraph that to Olly. I have no intention of telling him that someone attacked me. That's why I already got the truck window fixed."

"I get it, but you're so good at stuffing that all inside. I don't think I'd be able to pull it off. Peyton took one look at me after Bruce and I decided to separate and knew something was off." Sam sniffed and then took a quick sip of her brew to cover it.

"Yeah, well, I've had a lot of practice." Astrid patted the sore spot on the back of her head.

"I know you have, and I'm sorry." Sam squeezed Astrid's knee. "Do you think the two events from yesterday are related to Russ?"

Sam had lowered her voice and leaned in for the question, but Astrid slid a glance toward Olly anyway, still engrossed in SpongeBob. "I'm not sure. I mean, he's supposed to be secured away somewhere, starting a new life."

"I hope so, but do you think he'll ever give up on Olly?" Sam covered her mouth. "Sorry. I don't mean to give you more to worry about. Russ wouldn't dare pop his head up now. He's still in danger. Those people don't just forgive and forget."

Rubbing her chin, Astrid said, "That's exactly what concerns me."

The cartoon ended with Olly singing along to the theme song. Then he hopped up from the couch and twisted around. "Is it time to go, Mom?"

"Yes, it is. Thank your hosts before we leave." Astrid turned to Sam. "Thanks again."

"Don't thank me. If Anton and I had walked you to your truck, you never would've been..." Sam trailed off as Olly walked into the kitchen with two bowls, both half-filled with milk.

"I got Peyton's bowl, too." He put them in the sink, and Astrid's heart did a little dance.

"That's what I like to see."

Olly's face reddened to the roots of his blond hair, and his eyes widened. "Don't tell anyone, Mom."

"I swear, I won't." She drew a cross over her chest.

Sam held up her hand. "Peyton won't either. She'd be mortified."

"Mortified?" Olly tried out the word on his tongue.

"Embarrassed." Astrid tugged at his sleeve. "Get your sweatshirt."

Sam cupped her hand around her mouth and tilted her head back. "Peyton, say goodbye to your guest."

Peyton's voice carried down the stairs as she shrieked. "He's not my guest, Mom."

"Get down here, Peyton." Sam winked at Olly. "Told you."

With all the thanks and goodbyes out of the way and with Olly carrying a couple of slices of pizza wrapped in foil, Astrid followed him out to her truck. "That wasn't so bad, huh?"

Olly mumbled. "It was okay."

She jabbed him in the shoulder. "Admit it. You had fun."

Olly clambered into the truck and snapped his seat belt. "Yeah, Peyton's okay, but it's gonna be more fun at camp."

A flare of panic jumped in her breast. She didn't want to be away from Olly right now, but maybe he'd be safer in the woods with Porter Monroe and the rest of the Scouts than hanging around the house.

She forced her lips into a smile. "That's right. You need to pack up when we get home, so you're ready for pickup tonight. Remember what I told you."

"Stay with the group and follow the rules."

"Right on." She raised her fist for a bump, and Olly obliged.

Olly spent the rest of the ride home chattering about camp and all the activities lined up for them. Astrid made the appropriate noises at the right times, but her mind was jumping from the break-in at her house to the break-in of her truck.

The perpetrator hadn't stolen anything from either location. She'd bought the story about teens at the house getting spooked and dumping the drone in the trash, but that scenario didn't fly for the truck. She'd been assaulted.

She touched the back of her head and sucked in a breath

between her teeth. Maybe the person she'd surprised in her truck bed hadn't wanted to kill her, but he hadn't been afraid to take her down. Why? He could've just run off. She didn't have a chance at identifying him in his ski mask and gloves.

But perhaps he didn't want to take any chances. She slid a glance at Olly, describing how he planned to eat ten s'mores at the campfire. Anything bad that had ever happened in her life, except her brother's kidnapping twenty years ago, had been due to her association with her ex. Was this any different?

There had been speculation among law enforcement that Russ hadn't turned over all the drugs and money when he decided to rat out his buddies. The FBI had questioned her hard, but Russ had kept all of that from her. They weren't even married at the time, as the divorce had been finalized months before the testimony.

There was a good chance that Russ's associates didn't believe her. If anyone who had escaped the sting of the Dumas cartel, and there must've been a few, thought she had access to money and drugs, they wouldn't hesitate to track her down and force her to give it back. Was this just the beginning?

She flexed her sweaty hands on the steering wheel. She should've told West everything about her past instead of pretending she had no idea why someone would want to search her house and truck. She knew damned well why some criminal would want to toss the house of Russ Crockett's ex-wife.

By the time she pulled into the drive, Olly had grown silent. Had she missed her cue? She slid the truck into Park and turned her head toward him, giving him her full attention. "When we get inside, get your backpack and tell me what you want to wear. I'll do some laundry, and then we can get you packed up and ready to go."

With his chin at his chest, Olly rubbed the side of his thumb against the seam of his jeans. "Was there a dead guy at the cove?"

Astrid clamped her bottom lip between her teeth. It was impossible to keep anything from the kids on this island. "Where did you hear that?"

"Peyton told me. She heard it when she went into Mama Lucy's bedroom last night 'cuz she woke up and her mom wasn't home. She said her grandma was listening to something on her computer, and Peyton heard it."

"Yes, that's true. A guy walking his dog on the beach found the man's body." She squeezed her son's knee. "You don't have to worry about that. The police think it has something to do with drugs."

"When did the guy find him? Was he in the water or on the sand?"

Tilting her head, Astrid said, "He was discovered a little while before we got to Peyton's house. I don't know any of the details, but like I said, it was someone involved in drugs."

Had she blundered mentioning the drugs? How much had Olly known about his father's activities and why he'd had to go away?

"So, like, did the guy drown or something?"

Olly didn't even know the man had been murdered. She cut the engine and yanked the keys from the ignition. "Maybe he did. I'm not sure, Olly. Are you...concerned about it?"

"Nah." He shoved open the door and jumped to the ground. "Is my backpack in my closet?"

Before she had a chance to answer him, he was running toward the front door, clutching his pizza in front of him. She sighed. She was pretty sure the dead body at the cove would make its way into some scary campfire stories this week. Hopefully, Porter Monroe, the Scout leader, would have the good sense to steer the boys away from that and toward some good old-fashioned ghost stories.

She could handle the supernatural. It was the real-life monsters that scared her the most.

LATER THAT AFTERNOON, Logan Davidson's mother, Denise, shaded her eyes against the setting sun as she watched Olly and Logan hoist their gear into the back of her SUV. "I think it's easier this way. Have most of the boys in one pickup spot."

"Sure, sure. Makes sense to me." Of course Denise's place had to be the pickup spot. Denise was determined to be supermom, but Astrid was just as determined to get along with the mother of her son's best friend.

Crooking her finger at Olly, Astrid called. "You're not getting away without a hug."

Olly shrugged at Logan and then galloped back toward her, like a clumsy colt. He curled his arms around Astrid's waist and squeezed. "Be careful, Mom."

She hugged him tighter and patted him on the back. "That's my line. You don't have to worry about a couple of teenagers breaking into the house."

Wriggling out of her grasp, he stood on his tiptoes and planted a quick kiss on her cheek. "Bye."

"Have fun. Be careful. Love you."

He'd slammed the car door on her last words, and Denise chuckled. "Boys, huh? But I think we have it easier in the teen years than girl moms. I'm not looking forward to the arguments with Posey when she hits fourteen or fifteen."

Astrid didn't feel like opening the door to another soliloquy on the perfections of Posey Davidson, so she just nodded. "Thanks again for having the boys over, and call me if you need any help before the Scout leaders pick them up."

Denise chewed on her lip for a few seconds. "I'm kind of glad they're taking off this week. I hope the new sheriff makes an arrest in the Chase Thompson case before the boys come back. That one spooked Logan."

"It did?" Astrid raised her eyebrows. "Olly was asking questions about it, too. Do you think the kids were talking about it among themselves? Telling stories?"

"Not sure, but I hope it's not fodder for the campfire." Denise hoisted her purse onto her shoulder. "I'll talk to Porter about it before they leave."

"Thanks again, Denise."

Denise waved before ducking into the car, and Astrid kept waving until the car backed down the drive and disappeared.

She stayed on the porch, crossing her arms against the sudden chill. At least Olly wasn't the only kid worried about the dead body at the cove, so maybe his concern had nothing to do with his father's situation.

He also seemed more upset about the break-in than he'd let on. Why else tell her to be careful? He'd never said that to her before, and she hadn't even told him about the attack at her truck last night.

Releasing a long breath, she turned toward the house. She'd borrowed that drone from the office to get some aerial shots of a listing already on the market, and with Olly gone for the week, she'd better get to it tomorrow morning.

After the break-in, Astrid had secured the drone in Tate's safe. She probably should've put it in there when she brought it home the day before yesterday, but she hadn't anticipated anyone coming out here to break in at the precise time she'd forgotten to set the alarm.

She closed the door behind her and glanced at the security keypad on the wall. Had she forgotten to set it? That would be a rare mistake for her. She'd been security conscious ever since her separation from Russ a few years ago. Even though her brother didn't have cameras on the side door, the alarm would've gone off the minute someone smashed that window—if the security system had been armed.

She jogged upstairs and veered into the master suite, which Tate had made his own when he'd renovated this cabin. They'd all inherited a chunk of money from a wealthy uncle, and Tate had used his share to do a fantastic remodel of this cabin, which their parents had turned over to him. She hadn't minded being cut out. Tate's best friend had been kidnapped when they were children, and Tate had been traumatized. Her parents figured they owed him for that disruption of his childhood.

She ducked into his walk-in closet and knelt before the safe. Once she entered the combo, the heavy door swung open. The drone box dominated the space it shared with a few of Tate's weapons and some paperwork she ignored. She pulled it from the safe and locked up.

Clasping the box to her chest, she carried it downstairs and put it on the coffee table in the living room, where it had been when some thief decided to grab it. She hadn't had a chance to use it on any of her listings yet, but Davia

Reynolds, her boss at work, had assured her it was a breeze to use.

She opened the box and set the drone on the table while she fished for the instructions. She unfolded the little user manual and ran her finger along the small text on the glossy card. The agency planned to upgrade soon because this drone was already out of date—no live feeds, no video going straight to your phone or computer. This one used a physical memory card, but it still seemed high-tech to her.

As she read through the instructions, she located all the parts and buttons and switches. She assumed the drone had a memory card installed, but she couldn't open the slot and didn't want to push it.

When she felt ready, she grabbed a sweatshirt and carried the drone outside. She'd do a test run here before taking it out to the property, and she had about fifteen minutes before it got dark.

Standing in front of the cabin, she set the power and tried to launch the drone. It buzzed but didn't take flight. She set it beside her on the porch while she perused the directions again but no luck.

She knew Davia planned to meet some clients tonight in the office, so Astrid shot off a text to her boss, who'd used the drone before. If she could get some pointers tonight, she'd be ready to go tomorrow.

Davia replied that she'd be in the office for the next thirty minutes and would be happy to help Astrid with the drone.

Astrid made it to the office with time to spare, pulling into a space next to an SUV belonging to the Dead Falls Island Sheriff's Department. Davia hadn't mentioned that her client was a cop.

As Astrid approached the office, her step hitched as she

caught sight of Sheriff West Chandler talking to Davia, looking almost as sexy in his civilian clothes as he did in uniform. He should've told her he was looking to buy, so she could represent him. Maybe he'd decided to steer clear of her and her messy life.

Squaring her shoulders, she pushed through the door. "Hi, Davia. Glad I caught you. Hello, Sheriff."

"I was just showing my other clients out when Sheriff Chandler showed up." Davia's gaze darted from West to Astrid. "He's interested in seeing a few properties, and he requested you as his agent. Said he already talked to you."

"That's right." She nodded at West. They'd sort of talked, but he hadn't seemed to be in the market immediately. But she'd take the business. "Be happy to help."

West said, "Now I'm even more satisfied with my choice of real estate brokers. You're obviously motivated, to be working after hours."

"Don't get used to it." Astrid patted the box. "I'm just here to get some last-minute instruction from Davia on using the drone."

As West raised his eyebrows and cleared his throat, Astrid held her breath. She willed him with her death stare not to mention the almost-theft of the drone. She hadn't told Davia and didn't want to mention it—not yet.

"Okay, let's see what you're doing." Davia cleared a space on her desk and patted it.

Astrid pulled the drone from the box and placed it on the blotter gently, as if it hadn't already been through hell. "I set this. Turned on this switch and checked that this was on. No go."

Davia squinted at the drone and tapped its side. "No wonder it won't work. It's broken."

"Broken?" Astrid's heart jumped. "How can that be? You showed me how it worked before boxing it and letting me take it home the other night. It seemed okay then."

"You haven't tried to use it yet?" Davia wrinkled her nose at the drone perched on her desk.

"No. I mean, just a half hour ago when I tried to give it a test run. But I didn't break anything. It never made it off the ground."

Davia flicked a finger at the silent machine on her desk. "Between the time I gave it to you and the time you set it up for a test, someone used it. Someone launched it, and it looks like someone tried to bat it out of the sky."

Chapter Six

Astrid's face drained of all color, and her blue eyes widened. "That's not possible. I haven't tried it yet."

West bit the inside of his cheek. He'd kept mum earlier when it became clear that Astrid hadn't told her boss about the near-miss theft of the drone. He wasn't here to call anyone out, but this shed a different light on things. Had someone damaged the drone when they tossed it in the trash? Or maybe they damaged it before and that's *why* they tossed it in the trash.

Davia screwed up one side of her mouth. "Could you have dropped it in transit?"

"Dropped it?" Astrid twisted her fingers in front of her. "No, b-but someone took it from my house and dumped it my trash can."

"Oh." Davia's mouth remained in an *O* after she uttered the word.

Spreading her hands, Astrid said, "I know. I'm sorry. I...we just thought it was some teens who broke in, saw the drone, snatched it and then thought better of it."

"Do you think they might've had time to take it up?" Davia tapped her scarlet fingernails against the drone's gray body. "Even though I mentioned before that it could've been dropped, it really looks like someone smacked it."

West peered over Davia's shoulder and followed the path of her fingers. If you weren't familiar with the drone, you might miss the indentations on its side. He reached around her and poked at a flat button. "What's that? It looks bent."

"That's the button for the memory card slot. This drone is an old one that we were planning to replace anyway for one that does a live video feed to a phone or computer." She wedged her finger against the button. "Seems stuck."

Astrid dropped to the chair next to Davia's desk. "I'm so sorry, Davia. I don't know how that could've happened. I can't imagine how the thieves had time to fly the drone, wreck it, and then stuff it back in the box and in my trash can."

"Don't worry about it. This is a good excuse to fast-track that replacement." Davia pulled on her earlobe, rotating the diamond stud embedded there. "Look, I know Olly is a good kid and mine were, too, but they were no angels. Now that they're adults, they tell me all kinds of things they got up to—things I'd rather not know about. Do you think…?"

Davia left her words hanging, and Astrid wedged her fingers against her bottom lip. "Olly? You think Olly might have flown the drone?"

Waving her hands in the air, Davia said, "Just a thought, but boys, drones." She shrugged. "It's an irresistible combo. It's not a big deal, Astrid. The thing was on its last legs, anyway. I can tell corporate it finally crashed and burned, and we need that new one if they want us to stay on top of things out here—literally. A lot of the properties on this island need those bird's-eye view pictures for a sale. I gotta go. My hubby was irked enough that I stayed a little late for those clients on our date night. Can you lock up?"

"Sure, I have my keys." Astrid patted her purse hanging at her side. "I can pay to have it fixed, whether it was Olly or not. It was damaged under my care."

Davia flicked the drone with her finger. "It might be reparable, but don't knock yourself out. And go easy on Olly. The kid's had it rough."

West turned his head and pretended to inspect the drone as Astrid put her hand to her heart. "Thanks, Davia. I might still see about getting it fixed because I wanted to use it for my listing in Misty Hollow."

"You're gonna need all the help you can get with that property." Davia gave an exaggerated shiver. "Full disclosure, right?"

"I have it drawn up for the contract already. It's still a great piece of land—despite its history."

"Thanks for dropping by, Sheriff. Maybe you should try to sell Sheriff Chandler the Misty Hollow property." Davia winked at Astrid. "At least he might not be spooked."

When Davia swept out the door on a cloud of floral perfume, Astrid slumped against the back of the love seat. "I never thought of Olly. He was acting kind of weird that day. I thought he'd be more freaked out by the break-in. And then he was the one who conveniently found the drone in the trash."

West perched on the arm of the love seat next to her and crossed his arms. "When would he have had time to mess with the drone? Wasn't he at the Spring Fling with you? Didn't he come home with you where you discovered the theft together?"

"He wasn't with me at the Fling all day. I dropped him and his bike off at his best friend's house. They were riding their bikes most of the day, and then his friend's mother dropped them off at the Fling."

"Then how'd he get the drone?"

Her hand brushed his thigh as she raised her it to drag through her blond locks. "I *thought* I set the security system when we left that morning."

"What does that mean?" He shifted his leg, still tingling from her unintended contact.

"It means Olly and Logan could've ridden their bikes back to the house, used the key to get in and take the drone. Then Olly forgot to arm the system when he left." She smacked her hand on the cushion beside her. "That little sneak."

"Wait." He hopped up from the love seat and picked up the drone from Davia's desk. "Why'd he leave it in the trash, and why'd he break the window if he had a key?"

She drummed her fingers on the arm of the love seat he'd just vacated. "Not sure, but maybe when he returned with the drone, he remembered the camera at the front, so he went around to the side door. At that point, he could've seen the broken window, freaked out and stashed the drone in the trash to be collected at a later time. Or he and Logan could've broken the window by accident, got spooked and dumped the drone."

"You said the camera wouldn't work without the security system set."

She lifted her shoulders. "Either Olly never knew that, forgot or he believed he set the alarm when he left after taking the drone. Anything could be going through that kid's head. It has to be the one of those explanations. The drone was not broken when I checked it out of the office. I don't think a couple of thieves would've had the time or inclination to launch it."

"I don't know about that. We can't rule it out. Can you talk to Olly about it?"

"Not right now. He's on a Scout camping trip for the rest of the week. He'll be back before Easter." She bounded from the love seat and joined him at the desk. "If Olly or someone else launched the drone, we should be able to check that data card for the footage. That might tell us something."

"Except—" West tapped the side of the drone "—the damage to the drone affected the slot for the card. We can't get it out."

"Unless I can find someone to fix it. That might solve the mystery." She reached across him to stuff the drone back in the box, and her hair tickled the back of his hand. "I think I know someone who can handle the job."

"Right now?"

She checked her phone. "If I can catch him before he leaves his shop. He's actually an auto mechanic, but he knows his electronics and can fix anything. I mean, unless it's a software issue."

"I think it's definitely mechanical, and even if he can't fix the thing, maybe he can pop that sleeve open without doing further damage so you can retrieve the video card and find out where it was used last. That should be able to tell you if Olly or someone else flew it."

Astrid pulled her phone from her purse and tapped the display. A few seconds later, she gave him a thumbs-up. "Hi, Alexa. Is Jimmy still around? I have a job for him."

She cocked her head and listened before speaking again. "It's a drone. Can he look at it? I'll rush it right over before you guys close up shop for the day."

While Astrid finished her call, West packaged the drone back in the box. Even if Olly did take the drone out for a test drive and break the window on the kitchen door, it didn't explain the attack on Astrid last night. Something felt off to him.

"Okay." Astrid dusted her hands together. "Jimmy will have a look at it. The garage is still open, so I'll drop it off on my way home."

"Do you have plans for dinner?" Astrid's face showed as much surprise as he hoped he was hiding on his own face. That invitation came out of left field even if he did need more from this woman—more information, more conversation. "I was thinking we could grab a bite, and then you could show me this property at Misty Hollow."

"Are you serious?"

He patted his stomach. "About dinner? Hell, yeah. I'm starving."

"About the property at Misty Hollow." She wedged her hip against the edge of the desk and blinked. "Do you know the history of the place? Did you hear me and Davia talk about the disclosures?"

"Now, what kind of new sheriff would I be if I didn't familiarize myself with the crime on this island—current and past? I know all about the massacre committed by the foster son Brian Lamar aka Addison Abbott at that property thirty years ago."

"It doesn't scare you off?" A little smile touched the corner of her mouth.

"Brain Lamar is dead. Are you saying the place is haunted or doomed or something?"

Lifting one shoulder, she said, "Just figured it would be a tough sale. That's why I really, really wanted to use the drone. It's a fabulous space—despite its macabre history."

"I'd like to see it—after dinner." West's interest in the property wasn't completely sincere. He just figured he needed a cover for randomly inviting Astrid out for dinner. Might as well pretend it was business-related.

"It's going to be dark by then." She peeked out the window. "It's already dark."

"Best time to view a haunted property, wouldn't you say?"

"As long as I'm with the sheriff." Hunching her shoulders, she hugged herself. "That place is spooky."

"Then we'd better get going. You have any suggestions for dinner?" His gaze flickered over her casual outfit of jeans, running shoes and a hoodie. She looked fresh and pretty, but she'd look good in a potato sack.

"Pizza? We still might get a seat at Luigi's. A lot of families are off the island for spring break. Also, it's down the street from Jimmy's garage."

"Sounds perfect. I hate to admit that I've already been to Luigi's twice since I got to the island."

"No shame in craving a good pizza." She dangled her key chain. "I'll lock up and meet you there, after dropping off the drone."

He glanced out the window at the darkening sky. "I'll wait and follow you over to Jimmy's."

"Not necessary, but okay."

Something in his gut told him it *was* necessary, not that he could be Astrid Mitchell's bodyguard 24/7. He stood outside while Astrid locked up a few drawers and then secured the front door. When he walked her to her truck, he asked, "I didn't see your report today on the attack. Was there anything missing from your truck?"

"The lock on the toolbox was broken, and I searched through those tools in there, but I couldn't tell if anything was missing. My brother stashes some of his tools in my truck, so I'll have to ask him."

He held the door open for her as she hopped onto the driver's seat. "Have you checked with him about any possible missing items from the house?"

"Nope." She shook her head from side to side. "Not yet."

"You're avoiding it."

Resting her elbows on the steering wheel, she said, "My brother is a worrier. You have no idea. I don't want to set him off while he's busy in DC. The tools don't matter. I doubt he had anything of value in my truck."

"Does he have anything to worry about?" He curled his fingers around the edge of the door.

"If he doesn't, he'll find something." She grabbed the door handle of the truck and tugged. "Let's go."

West released the door, and she slammed it. Was that her way of telling him to mind his own business? As sheriff, her business *was* his business.

He followed her for a short ten-minute drive to Jimmy's Auto at the end of the main drag through town. He parked next to her and got out of his car. Might as well get to know as many residents of the island as possible. Also, if Jimmy looked at the drone and figured he couldn't fix it, they might as well force open the cover to the memory card slot and retrieve it and just hope they didn't damage anything.

The rolling door on the garage, securely closed, gleamed in the lights above it, which spilled onto a few cars parked on the side. A cheery glow emanated from the front office, though, and he could see two figures through the window.

Astrid marched to the door, oblivious of him on her heels. She almost let the door swing closed in his face, but he caught it, and she jumped.

"I didn't know you were coming inside."

"Thought I should meet Jimmy and his wife. I understand he works on our vehicles."

She searched his face for minute, as if not sure she could trust him. If she couldn't trust the new sheriff in town, who could she trust? He'd have to work on that. He used to be so good at inspiring trust in people—until he'd lost all that good faith with one action.

At the sound of a woman's voice from the back, Astrid looked away quickly. "Hey, Alexa. Thanks for waiting."

"Jimmy had to wrap up, anyway. Hello, Sheriff Chandler. I'm Jimmy's wife, Alexa Galvin."

He shook hands with the petite, dark-haired woman across the scarred counter, bearing stickers from oil and tire brands. "Good to meet you."

Jimmy came from the back and held up his clean hands before extending one to West. "You here to take a look at those contracts we have with the city for the vehicles?"

"If you have them."

"Alexa, hon, can you grab those for the sheriff while I take a look at Astrid's drone?"

A minute later, West had to drag his attention away from Astrid's conversation with Jimmy, as Alexa plopped some folders on the counter in front of him. "You can take these, Sheriff, as long as you return them."

"Absolutely." West grabbed the files from the glass top with no intention of reviewing them. He didn't even know if maintaining these contracts fell under his purview and not the city council's.

As he tucked the folders under his arm, Astrid smiled at him and clapped her hands. "Jimmy thinks he can fix it."

"Don't get too excited, Astrid." Jimmy ran a hand over his shaved head. "I'll have a look, but at least I can get that memory card out for you without breaking the whole thing and ruining it."

"I appreciate it, Jimmy."

West and Astrid left the Galvins to close up shop and meandered back to their cars.

West jerked his thumb to the side. "Walking distance."

"Yeah, that'll come in handy after we stuff our faces with pizza." Astrid patted her flat stomach.

He kept his mouth shut, but willowy Astrid didn't look like she needed to worry about working off calories.

They fell into step together as they walked to Luigi's, a bustling pizza place that catered to both seated diners and takeout. He knew all about the takeout.

His mouth watered as they stepped inside, and the scent of garlic curled around him. He'd been an oddball in Chicago, preferring a thin-crust pie to the deep-dish delicacy served throughout Chi-town—as if he needed another reason to abandon that city.

Standing on her tiptoes, even though she was probably one of the tallest people in the restaurant, Astrid surveyed the room. "Do you want to grab one of those tables, and I'll order at the counter?"

"Let's switch that around. You find a good table, and I'll place our order. Just let me know what you want."

"Pepperoni is fine with me and a glass of house red."

"Got it." He pivoted toward the counter and waited in a short line, as people threw curious glances his way. A buddy of his who'd left the Chicago PD a few years before he did and settled in as a small-town sheriff in Colorado had advised him to get to know as many people as possible on a personal level. Eat out in the local restaurants, shop locally, use local service people—see and be seen. West had known being the sheriff of an island department like Dead Falls would involve a lot of PR and people-pleasing. He couldn't complain about it now.

The young man at the counter adjusted his Luigi's pizza cap when West stepped up to the register. "Hey, Sheriff. What can we get you tonight? You plan on trying every combo we got?"

"Just about—" West zeroed in on the guy's name tag "—Evan, but tonight I just need a large pepperoni, a glass of your house red and a...soda."

He'd have to check with his friend on the rules for drinking alcohol in public. He was off the clock and in civvies, but was a small-town sheriff ever off the clock? He'd technically been off duty last night when Astrid had been attacked, even though he'd been questioning people in the Salty Crab about the Chase Thompson murder.

Evan took his order, handed him a plastic cup for the self-serve soda machine and gave him a number for his table. "The wine will be right out, Sheriff."

West nodded, aware of a few side-eye glances, and he wanted to say aloud the wine wasn't for him. He snatched up his cup and edged over to the soda machine. He'd probably never feel comfortable drinking in front of the good citizens of Dead Falls.

He joined Astrid at the table by the window and set down his drink next to the water glasses. "Mission accomplished. Wine's on the way."

"I guess I should make a full confession here."

His gaze jumped to her face as his hand jerked, the soda fizzing and the ice clinking in protest. Did she have something else to tell him about the drone? The break-in? Her ex-husband? "Oh?"

Leaning in close, she cupped a hand around her mouth. "I just had Luigi's pepperoni pizza last night."

He blinked and sucked down some soda. "I won't tell anyone. I'm the sheriff. I'm trustworthy."

The smile on her lips wobbled. "Those two statements could totally be mutually exclusive."

Before he could start down the path that might lead to a discussion of her ex, a young woman arrived with the wine. "Red wine?"

Astrid raised her hand, and the woman placed it on the table. "Enjoy."

Tilting the glass toward him, Astrid asked, "Should we toast to the drone's recovery? Or your arrival in town?"

"How about both?" He tapped his cup to hers and shoved the straw into his mouth.

As she sipped her wine, her eyes widened over the rim. "Look who followed us over here."

He turned his head toward the entrance and spotted Jimmy and Alexa from the garage waiting in the takeout line. Jimmy's eyes met his, and they nodded.

West asked, "Did Jimmy seem confident he could fix the drone?"

"Let's just say he was cautiously optimistic, but at least I trust him to pop out that memory card without destroying it. I don't know what that will solve, exactly, but maybe I can have some peace of mind that nobody actually broke into the house and that Olly caused the damage—if that's peace of mind."

"Except—" West toyed with his straw "—someone attacked you at your truck."

She swirled her wine before taking a sip. "Could be unrelated."

From the corner of his eye, he noticed someone charging toward their table. His muscles tensed and then relaxed when he saw Jimmy approaching them. West said, "Great minds think alike."

"Sorry to bother you, Sheriff. I know you're off duty and all, but I just got a notification on my phone that the security at my shop was breached. If you don't wanna come, that's okay, but I thought since you're already sitting here, and we were just at the shop…"

As the hair on the back of his neck stood at attention, West exchanged a quick glance with Astrid. "Of course I'll come. Astrid, can you stay for the food?"

"No way. I'm coming, too." She grabbed her purse and pointed at the waitress, who'd brought the wine. "Taylor, can you box up our order? We'll be back to pick it up later."

"Sure." Taylor's brown eyes sparkled as her gaze bounced between Jimmy and West. Probably hoping for all the details when they came back for the pizza.

The Galvins had driven from their shop to Luigi's, and Jimmy waved them into the back seat of the car, where West's knees almost hit his chin. "What kind of security system do you have, Jimmy?"

"Camera, alarm, the whole shebang." He pounded a fist on the steering wheel. "I hope all they took was petty cash. I can't afford to lose my tools. Can't do business without my tools."

West asked, "Did you see any camera footage on your phone?"

"It's not live. I can look at it later, but all I got on my phone was the alarm indicating a break-in."

"When we get there, let me go first in case someone's still hanging around." West felt for the weapon beneath his bulky flannel shirt.

Jimmy pulled up to the shop with the alarm blasting

into the night. West doubted any thief would stick around through this noise, but he ordered everyone to stay in the car.

He jumped out, his hand hovering over his gun at his waist. He yelled, "Police! Come out with your hands up."

With the toe of his shoe, he nudged the door with the shattered glass. It didn't budge, so he yanked the sleeve of his shirt over his hand and pulled open the door, the loose glass tinkling to the ground.

The lights had gone on as part of the alarm, and West stepped into the shop's office. He squeezed behind the counter, noting the closed register. Didn't mean they didn't open it and take the cash. Jimmy and Alexa would have to check that.

He was more interested in the drone. He and Astrid had had the same thought the minute Jimmy reported the break-in.

"All clear?" Jimmy called out as his work boots crunched the broken glass at the entrance to the shop.

"Yeah, don't touch anything, though." West turned toward Jimmy, Astrid hovering behind him. "Hey, did you leave Astrid's drone in the office?"

"You're kidding me." Jimmy stormed into the office, past West to a workbench between the office and the garage. He smacked the workbench, and all the tools rattled.

"Damn! Astrid, I'm sorry. Someone stole your drone."

Chapter Seven

The world tilted for Astrid, and she grabbed the corner of the counter. What the hell was going on? Why did someone want that drone so badly, and how'd they know she'd brought it here?

She glanced over her shoulder at Alexa still sitting in the car, her face pinched, and then into the darkness beyond the small parking lot. Had someone followed her from the office? That meant whoever took the drone knew where she worked.

Russ knew where she worked. Did Russ's former associates know?

Jimmy looked up from the register and shrugged. "They didn't take the petty cash."

"Check your tools in the garage, Jimmy." West pointed at the door between the office and the work area.

Cocking his head, Jimmy scratched his chin. "Doesn't look like they got as far as the garage. The door's still locked, and nothing looks broken, unlike my front door."

"Have a look anyway to be sure. You got a pair of gloves to put on?"

Jimmy used a pen to open a desk drawer. "Alexa keeps a stash because she doesn't like touching anything with grease on it. I told her she's in the wrong business."

With a pair of blue gloves on his hands, Jimmy eased open the door to the garage and elbowed on the lights. He called over his shoulder. "At least the cars are still here."

As the door closed behind him, Astrid spun around to face West. "Someone broke in here to steal that drone."

"Looks like it." He dragged a hand through his dark brown hair. "Could it just be someone who wants a drone and knows you have this one? It's not like there's a handy drone shop in town where someone could buy one."

Astrid sawed her bottom lip with her teeth. "Someone is that desperate for a drone that they'd break into my house, follow me from work and then break into Jimmy's Auto?"

"And search your truck and assault you when you caught him in the act. Not to mention, he had the drone and dumped it."

Lifting her shoulders, she spread her hands wide. "Doesn't seem plausible, does it? But I don't know what else is plausible. I guess now that he has the drone, even though it's broken, maybe he'll stop harassing me and anyone else who has it."

"Maybe it's not the drone he wants but whatever it recorded." West narrowed his eyes. "Who had the drone before you?"

"Not sure. There are only three of us in this Discovery Bay office." She held up three fingers. "Me, Davia and Sumit Rao. I can call and ask them, but Davia seemed pretty sure the drone had been launched after I picked it up. Maybe the thieves took it from my house and did fly it. Then they dumped it in the trash and are worried we can use the footage to track them down."

"Okay." West put his finger to his lips as Jimmy came in from the garage.

"Nope. Nothing." Jimmy tugged on the bill of his Seahawks cap, the blue glove still encasing his hand. "Whoever it was broke my window, snatched your drone and took off. Last laugh on him, man. Guess he didn't know you took the drone here for repair."

"I guess not." Astrid pointed to the smashed window. "I know a guy who can board that up for you tonight."

Jimmy lifted up his hands, showing both sides. "I can do that myself. I'll just have Alexa go back to Luigi's for our pizza while I work on it."

West said, "I can get someone to come out here first thing in the morning to check for prints. My guess is you're going to have a lot of prints on these doors."

"I'm sure we are, Sheriff, but I appreciate the effort." Jimmy shook his head at Astrid. "I'm real sorry about that drone, Astrid. I can include it when I file a claim for my broken window."

"I'll ask Davia, but I don't think that's necessary, Jimmy." She gestured outside to Alexa, who hadn't budged from the passenger seat of the car. "Should we tell Alexa to go ahead and pick up the pizza and meet you back here?"

"Could you? She can give you a lift back to Luigi's. Sorry I interrupted your dinner, but I guess it's good that you know the drone was stolen."

"Yeah, great." Astrid raised her brows at West. "Do you want to go back to Luigi's with Alexa to grab our pizza or just call it a night?"

"Call it a night? I'm still starving." West patted his stomach, flat beneath his T-shirt, visible now that he'd unbuttoned his flannel shirt to get to his weapon.

She should've known he'd be carrying, but now she felt

even safer in his presence. Of course, Russ was always packing, and that hadn't made her feel safe at all.

"Okay, but I'd rather we just drive our cars the few blocks to Luigi's. No offense, Jimmy, but I don't feel like leaving it in front of your shop."

"I don't blame you." He hitched up his beefy shoulders.

Astrid delivered Jimmy's message to Alexa, after assuring her nothing in the shop had been stolen except her drone, and then she and West hopped into their own cars and drove back to Luigi's.

After she parked, she joined West on the sidewalk where he waited for her. As he reached for the door of the restaurant, Astrid said, "I don't really need more pizza. You can take the whole thing, and I'll eat some leftovers I have at home."

Stepping in after her, he said, "Did you forget about the second part of this…outing? You were going to show me the Misty Hollow property by the light of the moon. Now we have moonlight *and* pizza. Maybe we can make a pizza offering to the ghosts and ghouls who show up."

Butterflies swirled in her stomach. Had he been about to call this a date? Weird, how all their so-called dates so far involved break-ins and assaults.

She waved at Alexa, two ahead of them in the takeout line, and said to West, "You're serious about looking at that property tonight."

"Unless you'd rather not." He pulled the receipt for their food out of his pocket. "Then I'll take my half of the pizza and head back to my rental."

"The customer is always right, or at least almost always, but there's no way I'd let you put an offer on that property without seeing it in the daylight."

"No way I ever would." He smacked his receipt on the counter and turned toward the teenager taking orders. "We had to leave in a hurry, and…"

Astrid supplied the name. "Taylor. I asked Taylor to box it up for us, Reggie."

"Oh, right." He wagged his pen at them. "Large pepperoni, right."

"That's right." She stopped Reggie as he started to turn toward a counter behind him stacked with pizza boxes. "Can you throw in some paper plates and napkins?"

"Sure will." Reggie gathered their order, piled it on the counter and grabbed a couple bottles of water out of the fridge. "These are on the house for keeping our community safe, Sheriff Chandler."

"Wow, thanks." Two spots of color formed on West's cheeks, and Astrid nudged him as they carried their food outside.

"Reggie's gesture embarrassed you?"

"In Chicago, kids his age are more likely to spit on you." His jaw tightened.

Was that why he'd left the big city for a small-town job? West didn't seem like the type of cop that would be sensitive about his PR, but maybe that's why he settled here.

She stumbled to a stop when she reached her truck. "Should we go separately? You can follow me. My place is located closer to Misty Hollow than town, and I'd hate for you to have to drive all the way back here to drop me off, and I wouldn't want to do it for you, either. If we each take our own vehicles, we can peel off from Misty Hollow after the séance."

He chuckled. "I didn't agree to any séance, but I'll follow you over. Can I take the food in my car so I can have a slice on the drive there? I wasn't kidding about my imminent starvation."

She plopped the bag with plates and napkins on top of the pizza box in his arms. "Of course, but I'm taking one of the waters with me."

A few minutes later as she pulled onto the main road that almost made a circle around the island, she glanced in her rearview mirror to make sure West was following her. Could she really put this drone mishap behind her? Davia wasn't too upset about it, and if the thief got what he wanted from Jimmy's Auto, he'd leave her alone. At this point, she didn't care who took the drone and what he… or she…filmed with it.

But why had this person left it in her trash can in the first place and why so desperate to get it back now?

She planned to make a call to the Scout leaders tonight to check up on Olly. The kids weren't allowed to bring their phones but if they were feeling homesick, they could talk to their parents. Should she question him about the drone and ruin his camping trip?

As she approached the waterfall, she flicked on her wipers and her turn signal. West's indicator light mimicked her own, letting her know he'd seen her direction. She headed across the bridge, the falls to her right, creating a white cascade in the darkness and a silent roar through her closed windows.

When she reached the other side of the water, she turned left onto the road that curved around the river through Misty Hollow. No new subdivision existed out this way, and only a few vacation cabins dotted the landscape. Beyond Misty Hollow, the Samish Reservation sprawled through the forest.

But between the falls and Samish land lay the property of Shannon Toomey, the niece of the man who'd been slaughtered here, along with his entire family, by his preteen foster child, Addison Abbott. Terrible story. Great property. Possible client.

She switched on her high beams as she approached the Keldorf property, the light sweeping over the burned-out husk of the barn. She'd suggested her client tear down the barn, at least, but Shannon refused to do anything to the property she'd inherited from her father, murdered by the same person who killed her uncle. Not surprising she didn't want to set foot on the place.

She parked her truck, leaving her headlights glowing, and West pulled up beside her, his lights joining hers. When he exited his vehicle with a flashlight in his hand, she raised both hands to her face.

"Are you seriously expecting a tour by flashlight?"

"I'm assuming there's no electricity, so, yeah." He aimed the beam at the barn. "Should we start there?"

"There is no there. It's a burned-out barn, nothing left inside."

"I'd like to check it out." He scanned the light back and forth around the charred barn, and the flickers almost looked like flames racing across the wood again. "It's part of the history of the property. I read the PI and child psychologist who broke the case were in here when Brian Lamar aka Addison Abbott tossed in a Molotov cocktail."

She wedged a hand on her hip. "You really do know your Dead Falls crime history."

"Shall we?" He cupped her elbow with his hand, the flashlight in his other hand leading their way toward the barn.

Astrid's shoes crunched the ground beneath as she squared her shoulders. She didn't need West's assistance to reach the hulking ruin, but she'd take it.

The firefighters had hacked through the barn door, leaving a gaping hole that looked like a screaming mouth.

Astrid shook her head. Fanciful musings. She'd better get her head on straight about this property if she hoped to sell it. She doubted West's commitment to the property. He'd just wanted to...what? Get her alone?

She of all people knew you couldn't trust a cop just because he was a cop—or a sheriff.

West ducked into the opening and whistled. "This place is small. Imagine being trapped in here with a raging fire."

"That PI and child psychologist are friends of mine." She shivered. "I couldn't believe it when it happened. I keep telling the owner, Shannon Toomey, to knock this down."

"Would she mind if you got someone to do it for her? Maybe she just doesn't want to deal with it but would be okay if someone made all the plans for her."

"Maybe." Astrid pivoted and flung her hand toward the house, another eyesore. "I can't imagine the buyer keeping any of this. People died in that house...children."

West spun her around and planted his hands on her shoulders. "You head back to your truck. I'll check out the house on my own, and then we'll eat some pizza overlooking the waterfall."

With his flashlight pointed at the ground, the moonlight illuminated his strong features. In this aspect, it looked as if he could take on just about anything—including ghosts.

She dug her heels in the ground. "I'm the Realtor here. I'll show you around."

It didn't take long to show West the main house. He poked his head into the rooms, empty and devoid of furniture now. Someone had even taken the cages where Mr. Keldorf had kept his finches. Addison Abbott had killed the birds, too.

When he'd seen enough, they stepped outside and Astrid locked up the front door, a replacement for the one that had been hanging on its hinges.

She brushed her hands together. "You've seen the worst of it now. Wait until you see the land in the light of day. That's what I was hoping to showcase with the drone footage."

"Maybe Davia will buy a replacement sooner rather than later. She didn't seem too eager for you to get the old one repaired."

"No, she didn't." Astrid patted her rumbling stomach. "I'm hungry. Do you want to follow me to the lookout over the falls? We can sit in the back of my truck and feast... on the pizza."

"Lead the way."

She practically sprinted to her vehicle. Why was she such a sucker for men in uniforms? West wasn't even wearing his tonight, and she was still flirting with him.

She'd put it down to her relief over the drone. She hadn't been thrilled that someone had broken into Jimmy's shop, but at least her intruder had gotten what he wanted. What did she care if someone snatched that drone, launched it and broken it? If they were that distressed about getting it back, let them have it and leave her alone.

Cranking on the engine of her truck, she waved out the window to West. His headlights trailed after her as she headed back onto the road. Before crossing the bridge, she turned left toward the falls and backed her truck into the overlook.

As she lowered the tailgate on the truck bed, West pulled up beside her. She retrieved the pizza from the cab of his truck, and West scrambled from his SUV with a blanket under his arm.

"Might as well be comfortable." He shook out the blanket and spread it over the truck bed. Then he turned and took the pizza and plastic bag from her.

As she hoisted herself into the truck bed, he hunched forward to help her, putting one hand under her arm. Then he crawled toward the cab and patted the blanket beside him. "I already had a slice, so you get first dibs on the pizza. Is it good cold?"

Placing her hand on top of the box, she said, "Let's call it lukewarm."

He dug into the plastic bag for some plates and napkins, pulling out a bottle of water, too. He settled his back against the cab and stretched his long, denim-clad legs in front of him, crossing them at the ankles.

With the box flipped open on her lap, she tore off two pieces of pizza and dropped them onto a paper plate. Sliding the box onto his thighs, she said, "Your turn."

"The falls are beautiful at night." He waved his slice in the direction of the water cascading in a sheer drop from the cliffs above it. "You ever go in the caves behind it?"

"When I was younger." She took a sip of water from her bottle. "Most of the teens on this island make that pilgrimage. I know Olly will do it one day, and I shudder to think about it. If you venture too far out of the caves, the rock is slippery with algae. One wrong move…"

West chewed, his eyes narrowing. "Not to mention a few suicides and murders."

"Exactly." She wiped her greasy fingers on a napkin. "That's the problem with this island. Great beauty can mask great danger—or evil."

"In the big city, you don't even get the benefit of nature's beauty—just the cold, hard, nasty truth." He ripped off another bite of pizza with his teeth, and she shot him a side glance.

He seemed easygoing enough, but sometimes a sliver of anger or anxiety peeked through the nice-guy sheriff veneer. He'd moved to Discovery Bay from Chicago for a reason, but she didn't really want to hear those reasons.

That sat in silence for several minutes, eating and watching the waterfall, her shoulder occasionally brushing against his as she reached for her water. She hadn't spent a night like this with a man in a long time. And maybe it meant nothing to him, but it felt like a small patch on her heart.

She jumped when his phone rang, placing her hand on her chest. Trouble on the island would follow him everywhere. Sheriff Hopkins, West's predecessor, didn't let it faze him or change his lifestyle. He always had other deputies handle the calls and the people of the island while he glad-handed with the Discovery Bay mayor, council and developers.

When West finished murmuring into the phone, he brushed off the thighs of his jeans. "Little trouble out by the trailer park. Hope you don't mind, but I feel as if I need to poke my nose into every situation at this stage of the game."

"I get it. Thanks for suggesting this. It was a nice break."

She pointed at the pizza. "I insist you take the rest home. Like I told you, I had Luigi's last night and with Olly gone, I can't handle the leftovers."

"You don't have to twist my arm." He got to his knees and folded the paper plates before stuffing them in the plastic bag and dropping their napkins in after the plates. "I'll take the trash with me and get rid of it on the way."

"You don't have to twist *my* arm." She dusted crumbs from her hands over the edge of the truck bed and gripped the sides to push to her feet.

West hopped out of the truck first. Holding the pizza box in one hand, he extended his other to help her down.

She accepted the support and jumped to the ground. He kept hold of her hand a few seconds after she'd gained purchase on the gravel and gave her fingers a slight squeeze. Or had she imagined that?

"Thanks for coming out to the property to take my mind off that damned drone. I know you're not really interested in the Misty Hollow murder house."

"You never know." He winked. "I'm a believer in new beginnings. I have to be."

Gathering her hair with one hand, she tilted her head. "I think we all have to be."

He slammed her tailgate, and the sound echoed over the water. "You're okay to get home by yourself?"

She snorted. "I grew up here, Sheriff. You should be asking yourself that question. It's dark out by the trailer park."

"Yeah, I have a surefire GPS in my car. Thanks for the tour, Astrid." His eyes seemed to sparkle in the darkness, but it was probably the moon playing tricks.

With her truck facing the road, Astrid pulled out ahead of

him. He trailed her across the bridge, and then she watched him make a left off the bridge while she turned right. When had pizza and bottled water ever tasted so good?

She bit her lip as she glanced at the time on the dashboard. Olly would probably be sleeping by now, but maybe he'd appreciate that she hadn't called to check on him his first night. She'd call one of the Scout leaders when she got home just to make sure all went well on the first day. They didn't have to tell Olly she called.

Now that the thieves had stolen the drone from Jimmy's Auto, she felt confident that they were the ones who'd launched the drone and not Olly. She had no clue why they hadn't thought about the memory card when they dumped it in her trash. They could've saved themselves a lot of trouble.

She dabbled her fingers against the small lump on the back of her head—and could've saved her some pain.

She veered onto the long drive leading to Tate's cabin and parked behind his Jeep. She climbed out of the truck and locked it. As she stepped toward the porch, she jerked her head toward a rustling noise from the bushes beyond the firepit.

A dog had been nosing around the property for the past few weeks, but Olly had scared him off when he ran after him to see if he had a collar. Maybe the dog had come back. They'd left some food for him, which was gone the following day, but that could've been any wild animal.

As she crept toward the bushes, she called softly. "Come out, baby. I'm not going to hurt you."

She crouched down, and someone slammed her from behind, knocking her to her knees. With his hand splayed across the back of her head, gloved fingers digging into her scalp, he shoved her forward, face in the dirt.

She scooped in a breath to scream and choked on the dirt she inhaled. She twisted her body to throw off her attacker, and that's when she felt it—a sharp point to her neck.

In a raspy voice, her assailant whispered in her ear. "Give me the memory card for that drone, or I'll slit your throat."

Chapter Eight

West reached for his phone on the console, his fingers tapping along the surface, surprised Deputy Fletcher hadn't called him with the update after separating the couple and talking to the victim.

Easing off the gas, West glanced at the console. Then the cup holder. Then the passenger seat. He felt the front pocket of his flannel shirt, and then hit the steering wheel with the heel of his hand. His phone must've fallen out of his pocket in the back of Astrid's truck.

He hadn't heard it ring since he left her, so it wasn't hiding in this vehicle. Knowing two deputies were already at the scene, West made a U-turn. He wouldn't even have to bother Astrid. He'd leave his car running and grab his phone from the truck bed. It had to be there.

In less than five minutes, he passed the bridge and kept going. He turned on his high beams so he wouldn't miss the entrance to her cabin. Not wanting to disturb her, he dialed back on the headlights as he turned onto the drive.

His lights swept over her truck as he pulled up beside it. Leaving his engine idling, he pushed open the door and planted one foot on the ground.

A scream pierced the air, and his body startled to attention. "Astrid?"

A commotion erupted on the other side of the firepit, a thrashing of bushes and someone choking. With his flashlight in the car and the headlights illuminating a different area, he pulled his weapon from its holster. He stalked toward the noise, his eyes straining to see into the dark. "Who's there? Come out."

"West!" Astrid staggered toward him, her hand to her throat. "He went into the woods."

He lowered his gun and rushed toward her, catching her with one arm. He led her toward the driveway into the glare of the headlights. "Are you all right? What happened to your neck?"

Her eyes widened, and she looked like the proverbial deer caught by surprise. "My neck. It's fine. Go get him."

He eyed the bushes where she'd come from, not even stirring now. "I can't chase after someone in the dark... and I'm not leaving you here by yourself. Let's sit on the porch. Tell me what happened."

As he put an arm around her and led her to the house, she leaned into him, her body conforming to his. He settled her on the step and swallowed hard when he spotted another drop of blood creeping down her throat. He touched the dark red bead with the tip of his finger. "What did he do?"

Her gaze darted to the forest. "He held a knife to my throat. He shoved my face into the ground."

Pointing to the cameras above them, he asked, "Do you think your security cameras caught anything?"

She shook her head and sucked in a breath. "He attacked me where you saw me—in the dark. The camera may have recorded the scuffle, but I doubt we'll be able to see anything of substance."

Brushing his knuckles down her cheek to dislodge some dirt, he asked, "What did he want? Did he say anything?"

A sob caught in her throat, and she coughed. "It's the drone again. He wants the memory card."

West's heart skipped a few beats. "He just stole the drone and presumably the memory card with it."

"Presumably."

"Did you have a chance to answer him? Tell him you didn't have it?" A pulse throbbed at the base of his throat.

"I told him I didn't have the card, that it was in the drone the last time I had it." She clasped a hand around her neck. "That's when he pricked me with the point of the knife… and then you drove up."

"Thank God I did. I think I dropped my phone in your truck bed." He drove a knuckle against his jaw. "What the hell is going on with this drone? This isn't some teenage kids trying to avoid incriminating themselves. And what happened to the memory card? It was there when you got the drone from Davia, right?"

"Of course it was." She pressed the heel of her hand to her forehead. "Everything was fine when I checked it out from the office—memory card in the slot, no dents or scratches, in working order. All hell broke loose when someone broke into my house to steal it, changed their mind and dumped it in my trash can. I thought this was over with the theft at Jimmy's."

"This is far from over. Once I get you settled in the house, I'll have a look out there with my flashlight." He tipped his head toward the black expanse of forest. He had zero confidence he'd find anything with the beam of his flashlight, but he couldn't sit here and do nothing after Astrid had been attacked—again.

She grabbed a wooden post and pulled herself to her feet. "I'm not settling anywhere. I'm coming with you. I know the forest better than you."

"Just stick with me." He didn't want to let this woman out of his sight.

"Wait. What happened to the call?" She ran her fingers through her hair, dislodging dirt and bits of debris from the ground.

"It was a domestic. A couple of my deputies were handling it. I'm sure they're doing fine." He jerked his thumb over his shoulder. "If my phone is, in fact, in the back of your truck, I'll give them a call."

As she brushed off her clothes, he turned off his idling SUV and grabbed his flashlight. He used it to scan the bed of Astrid's truck, and the light caught his phone's screen. "It's here. Must've been fate or something that made me forget it."

When she didn't answer, he spun around, his heart thumping. When her front door opened, he nearly sagged against the bumper of the truck in relief.

"Did you find your phone?" She jogged down the front steps, stuffing her arms into another jacket, a flashlight of her own clutched in one hand.

"Yeah, it was there." He held up one finger. "Hang on."

While making his call to Fletch, he kept his eyes on Astrid as she approached the tree line of the forest. West explained the situation and verified that the deputies had the domestic in hand. Then he pocketed his phone and joined Astrid.

"All set on that other call." He aimed his light at the ground. "Did it start here? Did you see where he came from?"

"I came over here to investigate a noise. He approached me from behind, so I couldn't see him. He had gloves on, and his voice sounded muffled so I'm guessing he was wearing the balaclava again."

"You think it's the same guy from last night?" He crouched down, examining the signs of a struggle—disturbed dirt, broken twigs, a drop of blood.

"I hope so. I'd hate to think there's more than one guy after me." As she rose to her feet she listed to the side, and West caught her around the waist.

"You sure you're up to this? I can handle a quick look by myself." He dropped his hand from her hip and took a step back, aware that everything about her was drawing him in closer. "Or are you worried about being in the house by yourself?"

She hooked her thumbs in her front pocket. "I'm okay in the house. The security system is good, and there are several guns in there—which I know how to use."

"I don't doubt it." He gestured with his flashlight. "If you want to lead the way, I'll be right behind you."

"If he came through the forest, which I think he did, he would've come this way. There's a path that we use." She held a branch to the side for him, and he stepped after her.

"What noise got your attention? I'd think after last night's attack, you might've been a little more careful."

She stopped suddenly, and he plowed into her back. "Sorry."

Twisting her head over her shoulder, she said, "I honestly thought my stalker was done with me after he got the drone from Jimmy's. I was almost happy he stole the damned thing. How was I supposed to know he wanted more?"

"Yeah, I get it." He held up his hands. "But what was the noise that lured you out?"

"Rustling in the bushes. I thought it was a dog that's been hanging around here recently. Olly scared him off last time, just when I thought he'd come to us. He looks a little ragged, and I was hoping to lure him in to feed him and maybe get him checked out by a vet, see if he's chipped." She shrugged.

"Instead, you're the one who got lured. Did you tell anyone about the dog?"

Her head snapped up. "No. I mean, I don't know. I guess so. You think the person who held a knife to my throat knew I'd come out for the dog?"

"He *was* able to get you away from the house and the cameras."

Looking at the ground and scanning it with his light, West followed Astrid as she moved forward.

She snorted. "I think that was just luck on his part. What he probably figured was that I'd been lured into a false sense of security because I no longer had the drone—and he was spot-on. I just can't figure out why this person is interested in that footage."

"Too bad the video wasn't uploaded to a computer or phone. Then we'd be able to find out. You need to ask your coworkers about what they captured on the drone." His pulse jumped and he tugged on the waistband of Astrid's jeans to stop her. "Hold on. Watch your step."

She paused with her foot raised, wobbling on one leg. "Literally, don't take another step?"

"My flashlight picked up something shiny right by your left foot. Do you see it?" He flickered the beam of his light at the ground and saw the gleam of something silver in the dirt. "There it is."

Astrid hopped out of the way, and West squatted, pulling on a glove he'd taken from his car. He sifted his gloved fingers through the leaves and pebbles until they stumbled on a rectangular shape. He rescued it, bobbling a lighter in his palm. "It's a lighter. Looks new and shiny."

Astrid crouched beside him, her knee banging against his thigh. "I recognize that."

"This belongs to you or someone you know?"

"We probably have one in the house. Turn it over. It's from the Salty Crab."

West nudged the lighter over in his palm. Yellow print stamped on the blue background proclaimed the lighter as property of the Salty Crab. "It looks new, not like it's been sitting out here for months or even weeks."

"You think it could belong to my assailant? I was getting ready to read Olly the riot act for stealing the lighter from the house and bringing it out here." She huffed out a breath, and the hair hanging over her shoulder stirred.

"We'd better check your house for the lighter first. Let's turn back." He dug a baggie from the pocket of his shirt and dropped the lighter inside. "I can check this for prints if you're not missing your lighter."

She started to rise, and then grabbed his arm, her fingers digging into his shirt. "Did you hear that noise?"

His muscles coiled as he cocked his head. Some leaves crackled and a twig snapped. As he moved his hand over his holstered weapon, the intruder whined and panted. He dropped his hand. "That's either your stray dog, or there's a wolf out here."

"We don't have wolves on the island. The population was eradicated years ago, and they haven't returned." She hunched forward. "Here, boy. C'mon out. I'll feed you."

The whining stopped, and a raggedy shepherd mix emerged from a clump of bushes.

Astrid whispered. "There you are. You want food?"

"Maybe he'll follow us. Too bad I don't have any of the pepperoni on me." West rose slowly. "Let's start walking."

As they turned, the dog stiffened his posture, and his eyes gleamed in the dark. With its pointy ears and sharp muzzle, this guy could pass as a wolf.

They crept back toward the house, and the dog followed them warily, ready to bolt at the slightest provocation.

When they reached the driveway, Astrid held her finger to her lips. "I'll go inside and get some food. I have left-over chicken."

"I'm not sure he'll be happy with my company alone. I'll come with you. Then you can direct me to your security footage, so that I can check the attack."

They both walked into the house with the dog frozen just steps from the porch. Astrid peeled off toward the kitchen and jabbed her finger at her laptop on the counter. "I'll get you logged on after I grab some chicken for my new best friend."

He sat at the counter in front of the computer as she ducked into the fridge. She emerged with a plastic bag in her hand, and then leaned over his shoulder.

She entered her password and clicked on a logo in the lower-left corner of the desktop. "You can look through the footage here from tonight."

He called after her. "Leave the front door wide open, and don't go running after that mutt into the woods if he takes off."

"How dare you call him a mutt." She clicked her tongue, but she left her door open.

As he started to scroll through the security cam footage, West could hear her murmuring to the beast. If that dog had an ounce of sense, he'd follow that woman anywhere.

After several seconds, the dog's nails clicked on the hardwood floor of the cabin, and Astrid shut the door. "Got him inside. He's ravenous. Probably thirsty, too."

"At least someone got lucky tonight." West pushed the laptop away from him, stood up and stretched.

At her wide-eyed gaze and pink cheeks, he clarified. "I did not get lucky with that recording. If you're looking, and I was, you can see sort of a scuffle of movement and maybe even a figure, but I can't make out a thing beyond that. He knew about the security camera."

"Yeah, because he avoided it the other day when he broke the window on the side door." Astrid knelt next to a bowl, the dog sniffing her heels, and shredded the rest of the chicken into it. She filled another bowl with water and placed it next to the food.

Whatever reservations the dog had earlier evaporated. Maybe he witnessed the attack on Astrid. He gobbled the food and took a few laps of water.

"You plan on keeping him here, right?" West eyed the beast and his sharp teeth.

"I do. I'm going to take him to the vet tomorrow, see if he's chipped. If he belongs to someone, I want to return him to his family." She wedged a hand on her hip. "Why? You called him a mutt before."

"He is a mutt, but he's a mutt who might just have your back out here by yourself."

She rolled her eyes. "I'm safe inside."

"You're not safe outside—at night. I'll feel a little better if the pooch is here with you. He looks like he can hold his own."

"Why, thank you, Sheriff."

He didn't miss her Southern twang...or her irony. "And if you do have a gun here, maybe you should load it and keep it with you. With Olly out of the house, that should be safe."

"Olly knows how to use a gun and knows all about gun safety. He knows better than to touch a gun—loaded or otherwise."

A sharp pain lanced West's temple, and he jabbed two fingers against it to massage it away. "You should always be careful."

Narrowing her eyes at him, she said, "Of course."

"I'm going to take this to the station with me." He dangled the baggie in the air before shoving it back into his pocket. "Maybe we can get some prints from this guy. We're still going to process Jimmy's garage."

"Lock your doors, arm yourself and you—" West crouched before the dog and chucked it under the chin "—earn your keep around here and act like a watchdog."

"I'll give him some more food, so he knows where his loyalty lies." Astrid took a tentative step toward the door.

How did you end an evening that was not quite a date and had turned into another rescue mission? He could see himself out and didn't expect a kiss or even a hug—didn't mean he didn't want one, or both. Astrid's phone buzzed on the counter, saving them both an awkward farewell.

She gave it a cursory glance, and then did a double take. "It's one of the Scout leaders."

Her panicked tone gave him pause, and he planted his feet on the floor. She didn't need any more stress tonight.

"Porter? What's wrong? Is Olly okay?"

West watched as her face regained some of its earlier color, and her chest heaved. "Okay, okay. That's fine. Do you think he's scared or homesick?"

She chewed on a nail as she listened. "Yeah, put him on. I'll wait."

He raised his eyebrows. "Everything okay?"

"Porter, one of the Scout leaders, just called to tell me Olly requested a phone call with me." She tapped the display to put the phone on speaker and refilled the dog's dish with more chicken.

Olly's high-low voice squawked out of the speaker, filling the kitchen. "Mom?"

"How's it going, kiddo? Miss me?" Astrid kept her tone light, but the crease between her eyebrows told a different story.

"Mom, I have to tell you something. I wanted to tell you before, but, umm, I thought maybe you wouldn't let me go on the camping trip."

Astrid's blue eyes flashed, but West couldn't tell if they signaled anger or fear.

"Go on. I'm sure it's not as bad as you think. Nothing we can't figure out together and deal with when you get home. Spill it, kiddo."

West marveled at her vocal control as the emotions played out over her face.

Olly continued, dragging out his words. "You know the drone?"

Astrid's body stiffened, and she picked up the phone. "Yes, I know the drone."

"I took it, Mom."

Astrid shot West a quick glance and swallowed. "When did you take it?"

"Logan and I rode our bikes back to the house. I had my key, so I let myself in."

"Wait, wait, wait." Astrid waved her hand in the air, and the dog perked up his ears. "How'd you get past the camera? It didn't pick you up."

"Ah, I didn't set the security system when we left earlier, so I just got in with the key. We took the drone and rode our bikes to the cliff over Crystal Cove. Then we flew the drone." He ended on a hiccup.

"Olly." Astrid sank to a stool at the kitchen island. "You broke it? How'd it get in the trash can at home?"

"Didn't have time to put it away when we got back, so I put it in the trash. I-I didn't break that window, though. I don't know how that happened, Mom. I swear. I didn't know someone would break in the house and that you'd be looking for the drone right away. So I sneaked outside to get it."

"But you broke it, Olly."

"I didn't really break it, Mom. It wasn't us."

"Don't make things worse by lying to me Olly. I know the drone is broken. I tried to use it today."

"I know, Mom, but we didn't break it. That man broke it."

Astrid put her hand flat against her chest as West moved closer to the phone. "What man, Olly?"

"That man on the beach at Crystal Cove—the same day that body was found."

Chapter Nine

A seed of dread formed in Astrid's gut, and one look at West's face told her he had the same feeling. She couldn't quite pinpoint her fear yet, but Olly's confession had sent a ripple of it down her back.

She peeled her tongue off the roof of her mouth. "What man, Olly?"

"Just some guy on the beach. I flew the drone off the cliff and it kinda dipped down, and we couldn't see it anymore. I thought maybe it went into the water. Me and Logan didn't want to get too close to the edge, but we moved to where we could see the rocks. I heard someone yelling, and I think he hit the drone with something. By the time I got it back up, it was flying funny. Then I landed it and saw the dent in the side. I'm sorry, Mom. I'll pay for it and everything out of my own money."

West cleared his throat. "Olly, this is Sheriff Chandler. Can you tell me what time you were on the cliff with the drone?"

Olly hiccupped again, and Astrid figured her son was freaking out about the sheriff on the line.

"Wh-what? Am I gonna get arrested for flying the drone?"

"Not at all, Olly." West massaged his temples. "Can you remember what time you were there?"

Olly released a noisy breath. "Naw. It was after my mom dropped me at Logan's house and before we rode back to his house so his mom could take us to the Spring Fling."

West mouthed some words at her that looked as if he were asking her if she could figure out the approximate time. She could, and she nodded.

"That's okay. That's good enough. One more question for you, Olly." West closed his eyes. "Did you see the man who yelled at you or what he was doing on the beach?"

Olly paused so long, Astrid thought he'd hung up. She said, "Olly?"

"Yeah, um, no. I really didn't see him. Maybe the top of his head. He was wearing a black beanie though, so I didn't see his hair. We didn't see anything else."

West pinched the bridge of his nose. "Did he see you?"

"N-no. We ducked down 'cuz he was yelling something at us, but we couldn't understand what he was saying."

Rubbing her aching jaw, Astrid asked, "And that's when you went home? You went right home after that and dumped the drone in the garbage can?"

"Yeah. Sorry, Mom. I felt bad, so I wanted to tell you. But we didn't break the window, and it wasn't broken when we were there." Olly yawned loudly.

"Okay, well, don't worry about it now. Have fun at camp, and we'll figure out how you're going to repay Davia for the drone. Got it?"

"Yeah, yeah. G'night. Bye, Sheriff."

Porter got back on the phone and assured Astrid that he'd see Olly back to his tent.

When Astrid ended the call, she placed the phone back

on the counter and stared at it. Without looking at West, she asked, "What are you thinking?"

He didn't answer right away, and her throat closed. She peeked at him from beneath her eyelashes. "Just say it. It can't be any worse than what I'm already thinking."

"Olly and Logan may have stumbled upon Chase's murder without knowing it. The killer saw the drone and struck out at it, hoping to bring it down, hoping the drone video wasn't going to someone's phone. He didn't mention hearing any popping sounds though, so he couldn't have heard the actual murder."

She clutched her neck with one hand. "When he couldn't knock down the drone, he followed them or somehow figured out where Olly lived and has been trying to get the drone back ever since."

"Thought he hit pay dirt in Jimmy's garage only to discover the video card wasn't in the drone."

"Where is it?" Astrid crossed her arms and dug her fingernails into her biceps. "That card was in the drone when I took it from the office. I checked."

"Maybe when the guy smashed the drone, the card fell out. We know he whacked the sleeve where you insert the card. It might be on that beach…or in the water."

She lifted her shoulders to her ears. "How do we tell *him* that? How far is he willing to go to find it? He broke into my house, attacked me at my truck, stole the drone from Jimmy's and went at me again in my own driveway."

"The good news is, if we find that card, we've solved Chase's murder."

"If we find it before he does." She rubbed her arms, feeling cold ever since Olly's call. "What if he thinks Olly and Logan got a good look at him?"

"He must know by now they didn't. They weren't the ones who reported Chase's body on the beach. The killer has to figure that two boys would call in a dead body." He cocked his head, his hazel eyes probing her face. "Why? Do you think Olly is lying about not seeing the man?"

She pinched her chin as she watched the dog dip his head for more water. "I don't think he was lying about that, but he seemed a little off to me—like maybe he wasn't telling me the whole truth and nothin' but."

"Kids lie all the time." West dashed a hand through his hair. "I-I mean, sometimes they lie about stupid stuff."

Astrid widened her eyes. "Do you have children?"

"Uh, no." He raised one hand. "But I was one."

"Well, I hope it's something minor like he ate too many s'mores tonight and got a stomachache and not that he witnessed a murder on the beach." She aimed a toe at the dog, collapsed at her feet. "What do you think? Should I let him stay inside tonight?"

"He looks like the type of dog that's not going to let anything get past him. Keep him inside…for security. And where's that weapon you were talking about before? One of your brother's guns in the safe?"

"Oh, no. I have my own. It's under my bed right now. When Tate, my brother, is home, I leave it in his safe, but when I'm here by myself I like to keep it handy." Astrid swallowed. She didn't want to reveal too much to West about her previous life with her ex stalking her. It would probably make him turn and run the other way, which maybe he should do, anyway.

"Arm your security system when I leave and keep your dog and your gun close." He crouched down and rubbed the dog's neck, prompting him to thump his tail on the kitchen floor without opening his eyes. "What are you going to name him?"

"I don't want to name him anything until I make sure he doesn't already have a home and a family looking for him. I haven't seen any lost-dog posters, though, and he's been hanging around here for a few weeks."

"Too bad he wasn't hanging around when your intruder dropped by."

"I hadn't fed him yet. Now he's going to have some fur in the game." She knelt beside West and scratched the dog behind his ear. "Are you going to look for the video card on the beach?"

"Might as well give it a try. Should probably check the bluff where Olly launched the drone, too. It could be anywhere." West pushed to his feet and wiped his hands on the thighs of his jeans. "I need to wash my hands. If I touch my face after touching dog, I'm gonna have itchy eyes."

"Help yourself." She waved her hand at the kitchen sink. "Do you have any leads in the Chase Thompson case? Any…witnesses, besides that drone, prints, weapons, clues?"

"A few things have come up." He squirted some lemon hand soap into his palm and lathered his hands under a stream of water. "I think the motive is most likely drugs. Chase was a small-time dealer. Almost everyone knows that. The question is if he graduated to the big leagues and got in over his head."

"So this person who's after me is most likely not a local, or at least not a Dead Falls resident. He may be local to Discovery Bay." She gave the dog a final pat before standing up next to West as he ripped a paper towel from the roll to dry his hands. "You'll keep me posted, won't you? I mean, about the memory card."

"I will keep you posted." He balled up the paper towel and held it up. She pointed to the drawer that pulled out for the kitchen trash can. After he tossed it, he brushed his hands together. "You going to be okay here tonight on your own?"

"As you mentioned—" she aimed a finger at the dog, lounging at her feet "—I'm not going to be on my own."

"You should come into the station tomorrow for another report about tonight's events. Might as well have a legal trail of all these incidents. Just in case."

"In case he kills me one of these times?" She'd tried to keep her voice light but she'd failed, and a rash of goose bumps pimpled her arms.

"Don't even joke about that, Astrid. I…we'll keep you safe." He chucked the dog under the chin and made a move toward the front door.

She followed West, and the dog's nails clicked on the hardwood floor as he trailed after both of them. Looked like the mangy mutt already didn't want to let her out of his sight.

She stepped out on the porch with him. "Thanks for the pizza and for coming back here—even if it was for your phone."

"And thanks for showing me the place at Misty Hollow. Not sure it's for me, but when I see something I like I'll let you know so you can rep me."

"You haven't seen anything you liked so far?"

"Oh, I wouldn't say that." He clumped down the steps of the porch and strode to his SUV.

With her heart beating faster than usual, she watched

him get into his vehicle and lift a hand in a wave. She waved back and slipped into the house. After setting the security system, she leaned against the door and eyed the dog, who thumped his tail once.

"Do you think he meant me, boy?"

THE FOLLOWING MORNING, Astrid awakened to a whine close to her ear. She jerked back, pulling her pillow in front of her as an inadequate shield. One glimpse of the wet nose at the edge of the bed, and memories of last night flooded over her.

She traced the small scratch on her throat with her fingertip. What would've happened if West hadn't forgotten his phone? The sheriff always seemed to be in the right place at the right time—for her.

At a second, more insistent cry, Astrid rolled out of bed and patted the dog's head, his fur rough and wiry beneath her fingers. "I hope you're house-trained and didn't have any accidents last night. Of course, that would totally be my fault."

He trotted after her as she went downstairs. She slid open the back door, and the dog dashed outside. He made a beeline for the woods and disappeared.

She sighed, leaving the sliding door open behind her. Maybe he was destined to be a wild dog. She'd try to lure him back later with more food, but she made a note to pick up a leash and collar so she could take him to the vet—if he'd let her.

At least there had been no more incidents last night. She twisted her head over her shoulder, taking in the wide-open door, and pivoted to close and lock it. The dog would be able to find his way back to the house if he wanted. He'd been sniffing around for weeks.

As she stuck a bowl of oatmeal in the microwave, her cell phone rang. Her shoulders tensed when she saw the unknown number. "Hello, this is Astrid."

"Astrid, this is Michelle Clark. I'm calling about the Misty Hollow property you have listed for sale."

Astrid opened and closed her mouth like a fish, grateful the client couldn't see her. They hadn't even posted aerial pictures of the property yet. Maybe she wouldn't need those drone pics after all. "Um, yes, of course. Would you like to see it? I have to warn you. It's a fixer. The owner didn't want to make any improvements before listing, but the asking price reflects that."

She clamped down on her lower lip. She was supposed to be talking up the property, not leading with all the bad.

"Understood, and I *would* like to see it. Are you available today? I'm on Dead Falls Island just for a few days and would love to have a look before I leave."

Astrid pulled back her shoulders. Time to get serious. "And I would love to show it to you. I'm available this afternoon. I can pick you up at your hotel—or wherever you're staying."

"That would be perfect. Let's make it three o'clock, and you can pick me up at the Bay View Hotel. Is that convenient for you?"

"I'll swing by there at three. Please call me if anything changes. Otherwise, I'll see you then, Michelle."

Astrid ended the call, clapped her hands and twirled around the kitchen. She'd make it up to Davia by selling this property in record time.

She spent the morning at the sheriff's station to make

a report about the attack last night. She'd craned her neck around the small station, but West was nowhere to be found.

She also stopped by the pet store and bought a collar and leash to corral her stray. While in the shop she perused the lost animals board, but nobody had posted missing a brown-and-black shepherd mix.

Her final stop before picking up her client was the office. She'd already called Davia that morning with the bad news about the stolen drone, but her boss hadn't seemed concerned at all. She had her eyes on a new toy, one that would send the video straight to a phone or computer.

Astrid sailed into the office and gave Davia a thumbs-up. "I'm showing the Misty Hollow property in about thirty minutes."

Sumit kicked his legs up on his desk, crossing them at the ankles. "Since you broke our drone, you'd better make good."

Astrid made a face at him. "You're just jealous because Shannon picked me."

"That dump?" Sumit snorted. "You can have it, sister, and good luck."

"Michelle Clark called here, asking for you. I gave her your number." Davia held up her hands, fingers crossed. "Let's hope she's serious, unlike the sheriff."

"How'd you know the sheriff wasn't serious?" Astrid flicked through some files on her desk just in case Michelle wanted to make an offer on the spot.

"Mmm, I just got the impression he wanted to spend a little more time with you." Davia winked broadly.

Astrid dropped a folder. "Are you kidding?"

"No. Are you clueless? Didn't you two go out to dinner?"

"If you call pizza at Luigi's out to dinner, and we were interrupted by Jimmy, anyway."

"That's a date in my book." Sumit crossed his hands behind his head. "In fact, that's a high-end date in my book."

"I didn't realize you ever got past coffee date one with any of your online honeys. Maybe you should start with Luigi's, and you'd make some progress."

"Did the new sheriff make progress with you?" Sumit formed pistols with both hands and pointed at her.

"That's enough, children." Davia pointed to the whiteboard. "Astrid, don't forget to put your details on the board."

"Of course." Anxious to get off the topic of her and West, Astrid walked to the whiteboard and uncapped a marker, the alcohol smell invading her nose. She wrote down the address of the property, the time of the showing, Michelle's name and phone number. The agents in the office never showed a property without notifying everyone else on this board…except last night. Sheriffs could be the exception, although Astrid knew more than most that a uniform didn't exempt the wearer from bad deeds.

"Maybe we won't even have to list this one." Davia held up a finger and answered her cell.

As Davia sweet-talked a client and Sumit grabbed his own call, Astrid slid all her files into her bag and waved to them on her way out of the office. Before she started the engine of Tate's Jeep, she texted Michelle that she was on her way.

Traffic on the main road crawled with tourists and outdoor enthusiasts, hitting the island for spring break. The hotels, restaurants, bars, bait shops and tour guides loved it, but the rest of the locals grinned with gritted teeth. The tourists were a necessary evil, but they did buy summer cabins on the island. Of course, if the big development company Bradford and Son had its way, they'd be looking at even more traffic.

She turned into the parking lot of the Bay View Hotel and spotted Michelle in front immediately, black hair pinned into a chic chignon at the nape of her neck and oversize black sunglasses tempering the glare of the overcast day.

Astrid glided up to the curb and rolled down the window. "Michelle? I'm Astrid Mitchell."

"Oh, you're good." She grabbed the handle of the passenger door. "How'd you know it was me?"

Astrid caught a whiff of Michelle's exotic perfume as she slid onto the leather seat. "You didn't look like you were waiting for a fishing or camping tour."

"Ah, yes. City girl." Michelle waved a hand over her black slacks and white blouse. Tapping her high heel, she asked, "I suppose these are unpractical for touring the property, aren't they?"

"There are a lot of unpaved areas of the property." Astrid wrinkled her nose. "I'd hate for you to ruin those beautiful shoes."

"Give me one moment?" Michelle held up one perfectly peach-colored manicured finger. "I'll run back inside and make a few adjustments."

"Take your time."

As she watched Michelle stride purposefully back to the hotel entrance, not one single wobble on those heels, Astrid tried to place the woman's accent. It was as exotic as her heavy perfume that still hung in the car.

A text notification came through on her phone, and she bit the inside of her cheek as she read West's message. He hadn't had any luck locating the drone's memory card on the beach or the bluff.

She texted him back that she'd have a look in and around her trash can on the side of the house. If Olly had stuffed the drone back in its box out there, maybe the card fell out.

By the time she put her phone down, Michelle was making a beeline for the Jeep, a pair of dark jeans encasing her long legs and a pair of low-heeled boots replacing the heels. She hadn't changed her white blouse or jacket, so she still looked elegant.

Michelle pulled open the door. "Better?"

"I think you'll be much more comfortable." Astrid plugged her dying phone into the car's charger and pulled back onto the road, apologizing for the traffic. "It's not much better in the summer, but the visitors are more spread out. Are you looking for a permanent residence or a vacation spot?"

"Vacation spot. My husband recently discovered boating and with that fishing." She rolled her dark eyes. "I told him the only condition was that I had to find or at least approve of the place."

"That sounds like a good deal."

Michelle's large, square-cut diamond glittered as she fluttered her hands around the car. "We make our compromises. Are you married?"

Astrid licked her dry lips. "Divorced."

Michelle clicked her tongue. "Ditto for me. Twice before Charles. So, we know, marriage is all about compromise."

Marriage was also about your husband not being a criminal and a thief. Astrid allowed a smile to curve her lips as she nodded.

It sounded like Michelle and her husband had money,

and that's all that mattered to this sale. The more money, the better. She couldn't have a penny-pinching client who would balk at the level of renovations needed to make this property habitable—and to erase its ghoulish past.

They chatted easily on the ride, and Michelle gasped as they approached Dead Falls. Her big diamond glistened like a drop of water from the falls as she put a hand to her mouth. "Can you stop on the bridge for a second so we can admire the view?"

"I can't stop on the bridge, but there's a lookout point to the right once we cross."

With no cars behind them, Astrid crawled across the bridge so Michelle could gawk. Once across, she turned right and backed into the turnout where she and West had parked last night. If he hadn't gotten that call, would the night have taken a romantic turn?

Michelle rolled down her window and stuck her head out. "This is lovely. I suppose there's no view of this from the property, is there?"

"I'm afraid not. It's not on an incline, but the good news is that you don't get as much moisture there as you do in this area."

"You're right." Michelle drew her head back inside the car and patted her hair. "This could give major frizz."

Astrid slid a glance at Michelle's perfect coif as she pulled back onto the road. "Just another five minutes."

She drove onto the property with less trepidation than last night. The structures didn't look as spooky during the day, but she'd have to tell Michelle the whole sordid story.

She pulled up and parked in the same spot as last night with a view of the main house and the charred barn, the other buildings visible in the rear. As she put a hand on

Michelle's arm, she said, "We need to discuss something before I show you the property and you potentially fall in love with it."

"Oh, sweetie—" Michelle flicked her long fingernails as an accent Astrid still couldn't place in person touched her words "—I know all about the storied history of this place. My husband, Charles, and I compromise, but he would never allow me to check out a place without doing his research. So, yes, I'm aware of the family massacre that took place here many years ago, and that the perpetrator, who'd gotten away with it, remained on this island and started killing single mothers in some sort of weird retribution."

"Whew." Astrid skimmed her fingertips across her forehead. "I'm glad to get that out of the way. I'm not looking forward to that part of this sale."

Michelle scooted her dark glasses to the edge of her nose. "Weren't you scared?"

"Me?" Astrid pressed her hand against her chest. "Why would I be scared?"

"He was going after single mothers, wasn't he?" She arched a perfect dark eyebrow.

Astrid jerked her head back. She'd told Michelle she was divorced but hadn't mentioned Olly. "How do you know I'm a single mom?"

Michelle pulled down the visor and tapped the picture of Olly wedged under the mirror. "I saw this earlier. He looks just like you."

"Oh." Astrid cracked a smile. "That's Olly. He's ten."

"Cute boy." Michelle readjusted her sunglasses. "So, weren't you afraid when Brian Lamar started killing single moms?"

"Not really." Astrid put her hand on the door handle and pulled it, cracking open the door. "The two women he murdered were involved with drugs, so a lot of us figured that was the link."

"So sad." Michelle shook her head. "I have a son who's an addict. No fun."

"I'm sorry to hear that." Astrid pushed open the door. "Now that the bad stuff is out of the way, let's focus on the good. Shall we?"

Their shoes crunched the gravel and dirt as they approached the main house. It didn't take long to show Michelle the house, as she'd already admitted they'd be tearing it down and rebuilding a new structure.

Michelle took a longer time surveying the aspect of the rest of the property and the outbuildings—its positioning, its views, the property line. The history didn't seem to faze her at all.

She had been snapping several photos with her phone and raised it for another shot. She cursed and dropped the phone in her bag. "I knew it was going to die on me. Charles will kill me if I don't get pictures of everything. Can I borrow your phone for a sec or tell you what pics I want?"

Patting her purse, Astrid said, "Mine was dying, too. I left it in the car on the charger, even though it's not charging now."

"I'll run and get it, sweetie." Michelle called over her shoulder. "Jeep unlocked?"

"It is, yes."

While Michelle returned to the car to get Astrid's phone, Astrid inspected the burned-out barn, the wood still giving off an acrid odor. She'd have to talk to Shannon again about knocking this down. It created an eyesore for any-one immediately coming onto the property.

Astrid jumped when Michelle came up behind her.

"Lost in thought?" Michelle handed Astrid's phone to her.

"Just thinking how I'm going to convince the seller to tear this down. If she doesn't mind, I might just hire my own crew of locals to do the job and write it off as the cost of doing business." Astrid navigated to her camera with her thumb. "What do you need?"

At Michelle's direction, Astrid took several photos of the property and texted them all to Michelle's number.

"Thank you so much." Michelle plucked the phone from her purse, seemed to remember it was dead and dropped it back inside. "Those should satisfy Charles."

"If he'd like to have a look himself, I'd be happy to make myself available."

Michelle answered, "Let's see what he thinks, first."

As they walked toward the car together, Michelle said, "It's certainly big enough for what we want. The views, even though we can't see the falls, are fantastic. There's so much we could do with this."

"I agree. It hasn't been utilized to its full potential. It's just waiting for the right owners to come along and—" Astrid snapped her fingers "—reimagine it."

"I like that notion." Michelle tripped to a stop, her head bending forward. "Oh!"

"Are you all right?" Astrid put a hand on Michelle's back.

"Did you drop this, sweetie?" Michelle crouched down and rose with her hand cupped.

Astrid peered into her palm and sucked in a quick breath. "I-it's a memory card."

Chapter Ten

A smear of blood from Naomi Wakefield's ragged fingernail, with its chipped blue polish, marred the sleeve of her hoodie as she folded her arms tightly against her chest.

West dragged his gaze away from the red spot and focused on Naomi's face, black smudges beneath her eyes, the tip of her nose a cherry red.

He cleared his throat. "When was the last time you saw Chase, Naomi?"

"That morning before he…died." She glanced over her bony shoulder into the forest. "You're not gonna tell anyone I talked to you, are you?"

"I already told you. There's no reason for me to go public, but if you provide some material evidence that can help convict someone, you'll need to testify in court. But let's not go there right now. I'm just trying to establish a timeline for Chase, and you seem to be the last person who saw him alive."

"Other than the guy who killed him." Her bloody thumb went back to her lips, and she bared her teeth to tug at her cuticle.

"What time did he leave your place?" As he waited for her answer, he took inventory of the sad woman before him—her pasty complexion, her jiggling leg, the random twitch of her left eye. Could the murder of her boyfriend prompt her to go to rehab for her meth addiction? Was that rock bottom enough for her?

Tucking a lock of stringy blond hair behind one ear, she said, "Maybe eleven o'clock, like in the morning. I just got up."

"Did he tell you where he was going or who he was meeting?" He nudged the can of Coke he'd brought for her just to get her to stop gnawing at her own flesh.

"No, but it was big. He was excited. I don't think this was the first time, though. He got his hands on some primo stuff a few weeks before. He'd been selling it around the island, even gave me a little taste of it." She spread her thin lips into a smile that stretched across her narrow face and revealed teeth too yellow for a woman her age.

Looked like he'd given Naomi more than a taste. "So, you think he was getting more of this product from someone?"

She hunched her shoulders and squeezed the can, denting one side. "Maybe. He didn't tell me nothing."

"Did you ever see Chase with another phone?" Chase's phone had been missing, but they were working with his carrier on getting the call record for it.

"He was always on the phone. He coulda had two. I accused him of using a burner to call his side chick." Her dull brown eyes flashed for a second. "Did you find his phone?"

"He didn't have it on him." Chase Thompson had more than one woman on call? West scratched his chin. "Did Chase have another girlfriend?"

"Seemed like it to me, but he said he didn't. He was a liar." She slammed the Coke can on the picnic table.

If Chase was seeing another woman, maybe West could

get her name out of Naomi. He coughed. "Could he have left his phone at your place?"

"Not that I know of. I could call it when I get home and listen for it ringing." She rubbed her hands against her thighs. "Can I go now?"

"You can go." He slipped her his card. "If you remember anything, give me a call. We can meet out here again if you like."

"Okay." She stuffed the card in the back pocket of her skinny jeans. "Can you wait here for a bit while I hike back to my car? I don't want anyone seeing you follow me out."

"Go ahead." He fished his phone from his pocket, which had been buzzing with texts. "Keep an eye out for Chase's phone, Naomi, and if you can think of the name of his other girlfriend, let me know."

"All right." She swiped the can from the table and hit the path through the forest back to her car.

West blew out a breath. That woman needed help. Maybe with Chase out of her life, she'd seek it.

He glanced at his phone, and his pulse jumped when he saw some text messages from Astrid from just a few minutes ago. He knew she'd been into the station to file a report about the incident last night, but he didn't know what she'd been up to the rest of the day—not that he had a right to know.

He tapped his phone to call her, and she answered before the first ring finished.

"West, do you have a minute? I'm not interrupting you, am I?"

Her breathy voice jacked up his senses. If she'd been attacked again, he'd have to put 24/7 security on her. "Just finished with something. What's up?"

"I found a memory card."

His protective instincts settled down, but his interest piqued. "*The* memory card?"

"That's just it. I don't know if it's the one from the drone, but what are the odds I randomly find a memory card on the ground?"

"That's what happened?" He pushed up from the picnic bench and paced toward the trail. "Where was it?"

"It was out at the Misty Hollow property. Isn't that weird? You and I were just there last night. We didn't see anything then, but of course, it was pitch black out there."

"Does it look like it could be from the drone?"

"I guess so. It's a standard memory card."

"Wait. Where are you? You haven't looked at it, yet?" He glanced back at the picnic table to make sure he hadn't left anything there, and then plowed onto the trail. He'd given Naomi enough time to get out of here.

"No. I'm sitting in the parking lot of the Bay View Hotel in town. Just dropped off my client. I was showing her around the property when she saw the memory card on the ground."

"The drone wasn't anywhere near there, was it? Misty Hollow isn't very close to where Olly was flying it over Crystal Cove and the cliffs above it."

"Doesn't mean Olly and Logan couldn't have ridden their bikes out that way." She huffed out a breath. "If I find out he went over the bridge and was in Misty Hollow, he's in big trouble—bigger trouble."

West broke through the short trail to the road, where his SUV sat solo. He hadn't expected to see Naomi's car even if he hadn't given her enough time to leave first. She'd been so nervous she'd parked on a different stretch of road and hiked in farther than he did.

"I'm coming over to your place. Do you have an adapter on your computer to read the card?"

"I'm sure I can find one. Tate has a lot of that sort of stuff around. If not, I can take it to the office. We've been transferring the drone images to our computers there with an adapter."

Sliding behind the wheel of his vehicle, West said, "I'm on my way. If you get there first and you can't find an adapter, let me know and I'll swing around to your office instead."

"Okay, I'll meet you there."

On the drive to Astrid's place, West got on his speakerphone with the station to take care of the day's business. Finding and arresting Chase Thompson's killer topped his list of priorities, but Astrid's stalker came in at a close second. He couldn't shake the feeling that his two most pressing matters were related.

He pulled up to the cabin and parked to the side, behind her truck. She must've taken her brother's Jeep to show the property, and he'd gotten here first. He'd use his time to check the woods where her attacker had disappeared last night.

He'd sent a deputy out today to have a look, but he hadn't found anything out of the ordinary, nothing indicating someone had made a quick escape through the trees. No prints on the lighter.

He slammed his car door and made his way to the tree line, looking at the ground on his way. Just like last night, he saw the area where Astrid had scuffled with the intruder—along with shoe prints from the deputy.

He ducked into the woods, his head on a swivel as he eyed the bushes and branches for any ripped clothing or threads. How had the guy made his getaway? Had he parked a vehicle somewhere in a clearing? He didn't have a handle on the layout of the forested area yet, but most of it was connected. He could've crashed through the trees from where he'd met Naomi and probably wound up here.

The path beneath his feet led deeper into the woods with a cut-through to the road. Astrid's attacker must've gone that way, back to…wherever. He couldn't have continued through the forest, unless he was some kind of mountain man living off the land.

West froze at the sound of heavy breathing filtering through the leaves. A whine came from the same direction, and West's tense muscles relaxed when he realized the heavy breathing was actually panting.

He gave a low whistle. "Is that you, boy? Did you get away again?"

The dog wasn't about to show himself to West, and he made a quick and stealthy retreat.

The sound of a car engine had him giving up the search and turning back toward the house to meet Astrid. When he stepped out of the forest, he almost ran into her.

She yelped and smacked a hand to her chest. "You scared me. Why are you creeping around in the bushes?"

"Hoping to find something we missed last night, or my deputy missed this afternoon."

"Did you?" She wedged a fist on her hip.

"Just the mutt. Did he escape again?"

"He stuck around last night inside with no complaint, but the minute I set him free this morning, he took off. I'm hoping to lure him back with some more food tonight.

I bought him a bag of dog food and a dish. I also got a leash just in case he'll let me domesticate him for a trip to the vet."

"I think he's domesticated but scared of something. I heard him but couldn't get him to show himself."

Narrowing her eyes, she said, "How'd you know it was him?"

"Unless your attacker is panting and whining, my money's on the dog."

"Okay." She rolled her shoulders. "Do you want to help me bring the dog food inside? Then I'll have a look for an adapter for this card. I have it in my pocket. I can't believe the memory card would be literally at my feet, but what else could it be?"

"Could be lookie-loos taking videos of the Misty Hollow Massacre site. You don't even know how long it's been sitting there. We could've easily missed it last night in the dark."

She screwed up one side of her mouth. "Who's taking video with an old camcorder instead of a phone? I don't think there are that many devices around that still use the SD cards."

"SD?"

"Secure digital."

"They're still in use." He ducked into the back of the Jeep and hoisted a forty-pound bag of dog food over his shoulder. "Oof! You're expecting the stray to come and stick around for a while, I see."

"I hope so. Olly's been after me to get a dog. I've been putting it off, but if this guy's going to fall into my lap, it must be a sign."

He followed her up the porch and watched as she unlocked the dead bolt on top before sliding the key into the lock on the door handle. She bumped the solid door with her hip, and he anxiously peered over her shoulder into the cavernous living room.

Pointing toward a long door in the kitchen, she said, "You can put the dog food in the pantry for now. I'm going to my brother's office upstairs to see if I can find something to read this card."

West nudged open the pantry door with the toe of his shoe and heaved the bag to the floor. His gaze darted around the well-stocked shelves. Astrid could hole up in this house for weeks without going out, if she needed to. He shook his head. Nobody was going to lay siege to Astrid in her home. He had to stop worrying so much about her...and her son. This job wasn't some kind of redemption gig for him.

"Found it!" Astrid's voice carried down the stairs on a note of excitement.

West closed the pantry and strode into the living room just as she jumped off the last step, waving an adapter between two fingers.

"I knew Tate would have something. I can just insert this into my laptop and slip the card into the slot." She woke up her laptop on the kitchen island and shoved the adapter into a port on the side of her computer.

The laptop beeped in recognition of the device, and Astrid pulled the memory card from her pocket and thumbed it into the slot.

West held his breath as the blue circle spun on the display. He eked out a tiny puff when the drive appeared on the monitor. Astrid double-clicked the icon, and then double-clicked on the unnamed folder.

When the folder opened showing a blank space, they both physically deflated. Astrid stated the obvious. "There's nothing there. It's empty."

West swallowed his disappointment. "Could the contents have been deleted already?"

"I suppose." She closed it and clicked on it again with the same result.

He shouldn't be giving her false hope that this thing was over. That road would only lead to more danger. "Although I doubt someone would delete the video and then drop the memory card where you could find it."

"U-unless they wanted me to know they found it." She drew her bottom lip between her teeth.

"Because they're such great guys, and they don't want you to worry after they attacked you not once, but three times?" He squeezed her shoulder to soften the blow of his words. "Look, I'm not sure what that card was doing at Misty Hollow—probably just some kind of weird coincidence. We're getting closer every day to solving Chase Thompson's murder and when we do, the people behind the attacks on you will have more to worry about than drone footage that may or may not show them committing murder."

"Are you?" She crossed her arms and wedged her fists against her body. "Getting close to finding his killer?"

They didn't have any witnesses or clues, but they had a good idea about the motive. "We're almost certain this is a drug deal gone bad, given Chase's ties to the Discovery Bay narcotics trade. It's a matter of making our way up the chain of command. Every drug cartel, big and small, has its hit squad—the people who provide the muscle."

Astrid hunched her shoulders as if to ward off a chill,

even though they were inside her kitchen. "I'm aware of how it works."

He raised his eyebrows in anticipation. Was she going to tell him all about her ex and his involvement in the drug trade as a crooked cop?

He paused through an awkward silence. She still didn't trust him.

Rubbing his hands together, he said, "We know how it works, too. These people killed someone in the middle of the day on a beach, a known drug dealer, who'd recently gotten a new supplier. It won't be hard to track them down. They're not that smart—but they are vicious."

She snapped the lid of her laptop closed with a sigh. "Which is not good news for me. I wish I could just post a sign on my door and car stating that I don't have the damned card."

"And I'm sure their question would be, if you don't have it, who does? Where did it go?"

Tapping her toe on the tiled floor, she asked, "Did you search for it already in all the likely places?"

"I did." He shook his head. "Like looking for a particular grain of sand on the beach. The tide could've taken it out if it fell out there. If it fell out on the cliff or on Olly's way home, it could be anywhere—windblown, buried under debris, crushed into the road by a tire."

"Yeah, well, I'm sorry for your investigation, but I hope that's exactly what did happen, and I hope those goons figure it out before they come at me again. If I had it and watched it, I would've turned it over to the police already." She flicked a lock of hair over her shoulder. "Not too smart, these drug dealers."

"I concur." He smacked his palm on the counter. "I'm

going to let you get back to your evening. I won't stop searching for it, and you keep things locked up tight out here. Watch yourself going to and from your vehicle."

Astrid puffed up her cheeks and blew out a breath. "Thanks for coming over. I probably should've checked the card before I called you."

"I'm glad you called. If it were the memory card from the drone, I would've wanted to be in on the first look." He took a step toward the front door and hesitated. "You sure you're going to be okay here tonight? I can have a deputy cruise by a few times."

"If someone's in the area, sure, but I know how thin the ranks of the DFSD are. I don't want to take away from a real crime in progress." She brushed past him on the way to the front door. "I'll be fine. This is a good security system…when it's activated."

His arm buzzed where she skimmed it with her own, and he followed her to the entryway. She disarmed the security and swung open the door, peering at the flood-lit drive.

Stepping onto the porch, he said, "Don't go outside at night."

"Ugh." She shoved her hair out of her face and closed her eyes. "I thought I was done living like that."

The tingling in his arm reached his fingertips, and he reached out to trace the line of her jaw. As her lashes fluttered, he ran his thumb along her bottom lip and her mouth parted at his touch. He ducked his head, but the sharp whine of a dog startled them both, and they sprang apart.

She blinked rapidly. "H-he came back."

"Sounds like it." West stretched his lips into a smile. That dog had the worst timing—and the weirdest bark.

The sun had just set, and West squinted through the dusky glow to locate the direction of the dog's yelps and whines.

Astrid squeezed his biceps. "He sounds like he's hurt, doesn't he?"

"Sounds like something's wrong." West whistled through his teeth. "C'mon, boy."

With a stealthy creep, the dog emerged from the other side of the Jeep, out of the woods where West had spotted him before. His eyes glowed in the low light, and West coaxed him with a whistle into the brighter lights fanning from the house.

Astrid descended the two steps of the porch and crouched. "Come. Do you want to eat?"

The dog's ears pricked at the sound of Astrid's voice, and he loped toward her, his tail wagging stiffly, the fur on his back standing at attention.

West breathed out a soft sigh. "He looks okay."

"He has something in his mouth." Astrid snapped her fingers. "That's right. Come over here and show me what you have."

As the dog trotted into the light, Astrid gasped. "He has blood on his face and mouth. He *is* hurt."

"Be careful. He might snap at you."

"You wouldn't do that, would you?" She made kissing noises, and that dog was no dummy. He walked toward her, the light fur on his face stained red with either his blood or the blood of the unfortunate creature he had in his mouth.

"I think he might've killed something. Don't try to take it from his mouth. He might bite you."

"Me and him are like this, now." She crossed her fingers as she took the last few steps to meet the dog, still emitting strange, feral noises from the back of his throat.

Astrid cupped her palm beneath the dog's mouth, pink drool hanging from his jowls. "Let me see what you have. Drop it."

With a shake of his head, the dog opened its maw, releasing his treasure in the center of Astrid's hand.

Astrid screamed and jerked her hand back.

As the dog wagged his tail and grinned, West scrambled down the steps to gawk over Astrid's shoulder at the dog's prized possession.

Astrid covered her mouth. "I-is that a finger?"

West grabbed a stick and nudged the fleshy item. His gut twisted. "Yep. It's a finger with blue-chipped nail polish."

Chapter Eleven

Gagging, Astrid staggered to her feet and folded her arms across her stomach. "Where did he get that? It looks… fresh to me."

West swore under his breath. "I'm pretty sure I know whose finger that is and if I'm right, it's definitely fresh."

"You do?" Astrid jerked up her head while the dog whined, still looking for kudos. "How can you identify someone from a finger?"

"Because I was just talking to its owner—Chase Thompson's girlfriend. I noticed the blue fingernail polish. Of course, I could be wrong."

"Good boy." Astrid patted the dog on the head. "Then it's Naomi Wakefield's. I've seen them together when she's strung out."

"Yeah, I'd say that's most of the time." He blocked the dog from picking up finger and said, "Can you get me a plastic bag? We can't let this beast mutilate the finger anymore. It's evidence. Then I'm calling a team out here to search for her body."

Astrid stopped, one foot on the first step of the porch, and twisted her head around. "Body?"

"You don't think old Spot here up and ripped off Naomi's finger while she was living and breathing, do you?"

He nudged the dog with his knee and hovered protectively over the finger.

"I was kind of hoping that maybe she's injured, and the dog took advantage of her. I don't want to think about the rest." She spun around and pushed through the front door. On unsteady legs, she grabbed a plastic bag from a drawer in the kitchen.

If Chase's killers murdered Naomi Wakefield because they suspected her of passing information to West, would they ever give up on their assumption that she had the video from the drone? But if she did have it, she'd have already turned it over to West and if the footage did ID the killers, they'd be in trouble by now. They had to assume she didn't have it. Didn't they?

She gripped the edge of the counter with one hand, the other pinching the plastic bag between two fingers, and took a deep breath.

When she went back outside, she waved the baggie at West, on the phone and giving orders. He nodded his thanks and took the bag from her. He ended the call as he crouched down, a glove on one hand.

He shook open the baggie and picked up the dog's prize with two fingers. He dropped it in the bag and sealed it. "I have a couple of deputies coming out to do a search of the forest between where Naomi and I met and where she left her car. I'm assuming she was ambushed on her way to her vehicle."

"Why? Did Naomi tell you anything about Chase?"

"Not much." He scratched the dog on top of the head. "Except she did mention she suspected Chase had another girlfriend."

"Doesn't sound like much to me. Maybe they just didn't like her talking to you."

Driving two fingers into his temple, West said, "We were careful. Nobody knew we were meeting. I made sure nobody was following me, and I figured she'd do the same because she was paranoid about being seen with me."

"It's not your fault." She touched his forearm, braided with veins and tensile strength as he clenched his fist.

West's voice had taken on a strange quality—not quite guilt but maybe regret. Cops weren't generally responsible for the safety of witnesses, unless some kind of commitment had been made to testify. God knows, her ex didn't care what happened to his witnesses, but West appeared to be an entirely different breed of law enforcement officer—at least so far.

He squeezed his eyes closed for a brief second and then seemed to emerge from his funk. "I'm going to use the dog before the team gets here to see if he can lead me to the body. I don't want any more animals carrying off pieces of it."

A chill touched the back of Astrid's neck. "The drug trade on this island is getting ridiculous. Sheriff Hopkins turned a blind eye too many times because he didn't want to be bothered."

"Or he was afraid." West lifted one shoulder. "Let's go, boy."

The dog stood at attention and pointed with his nose at the forest. West held the bloody finger, now encased in plastic, in front of the dog's face, and the dog took a few tentative steps toward the tree line.

West followed, but the dog stopped and whined, pinning Astrid with a hopeful look.

She twisted her lips into a frown. "He wants me to come along."

"You don't have to. I can wait for the team if the dog doesn't want to lead me to Naomi. I'm sure it's not going to be pretty."

"I'll close my eyes." She pulled her sweater around her and joined West. "Let's go, Sherlock. Show us the body."

As Astrid joined West, the dog trotted ahead of them, his nose alternately to the ground and up in the air. She lengthened her stride to keep up with West and the dog, who now seemed like a heat-seeking missile.

They tromped deeper into the woods, and West tried to hold back branches for her as they veered off the beaten track.

Panting, she pointed through a thicket of trees. "The road is going to be visible pretty soon. Did you meet with her on the other side?"

"I did. I parked north of the road, and I believe she parked on this side. She probably would've been safer coming and going with me. Probably would've been safer at the station. But she insisted on the cloak-and-dagger stuff." West smacked at a bug on his arm. "She must've been followed. They probably had their eyes on her as soon as they killed Chase."

"Poor girl. I don't mean to speak ill of the dead, but Chase Thompson was bad news for everyone he touched. If he was cheating on Naomi with someone else, that woman had better watch her back, too."

"Naomi thinks Chase may have had a burner phone for his affair. We're going to have to thoroughly search their place."

"Thought you would've done that already." Astrid tripped over a root and grabbed for West's arm.

He steadied her with a hand on her back. "We did, but we'll go through it again. We didn't find a phone on his body, and we still haven't gotten the records from the phone company regarding his activity. We..."

The dog started barking furiously ahead of them, and West whistled to call him back.

"I appreciate his efforts, but we don't want the mutt disturbing the crime scene any more than he has."

Clutching her stomach with one hand and standing on her tiptoes, Astrid, asked, "You're sure he led us to her body? Maybe it's just body...parts that he found."

"One way to find out." He squeezed her shoulder. "You can stay here."

"I-I can't really at this point." Some hard core in her heart overcame her trepidation about seeing a dead body. If this crime was linked to her and that drone, she had to see with her own eyes what these people were capable of.

The dog appeared before them, his eyes gleaming, his nostrils flared.

Astrid touched the soft fur on his head. "Let's go."

"Me first." West stepped in front of her and picked his way over the forest bed, following the dog. He stopped suddenly and held his hand behind him. "It's exactly what we expected. You don't need to see it."

As West got on his phone, Astrid sat heavily on a fallen log and pulled her hood up and around her face. This was all way too close for comfort. How did she keep getting pulled into drug violence when she never even touched the stuff?

The dog sat beside her, thumping his tail against the

log, and she stroked his back. "You're a good boy, Sherlock. Are you going to protect me from these maniacs?"

"Sherlock." West joined her on the log. "Is that what you named him?"

"Seems fitting, doesn't it?" She tipped her head toward the small clearing where she still refused to look. "Don't you have to do something...over there?"

"The less I do right now, the better. Deputies were already on their way from when I called them before. I just called in the precise location, and they'll be arriving soon with a forensic kit. We need to collect some evidence in the area."

"H-how was she killed?" Astrid swallowed, and then tried to take in a full breath of pine-scented air.

"Same way as Chase—bullet to the head, execution style, but not before they did a little damage." West clenched his jaw, and a muscle twitched. "Looks like they wanted some information out of her. That finger Sherlock brought to us? Let's just say, he's not the one who detached it from Naomi's hand."

Astrid curled her own fingers into fists, as if to protect them. "Do you think that's what they have in store for me if I don't give up that memory card?"

"You don't have it."

"Exactly." She jerked her thumb toward the clearing. "She probably didn't have anything to give them, either. Didn't stop them from chopping bits off of her."

A siren whooped from the road on the other side of the clearing, and West pushed up to his feet, smacking dirt from the seat of his khaki uniform pants. "Time to get to work. I'll have one of the deputies walk you back to your place, or better yet, drive you and Sherlock back."

She'd been kind of hoping West would do those honors himself, but he had another murder investigation on his hands.

She stood up next to him on wobbly knees. If he noticed her nerves, he didn't call her out. "Okay, I'm going to get home and call my son before they turn in for the night or make s'mores or whatever they're doing out there. Some nice, normal activity that doesn't involve dead bodies and severed fingers."

A bright spotlight illuminated the area, and Astrid squinted at the figures emerging from the source. One called out. "Sheriff?"

"On the other side of the clearing. Be careful where you're stepping. I'll come to you." West turned to Astrid and ran his hands down her arms, ending with a light clasp of both her hands. "Lock up when you get home and invite Sherlock inside with you. Give him a reward for his hard work. Don't worry about what's going on out here. These murders are drug-related, and the perpetrators have to know that if you had video of Chase's murder from that drone, you would've turned it over by now. I'm confident they'll leave you alone and at the rate they're killing people, we'll catch them. Are you ready?"

"For?" She didn't move a muscle for fear that West would drop her hands.

"I'm going to walk you across the crime scene to the road. Keep your head averted."

She nodded, and he took her hand, leading her to the clearing. She kept her gaze pinned on the deputies gathered at the edge of the crime scene, just outside the yellow tape they'd strung between the trees.

With a wink just for her, West turned her over to a

young deputy with instructions to drive her and Sherlock back to her place and wait until they both went inside. The deputy discharged his duty faithfully, and Astrid marched straight to the kitchen after she'd barricaded herself inside the cabin.

"West is right. You deserve a reward and a clean up." She rubbed Sherlock's chest as she wiped the blood from his face with a wet rag. Then she went to the pantry to open the bag of dog food. She dumped a healthy amount into a bowl and added some water to it. As she set it down, he cocked his head at her. "Don't look at me that way. I'll give you some of my chicken, too."

Missing her son and her brother, Astrid kept up a one-sided conversation with Sherlock as she made a quick dinner for herself. She carried her plate of chicken and rice to the island and dropped a few pieces of meat into Sherlock's bowl. "Is that better, Sherlock?"

While she ate, she checked her phone for any information about Naomi Wakefield, but the media hadn't caught on yet. She pushed her plate away and called Porter Monroe's cell phone.

He picked up after the first ring, probably already fielding calls from anxious parents. "Hello, Astrid."

"Hi, Porter. Everything good?"

"Yeah, the kids seem to be having a good time…"

She caught her breath at his pause. "But?"

"No, no. Olly's fine. Went fishing today and caught a few for lunch. The boys went swimming in the lake, and we had inner tubes for the river. Good times."

"You sort of hesitated at the end. Is something going on?" She tried to steady her breathing. Olly was safe and having fun.

"Olly seems out of sorts—nothing serious, nothing like depression or anything like that. No acting out. Just a little quieter than I'm used to seeing him."

Astrid chewed on her bottom lip. "Could be, you know, things with his father."

"I'm aware of the situation and figured his subdued demeanor might be the result of that." Porter huffed out a big breath. "Do you want to speak with him? He won't be singled out. Quite a few of the boys have already talked to their parents."

"Sure, if he wants to talk to me."

"Hang on."

Astrid jiggled her leg up and down while she waited through the silence. She whispered to Sherlock. "Maybe I should tell him about you to lift his spirits."

"Hey, Mom."

"Hi, Olly. Heard you caught some fish today." Even she could hear the false brightness of her tone. She grimaced at Sherlock.

"Yeah, it was a good spot. We cleaned 'em and ate 'em, too."

"Sounds yum." She cleared her throat. "Are you having fun?"

"Yeah, sure. Almost all my friends are here, except Ryan. He had to visit his grandparents in like Idaho or someplace."

"I'm sure he's having fun, too." Did Olly's tone sound flat? Tense? Or had Porter just put that idea in her head? She stared at Sherlock for a second.

"D-did you get that drone to work?"

Astrid bit her bottom lip. It wasn't like Olly to obsess over something he did wrong or bring it up. He usually tried to sweep that sort of thing under the rug. She had no intention of telling him that someone stole the drone from Jimmy's Auto.

"No. Davia's not going to bother. She wanted a newer, shinier model, anyway." She drummed her fingers on the counter. "That still doesn't mean you're off the hook, bud. I'm thinking you should do a little cleanup around the office when you get back—empty trash, do some shredding, whatever Davia needs."

"Okay. I can do that." The raised voices of kids almost drowned out his final words. "Gotta go, Mom."

He ended the call before she could respond or ask to speak to Porter. She tapped the cell phone against her chin. "That whole break-in must've upset him more than he let on, Sherlock. Don't know why he's so interested in that drone. Wish he'd stop asking about it, so I don't have to keep lying."

The phone buzzed in her hand, and she tapped it. "Did you forget something? Like, love you, Mom? Miss you?"

The silence on the other end of the line caused a cold ripple along her spine, and she pulled the phone away from her ear to check the calling number—not Porter's, unknown.

She licked her dry lips. "Hello?"

A woman's voice, both hushed and gravelly at the same time, answered. "We know you probably don't have the memory card from the drone, Astrid, but if you find it before we do and turn it over to that sheriff, you're going to suffer more than that junkie Naomi did, more than your traitorous ex will when we find him. By the way, where's Olly?"

Chapter Twelve

A fist squeezed her heart, and Astrid almost tipped off the stool. Gripping the edge of the island, she growled, "None of your damned business. You people must know by now I don't have the drone's memory card."

The woman hissed like a cat. "Because you would've turned it over to the sheriff by now. But you're looking for it, aren't you?"

"No. Th-the only reason I wanted to find it at first was to hand it over to you. I don't care about Chase Thompson. I don't care about your activities. And I don't care for law enforcement." Astrid locked her jaw. At least that's how she felt before Sheriff West Chandler landed on the island with his hot bod and hazel eyes and do-gooder spirit.

The woman clicked her tongue. "The amount of time you're spending with the sheriff puts a lie to that."

"That's because you've been stalking and attacking me. What do you want me to do? I told your…colleague the other night I didn't have it and didn't know where it was."

"You know what else tells me you're lying, Astrid?"

Astrid swallowed against a throat that felt like sandpaper. She managed to croak one word. "What?"

"When you did find a memory card, you ran right to the sheriff. You didn't hide it or destroy it. You called your buddy, Sheriff Chandler, to turn it over to him."

The knots twisting in Astrid's gut tightened. "I-I...did you plant that there to test me?"

"You failed." The woman's voice dropped, and she whispered. "Don't fail again."

Before Astrid could make an excuse or assure the woman she had no interest in the drone footage, her tormentor ended the call.

Astrid jumped from the stool, startling Sherlock. She cruised to every door and window in the place to double-check the locks and pull the drapes tight. They were watching her. They knew everything she'd been doing. Now they knew Olly's name and the fact that he was gone.

How long would it take them to find out where he was? A friendly woman pretending to have a son of her own asking about activities? There were enough tourists on the island for the spring holiday that someone like that could blend in with the rest.

Why had she mentioned Russ? Were these the same people who had been involved in her ex's case? The drug trade was a small network, just like any other profession. They probably knew each other. Were they actively trying to find Russ? She couldn't help them with that, either.

After checking her security system, she sank to the kitchen floor next to Sherlock, where he'd fallen asleep next to his bowl. They'd only want to get to Olly to punish her. She wouldn't give them any reason to do that.

She'd stop looking for the drone. She'd stop looking for that memory card. And she'd stop seeing West Chandler.

THE MORNING AFTER Astrid's stray found Naomi Wakefield's dead body, West woke up with a racing heart and a pounding headache. He stuffed some pillows behind his back, closed his eyes and took several deep breaths.

When the guilt tried to worm its way into his brain, he tried to shift his thoughts to all the people he'd helped throughout his career—at least that's what his therapist told him to do. He had the scenarios lined up in his head— saved a baby from a burning car, talked a husband out of slicing his wife's throat, foiled a gangbanger's hit on his teenage witness.

Those scenes marched through his brain, behind his closed eyes. But why did they always end with a dead four- teen-year-old holding an unloaded gun? Would Naomi's lifeless body join that image in his nightmares?

West cursed and rolled out of bed, tripping over a box. He had to spend a day unpacking and getting his rental house sorted out. He couldn't live out of boxes forever.

As he made his way to the kitchen to prepare some breakfast, he glanced at his phone. He'd had a late night at the crime scene and didn't want to disturb Astrid when he'd finished. He breathed easier when he didn't see any messages or phone calls from her. Everything must've been quiet at her place last night.

He'd resume his search for the drone's memory card, but he knew anything could've happened to it by now. Maybe a bird carried it away and tucked it into a new nest.

He cracked some eggs into a pan and turned on the heat. As he pushed the eggs around, he scrolled through his phone with his thumb. He nearly dropped his phone into the pan of eggs when he saw a text message from Naomi. How'd that happen? They'd found her phone in her pocket last night and as far as he knew, it was safely checked in to evidence. Nobody in the department would play a joke like that.

He turned off the eggs and tapped the message to read it. She'd texted him a name—Monique. Could that be Chase's chick on the side? The date and time stamp on the message showed today's date about ten minutes ago.

He made a quick call to the station to make sure that Naomi's cell phone had been checked into evidence and waited while the deputy on-call looked to verify it was still there. West let out the breath he was holding when the deputy returned with the good news.

Naomi's phone was password protected, so they'd turned it off. They'd let tech handle getting into the phone, but this message made that task even more urgent. Naomi must've put that message on a timer or something. Had she planned to clear out of town before Chase's killers could make the connection between her and their information about Monique?

He dumped the eggs onto a plate and forked big clumps into his mouth as he hunched over the counter. He washed it all down with a few gulps from the orange juice container.

He showered and dressed in his uniform in record time and hit the road to the station, which sat a little outside of the town. He would've expected the sheriff's station to be smack-dab in the middle of the main drag, but it occupied some prime real estate instead. A savvy sheriff in the past had some odd priorities—maybe that was before the drug trade hit Discovery Bay hard, and the deputies were still dealing with cats up trees and fights between neighbors. The good old days.

By the time he reached the station, he was craving caffeine and stopped at the coffee pot on his way to his office without even putting down his bag.

"Late night?" Deputy Robard raised her eyebrows at him.

"Chase Thompson's girlfriend, Naomi Wakefield."

"I heard." She shook her head. "You know that saying—lie with dogs, get fleas, or something like that. Chase was a dog."

"Yeah, Naomi was in a bad way when I talked to her." West dumped some vanilla creamer in his coffee and swirled it with a stir stick.

"Did she at least give you anything? They must've been worried that she would or did, but you'd think they would've killed her *before* she talked to you, not after."

"She didn't give me anything at the time, except the suspicion that Chase had another girlfriend. She couldn't tell me a name, but she gave it to me later, after she died." West patted his front pocket where he'd stashed his phone.

Robard's eyes popped open. "How'd she do that?"

"Text message."

"Before she died?"

"After."

"What the..." Robards took a gulp of her own coffee. "That's some voodoo right there."

"I think she sent the text on a time delay." He leveled a finger at her. "Don't you work tech?"

"In a pinch. Discovery Bay hosts a tech unit for all the islands, but I've been to the training."

"Perfect." He jerked his thumb toward the hallway. "Do you think you can get into Naomi's phone and find out if that's what happened? I don't want to assume the message is from her if it isn't. Could be someone else trying to trick us, send us down the wrong path."

Rubbing her hands together, she said, "Phone hacking. One of my favorite things to do."

"Go ahead and check it out of evidence and have a look. I'm mostly interested in if she delayed sending that message to me, but of course, have a look at her other messages, too. I'd be interested in her communications with Chase before he was murdered. We never found his phone, and his carrier hasn't sent us his records yet."

"Yeah, that always seems to take a while around here. I'll get right on that, sir."

West carried his coffee into his office and logged in to his computer. He pulled out his cell phone and dropped it on his desk. Still nothing from Astrid. A buzz of apprehension flitted in his ear, so he texted her. She'd been the victim of several attacks this week. Why wouldn't he check up on her?

He watched the message until it showed *delivered*, and then continued watching for a response. He sat up in his chair when he saw the three little dots flicker on his display. They disappeared. Reappeared. Disappeared again.

Huffing out a breath through his nose, he turned to his computer. She probably had a lot on her plate today if she planned to take in Sherlock. He hoped she would. That dog showed some real smarts last night and seemed to have bonded with Astrid already.

A few minutes later, Deputy Robard popped her head in his office, holding up Naomi's cell phone in its leopard-print case between her gloved fingers. "Got it, boss. I'll give it a whirl and let you know what I find."

"Thanks, Robard."

She cocked her head. "You can call me Amanda, boss."

"Right, Amanda. Thanks."

He'd have to get used to working in a smaller department where he'd be dealing with the same deputies every day on every case.

He spent the next thirty minutes reviewing the ballistics reports from Chase's and Naomi's murders. Same weapon had done them both, but Chase's murder had been more clinical, more businesslike. Naomi's had seemed more personal. Could she have known her killer? Maybe the murderer was just hell-bent on taking a little revenge because Naomi had spoken to him.

As he stretched his arms over his head and eyed the dregs of his coffee, Amanda tapped on his open door. Her bright eyes signaled good news.

"You got in?"

"I did." She tipped the phone back and forth. "She did a delayed send on that message to you. So that was her, for sure. Not much between her and Chase in the days leading up to his murder, but I'll type up a transcript, so you can go over it yourself."

"Good work, Amanda. I'm going to start looking for this Monique. Chase may have been keeping her a secret from Naomi for obvious reasons, but his friends might know something more about her. Unless Naomi timed another delayed text message to me with more information, the name is all I got."

"You've been to the Salty Crab?" Amanda wrinkled her nose as she said the name of the dive bar. "That was Chase's hangout. If Dead Falls Island has a wrong side of the tracks, it's all centered at the Crab."

"Yeah, I've had the pleasure, and it's my first stop.

The medical examiner hasn't performed a postmortem on Naomi yet, so I have time this afternoon." He grabbed his jacket from the hook behind his desk. "Let me know if you find out anything else of interest on Naomi's phone about Chase's activities or this other woman."

"Will do, boss."

He pushed to his feet behind his desk. "Uh, you can call me West."

"I'll stick with boss, for now." She gave him a mock salute.

He smiled to himself as he grabbed the keys to his SUV. The DFSD had gotten a bad rap under its previous sheriff, but he'd found nothing but dedicated, hardworking deputies so far. He planned to start with Chase's murder and clean up the drug trade on this island. Its proximity to the Canadian border had made it a hub for drug trafficking between the two countries, but he was determined to shut it down.

He drove into town and parked down the street from the Salty Crab. He didn't want to drive away business from the bar by taking up residence there. As he walked to the Crab, he glanced at his phone, and his stomach did a little dive when he saw no response from Astrid.

When he entered the bar, he blinked several times to adjust to the darkness. The bartender stood out, illuminated by the neon signs behind him flashing off the mirror, and he crossed his beefy, tattooed arms when he caught sight of West by the door. Different guy from the one the other night, who'd brought him towels for Astrid.

He was hoping the same bartender would be working, but maybe this one would be as helpful as the other guy. West bellied up to the bar, a few stools down from the only other patron seated there, and rapped his knuckles on the sticky wood top. "Coke, please."

The pumped-up guy swiped a wet cloth across the bar in front of West and tossed down a cardboard coaster, advertising a local brew. "I know you don't just wanna Coke. You got something to ask me about Naomi?"

West tipped his head. "What's your name?"

"Jackson Cross, and Naomi was a regular here along with her old man, Chase. The two of them…" He shook his head, his shaggy hair brushing his shoulders.

West asked, "Trouble?"

"Everyone knew Chase was dealing." Jackson held up both calloused hands. "But not in here, man. I wouldn't allow it. I had to keep riding him to take his business outside. Naomi wasn't much better." Jackson crossed himself and kissed a heavy cross dangling against his chest, along with several other chains. "RIP."

"Do you know if Chase was cheating on Naomi? Seeing another woman?"

Jackson selected a glass from a tray, scooped some ice into it and shot a steady stream of soda into it from a nozzle. He set it down on the coaster and dropped a straw on the bar next to it. "Can't say for sure. He could've had a couple of side chicks. You know when a guy's carrying product like that, the ladies who are that way inclined come running."

"Was someone named Monique one of those ladies?" West took a sip of his Coke, watching Jackson over the rim. The bartender's face didn't change.

"Monique? Doesn't ring a bell." Jackson scratched at his beard.

"I know Monique." The man sitting to West's right, hunched over a beer, turned his head.

As Jackson wandered off to help a customer waving him down at the end of the bar, West turned to fully face the skinny man next to him, slumped over the bar. "What's your name?"

The man shoved a mess of greasy blond hair behind one ear. "Benji Duran."

Benji didn't offer his hand, still wrapped around his sweating mug, so West kept his resting on his thigh. One quick move or one strong gust of wind, and this guy might topple over. "Benji, I'm Sheriff Chandler."

"I know who you are." Benji took a gulp of beer and wiped the foam from his mouth with the back of his hand. "You gonna find out who killed Chase and Naomi?"

"We're working on it." West took another sip of his drink. Benji didn't seem like a man you rushed. "So, you know Monique?"

"Oui, oui." Benji snorted at his own cleverness, and a fizz of beer bubbled from his left nostril.

West pulled his gaze away from Benji's red-tipped nose and focused on his watery blue eyes. "Is Monique really French, or are you just riffing on her name?"

"Naw, she's French. She's got a French accent and all. French Canadian." Benji grabbed a cocktail napkin and blew his nose.

Had he been one of Chase's customers or was booze his particular poison? Could he trust what came out of Benji's mouth? If he hoped to get anything out of Benji, he'd have to be specific.

"Did Monique hang out with Chase?"

"Yeah. Chase got all the fine ladies."

"Is Monique still here on Dead Falls Island?"

"I think so. I saw her yesterday."

West did the calculation in his head as he tipped his glass again. Monique was here a few days after Chase's murder. "Where did you see her? Does she come here to the Salty Crab?"

Benji shook his head and finished off his beer. Tapping the side of his glass, he asked, "You buying?"

"Jackson." West held up his hand in the air. "Another brewski for my man Benji."

West had to bite his tongue while Jackson swept Benji's empty mug from the table and replaced it with a fresh, frosty one, topped with foam, with Benji watching his every move with rapt attention, his tongue lodged in the corner of his mouth.

With his new beer in front of him, Benji closed his eyes and took a sip.

Benji's craving satisfied, West cleared his throat. "So, did you see Monique here at the Crab?"

"She never comes here."

West ground his back teeth. "Is that because Chase came here with Naomi?"

"Monique was too good for this dive." Benji flicked a hand dismissively at his surroundings. "She made Benji take her to the Harbor Restaurant and Bar where she drank dack…dack…" Benji gave up and took another slug of beer.

"Daiquiris?"

Benji tried to snap his fingers and failed. "Thas right."

"Is that where you last saw Monique? The Harbor?"

"I don't go in there. Overpriced beer."

West took a deep breath. "Where'd you see her, Benji? Do you know where she stays on the island?"

"Saw her on the street, man. Just walking. Tried to say hey, but she acted like she didn't know me."

"What does she look like?"

"Fine."

West rolled his eyes at Jackson, hovering nearby, and the bartender took pity on West.

Jackson smacked his dish towel next to Benji's drink, making Benji jump in his seat. "Benji, is Monique that black-haired woman who smokes those cigarettes with a cigarette holder? Calls everyone *mon cher* or some crap like that?"

Benji's chin dropped to his sunken chest. "Never called *me* that."

Jackson plowed on with more patience than West possessed. "That's her though, right? Long black hair. Wears that little rabbit fur jacket? Smokes like a chimney."

Benji mumbled. "That's Monique."

West mouthed a thank-you to Jackson, who shrugged.

"Dude's been coming in here for years. You eventually figure out how to talk to him once he's a few sheets to the wind." Jackson tugged on his beard. "So, I have seen her around. Just didn't know her name was Monique, and I never saw her with Chase. Didn't seem his type, but I suppose she was slumming to cozy up to our local dealer. She must have a bad habit. Can't tell you where she stays, though. I've just seen her around."

"Thanks for your help, Jackson." West dropped some bills on the bar to cover his soda and a few of Benji's beers. "Now I'll shove off and stop scaring away your clientele."

Back outside, West rubbed his eyes. All he had to do was search for a black-haired, chain-smoking, daiquiri-drinking fox named Monique...and try to run into her on the street.

As he loped back to his vehicle, he caught sight of a blond-haired fox instead, coming out of the local pet store.

Waving his hand to catch Astrid's attention, he veered to the left, making a beeline for where she stood on the sidewalk, outside the store.

Sensing his approach, her head jerked up. Her eyes widened in her face…and then she turned and ran.

Chapter Thirteen

Oh, damn. Oh, damn. What was *he* doing here? And in the middle of town, in the middle of the day where anyone could see them. She careened around the next corner, the plastic bag from the pet store hitting her leg. Feeling like a character in a chase film, she ducked into a souvenir shop.

She took up a position behind a carousel of magnets sporting the falls, the bay and the lighthouse, peering around the edge at the window. When West's solid frame strode past the glass, she crouched.

The clerk came from behind the counter, twisting her pink-tinged hair around one finger. "Can I help you?"

"No, ah, yes." Astrid peeled a magnet from the display and held it up. "I'll take this one."

"Okay, whatever." The young woman shuffled back to the counter and rang up Astrid's purchase.

Before leaving the store, Astrid poked her head into the street, scanning the sidewalk, right and left. Okay, this was ridiculous. She couldn't hide from the sheriff forever, could she?

She dropped the magnet into the bag with Sherlock's toys and chews and walked into the nearest coffeehouse. She snagged a seat by the window and pulled out her phone. She finally answered West's most recent text with a message to meet her at Tate's boat in the harbor in fifteen minutes, and she'd explain everything then. Would she? Could she?

She ordered a latte, and then sat by the window watching her phone's display. She wouldn't blame him if he blew her off. After everything he did for her, she turned and ran when she saw him. What would've happened last night if Sherlock hadn't interrupted their kiss? Because that *was* gonna be a kiss. Maybe that's why he thought she turned tail and scurried away—maybe that's why she should've.

West's answer came through at the same time the barista announced her latte. He'd meet her in thirty. She texted him quick directions and a smiley emoji to take away the sting of her flight.

Fifteen minutes later, she dumped her empty coffee cup in the trash can and headed toward the marina. She pulled into a parking space at the edge of the lot and shoved her bag under the seat. As she slid from her truck, she flipped up her hoodie and kept her head down.

She entered the gate to the boat slips, and her rubber-soled shoes smacked against the metal gangplank as she made a beeline for Tate's boat, *Fire Dancer*. She prepared the boat for launch by checking the bilge plug, pulling up the fenders and shoving the key in the ignition. Now she just needed her passenger.

She didn't have to wait long. A few minutes later, West strode down the ramp, the breeze lifting his dark hair above his sunglasses. When he spotted her on the boat, his gait slowed. He reached the slip and pointed at her. "Do you need the secret code word now?"

"There is no code word. Hop on." She turned on the engine, and the boat purred in the water.

Cocking his head, he said, "We're actually going out to sea? Are you going to dump my body overboard when you're finished with me?"

"Don't be ridiculous. You game, or no?" She patted the edge of the *Fire Dancer*.

"I'm in." He stepped onto the boat and sat on a cushion next to the motor. "Seriously, I don't have time for a pleasure cruise."

"This is business, not pleasure, Sheriff." She eased on the throttle and backed out of the slip. Then she swung the boat around and chugged into the sea lane.

Once they hit a rhythm, West turned from the bay to face her. "Why all the cloak-and-dagger stuff, and why did you run away from me in town?"

"I got a phone call last night after you left."

"Oh?" He shoved his sunglasses on top of his head.

"It was a woman warning me to stop looking for the drone's memory card."

"So, they've come to the conclusion you don't have it and don't know where it is."

"They figured I would've turned it over to you by now if I had it." She caught her hair in her hand as it blew across her face. "But they're watching me. They seem to know my every move."

He rubbed his knuckles against his clean-shaven jaw. "We figured that much. They know your truck. They know where you live and work."

"It's worse than that." Astrid waved to another boater as she tipped the steering wheel to the right to enter the open bay. "They planted that blank memory card at the Misty Hollow property as a test. I failed."

"How so?" West sat up straighter.

"They know I turned it over to you." She lifted her shoulders as a cool breeze blew through her. "They know more than my home and car. They're spying on me."

"What did you tell her?"

She widened her eyes. "What did you want me to say? I told her I was done looking for that card. That I didn't care what had happened to Chase Thompson."

Snapping his fingers, he said, "That's why you ran from me? It's not my breath or my aftershave?"

Should she tell him now, he always smelled great? And she knew for a fact he didn't mask his own natural, masculine scent with aftershave. Russ used to bathe in the stuff, and it made her gag—even before he turned into a criminal.

She nodded mutely. "I-I just figured it would look better if I weren't living in your pocket."

His eyebrows shot up to his hairline. "You've been living in my pocket? What does that even mean?"

"We *have* been spending a lot of time together." She dropped her lashes and hoped he'd mistake the pink in her cheeks for the wind.

"Because they keep making you a victim of their attacks."

"That's what I told her. I asked her if she expected me not to report the attacks against me to the sheriff."

"Did you mollify her?"

"I'm not sure." Astrid bit her bottom lip. "She made some veiled threats against Olly."

"She would. They would. They always threaten those you love most."

The boat hit a small wave, and a shimmer of water sprayed West. Sparkling droplets clung to the ends of his hair and his eyelashes. He dropped his glasses over his eyes again and licked the salt from his lips.

"I agree with her…and you. Stop taking any measures to find the drone, fix it or look for its missing parts. You don't need to be a part of this. It was just bad timing that Olly took the drone and flew it near the scene of a murder."

"Okay." Her hands rested lightly on the steering wheel. "Should I stop, I mean, should we stop seeing each other in public?"

With his head turned back toward the bay, he seemed not to have heard her. Suddenly, he whipped his head around. "This woman who called, what did she sound like?"

"She disguised her voice somewhat. She sounded gravelly, then whispery. I don't know if she was trying to sound threatening, or what, but I probably wouldn't recognize her voice if I heard her talking normally." She flicked a hand in the air. "And don't ask about a phone number. The call came up as an unknown number and when I tried to do a callback, it was blocked. I'm sure she's using a burner phone, so she can't be traced."

"Yeah, I'm sure she's just one of the drug cartel's many drones, excuse the pun, who goes out there and does what she's told. They probably used a woman to keep you off-balance."

"There was one thing weird about her speech." Astrid cut the speed on the boat and launched into a wide U-turn. "The way she pronounced my name."

"How'd she pronounce your name?"

"Well, the second syllable is a short *I* sound, and the accent is on the first syllable. She put the accent on the second syllable, and she mangled it by pronouncing the *I* like a long *E* sound. Like you'd pronounce an *I* in Spanish."

"Or French." West hit the boat's railing with his palm. "Could she have had a French accent?"

"Maybe. Why?"

"Chase Thompson's side chick was a French woman named Monique. From her description, she doesn't sound like Chase's type or vice versa. I was wondering what she'd be doing with a guy like Chase and figured it was his access to drugs. But…" Chase rubbed his jaw.

"But now you think it was to keep an eye on him." Astrid shifted the tiller to point the boat toward the entrance to the sea lane. "This Monique discovered Chase was skimming or stealing or whatever he was doing, she ratted him out to the big boss and set him up for murder."

"Could be."

"Have you met her yet?"

"Nobody knows where she's staying or even if she lives here permanently. I have a description and a possible hangout for her."

"What's the hangout?"

"The Harbor Restaurant and Bar. Must be around here, since we're at the harbor. Logical conclusion." West tapped his head.

Tilting her head back, Astrid pointed to the bluff above the harbor. "It's right up there. If she's sitting at her favorite bar, she could've looked right out the window and seen us together."

West came up behind her and reached over her shoulder, covering her hand with his. "There's no reason why we can't be seen together, Astrid. Just because we're a…couple, it doesn't mean you're actively looking for the drone footage or helping me in any way with that case."

She twisted her head over her shoulder and narrowed her eyes. "We're a couple? Since when?"

"Since now." Wedging a finger against her chin, he planted a salty kiss on her mouth.

Her knees almost buckled, and it had nothing to do with being on the deck of a boat. She let out a small gasp when he ended the kiss.

"Let's hope Monique and everyone else saw that." His soft lips, which had recently been caressing hers, quirked into a smile.

"So, you're suggesting we play at being a real couple so that everyone, including Monique and her cohorts, will assume what we have is personal instead of professional?"

"Something like that. Even though I'm the sheriff of Dead Falls Island, I'm allowed to have relationships and... friends."

"Well, then let's make sure everyone knows." She set the tiller on course and pivoted on her tiptoes, hooking one arm around West's waist.

He took the hint and bent his head to solidify their standing as a new couple by kissing her again. This one felt less showmance and more romance, but he could be a damned good actor.

He broke away and put his hand on the tiller. "Whoa, steady. You don't want to plow your brother's boat into the rocks."

"That would be even more convincing." She took over the steering and reduced the speed of the boat, although her heart had picked up the pace to make up for it.

"To launch our new status, I propose dinner tonight." He leveled a finger at the glass wall of the Harbor Restaurant. "Up there. And if Monique is there, even better. Let her see us enjoying a night out that has nothing to do with the drone or Chase's and Naomi's murders."

Combing her fingers through her tangled hair, Astrid asked, "And if Monique isn't there?"

West shrugged and winked. "The show must go on."

ASTRID HAD NO intention of telling Sam that all the fuss was for a fake date.

Sam squealed over their FaceTime call. "Wear the white silk blouse. With your blond hair, you always look like an ice queen in white."

Astrid held up the blouse under her chin and frowned into the mirror. "Do I want to look like an ice queen? Don't I want to look smokin' hot, instead?"

"What? And give him the impression that you're easy? You haven't done this for a while. Trust me." Sam took a sip of her wine.

"You've been separated for about four months now. How are you the expert?" Astrid slipped the blouse from the hanger and pulled it over her head, luxuriating in the softness against her skin.

"I read stuff." Sam shoved her hand into a bag of chips and crunched one between her perfect white teeth. "You're really taking advantage of your time with Olly gone. I can't wait until the Girl Scouts take their trip this summer—not that I won't miss Peyton. Do you miss Olly?"

"Of course. I'm going to give him a call before I go out. For some reason, he's kind of needy this trip. Wants to talk to me every night. I'm not complaining." Astrid dipped and hooked her fingers around the straps of a pair of high-heeled black sandals. "What do you think?"

"Killer." Sam licked her fingers. "But you'll be about six one in those. How tall is our hunky sheriff?"

"About that, I think. He's not the type to worry if a woman is taller than he is. He has more confidence than that."

"Unlike Russ." Sam covered her mouth with her greasy fingers. "Oops, sorry. Didn't mean to bring up bad juju before your first date in years."

"Doesn't bother me." Astrid sat on the edge of her bed and slipped her feet into the sandals. "Okay, I gotta go put some makeup on and give Olly that call before I leave."

"He's not picking you up?"

"I insisted we meet there. He'd have to double back."

"If you're driving, you can't get your drink on and invite him inside when he drops you off." Sam swirled her own wine before taking a gulp.

"I don't want to get tipsy, and I thought I was the ice queen."

Sam rolled her eyes. "You're the ice queen until he melts your core."

"You need to put away the trashy mags."

"All the trash is online now." Sam smoothed out the empty chip bag. "Seriously, though. If this date goes well, you should make sure West is okay with kids. I mean, after what he went through, maybe he's skittish about them."

Astrid dropped her makeup bag on the bed. "What are you talking about? What did he go through?"

"Wait. You've gone this far with him and haven't even done a search on him. Even *I* did a search on him, and I'm not even interested in dating him."

"You did a search on the sheriff?" The silky material of Astrid's blouse trembled as her heart pounded in her chest. "What did you discover?"

"Oh, Astrid. This is not the time to be telling you, right before a date with the man."

"You'd better spill it, Sam. What did you find out about West?"

"Oh, sister, he shot and killed a teenage boy."

Chapter Fourteen

Astrid's stomach dropped, and she clapped a hand over her mouth. "N-not on purpose. I mean, obviously not, or he'd be in prison. What happened?"

"It was some gang initiation thing where this teen had randomly shot into a crowd, hitting a toddler. When West went to apprehend the suspect, the kid pulled a gun on him. West shot him. Self-defense, right? That was the conclusion of the investigation. There were witnesses and everything."

"That's horrible for everyone." Astrid blinked back tears.

"What's worse is the gun the teen had was actually unloaded." She waved her hand. "Not that West could've known that."

Astrid shook her head. "What a tragic situation. Did the toddler die, too?"

"No, thank God, but West left the force after that."

"He must've been messed up." No wonder West seemed to bolt every time he saw Olly.

"Look, I'm sorry to be a downer. It wasn't West's fault, but he might have some lingering issues with preteen boys."

Astrid reached for her dresser and snatched up a tissue. She dabbed her nose. "I guess that's why he wanted to leave Chicago."

"Probably. I'll let you go. Bruce is calling tonight to set up a dinner to discuss reconciliation."

"And I'm all for it." Astrid aimed a kiss at the screen. "I'll talk to you later."

"Bye, girl."

Astrid sat on the bed, her makeup bag in her lap. Why hadn't West told her about his past? Maybe for the same reason she hadn't told him about hers. Had he already done a search on her like Sam did on him?

She slid off the end of the bed and leaned toward the mirror to apply her makeup. Then she navigated the stairs in her high heels, holding on to the banister. When she reached the kitchen, she placed a call to Porter's cell phone.

"Hello, Astrid. Perfect timing. I just sent the boys to wash up before helping with dinner. I'll get Olly for you."

Astrid backed up from Sherlock's nose. "Do not get my slacks dirty. I'll feed you before I go out."

"Hey, Mom."

"Hi. What did you do today?" She still hadn't told Olly about finding Sherlock again and feeding him, just in case the dog ran off, even though the vet assured her this morning he wasn't chipped.

Olly went into his typical recitation of events, bouncing from one topic to the next, usually with no timeline, rhyme or reason. She smiled as she listened to her son's scattered narrative.

As their conversation wound down and Olly started making noises about helping to clean the fish, he blurted out, "Did you fix the drone?"

She pursed her lips. "Olly, I told you not to worry about that. Davia is getting a new one from the company. Did the break-in at our house bother you? You can tell me. You can tell me anything, Olly. I-I know you've been through a lot with your dad."

Some noises from the background floated across the line, and Olly hiccupped. "I gotta go, Mom."

"Olly…"

Porter's voice interrupted her. "It's me, Astrid. Olly went outside to clean fish."

"Is he doing okay, Porter?"

"He's fine. Coming out of his shell a little, back to himself."

"Okay, I'll let you get to it."

She fed Sherlock, and then let him outside for the night wearing his new collar and tag. She'd eventually figure out a dog door situation, but not while she might still be the target of murdering drug dealers. She just had to hope Sherlock would stick around…and not bring home any more body parts.

She locked up the cabin and set off for her first date in years—even if West *had* asked her out to throw off the bad guys. A smile played across her lips. His ploy to get her to go out with him had to be one of the most creative she'd ever heard.

With parking at a premium on the bluff overlooking Dead Falls Harbor, Astrid left her truck with the lone valet parking attendant. She didn't even know what kind of car West drove outside of his DFSD SUV, so she had no clue if she beat him to the restaurant.

A flutter of apprehension skirted across her skin as she pulled open the door to the restaurant. If Monique was at her favorite bar tonight and saw her with West, what would the woman make of it? It's not like they'd be here to search for the drone or its memory card. Would it set Monique's mind at ease to think Astrid and West had other reasons to hook up…hang out? Or would it make her more concerned?

As Astrid approached the hostess table, West hopped off a barstool and intercepted her.

"I told the waitress I'd wait for you before taking our table. The busboy had to clean it off, anyway."

"It should be ready now, Sheriff Chandler." The pretty hostess in the slinky black dress batted her eyelashes at West.

Astrid held her breath, but West didn't seem to notice except to smile at the woman and thank her. Russ would've turned on the charm by this point and ended the evening with the woman's phone number in his pocket. Astrid gave her head a little shake. Not all cops were slick Romeos… but they all seemed to have secrets.

The hostess showed them to a table by the window, and the lights from the harbor twinkled, reflecting off the water, giving the whole scene an impressionist haziness.

West pulled out her chair. "Unless you prefer the other side of the table."

"This is fine." When the hostess left them, Astrid hunched forward, elbows on the table. "Did you spot the French woman in the bar?"

"I did not."

"So, without the appropriate audience, maybe we should wrap this up early."

West shook his head. "Where's your patience? She could show up at any time."

Through an appetizer of calamari, a beer for West and a strawberry daiquiri for her, the main course and a shared tiramisu, Monique still hadn't made an appearance, but several heads had turned their way, guaranteeing a mention in the Dead Falls gossip mill.

By the end of the evening, Astrid discovered that West had been engaged once but never married. He left his job as a police officer in Chicago due to stress, but he left the story hanging. It wasn't her place to chime in now. When she realized he had no intention of finishing it, she checked her phone. "Probably should call it a night, huh?"

"Mission accomplished." West leaned back in his chair and shook the ice in his water glass.

"I know." She cupped a hand around her mouth. "We got all the tongues wagging."

"That's not what I meant." His hazel eyes shifted to a deep green in the candlelight. "I'd been wanting to get to know you better since the day I met you at the Spring Fling—away from the danger and the threats and the fear. Like I said, mission accomplished."

She propped her chin in her hand. Could the same be said for her? West had kept a piece of himself hidden, hadn't wanted to reveal his real reasons for leaving Chicago. She'd done the same, though. She hadn't gone into any detail about her ex and didn't want to. Maybe it was best to keep things light for now, as they'd had so little of it since they'd met.

"So, let's show Monique and the rest of the bad guys that there's more to our relationship than hunting drones."

She skimmed her fork over the crumbs of tiramisu and licked it. "So, was this all a ruse?"

His gaze focused on her mouth, and then he swallowed. "Kind of. You can't allow thugs to dictate who you can and cannot see. You can't cower in your house until they decide you're no longer a target."

"I agree, or I never would've consented to this date."

He swept the napkin from his lap and crumpled it next to the empty dessert plate. "No running away from me in the street anymore?"

"Well, that depends." She laughed at his wide eyes.

"You, see? That's what I learned about you tonight." He wagged a finger at her. "You snort when you laugh."

West insisted on paying the bill and on following her home. When his car pulled in behind her truck, she pressed her hand against her belly and the butterflies raging inside.

Should she invite him in? Would he make a move? Should *she* make a move?

She stumbled from the truck and grabbed the door. Taking a deep breath, she made a decision and strode toward him.

He met her halfway and took her in his arms before she uttered one word. Wedging a knuckle beneath her chin, he tilted her head back and sealed his lips over hers. The taste of the tiramisu on his mouth made the kiss even sweeter.

If her knees felt weak before, they were positively jelly now. She sagged against him, wrapping her arms around his neck. How would they ever make it inside?

When they finally pulled apart, West said, "I'm sorry. I just couldn't wait any longer."

"Do you want to come inside?" She clawed inside her purse for her keys and found her phone buzzing instead. She fully intended to ignore the call until she saw it was Porter's phone.

"Sorry, this might be Olly or about Olly." She grabbed the phone and tapped it, her heart rate accelerating. "Hello?"

"Mom?"

She could barely make out Olly's whisper. "Speak up, Olly. I can't hear you. Is something wrong?"

Her son cleared his throat and continued in a louder stage whisper. "Mom, I buried it."

Blood pounded in her ears. "Buried what?"

"The memory card from the drone."

Chapter Fifteen

"What?!" Astrid's voice went up several octaves and even more decibels, as her face went completely white.

West's heart jumped to his throat. "What happened? Is Olly okay?"

She reached for his arm, and her fingernails dug into his skin. "Olly just told me he buried the drone's memory card."

Putting his hand on Astrid's stiff back, he nudged her toward the front door. "Let's get inside. Put the phone on speaker, so I can hear him."

Astrid put one foot in front of the other as she said, "Hold on a minute, Olly. Sheriff Chandler is with me. He wants to hear what you have to say."

Once on the porch, she spun around and yelped when Sherlock came up behind her and snuffled the back of her knees.

"It's okay. I have him." West hooked his fingers around the dog's collar and told him to stay.

Astrid's hands were shaking so badly, she couldn't put the key in the lock. West took the keys from her and unlocked the top and bottom. Sherlock trotted ahead of them and when West shut them all inside, Astrid rearmed the security system.

Carrying the phone in front of her as if it were a bomb,

she sat on the edge of the couch. She tapped the display and put the phone on the coffee table. "Okay, Olly. We're inside and I have the phone on speaker for Sheriff Chandler."

"Hey, Olly. Do you want to tell us what happened from the beginning? You're not in trouble. Nobody's in trouble." West took one of Astrid's fidgety hands in his own.

"I told you Logan and I took the drone, and some guy whacked it or something, so it was acting weird when we got it down. I tried to fix it, and that's when that little card fell out. I tried to put it back in, but that opening was bent or something. It wouldn't go back in, but I could jam the little door on the slot closed without the card in it. So, that's what I did. I put the card in my pocket."

Astrid darted a gaze at West and swept her tongue across her bottom lip. "Why didn't you just give it to me?"

"I forgot I had it until I was packing for the sleep-out. Then there was such a big deal about the drone, I was afraid to give it to you."

"That's what's been bothering you since you left?"

"Yeah, but since you told me Davia's buying another one, I figured I'd better tell you what happened." He paused, and it sounded like he gulped back some tears. "Sorry, Mom."

"Don't worry about it, Olly. I'm not happy with all this lying and secrecy, but you haven't done anything that can't be fixed." Astrid laced her fingers together and clamped her hands between her knees. "Why'd you bury the memory card?"

"Just didn't want anyone to catch me with it. You know how Mr. Monroe gets all nosy."

"Yeah, because that's his job. Nobody knows you have that card, or buried that card?"

"Only Logan, but he doesn't know where I buried it."

West hunched forward, elbows on his knees. "Where *did* you bury it, Olly?"

"I-I'm not really sure, Sheriff Chandler. Under some tree, down by the river where we were fishing."

West's eye twitched. Great. Possible evidence in a murder case buried in the mud somewhere.

He touched Astrid's arm as he spoke again. "Do you think you could show me, Olly?"

"Do you really want it that bad?" Olly whistled. "Do you think it might have who killed that guy on it?"

Astrid covered her mouth with her hand.

Stroking her arm, West answered Olly. "I don't really know, but I'd like to look at it, anyway."

Astrid blurted out. "Don't tell anyone about it, Olly. Y-you know, it could be a police thing, so just don't tell anyone, not even Mr. Monroe and not the other boys. Tell Logan to stay quiet, too. Just in case it messes up evidence."

"Yeah, sure." Olly blew out a long breath. "I'm glad I told you."

"Me, too. Enjoy yourself and don't think about it again. Sheriff Chandler will talk to Mr. Monroe about meeting you out there. He'll make up some reason."

"Oh." Olly sniffed. "You can't wait until camp is over in a few days?"

West said, "The memory card may already be corrupted, messed up. I just want to make sure it doesn't get any worse. It's all right, Olly. I'll talk to Mr. Monroe tomorrow morning about making my way out there. You can show me where it is then."

Astrid and Olly said their goodbyes, and Astrid ended the call. She sat still, staring at the phone in her hand. "All this time he had it. All this time he's been in danger."

"They don't know he has it. Why would they?" He rubbed a circle on her back. "I'll go out there tomorrow and hopefully Olly can tell me where he buried it. Once I have it, he…and you…will be safe—whether or not it contains the evidence we need."

Astrid growled and squeezed her hands together. "Ooh, I could strangle that kid. If he'd told me before he left and handed it over, none of this other stuff would've happened. Maybe even Naomi would be alive."

"Naomi's murder didn't have anything to do with the drone. The cartel must've believed that Naomi had information from Chase, information they couldn't afford getting out." The back rub turned to a caress of her shoulders. "Don't even think that. Olly did the right thing, and I'm going to take care of it tomorrow."

"I hope after all this, the footage actually proves useful."

"So do I." He pushed up from the couch, his hand still on her shoulder. "Go take a bubble bath, have a glass of wine, rub Sherlock's belly—whatever you need to do to relax. I'll get Monroe's phone number from you and call him tomorrow."

She grabbed his hand, her fingers threading through his. "Do you have to leave?"

A knot of desire formed in his belly. "I don't have to leave…if you don't want me to."

"You said whatever I need to do to relax." She stood up beside him and hooked her fingers in his belt loops. "I think I need you."

WHATEVER URGE CAME over him in the driveway when they got home seemed to claim him again, as he cupped the back of her head, sliding his fingers into her hair. She'd kicked off her heels when she sat on the couch to talk to Olly, so she and West no longer stood nose-to-nose. She compensated by rising on her tiptoes and pressing her mouth against his.

His lips parted, and she flicked the tip of her tongue inside his mouth as she pulled him closer. He groaned and deepened the kiss, moving his body against hers.

As Sherlock whined and thumped his tail against the floor, West whispered in her ear, "I don't need an audience."

She giggled but suppressed the snort this time. "You're right. It would probably traumatize him."

Taking West's hand, she took a step toward the stairs. Still connected, they walked up the staircase, West trailing behind her, the warmth emanating off his body.

When they got to her bedroom, West pulled his wallet and phone from his pocket and tossed them onto the nightstand. He removed his boots and socks, and started to unbutton his shirt while she watched him, her heart pounding.

"Let me." She shooed away his hands and took over the unbuttoning job. Her fingers were trembling so much, he probably could've made faster work of it, but she enjoyed savoring the anticipation.

When she had a few buttons left, West grabbed the hem of his shirt, plucked his T-shirt out of the waistband of his jeans and pulled the whole mess over his head. He let his clothes drop to the floor. "That's how it's done."

She smoothed her hands over his bare chest, the dark hair scattered there tickling her palms. "I like a man out of uniform almost as much as I like him in uniform."

"And here I thought you were giving up on cops." He traced his tongue along the lobe of her ear.

"Never say never." She tugged at his belt. "Do you have a shortcut for removing everything from the bottom half, as well?"

"Your turn." He fumbled with the small pearl buttons of her blouse until he had a couple open. Then he pinched the silky material between his fingers and lifted the blouse over her head.

She raised her arms to make it easy for him, and he twisted around to lay the blouse over the back of a chair. "It just looks so much nicer than my stuff, I didn't want to toss it on the floor."

"Should I be offended that you're thinking about the orderly disposal of my clothing and aren't lost in the moment, overcome with passion?"

Grabbing her wrist, he pressed her hand against the bulge in his jeans. "I'm so overcome with passion, I'm about to explode."

"Please don't." She cupped his crotch. "I have higher expectations than that."

"Don't worry. I plan to exceed every expectation you have." He flicked the bra straps from her shoulders and buried his face in the crook of her neck. "You smell like a fresh day in the forest in a field of wildflowers. Are there fields of wildflowers in the forest?"

"I'll show you sometime." She reached behind her and unclasped her bra. She let it fall to the floor and got goose bumps as West's gaze traced the curve of her breasts.

His hands replaced his gaze, and he skimmed his fingers along her skin, circling toward her nipples. Her breasts ached at his touch, and she arched her back for more contact.

He palmed her right breast, dipping his head to swirl his

tongue over her nipple. With her legs shaking, she wrapped an arm around his narrow waist and dug her nails into his back.

She gasped. "I can't do this standing up, Sheriff. If you're gonna take me, you'd better do it on the bed, horizontally."

"I can do horizontal." He took a step back from their heated contact and unbuckled his belt. Before she could add a helping hand, he'd peeled off his jeans and briefs, and they dropped to his knees…but her gaze landed north of his knees.

She circled her hand around his shaft and ran it up the length of him. He clenched his jaw and squeezed his eyes closed.

"I'm not doing this standing up, either." He wrapped both hands around her waist and swung her around to the bed where she landed with a plop. He kicked off the remainder of his clothing, and then he knelt before her and unzipped her black slacks.

As he tugged at the material, she lifted her hips. He pulled her slacks from her body and threw them over his shoulder. "Sorry, I don't give a damn about those pants right now."

"Right answer." Her words ended on a squeak as he parted her thighs with his rough palms and tickled her swollen folds with the tip of his tongue.

And she thought *he'd* have trouble holding himself together. The second his mouth touched her, her core tightened and every nerve ending throbbed in anticipation. Her fingers plowed through his hair, as she couldn't decide if she wanted him to stop or keep going forever.

Turned out forever meant minutes as her passion exploded, and a warm rush infused her senses. Like a hot river of lava, her release raced through her body, melting her previously tense muscles into sweet pudding.

She'd clasped her knees against West's head, and she didn't release him until her legs fell open in lethargic surrender. Running her finger down the bridge of her nose, she asked, "Did I cut off the circulation to your brain with my thighs?"

"If you did, I hardly noticed." He encircled her ankles with his long fingers and lifted her legs, resting her calves on his shoulders, damp with sweat. "That was a little fast. Are you ready for another?"

"We have all night, don't we?" She unwrapped her legs from his body and scooted back onto the bed, patting the mattress. "Join me."

Staying on his knees, he maneuvered to the nightstand and scooped up his wallet. He flipped it open and pulled out a foil packet of condoms. They unfurled as he jiggled them in the air. "I'm not saying I was hoping to get lucky tonight, but I did have some faith in the future—with you."

His words gave her pause and put the reins on her giddiness. The word *future* made her nervous. Could she have a future with this man or any other when the father of her son remained in witness protection, hiding from the people he double-crossed? If the future meant the next few hours, she could handle it.

"I-is this okay?" He cocked his head as his brows created a V over his nose.

"It's more than okay, Sheriff." She snatched the condoms from his fingers, detached the top packet and ripped it open with her teeth.

He entered her while pinning her with a gaze so full

of desire and hunger, she let go of every last reservation. She'd deal with the future…in the future.

THE FOLLOWING MORNING, Astrid woke up with West's arm heavy around her waist, his head on her pillow, his body crowding hers to the edge of the bed. She didn't even mind.

She inhaled the scent of him on her sheets, a little salty, a lot masculine, and stretched her legs, curling her toes in satisfaction. A passionate lover, West combined a tenderness with his fervent ardor, making her feel both desired and cherished.

She'd been in her early twenties when she'd married Russ and didn't know men could be sweet and fierce at the same time. She liked it.

Sherlock whined at the closed bedroom door, and she rolled off the mattress, landing on her bare feet. She'd assumed the dog was housebroken, but the poor thing had been cooped up for a while.

West stirred, and she tiptoed to the door and cracked it open. Sherlock's soft black nose snuffled into the space. Pushing the door wider, she said, "Sorry, boy. I'll let you out right now. Promise you won't run away—or drag anything home when you come back."

She yanked her terry-cloth robe from a hook on the back of the door and stuffed her arms in the sleeves. Belting the robe, she patted her thigh. "C'mon, Sherlock."

His nails clicked on the wood as he followed her downstairs. She sniffed the air and scanned the floor for any accidents. "You're a good boy, Sherlock."

She padded to the sliding door in the back and opened it enough to let Sherlock outside. With his tail waving, he scampered toward the tree line, and the forest sucked him into its interior.

Shoving her hands in her pockets, she watched until the shivering bushes where he disappeared stilled. She'd felt safe wrapped in West's arms last night. Maybe when he left, she'd have to invite Sherlock to hold vigil at the foot of her bed until West caught Chase's and Naomi's killer. He maybe could've done that a lot sooner if Olly hadn't kept that memory card a secret.

She couldn't help it. She studied Olly sometimes for signs that he shared his father's antisocial nature. He didn't. Her brother Tate had assured her that Olly's occasional lying and misbehavior did not veer from typical adolescent male conduct. Comparing notes with Sam, who'd helped raise her stepson Anton, and other boy moms, she tended to agree with Tate. At least Olly had come clean about everything.

"Is he coming back?"

Astrid whirled around, hand to her chest. "You scared me."

"Sorry." West held up his hands. "I thought you had regrets and were contemplating following Sherlock out to the woods until I left your house."

Her gaze flickered over his half-naked body, his tight briefs clinging to him in all the right places. She swallowed hard.

His stride ate up the space between them, and he slipped his hands inside her robe to shape her hips. "If you're gonna look at me like that, I might just have to carry you back upstairs."

Curling her arms around his neck, she stood on her tiptoes to reach his mouth with hers. She pressed her lips, still tender from their feverish kisses last night, against his.

She broke off the kiss and wedged her head beneath his chin. "I'd take you up on that, but you have something rather important to do today."

"That's why I came looking for you. Can you give me Porter Monroe's cell phone number, so I can let him know I'm coming out to the camp today?"

"My phone's charging on the kitchen counter." She pointed over his shoulder and disentangled herself from his arms. "I'll send you my contact info for Porter."

"Guess I'd better get my phone. I left it upstairs."

As he climbed the stairs, she watched the muscles of his backside bunch and release. Then she shook her head and called out. "And put some clothes on, will ya?"

She grabbed her phone and scrolled through her contacts. She tapped Porter's name to send it to West and checked her text messages. Her pulse quickened when she read one from Michelle Clark letting her know that she showed her husband the photos, and he was interested. This sale would be such a boost to her career—and she hadn't even needed the drone photos.

She texted Michelle back with some possible next steps, and then held her breath when she looked at her phone calls. No voice mails and nothing from any blocked numbers. Had Chase's drug contacts given up on her?

As long as they didn't know Olly was the one who had the memory card…if it was still any good. She wiped her sweaty palms against the terry cloth of her robe. The sexy interlude with West had wiped all the nagging thoughts from her mind, but it hadn't banished them completely.

West jogged down the stairs in bare feet, clutching his

phone, his jeans and T-shirt covering his assets—but now she knew what lurked beneath. He held up the phone. "Got it. Thanks. Coffee?"

"I can make some. Do you want some breakfast, too?" She set down her cell and turned to the cupboard for the coffee pods.

"Just some toast, if you have it. I can make it myself." He perched on a stool at the kitchen island and tapped his phone's display. He gave her a thumbs-up. "Porter Monroe? This is Sheriff Chandler."

West raised his eyebrows at Astrid and said, "No, not at all. You're not in any trouble. I need to drop by the camp today and speak with Olly Crockett. Can you make that happen?"

As Astrid put on the coffee, she kept one ear trained on West's conversation with Porter. She knew exactly why Porter thought the sheriff might be calling him with bad news.

West said, "I'll be sure to make it there by ten so that Olly can join the others for kayaking. Can you give me the directions? Yeah, yeah, that'll work."

When the call ended, West glanced at his phone. "He's texting the directions to me and to you, just in case I need a guide."

He pocketed the phone, and Astrid set a cup of coffee in front of him. "That Porter's a little paranoid, isn't he? I mean, I get why most people don't want to hear from law enforcement, but wow, he had his alibi all ready."

"Yeah, well, Porter has always enjoyed working with kids—even before he got married and had a daughter of his own. It led to a lot of suspicion around his activities. He was even questioned in the disappearance of some young boys."

He took a sip of his coffee, considering her words. "That explains his response. I should have you whispering in my ear all the time giving me the lowdown on all Dead Falls Island residents."

The lowdown on everyone but herself. He must already know about her ex's situation. She should at least explain to him how she wound up with a guy like Russ, but he owed her some truths, as well.

Cupping her mug, she stared into her coffee. "West, I know why you left Chicago and your department."

His hand jerked, and his coffee sloshed over the side. "I suppose everyone in town knows. It's easy to do a search. The incident was all over the news at the time."

"I didn't do the search. Somebody told me…but it's not like it's the talk of the town." She ran a thumb along the rim of her cup. "That must've been difficult for you."

A muscle twitched in the corner of his jaw. "It made me question everything. I wasn't sure I could continue in this career."

Touching his arm, she said, "The boy was pointing a gun at you. He'd shot a child before. You had no reason to think his gun wasn't loaded and that he'd shoot you, too."

"I know all of that." He clasped the back of his neck. "It didn't help much at the time."

"But now? Have you come to terms with it now?" She grabbed the coffee pot to get him a refill and get out of his space.

Before he could answer her, his phone rang, and he spun it around to face him. "Porter calling. Maybe he wants me there earlier."

He tapped his display twice. "Porter, I have you on speaker phone, and Olly's mom is with me. Change of time?"

"Oh, h-hello, Astrid. I'm afraid there's a problem, Sheriff."

Astrid put down the coffee pot, her hands suddenly unsteady. "What's the problem, Porter?"

"We can't find Olly."

Chapter Sixteen

"Can't find him?" Astrid gripped the edge of the counter, her mouth suddenly dry. "What does that mean, Porter? Did he go somewhere and not return, yet?"

"Not exactly like that, Astrid." Porter took a deep breath. "The boys get up at seven to wash up and start preparing breakfast. We do a head count when they're in the mess area of the campsite. We did the head count and came up short. When we asked if any of the boys noticed anyone missing, Logan Davidson said Olly wasn't in their tent this morning. He figured he'd gone into the bushes to take care of business."

West picked up the phone, speaking into it. "How long had Olly been gone between the time Logan woke up and when you asked at breakfast?"

Astrid chewed on her bottom lip, the coffee taste in her mouth rancid. She closed her eyes and took a deep breath. Olly just wandered off. He did that sometimes.

Porter responded, "Logan woke up a little before the seven a.m. camp-wide alarm. He washed, dressed and was in the mess area by seven fifteen. They all have to be there by that time."

"So, we're talking about twenty to thirty minutes?" West scratched at the stubble on his jaw.

"That's right." Porter coughed. "Before you ask, all of us Scout leaders were in our area of the camp. Nobody arose before our own alarm at six forty-five. A few of the teen camp counselors have already gone out looking for him. Olly does like to fish, and he kept telling us about a fishing spot he wanted to try. One of the teenage boys went down there."

"I'm going to head out there myself, Porter. Keep looking. I'll send in a few more deputies if he hasn't turned up by the time I get there. Keep me posted."

"You got it, Sheriff. A-and, Astrid. I'm sure there's nothing to worry about. Olly has a good sense of direction and a good set of skills. There must be some reason he went off on his own. Like I said before, he'd been a little out of sorts when he got here, but he was getting back on track. Maybe he wanted to make up for some lost time or something. I'm sure we'll find him."

Astrid cleared her throat in an effort to command her voice before answering. "Thanks, Porter."

When the call ended, West squeezed her shoulder. "Don't worry. I'll find him."

She knotted her fingers in front of her. "Do you think he went off in search of the memory card himself? Maybe he felt guilty about not telling me and burying it, so he figured he'd find it for you before you came."

"He could've done that. Porter didn't mention that Logan had said anything about the card." West tossed back another gulp of coffee and put his cup in the sink. "I'll talk to Logan when I get there. Maybe Olly told his friend more about that card than he let on to us. Maybe Logan knows exactly where Olly is and is keeping mum out of a sense of loyalty."

"When *you* get there?" Her cup clattered in the sink as it joined his. "When *we* get there. I can't sit around here all morning waiting for your phone call."

"Okay. You might have a better idea of where he might've gone, anyway, or Logan might feel more comfortable talking to you. I'll call out more deputies if Olly hasn't turned up in a few hours. He knows how to swim, right? He's been fishing in rivers and knows about currents?"

"He knows all that stuff, but he also knows not to go wandering off without telling an adult." Astrid folded her arms, digging her fingers into her biceps and dropping her gaze to the floor.

"What is it?"

"Last year, someone lured Olly out of his bed in the middle of the night by pretending to be his father. Olly didn't tell me about it. Just sneaked out of the house."

"He knows his father…isn't available right now, doesn't he? There's no way his father would be contacting him now."

So, Sam hadn't been the only one conducting searches. Astrid nodded, tears pricking the back of her eyeballs. "He knows, but…"

"But what?"

"But what if someone else lured him away?" She hunched her shoulders to her ears, every muscle in her body taut and aching. "What if the drug dealers know he has the memory card?"

"How could they? We didn't even know until last night when he called." West's voice sounded firm, but a muscle twitched in the corner of his clenched jaw, and he wouldn't meet her gaze.

The same scenario must've occurred to him, which

made it even more real to Astrid. Despite her seized-up muscles, her teeth began to chatter.

West folded her in his arms and stroked her hair. "That prospect seems unlikely. They don't know he has the memory card. Even if they suspect it, they don't know where he is or how to get there. The camp seems remote to me. Porter told me I'd never find it on my GPS. That's why he gave me detailed directions."

She pressed her nose against the front of his shirt and sniffled. "They just seem to know everything."

"We'll find him, Astrid. Maybe he'll return before we even get to the camp. He's a smart, resourceful boy." He pulled her away from his chest and winked. "Look how long he kept you in the dark about his antics with the drone."

She gave him a shaky laugh. "I'm going to take a quick shower and get dressed. You can use the bathroom off Tate's room."

She took the stairs two at a time to avoid breaking down in front of him. How could it be a coincidence that he went missing the morning after he told her about burying the memory card? Unless he really did go off on his own to find it before West got there. That's something Olly would do. He always tried to make things right. He'd always tried to fix things for her when she and Russ would fight, or rather when Russ would rage at her for no reason. It broke her heart. A child shouldn't have to fix anything for his parents.

When she reached the bathroom, she let the robe drop at her feet. She stepped in the shower and cranked on the hot water, allowing it to stream down her back in an attempt to wash away her guilt. She'd been frolicking in bed with West when her little boy needed her.

She showered quickly and poked her head out of the bathroom door. When she heard the water running from Tate's bathroom, she wrapped the robe around her and scurried across the hall to her bedroom.

Her gaze darted across the room. All evidence of her passionate night with West had disappeared. He'd even neatly draped her slacks over the back of the chair and picked up her underwear. The bed might be a little more tousled than usual—along with her feelings—but she'd have to put last night behind her...for now.

She pulled on a pair of jeans and a long-sleeved T-shirt and dug her hiking boots out of the closet. She was prepared to walk miles to find Olly.

Gray skies met her when she pulled open her blinds, so she yanked a flannel shirt from a hanger to wear beneath her jacket. In the shade of the forest, especially around the bodies of water, the air could turn chilly.

She scooped her hair into a ponytail and jogged downstairs. As she grabbed her jacket from the coat closet in the foyer, West clumped down the stairs in the clothes he wore yesterday.

Tilting her head, she said, "You might need a jacket."

"I have one in my car. We'll ride over together. I figure having a local with me will get us there faster."

"Any more calls from Porter...or anyone else?" She veered around him to grab Sherlock's bowl from the counter. She dumped three cups of dry kibble into his dish. "I'd better leave this on the porch for Sherlock."

"Haven't heard from Porter. I gave my desk sergeant a heads-up about the situation, though. He told me it's common for kids to take off or get lost in the woods, even during the organized camps."

"I know that." She disarmed the security system and swung open the door with a whistle on her lips. "But we both know this is not an ordinary circumstance for an ordinary boy."

"Then we'd better get going." West squared his jaw as he met her on the porch.

Sherlock hadn't responded to her whistle, so she set the dish down on the porch. Her gaze tracked along the tree line. "I hope he returns."

She meant Sherlock, but she was thinking about Olly.

WEST'S GUT CHURNED with anxiety as he drove toward the Scout camp in the forest, following Astrid's directions. He'd tried to keep a positive outlook for Astrid's sake, but Olly's disappearance on the heels of his information last night didn't bode well for the boy.

If anything happened to Astrid's son on his watch, that dark vortex of guilt would pull him back, erasing all the progress he'd made over the past several months. But was it really progress or just stuffing down and ignoring his feelings?

His lips twisted. He'd been to so many therapy sessions, he couldn't imagine what feeling he'd ignored. Dr. Charmaine had forced him to lay bare everything and examine it in the harsh light of truth. He didn't have one feeling left he hadn't analyzed and probed.

At least Astrid hadn't turned away from him in disgust when she confronted him about his past.

She tapped him on the thigh, bringing him out of his reverie. "Right, right, right after the bend. Pay attention, Sheriff, or you'll get us lost, too."

West sucked in a breath. "Do you think Olly is lost?"

"He could be." She pressed her hands against her bouncing knees. "I mean, maybe he started out looking for the spot where he buried the memory card. Then he took a few wrong turns and got lost. He did tell us last night he probably could tell you where he buried it. He didn't sound absolutely sure about the location. There are a lot of trees out there, and most of them look the same."

"That's possible." West kept his tone light and tried not to strangle the steering wheel, but Astrid shot him a side glance. He tried on a smile, which seemed to make things worse as her knees started bouncing again.

After their last turnoff, they reached a trailhead, and West recognized the crossed branches of a red alder that Porter had described to him as being the starting off point to the scout camp.

He'd given silent thanks to the previous sheriff for the tip about keeping hiking boots in both his personal car and DFSD vehicle. The street boots he'd worn to dinner last night wouldn't cut it in these woods. Next purchase should be a four-wheel drive vehicle for his personal use.

Twisting around, he reached into the back seat. "Sheriff Hopkins warned me about keeping appropriate footwear with me at all times on the island."

"How about that?" Astrid lifted her eyebrows at the pair of boots in his hand. "Sheriff Hopkins was good for something, after all."

West cracked open his door and swapped his shoes while Astrid wandered to his side of the car. As he tied the boots, he said, "You're all kind of rough on Hopkins. Was he really that bad?"

"Just not dedicated. Kind of lazy. Didn't want to go out

of his way." She shrugged and rubbed her hands together, her focus on the trail.

"Seems he knew what he was *supposed* to be doing because he gave me some good advice." He stomped his boots on the mushy ground. "A lot of cops think they can take a top job in a small town and ease into retirement."

"Is that what you figured?"

"I'd done my research. I knew Dead Falls Island offered a prime spot for drug trafficking between the US and Canada…and I'm not ready to retire yet." He slammed the car door. "Let's go find Olly."

They tromped up the trail and Astrid confirmed his suspicions. She was an outdoor girl through and through. She could probably survive in the wilderness on her own for days—he hoped her son followed in Mom's footsteps.

Fifteen minutes of uphill later, a scattering of army green tents appeared through the trees. Astrid strode into the campsite looking better than when they started, and he brought up the rear only slightly out of breath. A gym in the city didn't quite prepare you for this kind of exertion.

On the lookout for them, Porter rushed forward. "The teen Scouts haven't found anything yet."

Astrid did the introductions. "Porter Monroe, this is Sheriff West Chandler. Have you met yet?"

"Not yet." Porter grabbed West's hand in a firm grip. "Good to meet you, Sheriff. Sorry it's under these circumstances. This has never happened before on one of my trips."

"I'm sure Astrid doesn't blame you, Porter. Thanks for calling so quickly and taking decisive actions."

Astrid said, "Not at all, Porter."

West turned his head to watch the boys stuffing their

backpacks as they roughhoused, oblivious to the serious-
ness of their missing friend.

Porter jerked his thumb at them. "We figured we'd go
ahead with our regular activities. We don't want to spook
the boys."

"I agree, but we'd like to talk to Olly's friend Logan."

"I have him waiting for you in the counselors' tent."
Porter gestured for them to follow him. "He hasn't said
much since we questioned him earlier."

Drawing up beside Porter, Astrid asked, "Did Logan
seem scared or worried about Olly?"

"Nope, but Sheriff Chandler can determine that for himself." Porter whipped aside the flap of a large canvas tent,
and a boy with curly dark hair jerked his head up.

"Hi, Ms. Mitchell. Am I in trouble?" Logan's big brown
eyes darted toward West.

"Hi, Logan. You're not in any trouble. Are you having
fun at camp?" Astrid sat next to him on a camp chair.

"Yeah, sort of. Olly and I caught the biggest fishes yesterday."

"Did you eat them? Were they any good?" West dragged
a chair over and sat across from Astrid and Logan.

"Umm, yeah, they were okay. I don't really like fish."
Logan scrunched up his freckled nose.

Rolling his shoulders, West leaned back in the small
chair. He shifted his jaw back and forth, trying to loosen
the tension. If he came off as too intense, the kid wouldn't
open up to him—and he always tensed up around kids.

"Olly's your best friend, right?"

"Yeah." Logan's gaze shifted to Astrid, and she gave
him an encouraging smile.

West wanted to ease into the interrogation, but they didn't

have time to waste. "When was the last time you saw Olly, Logan?"

"At lights-out." Logan rubbed his nose with the back of his hand. "We were in our sleeping bags in our tent. We were talking, and then fell asleep. Tyler and Colt were in there, too."

Astrid asked, "Were you and Olly talking to Tyler and Colt?"

"Naw. They fell asleep before us."

"After you fell asleep, you didn't see Olly again?" West uncrossed his arms, letting them fall loosely in his lap.

"Nope." Logan cranked his head back and forth like a robot.

"Did you hear him get up at night or in the morning?" Astrid scooted a little closer to Logan and brushed his arm with her knuckles.

"Nooo." Logan drew out the word, and his face paled, making his freckles pop.

West didn't have kids, but he knew a liar when he saw and heard one. Spreading his hands, West said, "It's okay if you did hear something and didn't say anything to Mr. Monroe. Maybe you forgot. Did you forget, Logan?"

"Uh-uh." He shook his head hard this time and had to brush his floppy brown hair from his eyes.

"Logan." Astrid turned her body so that her knees bumped the boy's. "What did you and Olly talk about last night?"

Logan's brown eyes widened, looking like two saucers in his sharp face. "Nothing. Fishing."

Astrid squeezed Logan's knee. "It's okay to tell us, Logan. Olly already informed us that he mentioned the drone's memory card to you."

"That's right, Logan." West shrugged. "So we know all about that, and Olly's not in any trouble over it. I just figured that's what you two were talking about before you went to sleep. Right?"

"Yeah." Logan nibbled on a raggedy nail.

West eased out a long breath. "Okay, yeah. Olly told us he buried it but couldn't exactly remember where. Is that what he told you?"

"Uh-huh." Logan sat forward in his seat. "We were going to go hunting for it today if we could sneak away after the kayaking."

Astrid's smile tightened on her face, and she shoved an unsteady hand through her hair. "Do you think he went by himself to find it before breakfast?"

Logan dipped his head and swung one leg back and forth, the heel of his sneaker hitting the chair on the backswing. "N-no."

"Why do you say that?" A muscle at the corner of West's eye danced out of control, and he wanted to slap it into submission before it terrified Logan.

"He might've gone looking for it, but he didn't go alone." Logan twisted his head toward Astrid. "Am I gonna get in trouble?"

"Not at all, Logan." Astrid tucked her hands beneath her thighs. "What do you mean, he didn't go alone?"

Deciding on the truth, Logan straightened up in his chair and planted both feet on the ground. "I mean, I heard Olly leave last night…but he wasn't by himself. Some woman woke him up and took him away."

Chapter Seventeen

Astrid's blood felt ice cold running through her veins, and her head swam as she opened and closed her mouth like one of those fish the boys caught yesterday.

Luckily, Logan had locked onto West, probably trying to judge the sheriff's reaction.

West's twitching eye and tight jaw confirmed Astrid's thudding dread. He knew what she suspected. Chase's killers had somehow found out Olly had the drone's memory card and…what? What did they have planned for him? What if he couldn't lead them to the card?

When the silence seemed to have stretched on for an eternity, West cleared his throat. "Someone woke up Olly to help him find the memory card?"

"I guess." Logan licked his lips. "I didn't wanna say anything because I didn't wanna get Olly in trouble. He told me not to say anything to anyone about the drone thing. I thought maybe he called this woman to help him or something."

"Maybe he did." West ran a hand over his mouth and down the dark stubble on his chin. "Did you see the woman, Logan?"

"I pretended I was asleep because I didn't want to go with them. It's too cold at night."

"I agree. Good move." West gave Logan a thumbs-up. "Did you hear her voice?"

Logan lifted his shoulders to his ears. "They were whispering, but I could tell it was a girl."

Astrid couldn't take it anymore. She jumped up from the chair, knocking it over and making Logan jerk in his seat like a puppet. Wringing her hands in front of her, she asked, "Why'd Olly go with her, Logan? Why'd he just get up out of his sleeping bag and leave the tent in the middle of the night?"

Wrong move. Logan's skinny body stiffened, and he whipped his head toward the entrance to the tent, looking ready to bolt.

Astrid smoothed her hands against the thighs of her jeans. "I-I mean, did it seem like he knew her? I guess that's why he'd go with her, right, Sheriff Chandler?"

"Maybe. Better pick up that chair, or Mr. Monroe's gonna think we messed up the tent." West winked at Logan.

"Oh, we don't want that." Astrid smiled stiffly at Logan.

West gave her a little nod. "Can we get back to the woman's voice, Logan? You knew she was a female. Did you notice anything else about it?"

Logan squeezed his eyes closed and puffed out his cheeks. Astrid could kiss him for his level of concentration.

A breath hissed out of his puckered lips. "Yeah, she called him a funny name. I mean, she called him Olly, too, so I know she knew him, but she called him another name."

Astrid had taken her seat next to Logan again and gulped before asking. "What other name?"

Logan rolled his eyes upward and pressed his lips together. "Moshare."

"Moshare?" Astrid frowned. She'd been fearful of Logan's answer, but this didn't make sense.

West shifted in his too-small chair. "Moshare. Did she say it like this, Logan? *Mon cher*?"

West's French accent had Astrid curling her fingers around the arm of her jacket and holding her breath. West had told her yesterday that Chase's girlfriend was French, and her anonymous caller had pronounced Astrid's own name with a slight accent.

Logan screwed up one side of his face. "Yeah, I guess so."

"One more question, and then we'll let you join the others." West held up one finger. "What time did this woman come into the tent?"

Logan glanced longingly at the tent opening. "I dunno. It was dark. We can't have our phones, but I fell back asleep after they left."

"D-did Olly seem scared?" Astrid clenched her teeth and buried her fists in her lap.

"Olly scared?" Logan's eyes bugged out. "Naw. Olly's never scared, Ms. Mitchell."

West thrust out his hand to Logan. "Thanks, Logan. You did a good job."

Logan's cheeks flushed as he shook West's hand. Then he turned to Astrid. "When Olly comes back, tell him to come find me."

"I'll do that." Astrid gave him a misty smile and swiped her fingers beneath her nose.

As Logan hopped up, West put a finger to his lips. "Let's just keep this between us right now. We don't want everyone out there looking for the memory card, right?"

"I can keep a secret." Logan drew a cross on his chest.

She waited until Logan went outside the tent, and then covered her face with her hands, letting out a low moan. "They have him, don't they? Those drug dealers found out Olly had the memory card, and they took him."

West perched on the edge of the chair Logan just vacated, bumping his knees against hers. "They just want that card. They're not going to hurt him."

Lifting her head, she swiped a tear from her cheek. "What if he can't give them the card? What if he can't remember where he buried it? They didn't believe me when I told them I didn't have it."

"He's a kid. They'll figure he'll give it up if he knows where it is." West scratched his scruff, and the tic that had been fluttering at the corner of his eye moved to his jaw.

"What?" She dug her fingers into his thigh. "What are you thinking?"

"I'm just wondering how they discovered Olly had the card and how they found this campsite. You don't think…"

"I'm not thinking anything right now, and you're driving me further into a panic. Just spit it out."

"Maybe someone bugged your house when they broke in. How else did they find out? You didn't know Olly had that memory card until he called last night and told you."

Astrid gasped and gripped the seat of her chair. "Bugged my house? That's terrifying."

"I don't know. Would they have been that desperate that early?"

She replied, "That wouldn't explain it, anyway. We may have talked about Olly in the house having that card, but we didn't read out those directions that Porter texted to us."

Hearing his name, Porter poked his head in the tent. "Was Logan any help?"

Astrid glanced at West. Would he tell Porter that Olly had been kidnapped from his tent? Porter would panic and probably cause all the boys and their parents to panic, too, even though the kidnapper posed no danger to the other boys.

West pushed to his feet. "Not really. He and Olly talked in the tent before they fell asleep and when Logan woke up, Olly was gone. I am going to start a search though, and I'm calling in a few deputies. Obviously, stay alert for any signs of Olly."

"I'm so sorry, Astrid." Porter lifted his hat and ran a hand over his head. "I don't know why Olly would go off like that. Do you suspect any foul play, Sheriff?"

"Too soon to tell, Porter. You can tell the boys Olly wandered off, but just carry on."

"Okay. Anything more we can do, Sheriff, let us know."

Astrid cocked her head. "You told Logan to keep quiet, and you skirted the truth with Porter. What's your reasoning?"

"If Olly is tramping around the forest with this French woman, I don't want her spooked. I don't want to alert her that we're onto them. We'll search first, and I'll have a few of the deputies canvass the area." He snapped his fingers. "I do need more info from Porter, though. If Olly buried the card when he was on a Scout excursion, we need to know where they went yesterday so we can search that area."

"You should probably catch him before the boys head out." Astrid massaged her temples, as all the tension of the morning pounded in her head. "While you're talking to Porter, I can check the tent and Olly's sleeping bag. Maybe he left some kind of clue there."

"Porter already checked the tent, but definitely have a look."

"Don't leave without me. I'm going to search for Olly, too." Astrid straightened her spine. "I have a feeling Olly isn't just going to lead this woman to the card. He knows how important it is to your case. Maybe he'll stall her. He knows this forest well."

West clasped the back of his neck, a frown creasing his brow. "Hang on. You were making a point when Porter came in and interrupted us. You said, and I agree, that Monique and her cohorts couldn't have found out the location of the campsite from bugging your house because we didn't discuss those directions."

"That's right, unless they found out another way. I suppose they could've asked around town. You said that Monique was hanging around Dead Falls with Chase."

"Yeah, but where did we discuss both the fact that Olly had the memory card and buried it and the location of the campsite?"

Astrid swallowed. "My phone."

"Yeah."

"Y-you think my phone's bugged?" She pawed through her purse to find her cell and cupped it in her hand, eyeing it as if it was getting ready to bite her.

"It could be."

"How? Someone was able to do that remotely?" She tapped her phone to access it, clicking through the apps as if one of them could tell her someone was listening to her calls and reading her texts.

"That would take a high level of technical expertise to do it remotely, but…"

"You mean someone did it physically? How could that happen without my knowledge?"

West shrugged. "People leave their phones unattended all the time. One of my deputies informed me this week, it doesn't take long to bypass someone's security code on the phone if you know what you're doing."

She held her phone out to him. "Do you know what you're doing?"

"No, but my deputy Amanda does." He plucked it from her hand. "We can have her take a look, but can you think of any time this week when you left your phone?"

"A few times, but I don't believe some stranger could've picked up my phone, broken into it and bugged it."

"Think." He tapped his head. "Maybe it wasn't a stranger."

She blinked. "One of my friends? A coworker? No way."

When West's phone rang, Astrid started, her frayed nerves playing havoc with her reflexes. They needed to get out there now and start looking for Olly and this woman.

She pinned West with an expectant gaze when he answered his phone. Could this be some news already?

Maybe he felt the heat of her stare because he put the phone on speaker as he picked up the call. "Sheriff Chandler."

A low, rough voice rasped over the line. "Sheriff, this is Jackson Cross, the bartender at the Crab."

"Yeah, I remember. What can I do for you?"

Astrid tapped her foot. If this was some barroom brawl, she hoped West could send one of his deputies.

"Oh, me? I'm all good, but I have some information you might be interested in."

"Go on."

"That French broad Monique you were looking for?"

"Yeah?" West glanced at her, and she crossed her arms, holding on tight.

"She's here at the Salty Crab. Came in about ten minutes ago, looked around, took a seat by the window. Ordered a Bloody Mary and looks like she's waiting on someone."

"You're sure?"

"Absolutely." Jackson hacked. "That fool Benji's in here already drooling over his first beer of the day. Her appearance surprised the hell out of me, too. Told you she didn't come in here. Thought you might want to know."

"Thanks, Jackson. I'm coming right over. Call me if it looks like she's leaving."

"Will do, boss."

When West ended the call, he pocketed his phone and said, "We found Monique."

Astrid ran her tongue across her teeth, her mouth suddenly parched. "That's great but if Monique is in the Salty Crab, who the hell has Olly?"

Chapter Eighteen

"That's what we're going to find out." West took Astrid by the shoulders, his tone unwavering. He didn't know if he was trying to convince her or himself. He had to save this boy.

"You mean you're going to the Salty Crab right now? Now, while Olly is out there somewhere with God knows who?" She wrenched away from him and grabbed her purse. "I'm going to find him. This is more than a case to me. He's my boy. He's my world. I don't expect you to get it. He's not *your* child."

He staggered back. Her words lashed him, flaying his skin raw, peeling it back and leaving him exposed. He'd heard these cries before from another mother. There was nothing he could do about that mother's pain, but he'd fix this. He'd make it right.

He squeezed his eyes closed for a brief moment, and then scooped in a deep breath. "It's not logical for me to go thrashing through the woods looking for Olly, who's no longer with his abductor. Do you think they're on the trails, sharing water and gushing over the flora and fauna together? They're not going to be in the open, waiting for someone to find them. Olly's abductor will be hiding with him, staying off the main trails. Keeping quiet when they hear voices. Maybe even ready to take drastic measures when confronted."

Astrid's anger seemed to seep from her body, and her shoulders rolled forward. "I-I'm sorry. What do you have in mind?"

"You don't have to apologize to me. I get it. I know your impulse is to charge out there, shouting his name." He put a hand over his hammering heart. "It's mine, too, but Jackson gave us an opportunity. Monique is the one who lured Olly from the tent. She either knows where he is or knows who has him. I'd say she's a good starting point for narrowing down our search."

Astrid gave him a jerky nod. "I understand. But I'm coming with you. Maybe Monique is a mother. Maybe she'll listen to me."

West didn't want Astrid anywhere near Monique, but he didn't want to tell her that yet. He could take her along to the Crab and maybe send her off on another errand while he talked to Monique, as he doubted the woman would be susceptible to a mother's pleas.

"Okay, let's go."

On the way out of the campsite, West stopped to speak to the Scout leader left behind to find out where the group had gone the day before. The man also told him the teens were still canvassing the area, looking for Olly.

As West hiked back to his vehicle, he prayed that the young men wouldn't stumble across something they couldn't handle…and then he said the same prayer for himself.

THEY DROVE INTO TOWN, Astrid fidgeting beside him the entire journey. He reached over and put his hand over both of hers, entwined in her lap. "Let's take this slow and easy.

We can't go rushing in there accusing Monique of taking Olly and demanding his location. I don't even want her to know that we know."

"Okay, okay." Her lip quivered, but otherwise she looked ready to do battle.

He parked his car one block over from the Crab and called Jackson at the bar. "Is she still there?"

"Still here. On her second Bloody Mary, and her friend joined her. Man, we haven't had class like these two in this bar since the ribbon-cutting ceremony."

"Man in a suit?" Had the big bosses come out for a little kid and a drone?

"No, no, a woman. Black hair, like Monique's, dressed up in some expensive threads, high heels, long talons for fingernails, big gobs of jewelry, the whole nine yards."

"I'm on my way in shortly. Don't make a big deal out of seeing me there."

"C'mon, Sheriff. You know we don't like the law at the Salty Crab."

As West ended the call, Astrid grabbed his arm. "Oh my God. I think I know Monique's companion."

"What? You know the woman who's with Monique?"

"That description matches a client of mine, Michelle Clark." Astrid's grip tightened. "And she had access to my phone."

"When was this?"

"A few days ago." She released his arm and clamped a hand over her mouth. "It was when we found the blank memory card on the ground at the Misty Hollow property. Michelle probably put it there."

West's gaze tracked to the corner. He didn't want to

let either one of those women in the Crab out of his sight. "And the phone?"

"I'd left it in the car. She told me the battery on her own had died, and she wanted to continue taking pictures of the property to send to her husband. She insisted on going back to the car to get the phone." Astrid smacked her hand on the dash. "She must've done it then."

"Tell me everything you know about Michelle Clark."

When Astrid had finished telling him what little info she had on her client, he called the station to relay the information to Deputy Fletcher. "If Amanda's there, have her do a deep search on this woman."

Astrid turned to him, her hands excitedly flapping around her. "This is perfect, West. I pretend I don't know anything about either one of them or the phone. Seeing Michelle with Monique will give me an excuse to talk to both women."

"Then what?" West squeezed the back of his neck. He didn't like the idea of Astrid talking to those women. They were capable of anything.

"Then... I don't know. Maybe I can get information out of them. Maybe I can at least let them know that nobody is onto them."

Closing his eyes, West dug his fingers into his temples. "I have an idea."

ASTRID TOOK SEVERAL steadying breaths as she strode toward the Salty Crab. Before reaching the door, she adjusted the wire West had taped to her chest.

She jerked open the door and made a beeline for the bar, not looking at the smattering of customers in for a prelunch drink. She leaned on the bar and waved to the bartender, a man she'd seen in passing a few times around town.

"Hey, Jackson. Can you do me a Bloody Mary?"

"Absolutely, Astrid." He cocked his head. "A little early for you, isn't it?"

She let out a sigh. "Yeah, apparently my son decided to sneak out of his tent last night on the Scout trip. It's not the first time he's pulled a stunt like this, but it had better be his last."

"Sorry to hear that, Astrid. Sounds like you need that drink." Jackson winked at her.

Astrid glanced to her right, her gaze sweeping across the two women sitting at the window, their heads together in furious, whispered conversation. She felt like grabbing Monique by the hair and demanding answers. Instead, she did a double-take and widened her eyes. "Michelle? Just the person I need to see."

"Oh, hello, Astrid. I was going to call you today." Michelle scooted away from the table and the younger woman across from her.

Astrid had to pounce before Monique left. As Jackson put the drink in front of her, Astrid nodded her thanks and carried the glass to the table with the two women. She dragged a chair over from the next table.

"Did your husband have a chance to look at all the pictures?"

"He did." Michelle puckered her lips in a pout. "I'm still working on him."

Astrid deliberately shifted her eyes to Monique, sucking down the last of her Bloody Mary. She smiled and raised her eyebrows.

Michelle tapped her fingernails on the table. "This is Monique. She's staying at the Bay View, and we met over breakfast. I'm sorry, sweetie, I didn't catch your last name."

"Monique Girard." She held out her hand for a limp shake.

"If you're looking for property on the island, let me know." Astrid slid her card toward Monique, noting a long scratch on the young woman's face. Astrid tapped her own cheek. "Ouch. Cat get you?"

Monique shrugged. "I was on a hike earlier and a tree branch smacked me in the face. Should've been paying attention."

"Obviously." Michelle's red lips tightened, and then she stirred her drink, the ice clinking against the side of the glass. "Did I hear you mention something about your son, Astrid?"

That reminded Astrid that she'd better take a sip, even though she hated Bloody Marys. She stuck the straw in her mouth, and the tangy concoction hit the back of her throat. "Yeah, I got a call from the camp this morning that he'd sneaked out of his tent."

"Oh, no." Michelle clicked her tongue. "You must be worried."

"I am, but it's not like he hasn't done this before. He's made a habit of it, so I'm sure he's just trying to make life difficult for the Scout leaders. He knows the woods very well, so I'm not afraid that he's in danger from the elements." She lifted her drink. "I just need a break before I start looking for him. My nerves are frazzled."

"I'm sure they are. You have my sympathies." Michelle flicked her fingers. "I have a daughter myself who was always wayward, and I told you my son has issues. What are you going to do?"

Her color high, Monique shoved back her chair. "I have to leave now. Thank you for the drink, Michelle. Nice to meet you, Astrid."

"*Drinks*, sweetie." Michelle tapped Monique's empty glass. "You had two of those."

Monique laughed. "You're right. I'll owe you if I see you before you check out."

When Monique left, Michelle turned back to Astrid. "My husband had some additional questions. Do you have a minute now?"

"Of course." Astrid sat through Michelle's fake questions, knowing the other woman couldn't care less about the answers.

When Michelle's phone buzzed, she glanced at it. "Oh, I have to leave. I'll be in touch before I leave the island."

"I hope so."

Michelle settled her tab with Jackson and even paid for Astrid's drink, which was nice of her considering she'd kidnapped her son.

When the door shut behind Michelle, Astrid dipped her head. "Hope that was okay."

She didn't expect an answer from West, sitting in his car, as this was a one-way bug, so she pushed back from the table and approached the bar. "Thanks for playing along, Jackson. You've been a big help."

"I just hope the sheriff tells me what this was all about when it's over."

"I'm sure you'll hear about it. I'm sure everyone will hear about it." She exchanged her Bloody Mary for a Diet Coke and as she turned back to the window table Jackson snapped his fingers.

"When you walked in, you could see the two of them going at it."

"Yeah, they didn't look too happy." She cocked her head. "Could you hear what they were arguing about?"

He rubbed a spot on the bar with a cloth. "They were whispering or talking low, but every once in a while, the younger one would get excited and raise her voice. I heard her say something about how it wasn't her fault she lost something. Then the older woman would shush her."

"Lost something? Yeah, I guess that makes sense." Astrid returned to the table, waiting for the next step in the plan.

She didn't have to wait long for her phone to start buzzing. She answered it just as if she would if no one was listening in. "Hi, West. Any luck?"

"Sorry, Astrid. The teenage Scouts haven't found him yet."

She closed her eyes and moderated her tone. "I know he's done this before, but I just can't help thinking he went off to find the buried drone card so that he could give it to you to make up for keeping it. If he couldn't remember where he left it, he might be looking for it now. O-or he could've gotten hurt and can't make his way back."

The little sob at the end was for real.

"You said he knows the forest. Where would he go if he couldn't find his way back to the camp?"

"He'd go to the falls, West. All the kids know how to get to the falls. Hell, maybe he even put the memory card there and didn't want to tell me because he's not supposed to go to the falls by himself. It's about three miles from the camp, but that's nothing to Olly." She held her breath, waiting for West's response, the response that would hopefully lure Olly's captors to a specific location—as long as her son was still leading them on a wild goose chase out there.

"In the caves? Do you think he's in those caves behind the falls?"

She drew in a breath. "Yes. That would make total sense.

He told me he couldn't remember where he buried the card because he didn't want to admit he'd been to those caves. He didn't want to tell you, either, when you arrived, so he figured he'd get the card himself. That has to be it, West. He has to be at those caves. Maybe he got stuck and can't make his way out."

"Then that's where we'll start looking. Where are you? I'll pick you up."

"I'm at the Salty Crab. I'm sorry, but I needed a drink."

"Totally understandable. I'll swing by and pick you up."

"Hurry, West. I'm starting to get worried."

When they ended the call, Astrid slipped her phone into her purse, feeling as if she had ticking time bomb in there. Would Michelle and Monique take the bait and send their goons to the falls with Olly? What would Olly make of it? If he'd left the card somewhere else, he'd be happy to go along with them to lead them astray.

But what if that's exactly where he *did* leave the card? Would he try to dissuade them from heading to the falls? Would he be able to bluff them? Would they hurt him if they figured that out? He was just a kid.

She pushed away from the table and waved to Jackson on her way out the door. "Thanks, again."

West pulled up ten minutes later, and Astrid practically lunged at the car door. She yanked at the door handle before he unlocked it so by the time he did, it swung open hard. "Sorry, sorry."

"It's okay. You did good in there. I heard everything clearly. Let's hope Michelle heard everything clearly over the phone."

It took her three tries to snap her seat belt. When she heard the click, she said, "Let's hope Olly's okay, and that they take the bait and lead him to the falls. We don't even know if he's already shown them the card. What if they already have the card, and they did something to Olly?"

"We can't think like that. There's no reason for them to hurt Olly, once he gives them the card. As far as ID'ing them?" He lifted his shoulders. "They'll most likely be long gone off this island. I have a question for you about your meeting."

"Yeah?" She licked her lips.

"You mentioned something about Monique getting scratched by a cat, and she responded that she'd been hit with a tree branch. What did that scratch look like?"

"Pretty much like what she said. If you're not paying attention when you're hiking out here, those little branches can snap back and get you."

"It looked fresh?"

She nodded. "What are you thinking?"

"Another question." He raised one finger. "You were still wired when you were talking to Jackson. He said he overheard Monique saying that she lost something."

"That's right. I guess she was telling Michelle it wasn't her fault that she lost the memory card."

"But she didn't lose the memory card." He drummed his thumbs on the steering wheel. "They never had the memory card. They took the drone, but nobody lost that either."

"So what did she lose?"

West shot her side glance. "Olly?"

"She lost Olly?" Astrid gripped the sides of her seat with both hands, the leather slippery beneath her damp hands.

"It's just a guess. She has an injury. How'd she get it? Chasing Olly? Maybe that's why she's back in town—she lost him."

"Why hasn't he contacted me, then? Why not go back to the camp?"

"He doesn't have a phone. He's scared. He doesn't know who's out there looking for him." He brushed her cheek with his thumb. "Just a thought."

She folded her hands in her lap and squeezed so hard, her knuckles turned white. "I'm not sure this makes me feel better. If Monique lost Olly, then instead of going after him herself, she passed the duty off to someone else, probably the same person who murdered Chase and Naomi, the same person who attacked me. In other words, some vicious killer is searching for Olly, someone who chopped off a woman's finger. They may have already found him. Maybe that's the phone call Michelle was waiting for at the Crab."

"Michelle and Monique wouldn't still be in town casually sharing a drink if Olly's captor had satisfied their goal. They must still be out there, either together or separate, and hopefully Michelle's lackey is working his way to the falls right now—with or without Olly."

"And if you can corral Michelle's henchmen at the falls, we can do a proper search for Olly without worrying about the bad guys getting to him first."

"Exactly. Or they still have him, and they're marching him to Dead Falls as we speak."

Astrid grabbed his arm. "And you'll stop them, West? You'll keep them from hurting Olly?"

"I will. I swear I will, Astrid." He gritted his teeth. "Or die trying."

Astrid flickered a gaze to West's face. She'd been wrong to think that West didn't care about rescuing Olly. His life depended on it.

Chapter Nineteen

As they crossed the bridge, Dead Falls on their right, West flexed his fingers on the steering wheel and tilted his head back and forth, stretching his neck. He would be no good to Olly if his nerves got the better of him. He had to stop these people. He had to make it safe for Olly.

Astrid urged him past the regular turnout for the falls and farther up the road toward Misty Hollow. "I'll show you a place where you can park your vehicle out of sight of anyone on the road. It's a longer hike to the falls but worth it if you want to stay off the radar—and we do."

"Lead the way." He followed her directions and backed his SUV into a small outlet, where the bushes draped over the back of his vehicle. "Almost camouflaged."

Rubbing her hands together for warmth, Astrid asked, "What's the plan?"

"If we beat them here, we hide out in the caves behind the falls and wait. If they're already here, we'll draw as close as we can to figure out if Olly's with them. Then I'll handle it."

Her gaze dropped to the weapon on his hip, and she nodded. Did she trust him around her son with a gun? Now that she knew the truth about him, did she trust him around her son at all?

They stepped from the SUV and stood still, listening. The rush of the falls drowned out most sound except for the chirping of the birds that dipped in and out of the spray. West whispered, "I don't know if we could hear human voices even if they were yelling."

"Believe me, you can hear them. Doesn't mean they're not whispering like us…or searching." She crooked her finger. "Follow me."

As she pushed aside some foliage to reveal a narrow path, West crept behind her, hot on her heels. Their hiking boots, which they still wore from this morning, crunched the sticks and rocks on the ground as they traversed the rugged trail.

The steep grade of the incline had West's calves burning, but he churned his legs, determined to reach the top with Astrid…and save her son.

When they reached the ledge shelf that snaked behind the falls, Astrid scrabbled over several rocks. West took the same path, as the spray of the water coated his hair and stuck to his lashes.

Astrid seemed to disappear into the rock face until West drew level with her and saw the mouth of the cave to his left. He ducked inside and plastered himself against the rough granite wall.

A beer bottle tipped over and rolled toward the edge, and West grabbed it and pulled it back into the cave. "You'd think these kids could at least clean up after themselves."

"They usually do. We did." She squinted through the sheet of water. "Unless they come up the back way like we did, we should be able to see their approach—if they took our hint."

"So, we wait." West crouched on his haunches, resting his forearms on his thighs.

"How long should we give them?" Astrid slid down the wall of the cave and sat, knees up, with one arm wrapped around her legs.

"As long as it takes, Astrid."

She cranked her head to the side and peered into the cave. "I don't see how he could've actually buried it in the cave. It would've taken him too long to get here, bury it and then return to the campsite."

"The goons who have him don't need to know that, and if he did bury it elsewhere, he's not about to tell them now. He's been leading them on some kind of wild-goose chase. He has to be. Michelle and Monique wouldn't be hanging around Dead Falls otherwise." He reached into the pocket of his jacket and cupped a memory card in his palm.

"Where'd you get that?" Astrid poked at the object in his hand.

"I swung by the station to grab it before I went to the Salty Crab to pick you up." He juggled it in his hand. "Might as well have a decoy."

She put a finger to her lips. "Shh. I hear something."

West closed his eyes and strained his ears to pick up sound outside the rushing water, and a man's voice carried over the tops of the trees. He whispered. "They're here. Can you see anything?"

Astrid scooted closer to the cave's entrance on her knees, her hand pressed against the wall, beads of moisture sparkling in her blond hair as she poked her head outside. She held up one finger.

West asked, "One man?"

She nodded and then collapsed back inside the cave. "Olly is with him. Thank God."

West closed his hand around the memory card. "We'll lure him with this and then make a trade."

"D-do you think he'll go for it? He's not going to know if this is the card from the drone or not."

"We'll play it by ear." West swallowed. "Do you trust me?"

Her lashes fluttered. "I do."

He dug his phone out of his pocket. He had alerted his deputies to be on call for a possible incident at the falls. Now that he had his quarry in sight, he could call in the reinforcements.

He tapped his phone's display and swore. "You didn't tell me we wouldn't get service up here."

"It's spotty." She tried her own phone with no luck. "Does this mean the cavalry isn't coming? We have to do this on our own?"

"That's exactly what it means." He tensed his muscles and drew closer to the cave's entrance. "We'll wait until they climb to the end of the trail and then make our presence known. I don't want them all the way on the ledge—too many things could happen."

A steely resolve took over his body. It was the same determination he'd felt the night he went after the shooter of a toddler—before he knew that shooter was a fourteen-year-old boy. It was the same determination a cop needed to do his job to protect people. He hadn't felt it in a while.

"Come on, pick it up. That memory card had better be here, kid. I know what you've been doing—leading me around like I'm some kind of idiot. But I got inside knowledge about this place, so don't tell me you didn't leave it here. I know you did."

Olly's up-and-down adolescent voice rang out clearly. "I told you I buried it under a tree. If you'd let me keep looking at that other place, I would've found it."

West made his move when he could see both Olly and his captor clearly heading for the dangerous ledge. Bending over, he emerged from the cave, holding up the memory card. "We already found it, Olly."

The tall, muscular man hustling Olly up the trail took a step back and raised his gun. "What the hell?"

Planting his boots firmly on the ledge, West said, "We figured out where you put it, Olly. Your mom did."

Astrid popped up beside him as Olly let out a yelp. "I knew you'd left it here, Olly. You would never forget where you buried something in the woods. You were just afraid to tell me you'd been up here on your own. Isn't that right?"

West could feel the tension radiating off Astrid's body. Would Olly understand? Would he play along?

The boy let out a big sigh. "Yeah, you got me. I put it in the cave. I didn't even bury it. I was gonna take Sheriff Chandler up here this morning to show him, but that woman got me."

"What happened to her? Did she get you out of your tent and then hand you over to this man?"

"Sort of." Olly grinned. "I pushed her and got away for a bit, but this guy was waiting and grabbed me. I pretended I couldn't remember where I buried it."

The man shoved Olly, and Astrid gasped. "Shut up, kid. I knew what you were doing. I was just giving you a chance before I started *making* you tell me."

"So, whaddya say?" West waved the memory card in the air. "The card for the boy."

The man snorted and clamped one hand on the beanie covering his head. "You gotta be kidding me. I don't know what's on that card."

"And you're not going to know unless you let Olly go."

"He's our ace in the hole, Sheriff. We're not letting him go."

Astrid cried out, one arm reaching forward as if to pull her son to her chest.

"Then you're not getting the card. I'll take it back to the station, play it and find out exactly what happened to Chase Thompson."

"If that's more important to you than this boy's life, go for it." He raised his gun and leveled it at Olly's head.

Olly seemed to shrink next to his captor as West's gaze zeroed in on the man's face. Every nerve ending buzzed with adrenaline.

"If you don't hand over the card, I'll take this annoying kid with me. We'll make our getaway, regardless of what you find on the video from that drone." He shrugged one solid shoulder. "And then we'll kill him."

A strangled noise came from Astrid's throat, and she threw out an arm to brace herself.

West narrowed his eyes. "You won't get that far. Do you think we came up here alone? I have my deputies surrounding this area, ready to take you down like a dog."

"Not when I come out of here with this kid at gunpoint. These small-town hicks. They ain't got the guts, my friend. They're not going to take that risk."

From the corner of his eye, West could sense Astrid making some motions with her hands. Olly's captor hadn't noticed, all his attention on the weapon at Olly's head and West's own gun, now in his hand.

West coiled his muscles, his finger twitched on the trigger. A second later, Olly dropped to the ground, out of sight amid the foliage.

Just like he'd been trained. Just like he always would. West took the shot.

Epilogue

Olly grabbed Sherlock's scruff and wrestled the big dog to the ground. Sherlock went happily, his tongue lolling out of his mouth, his brown eyes pinned adoringly on his best friend.

When Olly poked his head up, he said, "I don't get it, Mom. Why'd you think I took the card to the caves behind the falls?"

"I wasn't absolutely sure, Olly, but since Michelle was bugging my phone, we figured we'd put it in her head that it could be there. That way, we had a meeting point. Otherwise, we didn't know where to start looking for you."

"We did hear some of the teen Scouts calling my name, but—" Olly buried his nose in Sherlock's fur "—Jerome put that gun against my head."

"I'm so sorry you had to go through that, Olly. You must've been scared."

"Scared but incredibly brave." West carried a plate of graham crackers, chocolate squares and marshmallows to the firepit. "How did you get the idea to lead Jerome around to different places to buy time?"

"Saw it in a movie once." Olly rubbed his hands together before sweeping everything he'd need for a s'more off the plate. "I hid it pretty good, didn't I? Only I'd know where to find it. What was on the memory card, anyway?"

West clicked his tongue. "I can't discuss the case, Olly."

Olly wedged his tongue in the corner of his mouth as he slid a marshmallow onto the skewer. "Did that guy… Jerome…did he die? There was a lot of blood."

West shot her a quick glance and waved at some smoke in front of his face. "Naw, but he's going to be spending a lot of time behind bars."

Astrid leveled her finger at Olly. "That is the last one, dude. You're going to get a stomachache."

"This is nothin'. You shoulda seen how many Logan and I ate at camp."

"I'm sure it was a massive amount." She reached over and ruffled his messy hair. "Don't forget, you have an appointment with Dr. Maddox tomorrow."

"I know." He squished two graham crackers together. "All we do is talk."

"It's good to talk." West twirled his own marshmallow into the fire. "I had a lot of talking appointments like that. It made me feel better about a lot of things."

"Really?" Olly's eyes grew round.

"Absolutely."

Astrid mouthed a thank-you in West's direction. She wasn't sure how much West's therapy had helped him, but shooting and killing Jerome and rescuing Olly in the process had done wonders for putting him at ease around her son.

Olly smacked his lips as he finished his gooey concoction. "Okay, I'm going to bed."

"Do you want me to tuck you in?"

"Mom!" Olly crushed his paper plate in his hand. "I can go to bed by myself."

"Okay, take Sherlock with you. He just had a bath, so he can sleep at the foot of your bed."

"Sweet!" Olly gave a short whistle, and Sherlock jumped to his feet. As Olly and Sherlock trotted up the steps, Olly called over his shoulder. "Night, Sheriff Chandler, Mom."

"Good night, Olly."

"Good night, sweetie. Leave the front door open."

When Olly disappeared into the house, Astrid dragged her chair closer to West's. "Thanks for keeping things vague for Olly. I'm not sure he needs to know a dead man dropped next to him."

"I didn't think so." West took her hand and pressed a kiss against her palm. "Thanks for trusting me with your son."

"You're his hero now. I hope you're ready for that."

"He'll get over that soon enough."

Running her thumb over his knuckles, she said, "I know you had to keep things vague for Olly, but that doesn't mean you have to keep things vague for me, too. Does it?"

"What do you mean?" His eyebrows shot up to his hairline in a manner that told her he'd been thinking of something other than the case.

"I mean—" she blew out the flaming marshmallow on the end of his skewer "—what was on that memory card? Did Olly actually capture Chase's death on the drone?"

"I can tell you. It's going to come out soon, anyway." West stretched his legs, wedging his boots against the rock encircling the firepit. "The drone *did* catch the aftermath of Chase's murder, and now it makes sense why Michelle Clark, whose real name is Claire La Croix, was so desperate to get her hands on the footage. Her daughter, Monique La Croix, is the one who shot Chase."

"Wait, wait." Astrid's hands nervously fluttered over the

flames. "I know the La Croix name. Pierre Dumas has a sister named La Croix. Dumas was the dealer my ex ratted out."

"Exactly. With Dumas in prison, his sister Claire took over the family business and brought her daughter in with her."

Astrid pressed her palms on either side of her face. "And she knew? Michelle, I mean Claire, knew who I was all that time?"

"She did, although I'm not sure she held much of a grudge against you or your ex. She liked being in control, but she didn't want to see her daughter go down for murder."

"Monique cozied up to Chase to keep an eye on him, and then discovered he was skimming. Is that what happened?"

"Pretty much, but there's more to the drone story."

"More?" She reached for the glass of wine she'd parked under her chair. "I'm gonna need another hit of this."

"Not only did the drone catch Monique with Chase's dead body on the beach, but it also showed her stashing the drugs in a cave. They did not want us to find that hideaway. So the drone gave us Chase's killer and the drop-off/pickup point the Dumas cartel was using."

"That explains a lot." She ran her nails up his muscled thigh beneath the denim of his worn jeans. "I'm just glad you were here instead of Hopkins when this all went down. The arrests of Claire and her daughter are going to put a serious damper on the drug trade on Dead Falls Island."

"Is that the only reason you're glad I'm here?" Despite West's concerted effort on his s'more, he was making a mess of it.

She sighed and slid his plate from his lap to hers. She placed the chocolate square on top of the gooey marshmallow and squished the other graham cracker on top. "Well, that and the opportunity to turn you into an outdoorsman, city boy."

"I welcome your…efforts." He plucked the treat from the plate and took a bite. "You know, I guess I have been pretty vague with you."

Her heart pounded as she watched his tongue dab at the stickiness on his lips. "I've been guilty of the same. I was afraid to tell you about Russ. Afraid to admit how gullible I was with him."

"We all make mistakes in relationships. I didn't tell you that my girlfriend in Chicago dumped me after the shooting incident, either." He shrugged and licked his fingers. "But I'm done making those mistakes, and I want to be perfectly clear with you."

"About?" She reached out and stroked a smudge of chocolate from the corner of his lip. Then she sucked the sweetness from her thumb.

He dropped his plate on the ground and pulled her into his lap. "About my feelings for you. I'm falling in love with you. Is that clear enough?"

The pounding of her heart turned into skipping as she cupped his face with one hand. "Perfectly, as long as you're okay with a mischievous boy and a mangy dog as part of the package."

"I wouldn't take that package any other way." He pressed his mouth against hers, giving her a sweet, sticky kiss to seal the deal.

As she snuggled closer against his chest, she figured she'd just have to give cops another try—at least this one.

* * * * *

Don't miss the stories in this mini series!

A DISCOVERY BAY NOVEL

Captured At The Cove
CAROL ERICSON
August 2024

What Lies Below
CAROL ERICSON
September 2024

MILLS & BOON

INTRIGUE

Seek thrills. Solve crimes. Justice served.

Available Next Month

Conard County: Covert Avenger Rachel Lee
Colorado Kidnapping Cindi Myers

....

The Killer Next Door Amanda Stevens
What Lies Billow Carol Ericson

....

K-9 Defender Julie Miller
Hometown Homicide Denise N. Wheatly

Larger Print

Keep reading for an excerpt of a new title
from the Intrigue series,
HIGH MILE MYSTERY by Cindi Myers

Chapter One

The storm-swelled creek roared like a jet engine readying for takeoff as it rushed through the narrow canyon. The normally shallow trickle of water was now a torrent, tearing great chunks of earth and rocks from its banks and carrying broken branches and whole trees along in its wake. On the other side of the cataract, a group of campers clustered around several vehicles, cut off from escape by the rushing water.

Zach Gregory stopped at the edge of the water, alongside his fellow Eagle Mountain Search and Rescue members, and studied the situation. They had to find a way to get the stranded campers to this side of the swollen creek, even as rain continued to pour. He counted at least six adults, several children and three dogs. All of them were drenched. Even in rain gear, Zach felt cold and damp, rain lashing his face and seeping past his collar and down the back of his neck. He moved up alongside fellow SAR volunteer Caleb Garrison. "How are we supposed to get over to the camp?" he shouted to be heard above the din of the water.

Caleb pointed downstream. Zach followed his gaze and leaned forward to get a better look. The creek channel widened into an open area, the water forming a wide pool, the current much less swift. Newly elected SAR captain Danny Irwin motioned for the group to move toward this pool, and they set out, splashing through puddles and slipping in mud and on slick rock as they shouldered the rescue gear they had carried from the nearest road. The main route to the campground was washed out, and the weather had been deemed too bad to risk bringing in a helicopter to airlift the stranded campers. With conditions only expected to worsen, the forest service, Rayford County Sheriff's Department and Eagle Mountain Search and Rescue had decided to attempt a land evacuation.

Away from the swiftest water, the roar dulled enough to make conversation possible. "We're going to shoot a line across to that group of trees over there." Danny indicated the clump of piñons up the bank. "We'll attach instructions for someone on the other side to secure the line. Then we'll send a group over to assess everyone and send them back across, one at a time."

Someone unpacked the chunky, red line-throwing gun, which used compressed air to propel a coil of strong cable across a chasm. Volunteer Ryan Welch handled firing the gun. A crowd had gathered on the opposite bank, and two men ran to retrieve the other end of the line as soon as it hit the trees. They unwrapped the note and sent a thumbs-up signal across, then began fastening their end to the trees, while Ryan and Eldon Ramsey secured the cable on this side.

"Think it will hold?" Ryan asked Danny when the line was secure.

"Only one way to find out." Danny looked around. "Any volunteers to go first?"

Silence as they contemplated the turbulent gray water rushing beneath the thin line. Fall into that, and even with a life jacket, you could be in trouble.

"I'll go." Zach stepped forward.

Danny looked him up and down. "I guess if the line will hold you, it will hold anyone," he said. "Get suited up, and we'll give it a try."

Five minutes later, fitted with a helmet and personal flotation device, Zach slipped a harness over his hips, clipped onto the line and grabbed hold of the strap attached to a pulley on the line. Tony Meisner clapped him on the back. "Ready?"

Zach barely had time to nod before Tony pushed him and he was sliding down the line across the water. The cable sagged beneath his weight, and he felt spray from the churning water splash onto his legs as he skimmed over the creek. But the cable held. If not for the driving rain and heavy pack on his back, it might have been a fun trip, like riding a zip line on vacation.

Two men rushed to greet him as he landed on the opposite shore and helped him off the line. The radio attached to his shoulder crackled. "I'm sending Hannah and Sheri over next, so get ready," Danny said.

Paramedic Hannah Richards and former captain Sheri Stevens arrived in quick succession. They were greeted by a growing crowd as additional campers gathered beside the creek. Zach followed Sheri and Hannah into a chaos of wet and anxious campers. Dogs barked, children cried and everyone seemed to be talking at once. Everyone was muddy, wet and frightened. "We woke up, and there was water running through our tent," one man told Zach. "My oldest boy left the tent to go pee, and he almost fell in the river."

"There's a tree down on an RV at the back of the campground," another man said. "I think someone might be hurt."

"My husband was hurt by a falling branch," a woman said. She hefted a toddler on her hip. The child—a girl, judging by the pink barrettes in her hair—stared at Zach, her thumb in her mouth. "He's over by our trailer, but someone needs to look at him."

Hannah keyed her radio. "We've got some terrified kids over here," she said. "And some of the adults aren't in much better shape. Apparently, a tree came down on an RV, and there may be injuries or people trapped inside. We've got other injuries from falling trees. We need people over here to administer first aid. And a couple of people to ride with the kids back across wouldn't hurt."

"I'll send people over, and we'll start the process of getting people over to this side," Danny said.

"Zach, start gathering people who are ready to get out of here," Sheri said. "Make sure they know they've got to ride across that line, so only a small backpack or a bag they can carry in one hand can go with them. Everything else has to stay here."

"I can't leave my dogs," one woman wailed.

"We'll get the dogs out, too," Sheri said.

Ten minutes later, Zach was sending the first of the campers back across the line. As the woman started across the water, Hannah approached Zach, carrying a blanket-wrapped small child. "This is Micah," she said. "He's three, and he's suffering from hypothermia. I've tucked some hot packs in around him, but he needs to get to someplace warm and dry ASAP. I'm sending his mom right behind you." She put the child into Zach's arms.

Zach stared down into a pair of frightened brown eyes. Micah had his thumb stuffed into his mouth and said nothing, though tears—or maybe raindrops—slid down his flushed cheeks.

"It's okay, baby." A petite woman, dark hair plastered to her head, stood on tiptoe and stroked Micah's face. Then she looked up at Zach. "Don't drop him," she said.

Zach tightened his grip on the child. "I won't."

Traveling back across the river was much slower than the original traverse, since it required being towed uphill by volunteers on the other side. Halfway across, Micah began to squirm and wail. Zach held tight and tried to talk soothingly, though he was terrified he would drop the squirming child, despite them being clipped into safety lines He sagged with relief when fellow team member Carrie Andrews stepped forward to take the boy from him, then he stepped to one side a few moments later to allow Micah's mom to reunite with her son.

The next hour was a blur of traveling back and forth across the flooded creek. The rain stopped and the sun came out, and Zach began to sweat in the heavy rain gear, but it was too much trouble to divest himself of pack, life vest and harness, so he left everything on and focused on the work. He carried another child across, transported medical gear and escorted a frantic, snapping golden retriever who was determined not to be harnessed to anything. Zach was only able to get the dog to cooperate when someone produced a packet of beef jerky, which Zach fed, bit by bit, to the trembling dog all the way back across the water.

After the dog, there were only two more adults to get back across, and they didn't need Zach's help. He shed the harness and layers of gear and drank a bottle of water someone handed him. A tall blonde woman he hadn't seen before, one of the campers, he supposed, moved through the volunteers. "Thank you so much," she said to each one. When she got to Zach, she took his hand. "You were amazing."

"I was happy to do it," Zach said. It felt good to help other people, to make a difference.

She smiled, showing dimples. "I'm Janie. What's your name?"

"Zach. Zach Gregory."

"Well, Zach Gregory, you and the other volunteers are real heroes," she said, then surprised him with a hug.

He stepped back, a little embarrassed but also pleased. He hadn't joined Search and Rescue for the adulation, but who didn't like to feel they had done something good for someone else?

"How is it you rate a hug and all I get is a handshake?" Caleb grinned at Zach after the woman had moved away.

"I guess I'm just lucky."

"Right. I'm sure that's all it was." Caleb punched him in the shoulder, then moved on to help gather up their gear.

Zach bent and picked up his harness, helmet and rain gear. At six foot four and 230 pounds, he was used to attracting attention, and women seemed to like his looks, but he preferred to stay in the background.

"You did great out there today," Sheri said as she

joined him in collecting gear. "You stayed calm, and you kept everyone else calm."

"Thanks." This was the kind of praise Zach preferred—for the job he did, not for how he looked.

"Uh-oh." He and Sheri both turned at this exclamation from Ryan. Across the river, Hannah, Eldon, Deputy Jake Gwynn and Forest Ranger Nate Hall stood around a fifth figure on the ground.

"Jake and Nate went to search the RV that was damaged by the fallen tree," Sheri said. "They must have found someone hurt."

They hurried to join Danny, who was on the radio. "We'll send a litter over," Danny said. "Secure the body, and we'll bring it over."

"Is there a fatality?" Sheri asked when Danny ended the transmission.

He nodded. "I don't have any details. Jake and Nate found her near a van hit by a fallen tree."

While some team members prepared to bring the body to this side of the creek, Zach and the others gathered their gear and escorted the rest of the civilians up the trail to the road, where sheriff's deputies and Forest Service employees, along with a few of the campers' relatives and friends, waited to drive them back to the town of Eagle Mountain.

They were packing up to leave when a solemn procession came up the trail—Ranger Hall, followed by Jake, Eldon, Hannah and Danny with the litter bearing a wrapped body. They stopped beside the Search and Rescue vehicle and lowered their burden. Sheriff Travis Walker, in muck boots and a yellow slicker over his khaki uniform, came to meet them. "What have you got?" he asked.

"Her ID says her name is Claire Watson, from Maryland," Jake, who was a sheriff's deputy as well as a Search and Rescue volunteer, said. "None of the other campers seem to know her. We found her under a tree just outside of a rental van. She was probably trying to get away when the tree caught and pinned her." He folded back the blanket covering her. "You can see she was hit pretty hard in the back of the head."

Zach started to look away, but something about the woman's thick brown hair and high white forehead made him look again. He shuddered and went cold all over. "Cammie!"

He didn't realize he'd said the name out loud until the sheriff put a hand on his shoulder. "Do you know her?" Travis asked.

Zach took a step closer and stood over the body. This couldn't be real. He put out a hand as if to touch her, but Travis grabbed his arm and held it. "Zach," he said, his voice firm. "Zach, do you know this woman?"

Zach sucked in a breath, trying to pull himself together. He nodded, then said, "Yes," though the word came out as more of a croak. He was vaguely aware of the other team members gathered around, staring at him.

"How do you know her?" Travis asked.

Instead of answering the sheriff, Zach looked at Jake. "Could I see her arm?" he asked. "Her left arm."

Jake glanced at Travis, who nodded. Jake bent and peeled back the blanket enough to untuck the dead woman's arm. She was wearing a long-sleeved fleece top, blue with white trim. Zach swallowed hard. "Is there a tattoo?" he asked. "Just above her left wrist?"

Jake pushed up the sleeve, and suddenly Zach couldn't breathe. He stared at the blue-and-green butterfly tat, no larger than a dollar coin, the name Laney in script beneath it. He closed his eyes, and Travis gripped his shoulder, steadying him. "Do you know her?" Travis asked again.

Jake nodded and opened his eyes. "That's my sister," he said. "That's Camille. Camille Gregory."

"When was the last time you saw your sister?" Travis asked.

Zach choked back a moan. This couldn't be happening. How could it possibly be happening? Travis repeated the question. Zach forced himself to look at the sheriff. "Four years ago," he said. "At her funeral." Then, to make sure Travis understood, "My sister, Camille, died four years ago."

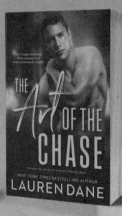

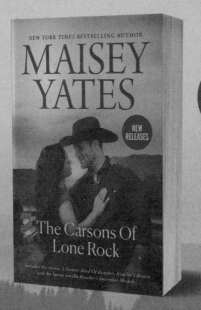

Subscribe and fall in love with a Mills & Boon series today!

You'll be among the first to read stories delivered to your door monthly and enjoy great savings.

WE SIMPLY LOVE ROMANCE

MILLS & BOON